HELEN SIMONSON was born in Slough and grew up near Reading. As a teenager, she moved to the small village in East Sussex, near Rye, which she still thinks of as home. A graduate of the London School of Economics, and a former advertising executive, she turned to fiction as a second career and recently completed a masters degree in creative writing. Helen currently lives in the Washington D.C. area with her American husband and two sons. *Major Pettigrew's Last Stand* is her first novel.

www.helensimonson.co.uk

Helen Simonson

BLOOMSBURY
LONDON · BERLIN · NEW YORK · SYDNEY

First published in Great Britain 2010
This paperback edition published 2010

Copyright © 2010 by Helen Simonson

The moral right of the author has been asserted

Bloomsbury Publishing Plc
London, Berlin, New York and Sydney

36 Soho Square, London, W1D 3QY

A CIP catalogue record for this book is available from the British Library

ISBN 978 1 4088 0955 6

10 9 8 7 6 5 4 3 2

Printed in Great Britian by Clays Ltd, St Ives plc

www.bloomsbury.com/helensimonson

for John,
Ian, and Jamie

Chapter One

Major Pettigrew was still upset about the phone call from his brother's wife and so he answered the doorbell without thinking. On the damp bricks of the path stood Mrs Ali from the village shop. She gave only the faintest of starts, the merest arch of an eyebrow. A quick rush of embarrassment flooded to the Major's cheeks and he smoothed helplessly at the lap of his crimson, clematis-covered housecoat with hands that felt like spades.

'Ah,' he said.

'Major?'

'Mrs Ali?' There was a pause that seemed to expand slowly, like the universe, which, he had just read, was pushing itself apart as it aged. 'Senescence', they had called it in the Sunday paper.

'I came for the newspaper money. The paper boy is sick,' said Mrs Ali, drawing up her short frame to its greatest height and assuming a brisk tone, so different from the low, accented roundness of her voice when they discussed the texture and perfume of the teas she blended specially for him.

'Of course, I'm awfully sorry.' He had forgotten to put the week's money in an envelope under the outside doormat. He started fumbling for the pockets of his trousers, which were somewhere under the clematis. He felt his eyes watering. His pockets were inaccessible unless he hoisted the hem of the housecoat. 'I'm sorry,' he repeated.

'Oh, not to worry,' she said, backing away. 'You can drop it in at the shop later—sometime more convenient.' She was already turning away when he was seized with an urgent need to explain.

'My brother died,' he said. She turned back. 'My brother died,' he repeated. 'I got the call this morning. I didn't have time.' The dawn chorus had still been chattering in the giant yew against the west wall of his cottage, the sky pink, when the telephone rang. The Major, who had been up early to do his weekly housecleaning, now realised he had been sitting in a daze ever since. He gestured helplessly at his strange outfit and wiped a hand across his face. Quite suddenly his knees felt loose and he could sense the blood leaving his head. He felt his shoulder meet the doorpost unexpectedly and Mrs Ali, quicker than his eye could follow, was somehow at his side propping him upright.

'I think we'd better get you indoors and sitting down,' she said, her voice soft with concern. 'If you will allow me, I will fetch you some water.' Since most of the feeling seemed to have left his extremities, the Major had no choice but to comply. Mrs Ali guided him across the narrow, uneven stone floor of the hallway and deposited him in the wing chair tucked just inside the door of the bright, book-lined living room. It was his least favourite chair, lumpy cushioned and with a hard ridge of wood at just the wrong place on the back of his head, but he was in no position to complain.

ι ɂ ɉ

'I found the glass on the draining board,' said Mrs Ali, presenting him with the thick tumbler in which he soaked his partial bridgework at night. The faint hint of spearmint made him gag. 'Are you feeling any better?'

'Yes, much better,' he said, his eyes swimming with tears. 'It's very kind of you . . .'

'May I prepare you some tea?' Her offer made him feel frail and pitiful.

'Thank you,' he said. Anything to get her out of the room while he recovered some semblance of vigour and got rid of the housecoat.

It was strange, he thought, to listen again to a woman clattering teacups in the kitchen. On the mantelpiece his wife, Nancy, smiled from her photo, her wavy brown hair tousled, and her freckled nose slightly pink with sunburn. They had gone to Dorset in May of that rainy year, probably 1973, and a burst of sunlight had briefly brightened the windy afternoon; long enough for him to capture her, waving like a young girl from the battlements of Corfe Castle. Six years she had been gone. Now Bertie was gone, too. They had left him all alone, the last family member of his generation. He clasped his hands to still a small tremor.

Of course there was Marjorie, his unpleasant sister-in-law; but, like his late parents, he had never fully accepted her. She had loud, ill-formed opinions and a north country accent that scraped the eardrum like a dull razor. He hoped she would not look for any increase in familiarity now. He would ask her for a recent photo and, of course, Bertie's sporting gun. Their father had made it clear when he divided the pair between his sons that they were to be restored in the event of death, in order to be passed along intact within the family. The Major's own gun had lain solitary all these years in the double walnut box, a depression in the velvet lining indicating the absence of its mate. Now they would be restored to their full value—around a hundred thousand pounds, he imagined. Not that he would ever dream of selling. For a moment he saw himself quite clearly at the next shoot, perhaps on one of the riverside farms that were always plagued with rabbits, coming up to the invited group, bearing the pair of guns casually broken over his arm.

'Good God, Pettigrew, is that a pair of Churchills?' someone would say—perhaps Lord Dagenham himself, if he was shooting

3

with them that day—and he would casually look, as if he had forgotten, and reply,

'Yes, matched pair. Rather lovely walnut they used when these were made,' offering them up for inspection and admiration.

A rattling against the doorjamb startled him out of this pleasant interlude. It was Mrs Ali with a heavy tea tray. She had taken off her green wool coat and draped her paisley shawl around the shoulders of a plain navy dress, worn over narrow black trousers. The Major realised that he had never seen Mrs Ali without the large, stiff apron she always wore in the shop.

'Let me help you with that.' He began to rise from the chair.

'Oh, I can manage perfectly well,' she said, and brought the tray to the nearby desk, nudging the small stack of leather books aside with one corner. 'You must rest. You're probably in shock.'

'It was unexpected, the telephone ringing so absurdly early. Not even six o'clock, you know. I believe they were all night at the hospital.'

'It was unexpected?'

'Heart attack. Quite massive apparently.' He brushed a hand over his bristled moustache, in thought. 'Funny, somehow you expect them to save heart attack victims these days. Always seem to on television.' Mrs Ali wobbled the spout of the teapot against a cup rim. It made a loud *chonk* and the Major feared a chip. He recollected (too late) that her husband had also died of a heart attack. It was perhaps eighteen months or two years now. 'I'm sorry, that was thoughtless—' She interrupted him with a sympathetic wave of dismissal and continued to pour. 'He was a good man, your husband,' he added.

What he remembered most clearly was the large, quiet man's restraint. Things had not been altogether smooth after Mr Ali took over old Mrs Bridge's village shop. On at least two occasions the Major had seen Mr Ali, on a crisp spring morning, calmly scraping spray paint from his new plate glass windows. Several times, Major Pettigrew had been in the store when young boys on a dare would stick their enormous ears in the door to yell 'Pakis go home!' Mr

Ali would only shake his head and smile while the Major would bluster and stammer apologies. The furore eventually died down. The same small boys slunk into the store at nine o'clock at night when their mothers ran out of milk. The most stubborn of the local working men got tired of driving four miles in the rain to buy their national lottery tickets at an 'English' shop. The upper echelons of the village, led by the ladies of the various village committees, compensated for the rudeness of the lower by developing a widely advertised respect for Mr and Mrs Ali. The Major had heard many a lady proudly speak of 'our dear Pakistani friends at the shop' as proof that Edgecombe St Mary was a utopia of multicultural understanding.

When Mr Ali died, everyone had been appropriately upset. The village council, on which the Major sat, had debated a memorial service of some kind, and when that fell through (neither the parish church nor the pub being suitable) they had sent a very large wreath to the funeral home.

'I am sorry I did not have an opportunity to meet your lovely wife,' said Mrs Ali, handing him a cup.

'Yes, she's been gone some six years now,' he said. 'Funny really, it seems like both an eternity and the blink of an eye all at the same time.'

'It is very dislocating,' she said. Her crisp enunciation, so lacking among many of his village neighbours, struck him with the purity of a well-tuned bell. 'Sometimes my husband feels as close to me as you are now, and sometimes I am quite alone in the universe,' she added.

'You have family, of course.'

'Yes, quite an extended family.' He detected a dryness in her tone. 'But it is not the same as the infinite bond between a husband and wife.'

'You express it perfectly,' he said. They drank their tea and he felt a sense of wonder that Mrs Ali, out of the context of her shop and in the strange setting of his own living room, should be revealed as a woman of such great understanding. 'About the housecoat,' he said.

'Housecoat?'

'The thing I was wearing.' He nodded to where it now lay in a basket of *National Geographics*. 'It was my wife's favourite housecleaning attire. Sometimes I, well . . .'

'I have an old tweed jacket that my husband used to wear,' she said softly. 'Sometimes I put it on and take a walk around my garden. And sometimes I put his pipe in my mouth to taste the bitterness of his tobacco.' She flushed a warmer shade and lowered her deep brown eyes to the floor, as if she had said too much. The Major noticed the smoothness of her skin and the strong lines of her face.

'I still have some of my wife's clothes, too,' said the Major. 'After six years, I don't know if they still smell of her perfume or whether I just imagine it.' He wanted to tell her how he sometimes opened the closet door to thrust his face against the nubby suits and the smooth chiffon blouses. Mrs Ali looked up at him and behind her heavy-lidded eyes he thought she too might be thinking of such absurd things.

'Are you ready for more tea?' she asked and held out her hand for his cup.

When Mrs Ali had left, she making her excuses for having invited herself into his home and he making his apologies for inconveniencing her with his dizzy spell, the Major donned his housecoat once more and went back to the small scullery beyond the kitchen to finish cleaning his gun. He was conscious of tightness around his head and a slight burn in the throat. This was the dull ache of grief in the real world; more dyspepsia than passion.

He had left a small china cup of beeswax warming on its candle stand. He dipped his fingers in the hot oil and began to rub it slowly into the burled walnut root of the gun stock. The wood became silk under his fingertips. He relaxed into his task and felt his grief ease, making room for the tiniest flowering of a new curiosity.

Mrs Ali was, he half suspected, an educated woman, a person of culture. Nancy had been such a rare person, too, fond of her books and of little chamber concerts in village churches. But she had left him alone to endure the blunt tweedy concerns of the other women of their acquaintance. Women who talked horses and raffles at the hunt ball and who delighted in clucking over which unreliable young mother from the council cottages had messed up arrangements for this week's play group at the Village Hall. Mrs Ali was more like Nancy. She was a butterfly to their scuffle of pigeons. He acknowledged a notion that he might wish to see Mrs Ali again outside of the shop, and wondered whether this might be proof that he was not as ossified as his sixty-eight years, and the limited opportunities of village life, might suggest.

Bolstered by the thought, he felt that he was up to the task of phoning his son, Roger, in London. He wiped his fingertips on a soft yellow rag and peered with concentration at the innumerable chrome buttons and LED displays of the cordless phone, a present from Roger. Its speed dial and voice activation capabilities were, Roger said, useful for the elderly. Major Pettigrew disagreed on both its ease of use and the designation of himself as old. It was frustratingly common that children were no sooner gone from the nest and established in their own homes, in Roger's case a gleaming black-and-brass-decorated penthouse in a high-rise that blighted the Thames near Putney, than they began to infantilise their own parents and wish them dead, or at least in assisted living. It was all very Greek, the Major thought. With an oily finger, he managed to depress the button marked '1—Roger Pettigrew, VP, Chelsea Equity Partners,' which Roger had filled in with large, childlike print. Roger's private equity firm occupied two floors in a tall glass office tower in London's Docklands; as the phone rang with a metallic ticking sound, the Major imagined Roger in his unpleasantly sterile cubicle with the battery of computer monitors and the heap of files for which some very expensive architect had not bothered to provide drawers.

Roger had already heard.

'Jemima has taken on the call-making. The girl's hysterical, but there she is, calling everyone and his dog.'

'It helps to keep busy,' suggested the Major.

'More like wallowing in the whole bereaved-daughter role, if you ask me,' said Roger. 'It's a bit off, but then they've always been that way, haven't they?' His voice was muffled and the Major assumed this meant he was once again eating at his desk.

'That's unnecessary, Roger,' he said firmly. Really, his son was becoming as unedited as Marjorie's family. The city was full of blunt, arrogant young men these days and Roger, approaching thirty, showed few signs of evolving past their influence.

'Sorry, Dad. I'm very sorry about Uncle Bertie.' There was a pause. 'I'll always remember when I had chicken pox and he came over with that model plane kit. He stayed all day helping me glue all those tiny bits of balsa together.'

'As I recall you broke it against the window the next day, after you'd been warned against flying it indoors.'

'Yeah, and you used it as kindling for the kitchen stove.'

'It was broken to pieces. No sense in wasting it.' The memory was quite familiar to them both. The same story came up over and over at family parties. Sometimes it was told as a joke and they all laughed. Sometimes it was a cautionary lecture to Jemima's wilful son. Today the hint of reproach was showing along the seams.

'Will you come down the night before?' asked the Major.

'No, I'll take the train. But listen, Dad, don't wait for me. It's possible I might get stuck.'

'Stuck?'

'I'm swamped. There's a big flap on. Two billion dollars, tricky buyout of the corporate bonds—and the client's nervous. I mean, let me know when it's finalised, and it'll go in my calendar as a "must", but you never know.' The Major wondered how he was usually featured in his son's calendar. He imagined himself flagged with a small yellow sticky note—important but not time sensitive, perhaps.

The funeral was set for Tuesday.

'It seemed good for most people,' Marjorie said on her second call. 'Jemima has her evening class on Mondays and Wednesdays and I have a bridge tournament on Thursday night.'

'Bertie would want you to carry on,' the Major replied, feeling a slight acid tone creep into his voice. He was sure the funeral had also been scheduled around available beauty appointments. She would want to make sure her stiff wave of yellow hair was freshly sculpted and her skin toned or waxed—or whatever she did to achieve a face like stretched leather. 'I suppose Friday is out?' he added.

He had just made a doctor's appointment for Tuesday. The receptionist at the surgery had been very understanding given the circumstances and had immediately insisted on moving a perennially asthmatic child to Friday in order to squeeze in his ECG. He didn't like the idea of cancelling.

'The Vicar has Youth-in-Crisis.'

'I assume the youth are in crisis every week,' said the Major sharply. 'It's a funeral, for God's sake. Let them put the needs of others ahead of their own for once. It might teach them something.'

'The funeral director felt that Fridays were inappropriately festive for a funeral.'

'Oh . . .' He was rendered speechless and defeated by the absurdity. 'Well, I'll see you Tuesday, then, about four o'clock?'

'Yes. Is Roger going to drive you?'

'No, he'll come straight from London by train and take a taxi. I'll drive.'

'Are you sure you'll be all right?' asked Marjorie. She sounded quite genuinely concerned and the Major felt a rush of emotion for her. She too was alone now, of course. He was sorry he had felt so furious at her and assured her gently that he was quite able to drive himself.

'And you'll come back to the house afterward, of course. We'll have drinks and a few nibbles. Nothing elaborate.' He noticed she did not ask him to stay. He would have to drive home in the dark. His empathy shrivelled away again. 'And perhaps there is something of Bertie's you'd like to have. You must have a look.'

'That's extremely thoughtful of you,' he said trying to dampen the eagerness that brightened his voice. 'Actually I was meaning to talk to you about that at some appropriate time.'

'Well, of course,' she said. 'You must have some *small* token, some memento. Bertie would have insisted. There are some quite new shirts he never wore . . . Anyway, I'll have a think.'

When he hung up the phone it was with a feeling of despair. She truly was a horrible woman. He sighed for poor Bertie and wondered whether he had ever regretted his choice. Perhaps he had not given the matter much attention. No one really contemplates death when making these life decisions, thought the Major. If they did, what different choices might they make?

ت ؟ ر

It was only a twenty-minute drive from Edgecombe St Mary to the nearby seaside town of Hazelbourne-on-Sea where Bertie and Marjorie lived. The town was a commercial hub for half the county and always busy with shoppers and tourists, so the Major had made careful calculations as to traffic on the bypass, possible parking difficulties in the narrow streets by the church, time required to accept condolences. He had determined to be on the road no later than one thirty. Yet here he was sitting in the car, in front of his house, unmoving. He could feel the blood flowing, slow as lava, through his body. It seemed as if his insides might be melting; his fingers were already boneless. He could exert no pressure on the steering wheel. He worked to quell his panic with a series of deep breaths and sharp exhales. It was not possible that he should miss his own brother's funeral and yet it was equally impossible to turn the ignition key. He wondered briefly whether he was dying. Pity, really, that it hadn't happened yesterday. They could have buried him with Bertie and saved everyone the trouble of coming out twice.

There was a knock on the car window and he turned his head as if in a dream to see Mrs Ali looking anxious. He took a deep breath and managed to land his fingers on the power window button. He had been a reluctant convert to the mania for power everything. Now he was glad there was no handle to crank.

'Are you all right, Major?' she asked.

'I think so,' he said. 'I was just catching my breath. Off to the funeral, you know.'

'Yes, I know,' she said, 'but you're very pale. Are you all right to drive?'

'Hardly a choice, my dear lady,' he said. 'Brother of the deceased.'

'Perhaps you'd better step out and get some fresh air for a minute,' she suggested. 'I have some cold ginger ale here that might do you good.' She was carrying a small basket in which he could see the bright sheen of a green apple, a slightly oily paper bag that suggested cakes, and a tall green bottle.

'Yes, perhaps for a minute,' he agreed, and stepped from the car. The basket, it turned out, was a small care package she had meant to leave on his doorstep for his return.

'I didn't know if you'd remember to eat,' she said as he drank the ginger ale. 'I myself did not consume anything for four days after my husband's funeral. I ended up in the hospital with dehydration.'

'It's very kind of you,' he said. He felt better for the cold drink but his body still ran with small tremors. He was too worried to feel any humiliation. He had to make it to Bertie's funeral somehow. The bus service ran only every two hours with reduced service on Tuesdays and last bus back at five p.m. 'I think I'd better see if there's a taxi available. I'm not sure I'm fit to drive.'

'That is not necessary,' she said, 'I'll drive you myself. I was on my way to Hazelbourne anyway.'

'Oh I couldn't possibly . . .' he began. He didn't like being driven by a woman. He hated their cautious creeping about at junctions, their heavy-handed indifference to the nuances of gear changing, and their complete ignorance of the rearview mirror. Many an afternoon he had crept along the winding lanes behind some slow female driver who blithely bobbed her head to a pop radio station, her stuffed animals nodding their own heads in time on the rear shelf. 'I couldn't possibly,' he repeated.

'You must do me the honour of letting me be of service,' she said. 'My car is parked in the lane.'

She drove like a man, aggressively changing gear into the turns, accelerating away, swinging the tiny Honda over the hills with relish. She had opened her window slightly and the rush of air blew ripples in her rose silk headscarf and tossed stray black locks of hair across her face. She brushed them away impatiently while gunning the car into a flying leap over a small humpbacked bridge.

'How are you feeling?' she asked, and the Major wasn't sure how to answer. Her driving was making him slightly sick, but in the excited, pleasant manner that small boys on roller coasters felt sick.

'I'm not feeling as washed out as before,' he said. 'You drive very well.'

'I like to drive,' she said, smiling at him. 'Just me and the engine. No one to tell me what I should be doing. No accounts, no inventory—just the possibilities of the open road and many unseen destinations.'

'Quite,' he said. 'Have you made many road trips?'

'Oh, no,' she replied. 'Generally I drive into the town every other week to pick up supplies. They have quite a selection of Indian specialty shops on Myrtle Street. Other than that, we use the car mainly for deliveries.'

'You should drive to Scotland or somewhere,' he said. 'Or there are always the autobahns of Germany. Very pleasant driving, I hear.'

'Have you driven much in Europe?' she asked.

'No, Nancy and I talked about it. Driving through France and perhaps up into Switzerland. We never got around to it.'

'You should go,' she said. 'While you have the chance.'

'And you,' he asked. 'Where would you like to go?'

'So many places,' she said. 'But there is the shop.'

'Perhaps your nephew will soon be able to run the shop by himself?' he asked. She laughed a not altogether happy laugh.

'Oh, yes,' she said. 'One day very soon he will be quite able to run the shop and I shall be superfluous.'

The nephew was a recent and not very pleasant addition to the village shop. He was a young man of twenty-five or so. He carried himself stiffly, a hint of insolence on his gaze, as if he were always prepared to meet some new insult. He had none of Mrs Ali's quiet, graceful acquiescence and none of the late Mr Ali's patience. While the Major recognised on some level that this was perhaps his right, it was awkward to ask the price of the frozen peas from a man waiting to be insulted in this very manner. There was also a hint of restrained severity in the nephew toward the aunt, and of this the Major did not approve.

'Will you retire?' he asked.

'It has been suggested,' she said. 'My husband's family lives up north and hopes I will consent to live in their home and take my rightful place in the family.'

'No doubt a loving family will compensate for having to live in the north of England,' said Major Pettigrew, doubting his own words. 'I'm sure you will enjoy being the revered grandmother and matriarch?'

'I have produced no children of my own and my husband is dead,' she replied, an acid tone in her voice. 'Thus I am more to be pitied than revered. I am expected to give up the shop to my nephew, who will then be able to afford to bring a very good wife from Pakistan. In exchange, I will be given houseroom and, no doubt, the honour of taking care of several small children of other family members.'

The Major was silent. He was at once appalled and also reluctant to hear any more. This was why people usually talked about the weather. 'They surely can't force you . . .' he began.

13

'Not legally,' she said. 'My wonderful Ahmed broke with family tradition to make sure the shop came to me. However, there are certain debts to be paid. And then again, what is the rule of law against the weight of family opinion?' She made a left turn, squeezing into a small gap in the hurtling traffic of the coast road. 'Is it worth the struggle, one must ask, if the result is the loss of family and the breaking of tradition?'

'It's downright immoral,' said the outraged Major, his knuckles white on the armrest. That was the trouble with these immigrants, he mused. They pretended to be English. Some of them were even born here. But under the surface were all these barbaric notions and allegiances to foreign customs.

'You are lucky,' said Mrs Ali. 'You Anglo-Saxons have largely broken away from such dependence on family. Each generation feels perfectly free to act alone and you are not afraid.'

'Quite,' said the Major, accepting the compliment automatically but not feeling at all sure that she was right.

❧

She dropped him on the corner a few yards from the church, and he scribbled down his sister-in-law's address on a piece of paper.

'I'm sure I could get a bus back or something,' he said, but they both knew this was not the case so he didn't press his demurral. 'I expect we'll be done by six o'clock, if that's convenient?' he added.

'Certainly.' She took his hand a moment in hers. 'I wish you a strong heart and the love of family this afternoon.' The Major felt a warmth of emotion that he hoped he could keep alight as he faced the awful starkness of Bertie in a walnut box.

❧

The service was largely the same mix of comedy and misery he remembered from Nancy's funeral. The church was large and dismal. It was mid-century Presbyterian, its concrete starkness unrelieved by the incense, candles, and stained glass of Nancy's beloved St Mary's C of E. No ancient bell tower or mossy cemetery here, with compensating beauty and the peace of seeing the same names carved on stone down through the ages. The only comfort was the small satisfaction of seeing the service well attended, to the point where two rows of folding chairs were occupied in the back. Bertie's coffin lay above a shallow depression in the floor, rather like a drainage trough, and at some point in the service the Major was startled by a mechanical hum and Bertie's sudden descent. He didn't sink more than four inches, but the Major stifled a sudden cry and involuntarily reached out a hand. He hadn't been prepared.

Jemima and Marjorie both spoke. He expected to be derisive of their speeches, especially when Jemima, in a wide-brimmed hat of black straw more suitable for a chic wedding, announced a poem composed in her father's honour. But though the poem was indeed atrocious (he remembered only a surfeit of teddy bears and angels quite at odds with the severity of Presbyterian teachings), her genuine grief transformed it into something moving. She wept mascara all over her thin face and had to be half carried from the lectern by her husband.

The Major had not been asked in advance to speak. He considered this a grave oversight and had prepared extensive remarks over and over during the lonely insomnia of the intervening nights. But when Marjorie, returning to her seat after her own short and tearful goodbye to her husband, leaned in and asked him if he wanted to say anything, he declined. To his own surprise, he was feeling weak again and his voice and vision were both blurry with emotion. He simply grasped both her hands for a long moment and tried not to allow any tears to escape.

After the service, shaking hands with people in the smoked-glass lobby, he had been touched by the appearance of several of his and Bertie's old friends, some who he had not seen in many years. Martin James, who had grown up with them both in Edgecombe, had driven over from Kent. Bertie's old neighbour Alan Peters, who had a great golf handicap but had taken up bird-watching instead, had driven over from the other side of the county. Most surprisingly, Jones the Welshman, an old army friend of the Major's dating all the way back to officer training, who had met Bertie a handful of times one summer and had continued to send them both cards every Christmas, had come down from Halifax. The Major gripped his hand and shook his head in wordless thanks. The moment was spoiled only by Jonesy's second wife, a woman neither he nor Bertie had had a chance to meet, who kept weeping brokenheartedly into her large handkerchief.

'Give it over, Lizzy,' said Jones. 'Sorry, she can't help it.'

'I'm so sorry,' wailed Lizzy, blowing her nose. 'I get this way at weddings, too.' The Major didn't mind. At least she had come. Roger had not appeared.

Chapter Two

Bertie's house—he supposed he should have to start thinking of it as Marjorie's house now—was a boxy split-level that she had managed to torque into some semblance of a Spanish villa. The lumpy brick pergola and wrought-iron railings of a rooftop patio crowned the attached double garage. An attic extension with a brick-arched picture window presented a sort of flamenco wink at the seaside town that sprawled below. The front garden was given over mostly to a gravel driveway as big as a car park and the cars were lined up two abreast around a spindly copper fountain in the shape of a very thin, naked young girl. The late afternoon was growing chilly, the clouds swelling in from the sea, but upstairs on the second floor, Marjorie still had the doors from the tiled living room open to the rooftop patio. The Major stayed as deep into the room as possible, trying to suck some warmth from lukewarm tea in a small polystyrene cup. Marjorie's idea of 'nothing elaborate' was a huge banquet of spoon-dripping food—egg salad, lasagna, a wine-soaked chicken stew—served entirely on paper plates. All around the room people cradled sagging plates in their palms, plastic glasses and cups of tea set down haphazardly on window ledges and the top of a large television.

Across the room he caught an undulation in the crowd and followed the stir to see Marjorie embracing Roger. Major Pettigrew's heart jumped to see his tall brown-haired son. So he had come after all.

Roger made copious apologies for his lateness and a solemn promise to help Marjorie and Jemima select a headstone for Uncle Bertie. He was charming and smooth in an expensive, dark suit, unsuitable gaudy tie, and narrow, highly polished shoes too dapper to be anything but Italian. London had polished him to an almost continental urbanity. The Major tried not to disapprove.

'Listen, Dad, Jemima had a word with me about Uncle Bertie's shotgun,' said Roger when they had a moment to sit down on a hard leather sofa to talk. He twitched at his lapel and adjusted the knees of his trousers.

'Yes, I was meaning to talk to Marjorie about it. But it's not really the time, is it?' He had not forgotten about the question of the gun, but it didn't seem important today.

'They understand perfectly about the value of it. Jemima is quite up on the subject.'

'It's not a question of the money, of course,' said the Major sternly. 'Our father was quite clear in his intentions that the pair be reunited. Family heirlooms, family patrimony.'

'Yes, Jemima feels that the pair should be reunited,' said Roger. 'A little restoration may be needed, of course.'

'Mine is in perfect condition,' said the Major. 'I don't believe Bertie quite took the time with his that I did. Not much of a shooting man.'

'Well, anyway,' said Roger, 'Jemima says the market is red hot right now. There aren't Churchills of this quality to be had for love or money. The Americans are signing up for waiting lists.' The Major felt a slow tightening in the muscles of his cheeks. His small smile became quite rigid as he inferred the blow that was to come. 'So, Jemima and I think the most sensible course of action would be to sell them as a pair right now. Of course, it would be

18

your money, Dad, but since you are planning to pass it on to me eventually, I assume, I could really use it now.'

The Major said nothing. He concentrated on breathing. He had never really noticed how much mechanical effort was involved in maintaining the slow in-and-out of the lungs, the smooth passage of oxygen through the nose. Roger had the decency to squirm in his chair. He knew, thought the Major, exactly what he was asking.

'Excuse me, Ernest, there's a strange woman outside who says she's waiting for you?' said Marjorie, appearing suddenly and putting her hand on his shoulder. He looked up, coughing to hide his wet eyes. 'Are you expecting a dark woman in a small Honda?'

'Oh, yes,' he said, 'that's Mrs Ali come to pick me up.'

'A woman taxi driver?' said Roger. 'You hate women drivers.'

'She's not a taxi service,' snapped the Major. 'She's a friend of mine. She owns the village shop.'

'In that case, you'd better have her come in and have some tea,' said Marjorie, her lips tight with disapproval. She looked vaguely at the buffet. 'I'm sure she'd like a piece of Madeira cake—everyone likes Madeira cake, don't they?'

'I'll do that, thank you,' said the Major, rising to his feet.

'Actually, Dad, I was hoping I could drive you home,' said Roger. The Major was confused.

'But you came by train,' he said.

'Yes, that was the plan,' said Roger, 'but things changed. Sandy and I decided to drive down together. She's out looking at weekend cottages right now.'

'Weekend cottages?' It was too much to take in.

'Yes, Sandy thought since I had to come down anyway . . . I've been on at her about getting a place down here. We could be nearer to you.'

'A weekend cottage,' repeated the Major, still struggling with the implications of this person named Sandy.

'I'm dying for you to meet her. She should be here any minute.' Roger scanned the room in case she had suddenly come in. 'She's

American, from New York. She has a rather important job in the fashion business.'

'Mrs Ali is waiting for me,' said the Major. 'It would be rude—'

'Oh, I'm sure she'll understand,' interrupted Roger.

❦

Outside the air was chill. The view of the town and the sea beyond was smudged around the edges with darkness. Mrs Ali had parked her Honda just inside the curly iron gates with their depictions of flying dolphins. She waved and stepped from the car to greet him. She was holding a paperback and half a cheeseburger wrapped in its garish, oily paper. The Major was venomously opposed to the awful fast-food places that were gradually taking over the ugly stretch of road between the hospital and the seafront, but he was prepared to find her indulgence charmingly out of character.

'Mrs Ali, won't you come in and have some tea?' he said.

'No, thank you, Major, I don't want to intrude,' she said. 'But please don't rush on my account. I'm quite fine here.' She indicated the book in her hand.

'We have quite a buffet inside,' offered the Major. 'We even have homemade Madeira cake.'

'I'm quite happy, really,' she said, smiling at him. 'You take your time with your family and I'll be waiting when you're ready.'

The Major was miserably confused. He was tempted to climb in the car and go right now. It would be early enough when they got back to invite Mrs Ali in for tea. They could discuss her new book. Perhaps she might listen to some of the funnier aspects of the day.

'You're going to think me impossibly rude,' he said. 'But my son managed to come down after all, by car.'

'How lovely for you,' she said.

'Yes, and he would like—of course I told him I'd already arranged to go home with you. . . .'

'No, no, you must go home with your son,' she said.

'I'm most awfully sorry,' he said. 'He seems to have acquired a girlfriend. Apparently they've been looking at weekend houses.'

'Ah.' She understood right away. 'A weekend house near you? How wonderful that will be.'

'I might see what I can do to help them with that,' he said, almost to himself. He looked up. 'Are you sure you won't come in and have some tea?' he asked.

'No, thank you,' she said. 'You must enjoy your family and I must be getting back.'

'I really am in your debt,' he said. 'I can't thank you enough for your gracious assistance.'

'It's nothing at all,' she said. 'Please don't mention it.' She gave him a slight bow, got in the car, and reversed it in a tight circle that flung gravel in a wide arc. The Major tried to wave but felt dishonest, causing the gesture to fail mid-arm. Mrs Ali did not look back.

As her little blue car pulled away, he had to resist the urge to run after it. He had held the promise of the ride home as if it were a small coal in his hand, to warm him in the dark press of the crowd. The Honda braked at the gate and the tyres squirted gravel again as it lurched to avoid the sweeping oval headlights of a large black car, which showed no shift or sudden braking. It only slid up the driveway and parked in the large open space the other guests had politely left clear in front of the door.

The Major, trudging back up the gravel incline, arrived slightly out of breath just as the driver reholstered a silver lipstick and opened her door. More from instinct than inclination, he held the door for her. She looked surprised and then smiled as she unfolded tanned and naked legs from the close confines of the champagne leather cockpit.

'I'm not going to do that thing where I assume you're the butler and you turn out to be Lord So-and-So,' she said, smoothing down her plain black skirt. It was of expensive material but unexpected brevity. She wore it with a fitted black jacket worn over nothing—at least, no shirt was immediately visible in the cleavage, which, due to her height and vertiginous heels, was almost at the Major's eye level.

'The name is Pettigrew,' he said. He was reluctant to admit anything more before he had to. He was still trying to process the assault of her American vowels and the flash of impossible white teeth.

'Well, that narrows it down to the right place,' she said. 'I'm Sandy Dunn. I'm a friend of Roger Pettigrew?' The Major considered denying Roger's presence.

'I believe he is talking with his aunt just now,' he said, looking over his shoulder at the open hallway as if by the merest glance he could map the invisible crowd upstairs. 'Perhaps I should get him for you?'

'Oh, just point me in his general direction,' she said, and moved past him. 'Is that lasagna I smell? I'm starving.'

'Do come in,' he said.

'Thanks,' she said over her shoulder. 'Nice to meet you, Mr Pettigrew.'

'It's Major, actually . . .' he said, but she was already gone, stiletto heels clicking on the garish green and white tiles. She left a trail of citrus perfume in the air. It was not unpleasant, he thought, but it hardly offset the appalling manners.

❧ ❧ ❧

The Major found himself loitering in the hall, unwilling to face what was inevitable upstairs. He would have to be formally introduced to the Amazon. He could not believe Roger had invited her. She would no doubt make his prior reticence out to be some sort of idiocy. Americans seemed to enjoy the sport of publicly humiliating one another. The occasional American sitcoms that came on TV were filled with childish fat men poking fun at others, all rolled eyeballs and metallic taped laughter.

He sighed. Of course, he would have to pretend to be pleased, for Roger's sake. Best to brazen it out rather than to appear embarrassed in front of Marjorie.

Upstairs, the mood was slowly shifting into cheerfulness. With their grief sopped up by a heavy lunch and their spirits fuelled by several drinks, the guests were blossoming out into normal conversations. The minister was just inside the doorway discussing the diesel consumption of his new Volvo with one of Bertie's old work colleagues. A young woman, with a squirming toddler clasped to her lap, was extolling the benefits of some workout regime to a dazed Jemima.

'It's like spinning, only the upper body is a full boxing workout.'

'Sounds hard,' said Jemima. She had taken off the festive hat and her highlighted hair was escaping from its bun. Her head slumped toward her right shoulder, as if her thin neck was having difficulty holding it up. Her young son, Gregory, finishing a leg of cold chicken, dropped the bone in her upturned palm and scampered off toward the desserts.

'You do need a good sense of balance,' the young woman agreed.

It was nice, he supposed, that Jemima's friends had come to support her. They had created a little clump in the church, taking over several rows toward the front. However, he was at a loss to imagine why they had considered it appropriate to bring their children. One small baby had screamed at random moments during the service and now three children, covered in jam stains, were sitting under the buffet table licking the icing off cupcakes. When they were done with each cake, they slipped it, naked and dissolving with spit, back onto a platter. Gregory snatched an untouched cake and ran by the French doors where Marjorie stood with Roger and the American. Marjorie reached a practised hand to stop him.

'You know there's no running in the house, Gregory,' she said, grabbing his elbow.

'Ow!' he squealed, twisting in her grip to suggest she was torturing him. She gave a faint smile and pulled him close to bend down and kiss his sweaty hair. 'Be good now, dearie,' she said and released him. The boy stuck out his tongue and scuttled away.

'Dad, over here,' called Roger, who had spotted him watching. The Major waved and began a reluctant voyage across the room between groups of people whose conversations had whipped them into tight circles, like leaves in a squall.

'He's a very sensitive child,' Marjorie was telling the American. 'High-strung, you know, but very intelligent. My daughter is having him tested for high IQ.' Marjorie did not seem at all offended by the interloper. In fact, she seemed to be doing her best to impress her. Marjorie always began impressing people by mentioning her gifted grandson. From there, she usually managed to work the conversation backward to herself.

'Dad, I want you to meet Sandy Dunn,' said Roger. 'Sandy's in fashion PR and special events. Her company works with all the important designers, you know.'

'Hi,' said Sandy extending her hand. 'I knew I was right about the butler thing.' The Major shook her hand, and raised his eyebrows at Roger, signalling him to continue with the introduction, even though it was all in the wrong order. Roger only gave him a big vacant smile.

'Ernest Pettigrew,' said the Major. 'Major Ernest Pettigrew, Royal Sussex, retired.' He managed a small smile and added, for emphasis: 'Rose Lodge, Blackberry Lane, Edgecombe St Mary.'

'Oh, yes. Sorry, Dad,' said Roger.

'It's nice to meet you properly, Ernest,' said Sandy. The Major winced at the casual use of his first name.

'Sandy's father is big in the insurance industry in Ohio,' said Roger. 'And her mother, Emmeline, is on the board of the Newport Art Museum.'

'How nice for Ms Dunn,' said the Major.

'Roger, they don't want to hear about me,' said Sandy. She tucked her hand through Roger's arm. 'I want to find out all about your family.'

'We have quite a nice art gallery in the Town Hall,' said Marjorie. 'Mostly local artists, you know. But they have a lovely Bouguereau painting of young girls up on the Downs. You should bring your mother.'

'Do you live in London?' asked the Major. He waited, stiff with concern, for any hint that they were living together.

'I have a small loft in Southwark,' she said. 'It's near the new Tate.'

'Oh, it's an enormous place,' said Roger. He was as excited as a small boy describing a new bike.

For a moment, the Major saw him at eight years old again, with a shock of brown curls his mother refused to cut. The bike had been red, with thick studded tyres and a seat with springs like a car suspension. Roger had seen it at the big toy store in London, where a man did tricks on it, right on a stage inside the main door. The bike had completely pushed from his mind all memory of the Science Museum. Nancy, weary from dragging a small boy around London, had shaken her head in mock despair as Roger tried to impress upon them the enormous importance of the bike and the necessity for purchasing it at once. They had, of course, said no. There was plenty of room to adjust the seat on Roger's existing bicycle, a solid-framed green bike that had been the Major's at a similar age. His parents had stored it in the shed at Rose Lodge, wrapped securely in burlap and oiled once a year.

'The only problem is finding furniture on a big enough scale. She's having a sectional custom made in Japan.' Roger was still boasting about the loft. Marjorie looked impressed.

'I find G-Plan makes a good couch,' she said. Bertie and Marjorie had acquired most of their furniture from G-Plan—good solid upholstered couches and sturdy square-edged tables and chests of drawers. The choice might be limited, Bertie used to say, but they were solid enough to last a lifetime. No need to ever change a thing.

'I hope you ordered it with slipcovers,' Marjorie advised. 'It lasts so much better than upholstery, especially if you use antimacassars.'

'Goatskin,' said Roger. There was great pride in his voice. 'She saw my goatskin lounger and said I was ahead of the trend.'

The Major wondered whether it was possible he had been too strict with Roger as a child and thereby inspired his son to such excesses. Nancy, of course, had tried to spoil him rotten. He had been a late gift to them, born just as they had given up all hope of having children, and Nancy could never resist making that little face smile from ear to ear. It was he who had been forced to put a stop to many an extravagance.

'Roger really has an eye for design,' said Sandy. 'He could be a decorator.' Roger blushed.

'Really?' said the Major. 'That's quite an accusation.'

They left soon after, Sandy handing her car keys to Roger to drive. She took the passenger side without comment, leaving the Major to sit in the back.

'Are you all right back there, Dad?' asked Roger.

'Fine, fine,' said the Major. There was a thin line, he reflected, between comfort and smothering. The car's back seat seemed to mould itself around his thighs. The ceiling also curved close and pale. The sensation was of being a large baby riding in a rather luxurious pram. The quiet engine contributed its own hummed lullaby, and the Major struggled against an encroaching drowsiness.

'I'm so sorry Roger was late today,' said Sandy, turning around to smile at him through the gap in the seats. Her bosom strained at the seatbelt. 'We were looking at a cottage and the realtor—I mean the estate agent—was late.'

'Looking at a cottage?' he said. 'What about work?'

'No, that all got resolved,' said Roger, keeping his attention fixed on the road. 'I told the client I had a funeral and he could push things back a day or get someone else.'

'So you looked at cottages?'

'It was my fault entirely, Ernest,' said Sandy. 'I thought I'd scheduled plenty of time to fit it in before I dropped Roger off at the church. The estate agent messed things up royally.'

'Yes, I'm going to call that agent tomorrow and let her know just how offended I am that she made me so late,' said Roger.

'No need to cause a ruckus, darling. Your aunt Marjorie was extremely gracious about it.' Sandy put a hand on Roger's arm and smiled back at the Major. 'You all were.' The Major tried but failed to summon his rage. In his sleepy state, he could only come up with the thought that this young woman must be very good at her public relations job.

'Touring cottages,' he murmured.

'We shouldn't have gone, I know, but these cottages get snapped right up,' said Sandy. 'Remember that cute place near Cromer?'

'We've only looked at a few places,' said Roger, his eyes giving an anxious glance in the rearview mirror. 'But this area is our priority.'

'I admit it's more convenient than the Norfolk Broads or the Cotswolds,' said Sandy. 'And of course for Roger you're the big attraction.'

'An attraction?' said the Major. 'If I'm to outrank Norfolk, perhaps I'd better start offering cream teas in the garden.'

'Dad!'

'Oh, your father is so funny,' said Sandy. 'I just love that dry humour.'

'Oh, he's a joke a minute, aren't you, Dad?' said Roger.

The Major said nothing. He relaxed his head against the leather seat and gave himself up to the soothing vibrations of the road. He felt like a child again as he dozed and listened to Roger and Sandy talking together in low voices. They might have been his parents, their soft voices fading in and out, as they drove the long miles home from his boarding school for the holidays.

They had always made a point of coming to pick him up, while most of the other boys took the train. They thought it made them good parents, and besides, the headmaster always held a lovely reception for the parents who came, mostly ones who lived nearby. His parents enjoyed the mingling and were always jubilant if they managed to secure an invitation to Sunday luncheon at some grand house. Leaving late in the afternoon, sleepy with roast beef and trifle, they had to drive long into the night to get home. He would fall asleep in the back. No matter how angry he was at them for sticking him with lunch at the home of some boy who was equally eager to be free of such obligations, he always found the trip soothing; the dark, the glow of the headlamps tunnelling a road, his parents' voices held low so as not to disturb him. It always felt like love.

'Here we are,' said Roger. His voice was brisk. The Major blinked his eyes and struggled to pretend he had been awake the whole time. He had forgotten to leave a light on and the brick and tile façade of Rose Lodge was barely visible in the sliver of moonlight.

'What a charming house,' said Sandy. 'It's bigger than I expected.'

'Yes, there were what the Georgians called "improvements" to the original seventeenth-century house which make it look more imposing than it is,' said the Major. 'You'll come in and have some tea, of course,' he added, opening his door.

'Actually, we won't come in, if you don't mind,' said Roger. 'We've got to get back to London to meet some friends for dinner.'

'But it'll be ten o'clock before you get there,' said the Major, feeling a ghost of indigestion just at the thought of eating so late.

Roger laughed. 'Not the way Sandy drives. But we won't make it unless we leave now. I'll see you to the door, though.' He hopped out of the car. Sandy slid over the gear shift into the driver's seat, legs flashing like scimitars. She pressed something and the window whirred down.

'Good night, Ernest,' she said, holding out her hand. 'It was a pleasure.'

'Thank you,' said the Major. He dropped her hand and turned on his heel. Roger scurried behind him down the path.

'See you again soon,' called Sandy. The window whirred shut on any further communication.

'I can hardly wait,' mumbled the Major.

'Mind your step on the path, Dad,' said Roger behind him. 'You ought to get a security light, you know. One of those motion-activated ones.'

'What a splendid idea,' he replied. 'With all the rabbits around here, not to mention our neighbourhood badger, it'll be like one of those discos you used to frequent.' He reached his door and, key ready, tried to locate the lock in one smooth move. The key grated across the plate and spun out of his fingers. There was the clunk of brass on brick and then an ominous quiet thud as the key landed somewhere in soft dirt.

'Damn and blast it,' he said.

'See what I mean?' said Roger.

Roger found the key under the broad leaf of a hosta, snapping several quilted leaves in the process, and opened the door with no effort. The Major passed into the dark hallway and, a prayer on his lips, found the light switch at first snap.

'Will you be okay, Dad?' He watched Roger hesitate, one hand on the doorjamb, his face showing the nervous uncertainty of a child who knows he has behaved badly.

'I'll be perfectly fine, thank you,' he said. Roger averted his eyes but continued to linger, almost as if waiting to be called to account for his actions today or to have some demands made of him. The Major said nothing. Let Roger spend a couple of long nights tossing with a prickling conscience along with those infernal and shiny American legs. It was a satisfaction to know that Roger had not yet lost all sense of right and wrong. The Major was in no mind to grant any speedy absolutions.

'Okay, I'll call you tomorrow.'

'It's not necessary.'

'I want to,' insisted Roger. He stepped forward and the Major found himself teetering in an awkward angular hug. He clung to the heavy door with one hand, both to keep it open and to prevent himself falling. With the other he gave a couple of tentative pats to the part of Roger's back he could reach. Then he rested his hand for a moment and felt, in his son's knobby shoulder blade, the small child he had always loved.

'You'd better hurry now,' he said, blinking hard. 'It's a long drive back to town.'

'I do worry about you, Dad.' Roger stepped away and became again the strange adult who existed mostly at the end of the telephone. 'I'll call you. Sandy and I will work out our schedules so we can come down and see you in a couple of weeks.'

'Sandy? Oh, right. That would be delightful.' His son grinned and waved as he left, which reassured the Major that his dryness of tone had remained undetected. He waved back and watched his son leaving happy, convinced that his ageing father would be buoyed up by the prospect of the visit to come.

Alone in the house he felt the full weight of exhaustion settle on him like iron shackles. He considered stopping in the living room for a reviving brandy, but there was no fire in the grate and the house suddenly seemed chill and dark. He decided to go straight to bed. The small staircase, with its faded oriental runner, loomed as steep and impassable as Everest's Hillary Steps. He braced his arm on the polished walnut banister and began to haul himself up the narrow treads. He considered himself to be generally in good health and made a point of doing a full set of stretching exercises every day, including several deep knee bends. Yet today—overcome by the strain, he supposed—he had to pause halfway up the stairs to catch his breath. It occurred to him to wonder what would happen if he passed out and fell. He saw himself lying splayed out across the bottom treads, head down and blue in the face. It might be days before he was found. He had never thought of this before. He shook his shoulders and straightened up his back. It was ridiculous to think of it now, he reprimanded himself. No good acting like a poor old man just because Bertie had died. He took the remaining stairs with as regular and fluid a step as he could manage and did not allow himself to puff and pant until he had gained his bedroom and sunk down on the soft wide bed in relief.

Chapter Three

Two days passed before it occurred to the Major that Mrs Ali had not called in to check on him and that this had caused him a certain disappointment. The paper boy was quite well again, judging by the ferocity with which the *Times* was thrown at his front door. He had had his share of other visitors. Alice Pierce from next door had come round yesterday with a hand-painted condolence card and a casserole dish of what she said was her famous organic vegetarian lasagna and informed him that it was all over the village that he had lost his brother. There was enough of the pale brown and green mush to feed an army of organic vegetarian friends. Unfortunately, he did not have the same kind of Bohemian friends as Alice and so the dish was now fermenting in his refrigerator, spreading its unpleasant plankton smell into the milk and butter. Today, Daisy Green, the Vicar's wife, dropped by unannounced with her usual entourage of Alma Shaw and Grace DeVere from the Flower Guild and insisted on making him a cup of tea in his own house. Usually it made the Major chuckle to see the trinity of ladies going about the business of controlling all social and civic life in the village. Daisy had seized the simple title of Flower Guild chairwoman and used it to endow herself with full noblesse oblige. The other ladies swam in her wake like frightened ducklings, as she flew about offering unsolicited advice and issuing petty directives which somehow people found it easier to follow than refuse. It amused him that Father Christopher, the Vicar, thought he chose his own sermons and that Alec Shaw, retired from the Bank of England, was made to join the Halloween Fun Committee and host junior pétanque on the village green despite being almost medically allergic to children. It amused him less when, treating their spinster friend as a project, Daisy and Alma would ask Grace to play her harp or greet people at the door at various charity events, while consigning certain other unattached ladies to cloakroom and tea serving duties. Even today, they had conspired to make a presentation of Grace. She was fully primped, her slightly elongated face made papery with pale powder and a girly pink lipstick, a coquettish scarf tied in a bow under her left ear as if she were off to a party.

Grace was actually quite a sharp and pleasant woman at times. She was very knowledgeable about roses and about local history. The Major remembered a conversation they had enjoyed in the church one day, when he had found her carefully examining seventeenth-century wedding records. She had worn white cotton gloves to protect the books from her fingers and had been unconcerned about her own clothes, which had been coated with soft dust. 'Look,' she had whispered, a magnifying lens held close to the pale brown ink scribbles of an ancient vicar. 'It says, "Mark Salisbury married this day to Daniela de Julien, late of La Rochelle." This is the first record of Huguenots settling in the village.' He had stayed with her half an hour or so, watching her page reverently through the subsequent years, looking for hints and clues to the tangle of old families in the area. He had offered to lend her a recent history of Sussex that might be of use, only to find that she had a copy already. She also owned several more obscure and wonderful old texts that he ended up borrowing from her. For a brief while, he had considered pursuing their friendship. However, Daisy and Alma had no sooner learned of the conversation than they had begun to interfere. There were coy comments in the street, a whispered word or two at the golf club bar. Finally they had sent Grace to a luncheon date with him, all made up and forced into a hideous silk dress. She looked as ruched and tied as a holiday pork roast. They must have filled her head with advice on men, too, so that she sat and made frozen conversation all through her green salad (no dressing) and plain fish, while he chewed a steak and kidney pie as if it were shoe leather and watched the hands of the pub clock creep unwillingly around the dial. He remembered that he had dropped her at her door with mingled relief and regret.

Today, Grace was left to keep him pinned in the living room with whispery conversation about the weather while Daisy and Alma clattered the cups and banged the tray and talked to him at the tops of their voices from the kitchen. He caught Grace shifting her eyes to the left and right around the room and knew all three of them were inspecting him and his house for signs of neglect and decline. He squirmed in his chair with impatience until the tea was brought in.

'There's nothing like a good cup of tea from a real china pot, is there?' said Daisy, handing him his cup and saucer. 'Biscuit?'

'Thank you,' he said. They had brought him a large tin of assorted 'luxury' biscuits. The tin was printed with views of thatched cottages of England and the biscuits were appropriately tumescent; stuffed with fudge, dribbled with pastel icing, or wrapped in assorted foils. He suspected that Alma had picked it out. Unlike her husband, Alec, who was proud of his history as an East End boy, Alma tried hard to forget her origins in London; but she sometimes betrayed herself with a taste for showy luxuries and the sweet tooth of someone who grew up without quite enough to eat. The other ladies, he suspected, were hiding their mortification. He selected an undecorated shortbread and took a bite. The ladies settled themselves on chairs, smiling at him with compassion as if watching a starving cat lap from a saucer of milk. It was somewhat difficult to chew under the scrutiny and he took a large swallow of tea to help the sandy biscuit down. The tea was weak and tasted of paper. He was rendered speechless by the realisation that they had brought their own teabags as well.

'Was your brother older than you?' asked Grace. She leaned toward him, her eyes wide with compassion.

'No—younger, actually, by two years.' There was a pause.

'He was ill for some time?' she asked hopefully.

'No, quite sudden, I'm afraid.'

'I'm so, so very sorry.' She fussed with her fingers at the large green stone brooch at her high-collared neck. She cast her eyes down at the carpet, as if looking for a thread of conversation in the geometric patterns of the faded Bokhara. The other ladies busied themselves with their teacups and there was a palpable desire in the room for the conversation to move on. Grace, however, could not find her way out.

'Was his family with him at the end?' she said, looking at him desperately. He was tempted to tell her that no, Bertie had died alone in an empty house and been discovered weeks later by the charlady from next door. It would be satisfying to puncture the vapid conversation with the nail of deliberate cruelty. However, he was aware of the other two women watching her struggle and doing nothing to help.

'His wife was with him when they took him to the hospital and his daughter was able to see him for a few minutes, I understand,' he said.

'Ah, that's wonderful,' she said.

'Wonderful,' echoed Daisy, and smiled at him as if this wiped away any further obligation to be sad.

'It must be a great comfort to you to know he died surrounded by family,' added Alma. She took a large bite from a fat dark chocolate biscuit. A faint chemical odour of bitter orange reached the Major's nostrils. He would have liked to reply that this was not so, that he was pierced with pain that no one had thought to call him until it was all over and that he had missed saying goodbye to his younger brother. He wanted to spit this at them, but his tongue felt thick and useless.

'And of course he was surrounded by the comfort of the Lord,' said Daisy. She spoke in an awkward rush as if she were bringing up something vaguely impolite.

'Amen,' whispered Alma, selecting a crème sandwich.

'Oh, go to hell,' whispered the Major into the translucent bottom of his teacup and covered his muttering with a cough.

'Thank you so much for coming,' he said, waving from the doorstep and feeling more generous now that they were leaving.

'We'll come again soon,' promised Daisy.

'Lovely to see the Vierge de Cléry still blooming,' added Grace, touching her fingertips to a nodding stem of white cabbage rose as she slipped through the gate behind them. He wished she had spoken about the roses earlier. The afternoon might have passed more pleasantly. Of course it wasn't their fault, he reminded himself. They were following the accepted rituals. They were saying what they could at a time when even the finest poetry must fail to comfort. They were probably genuinely concerned for him. Perhaps he had been too churlish.

It surprised him that his grief was sharper than in the past few days. He had forgotten that grief does not decline in a straight line or along a slow curve like a graph in a child's math book. Instead, it was almost as if his body contained a big pile of garden rubbish full both of heavy lumps of dirt and of sharp thorny brush that would stab him when he least expected it. If Mrs Ali had dropped in—and he felt again the slight pique that she had not—she would have understood. Mrs Ali, he was sure, would have let him talk about Bertie. Not the deceased body already liquefying in the ground, but Bertie as he was.

The Major stepped out into the now empty garden to feel the sun on his face, shutting his eyes and breathing slowly to lessen the impact of an image of Bertie in the ground, cold green flesh softening into jelly. He folded his arms over his chest and tried not to sob aloud for Bertie and for himself, that this should be all the fate left to them.

The warmth of the sun held him up and a small brown chaffinch, worrying the leaves of the yew, seemed to chide him for being lugubrious. He opened his eyes to the bright afternoon and decided that he might benefit from a short walk through the village. He might stop in at the village shop to purchase some tea. It would, he thought, be generous of him to make a visit and give the busy Mrs Ali a chance to make her excuses for not coming to see him.

ᘛ ᘚ ᘘ

He had been many decades, as man and boy, in the village of Edgecombe St Mary, and yet the walk down the hill to the village never ceased to give him pleasure. The lane was steeply cambered to either side, as if the narrow tarmac were the curving roof of some buried chamber. The dense hedges of privet, hawthorn, and beech swelled together as fat and complacent as medieval burghers. The air was scented with their spicy dry fragrance overlaid with the tang of animals in the fields behind the cottages. Garden gates and driveways gave glimpses of well-stocked gardens and thick lawns studded with clover clumps and dandelions. He liked the clover, evidence of the country always pressing in close, quietly sabotaging anyone who tried to manicure nature into suburban submission. As he rounded a curve, the hedges gave way to the plain wire fence of a sheep field and allowed a view of twenty miles of Sussex countryside spreading beyond the roofs of the village below. Behind him, above his own house, the hills swelled upward into the rabbit-cropped grass of the chalk downs. Below him, the Weald of Sussex cradled fields full of late rye and the acid yellow of mustard. He liked to pause at the stile, one foot up on the step, and drink in the landscape. Something—perhaps it was the quality of the light, or the infinite variety of greens in the trees and hedges—never failed to fill his heart with a love of country that he would have been embarrassed to express aloud. Today, he leaned on the stile and tried to let the colours of the landscape soak in and calm him. The business at hand, of visiting the shop, had somehow quickened his heart and overlaid the dullness of grief with an urgent and not unpleasant flutter. The shop lay only a few hundred yards downhill of his position, and the wonders of gravity helped him as he thrust away from the stile and continued to stride down the hill. He made the turn past the Royal Oak at the bottom, its timbered façade almost entirely obscured by hanging baskets of improbably coloured petunias, and the shop came into view across the gently rising roundel of the village green.

The orange plastic sign, 'Supersaver SuperMart,' winked in the low September sun. Mrs Ali's nephew was pasting to the plate glass window a large poster advertising a sale on canned peas; the Major hesitated in mid-stride. He would rather have waited until the nephew was not around. He did not like the young man's perpetual frown, which, he admitted, might be the simple result of unfortunately prominent eyebrows. It was a ridiculous and indefensible dislike, the Major had more than once admonished himself, but it caused his hand to once again tighten around the head of his cane as he marched over the grass and in at the door. The shop bell's tinkle made the young man look up from his task. He nodded and the Major gave a slightly smaller nod in return and looked around for Mrs Ali.

The store contained a single small counter and cash register up front, backed by a display of cigarettes and a lottery machine. Four narrow but clean aisles stretched back through the low-ceilinged rectangular room. They contained a well-stocked but plain selection of foods. There were beans and bread, teabags and dried pasta, frozen curries and bags of curly chips and chicken nuggets for children's suppers. There was also a large array of chocolates and sweets, a card section, the newspapers. Only the canisters of loose tea and a dish of homemade samosas hinted at Mrs Ali's exotic heritage. There was an awkward extension in the back that contained a small area of bulk items like dry dog food, potting soil, some kind of chicken pellets, and plastic-wrapped multipacks of Heinz baked beans. The

Major couldn't imagine who purchased bulk items here. Everyone did their main shopping at the supermarket in Hazelbourne-on-Sea or drove to the new superstore and outlet centre in Kent. It was also possible to hop over to France on a cheap ferry, and he often saw his neighbours staggering home with giant boxes of washing powder and strangely shaped bottles of cheap foreign beer from the Calais hypermarket. For most people, the village shop was strictly for when one had run out of something, especially late at night. The Major noticed that they never thanked Mrs Ali for being open until eight on weeknights and also on Sunday mornings, but they loved to mumble about the prices being high and they speculated about Mrs Ali's income from being an authorised lottery dealer.

He did not hear or sense Mrs Ali's presence in the empty store and so, rather than scour each aisle, the Major made his way as casually as possible back toward the bulk sales area, quite ignoring the tea canisters near the front counter and cash register. Beyond this area was the shop office, a small area hidden behind a curtain of stiff vertical vinyl panels.

He had inspected the prices on each stack of bulk items and had shifted to reviewing the ham-and-egg pies in the back-wall dairy case when Mrs Ali finally appeared through the vinyl, carrying an armful of Halloween-themed boxes of mini apple pies.

'Major Pettigrew,' she said with surprise.

'Mrs Ali,' he replied, almost distracted from his purpose by the realisation that American Halloween hoopla was making inroads into British baked goods.

'How are you?' She looked around for somewhere to put the boxes.

'Fine, fine,' he said. 'I wanted to thank you for your kindness the other day.'

'No, no, it was nothing.' She seemed to want to wave her hands but, encumbered by the pies, she could only waggle her fingertips.

'And I wanted to apologise—' he began.

39

'Please don't mention it,' she said, and her face tightened as she looked past his shoulder. The Major felt between his shoulder blades the presence of the nephew. He turned around. The nephew seemed bulkier in the narrow aisle, his face shadowed by the bright daylight from the shop front. The Major moved aside to let him pass, but the young man stopped and also stepped aside. An invisible pull invited the Major to pass him and exit the shop. His body, stubborn with the desire to stay, kept him planted where he was.

He sensed that Mrs Ali did not wish him to go on with his apologies in front of her nephew.

'Again, I just wanted to thank you both for your kind condolences,' he said, particularly pleased with the 'both,' which dropped in softly, like a perfectly putted golf ball. The nephew was forced to nod his head in appreciation.

'Anything we can do, you must just ask, Major,' said Mrs Ali. 'Beginning, perhaps, with some fresh tea?'

'I am running a little low,' said the Major.

'Very well.' She lifted her chin and spoke to the nephew while looking at a space somewhere over his head. 'Abdul Wahid, would you fetch the rest of the Halloween specials and I'll take care of the Major's tea order?' She marched past both of them with her armful of cake boxes and the Major followed, squeezing by the nephew with an apologetic smile. The nephew only scowled and then disappeared behind the vinyl curtain.

Dumping the boxes on the counter Mrs Ali rummaged behind it for her spiral-bound order book and began to leaf through the pages.

'My dear lady,' began the Major. 'Your kindness to me—'

'I would rather not discuss it in front of my nephew,' she whispered and a brief frown marred the smoothness of her oval face.

'I don't quite understand,' said the Major.

'My nephew has recently returned from his studies in Pakistan and is not yet reacquainted with many things here.' She looked to make sure the nephew was out of earshot. 'He is having some worries about his poor auntie's well-being, you know. He does not like it when I drive the car.'

'Oh.' It was slowly dawning on the Major that the nephew's concerns might include strange men such as himself. He felt disappointment sag his cheeks.

'Not that I have any intention of paying the least heed, of course,' she said, and this time she smiled and touched a hand to her hair as if to check that it was not escaping its tightly coiled, low bun. 'Only I'm trying to re-educate him slowly. The young can be so stubborn.'

'Quite. I quite understand.'

'So if I can do anything for you, Major, you must just ask,' she said. Her eyes were so warm and brown, the expression of concern on her face so genuine that the Major, after a quick look around himself, threw caution to the winds.

'Well, actually,' he stammered. 'I was wondering if you were going to town later this week. It's just that I'm still not feeling well enough to drive and I have to stop in and see the family solicitor.'

'I usually go in on Thursday afternoons but I can possibly—'

'Thursday would be fine,' said the Major quickly.

'I could pick you up around two o'clock?' she asked.

The Major, feeling very tactful, lowered his voice. 'Perhaps it would be most convenient if I waited at the bus stop on the main road—save you driving all the way up to me?'

'Yes, that would be perfectly convenient,' she said, and smiled. The Major felt that he was in danger of smiling like a fool.

'See you Thursday, then,' he said. 'Thank you.' As he left the shop, it occurred to him that he had failed to buy any tea. It was just as well really, since he was amply stocked for his own needs and visited only by those who brought their own. As he strode back across the village green, he was aware of a lighter step and easier heart.

Chapter Four

Thursday morning, the Major surfaced from sleep to the sound of rain hammering at the eaves like fists. It was also dripping, in an infuriatingly random and unmusical pattern, onto the weak spot on the windowsill where the wood was beginning to soften. The bedroom swam in blue darkness and from the stuffy cocoon of his blankets he could picture the clouds dropping their heavy loads of water as they bumped against the flank of the Downs. The room, with its heavy beams, seemed to be actively sucking in all the damp. The blue-striped wallpaper looked yellow in the strange rainy light and ready to peel itself off the thick plaster walls under the weight of the moist air. He lay in a stupor, sunk in the clumped duck-down pillow, and watched his hopes for the day being washed away down the bubbled glass of the window.

He cursed himself for having assumed the weather would be sunny. Perhaps it was the result of evolution, he thought—some adaptive gene that allowed the English to go on making blithe outdoor plans in the face of almost certain rain. He remembered Bertie's wedding, almost forty years ago: an alfresco luncheon at a small hotel with no room in the boxy dining room for fifty guests seeking shelter from a sudden thunderstorm. He seemed to remember Marjorie crying and an absurd amount of wet tulle whipped around her angular frame like a melting meringue. He was not usually such a fool about rain. When he played golf, he made sure to carry a pair of his old army gaiters with him, ready to strap them around his socks at the first sign of a shower. He kept a rolled-up yellow raincoat in the boot of his car and had a collection of stout umbrellas in the front hall rack. He had been teased at many a cricket match, on blazing hot days, for always carrying a small folding stool that held a plastic poncho in a zippered side pocket. No, he had not even considered the question of weather or so much as looked at the paper or the six o'clock news because he had wanted today to be sunny and, like King Canute demanding that the sea withdraw, he had simply willed the sun to shine.

The sun was to have been his excuse to turn a borrowed car ride into something more. An invitation to walk the seafront would have been entirely appropriate, given the beauty of the day. Now a walk was out of the question and he was afraid that an invitation to afternoon tea in a hotel would reflect too much presumption. He sat up rather suddenly and the room swam around him. What if Mrs Ali used the rain as an excuse to telephone and cancel entirely? He would have to reschedule his meeting with Mortimer or drive himself.

Assuming she did not cancel, there were certain adjustments to be made to his grooming and wardrobe. He got up, slipped his feet into Moroccan leather slippers, and padded over to the large pine wardrobe. He had planned on a tweed jacket, wool slacks, and a splash of celebratory aftershave. However, the tweed gave off a faint odour when moist. He didn't want to fill Mrs Ali's small car with a smell like wet sheep dipped in bay rum. He stood for a moment and ruminated.

In the dresser mirror on the opposite wall he caught the dark image of his face, barely lit by the dull morning. He peered closer, rubbing his short, bristled hair and wondering how he could possibly have become so damn old looking. He tried a smile, which got rid of the dour look and slight jowls but crinkled the skin around his blue eyes. He was partly convinced that it made an improvement and tried several degrees of smile before he realised he was being absurd. Nancy would never have put up with him being so vain and neither, he was sure, would Mrs Ali.

Reconsidering his wardrobe possibilities, he decided that today would be the perfect opportunity to wear the expensive acrylic sweater that Roger had given him last Christmas. He had thought its slim fit and black-on-black diamond pattern too young, but Roger had been enthusiastic.

'I got this directly from an Italian designer we financed,' he had said. 'All over London there are waiting lists for his pieces.' The Major, who had bought Roger a waxed-cotton rain hat from Liberty and a rather smart leather edition of Sir Edmund Hillary's account of Everest, thanked Roger graciously for the wonderful thought. He thought it rude to air his opinion of men who would put their name on a waiting list for a jumper, and besides, it was obviously a big sacrifice for Roger to give it away. After the New Year, he had consigned the pink-and-green-striped box to the top shelf of the wardrobe. Today, he felt that a little youthful style might be just the thing to counter a potentially damp social setting.

Rummaging among the tightly packed hangers for a clean white shirt, he thought again that it was probably time he went through his wardrobe and threw some things out. He thought of Marjorie stripping her built-in closets of Bertie's clothes. She was a practical woman, Marjorie. This was probably to be admired. He envisioned the boxes, labelled in fat black pen, full of clothes for the next church jumble sale.

❧ ❦ ❧

He was unusually fidgety by lunchtime and jumped when the phone rang. It was Alec wondering whether he was up to playing a round of golf despite the rain.

'I'm sorry I haven't called you before,' Alec said. 'Alma gave me a full report. Said you appeared to be holding up?'

'Yes, thank you,' he said.

'I should have called you sooner.' The Major smiled to hear Alec strangling himself on his own awkwardness. They had all stayed away; not just Alec, but Hugh Whetstone, who lived in the next lane, and the entire golf club group. He didn't mind. He had done the same in the past; stayed away from the nuisance of other people's losses and let Nancy deal with it. It was understood that women dealt better with these situations. When old Mrs Finch died, just down the lane, Nancy had brought soup or leftovers to Mr Finch every day for two or three weeks after the funeral. The Major had only raised his hat once or twice when he met the old man while out walking. Old Finch, as emaciated as a stray cat and looking completely unfamiliar with his whereabouts, would give him a blank stare and continue walking in wobbly curves along the middle of the lane. It was quite a relief when his daughter put him in a home.

'I have to pop into town and see the family solicitor,' he said. 'Maybe next week?' He tried to play golf once a week—a challenge in the unpredictable autumn weather. With Bertie's death, he had not been near the club in nearly two weeks.

'Ground may be soggy today, anyway,' said Alec. 'I'll get us an early tee-off time for next week and we'll see if we can't get in a full round before lunch.'

꒰ ꒱ ꒰

By two o'clock the clouds had given up their roiling and simply sat down on the land, transforming the rain into a grey fog. It was like a cold steam room and it pinned in place every odour. The Major was still screwing up his nose against the ripe smell of urine long after a wandering collie dog had left his mark on the corner post of the wooden bus shelter. The rough three-sided wooden shed with its cheap asphalt roof offered no protection from the fog and leached its own smell of creosote and old vomit into the dampness. The Major cursed the human instinct for shelter that made him stand under it. He read the deeply gouged historic record left by the local youth: 'Jaz and Dave'; 'Mick loves Jill'; 'Mick is a wanker'; 'Jill and Dave.'

Finally the small blue car came up over the swell of the hill and pulled up. He saw her wide smile first and then the scarf of brilliant peacock blues and greens loose on her smooth black hair. She reached over to release the passenger door for him and he bent down to climb in.

'I'm sorry, let me just move these,' she said, and scooped two or three plastic-covered library books out of his way.

'Thank you.' He tried to settle, without too much creaking, into the seat. 'Let me hold those for you.' She gave him the books and he was conscious of her long smooth fingers and short nails.

'Are we ready?' she asked.

'Yes, thank you. It's very kind of you.' He wanted to look at her but he was very aware of the narrow confines of the car. She put the car in gear and pulled sharply away from the curb. The Major held on to the door while fixing his gaze on the books.

They were thick, the covers old and blank under the yellowed plastic. He turned them sideways: a Colette novel, de Maupassant stories, a poetry anthology. To the Major's surprise, the de Maupassant was in French. He flicked though a few pages; there was no English translation.

'You certainly didn't get these books from the mobile library van,' he observed. Mrs Ali laughed and the Major thought it sounded like singing.

Every Tuesday a large green and white travelling library would take up position in a lay-by near the small estate of council houses on the edge of the village. The Major generally preferred to read from his own library, where Keats and Wordsworth were soothing companions and Samuel Johnson, though a good deal too self-important, always had something provocative to say. However, he thought the concept of the mobile library was a valuable one, so he visited regularly to show his support, in spite of having quickly exhausted the slim selection of older novels and being completely horrified by the lurid covers of the bestsellers and the large shelf of romance novels. On his last visit to the van, the Major had been browsing a fat book on local birds while a small boy with a green and dripping nose sat in the ample lap of his young mother and sounded out words in a board book about trains. The Major and the librarian were just exchanging a smile that said how nice it was to see a child doing something other than watching TV, when the boy took exception to something in the book and ripped the back cover right off. His mother, furious and blushing under the shocked look of the librarian, slapped the boy soundly. The Major, trapped behind both the prostrate child hiding under a table and the large backside of the cursing mother who was trying to drag him out where she could smack him more conveniently, could only hold on to a metal shelf himself and try to keep his sanity as the boy's howls reverberated around the metal van like a war.

'I go to the library in town, of course,' said Mrs Ali, calmly overtaking a towering hay wagon on the briefest stretch of open road between two blind curves, 'but even then I have to order most of what I want.'

'I've tried to order a book once or twice,' said the Major. 'I remember I was trying to track down a particular edition of Samuel Johnson's essays for the *Rambler,* not widely available, and was quite disappointed that the librarian didn't seem to appreciate my request at all. You'd think that after stamping the flyleaves of cheap novels all day, they'd relish the challenge of tracking down some wonderful old classic, wouldn't you?'

'Try ordering foreign languages,' said Mrs Ali. 'There's one librarian who peers at me as if I'm committing treason.'

'You speak other languages besides French?' asked the Major.

'My French is very bad,' she said. 'I'm more fluent in German. And Urdu, of course.'

'Your family's first language?' said the Major.

'No, I'd say English was my family's first language,' she said. 'My father insisted on European languages. He hated when my mother and grandmother would gossip in Urdu. I remember when I was a young girl, my father had this unshakeable belief that the

United Nations would evolve into a world government.' She shook her head and then raised her left hand from the wheel to waggle a finger at the windscreen. '"We will speak the languages of diplomacy and take our rightful places as world citizens," she said, in a serious sing-song. Then she sighed. 'He died still believing this, and my sister and I learned six languages between us in honour of his memory.'

'That's very impressive,' said the Major.

'And generally quite useless in the running of a small shop,' said Mrs Ali with a sad smile.

'There's nothing useless about reading the classics,' said the Major, weighing the books in his hand. 'I salute your continued efforts. Too few people today appreciate and pursue the delights of civilised culture for their own sake.'

'Yes, it can be a lonely pursuit,' she said.

'Then we—the happy few—must stick together,' said the Major. She laughed, and the Major turned his head to look out of the window at the fog-soaked hedges of the lanes. He was aware that he no longer felt chilled. The hedges, far from being grim and soggy were edged to the last leaf in drops like diamonds. The earth steamed and a horse under a tree shook its mane like a dog and bent to nibble freshly moistened dandelions. The car broke from the hedged lane and crested the last rise of the hill, where the road widened. The town spread down the folded valley, opening out along the coastal plain. The sea lay grey and infinite beyond the sharp edge of the beach. In the sky, a rent in the fog let down pale shafts of sunlight to gleam on the water. It was as beautiful and absurd as an illustrated Victorian hymnal, lacking only a descending archangel trailing putti and rose garlands. The little car picked up speed as it headed down and the Major felt that the afternoon was somehow already a success.

❧

'Where would you like me to drop you?' she asked as they joined the slow curl of traffic into town.

'Oh, anywhere convenient.' As he said this he felt somewhat flustered. It actually mattered a great deal to him where she set him down—or rather, where they would later meet and whether he might have the opportunity to ask her to join him for tea—but he felt it would be rude to be too specific.

'I usually go to the library and then I run my errands and do some shopping up on Myrtle Street,' she said. He wasn't quite sure which was Myrtle Street, but he thought it was up on the hill, at the poorer end of town, probably just beyond the popular Vinda Linda's Curry House Take-Away by the hospital. 'But I can drop you anywhere, as long as we pick somewhere before I have to go round again.'

'Ah yes, the dreaded one-way system,' he said. 'I remember my wife and I were trapped in the one at Exeter once. She broke her finger falling off a horse and we spent an hour circling around looking at the hospital, but not able to find an entrance from our direction. Trapped like a ball bearing in a plastic maze.' He and Nancy had laughed later, imagining Dante redesigning Purgatory into a one-way system offering occasional glimpses of St Peter and the pearly gates over two separate sets of dividing concrete barriers. As he spoke, he noticed, with a twinge of conscience, that it had already become comfortable to speak of his wife to Mrs Ali—that their shared loss had become a useful connection.

'How about the shopping centre?' suggested Mrs Ali.

'How about the seafront? Would that take you out of your way?' He knew that of course it would. The seafront was steps away on foot, but the traffic system demanded an extra turn to the left followed by a long loop down through the old town to the fishing strand. Her errands lay well inland and uphill from here. Everyone's life was inland and uphill these days, as if the whole town had turned its back on the sea.

'The seafront will be fine,' she said, and very soon pulled the car into the small pay-and-display car park right behind the beach. She left the engine running and added, 'Pick you up in an hour and a half?'

'That will be perfect,' he said, handing her the books and reaching to open the door. His mind raced with casual ways of requesting that she join him for tea, but he did not seem able to bring any of them to actual speech. He cursed himself for an idiot as she sped away again, waving.

ٹ ؟ ﻉ

The offices of Tewkesbury and Teale, Solicitors, were in a lemon-coloured Regency villa fronting on a small square two streets behind the sea. The centre of the square featured a tightly pruned garden, complete with dry fountain and small rope-edged lawn, smug behind high wrought-iron fence and gates. The villas, now offices, seemed to contain just the same sort of people for whom they were originally built. They were lawyers, accountants, and the occasional actress beyond her prime, all of whom cultivated an air of establishment that was slightly marred by the almost audible hum of social ambition. Mortimer Teale had the same, slightly appalling character.

The Major, who was early for his appointment, watched the bow window of the adjacent interior design shop, where a stout woman in a green brocade suit punched and prodded at a cornucopia of overstuffed pillows. Two small yapping dogs with beards darted and snatched at the braids and tassels. The Major worried that if he watched too long he would see one of them choke on a silk-covered button. He strolled a few doors down; at a strawberry-pink villa full of accountants, a youngish man, wearing a loud chalk-stripe suit and talking into a mobile phone the size of a lipstick case, ran out to a smart black sports car. The Major noted that his vigorous wave of gelled black hair was actually swept back to hide a balding patch on the back of his head. Somehow the man reminded him, uncomfortably, of Roger.

Old Mr Tewkesbury, Mortimer's father-in-law, had represented, if not a different breed entirely, then at least a happily mellowed and more intelligent version of the square's inhabitants. The Tewkesburys had been lawyers here since before the turn of the century and had been the Pettigrew family lawyers for nearly as long. They had grown in stature along the way by performing admirably in their work and declining all opportunities at self-aggrandisement. Father, son, and grandson had quietly given of their time to civic duties (free legal advice to the town council being just one of their causes) but had resisted all calls to stand for office, lead a committee, or appear in the paper. As a boy, he remembered, he had been impressed by Tewkesbury's unhurried speech, sober clothes, and heavy silver fob watch.

He had been puzzled, as had Bertie, when Tewkesbury took in Mortimer Teale as an associate. Teale had come out of nowhere to attach himself to the Tewkesbury daughter and only heir, Elizabeth. People said he was from London, which they mentioned with a twist of the lips as if London were the back alleys of Calcutta or some notorious penal colony, like Australia. Mortimer favoured loud ties, liked his food to the point of fussiness, and bowed and scraped in front of clients in a way that gave the Major his only opportunity, outside of the *Sunday Times* crossword, to use the word 'oleaginous'. He had married Elizabeth, and had squatted like a well-fed cuckoo in the midst of the Tewkesbury clan until he had managed to bury old Tewkesbury. Rumour was that he had added his name to the brass doorplate while the family was at the funeral.

The Major had considered finding himself a new solicitor but had not wanted to break with his own family's tradition. In more honest moments, he admitted to himself that he had not wanted to face telling Mortimer. Instead, he had reminded himself that Mortimer had done nothing but excellent work, which was true, and that it was uncharitable to dislike a man for wearing purple spotted pocket squares and having sweaty palms.

~ ❧ ~

'Ah, Major, so nice to see you even under such sad, sad conditions,' said Mortimer, advancing across the deep green office carpet to clasp the Major's hand.

'Thank you.'

'Your brother was a fine, fine man and it was a privilege to call him a friend.' Mortimer threw a glance at the wall, where pictures of himself with various local officials and minor dignitaries were hung in gilded frames. 'I was telling Marjorie only yesterday that he was a man who could have achieved much prominence if he had had the inclination.'

'My brother shared Mr Tewkesbury's dislike of local politics,' said the Major.

'Quite right,' said Mortimer, settling back down at his mahogany desk and waving at a club chair. 'It's an appalling mess. I keep telling Elizabeth I would resign completely if they would let me.' The Major said nothing. 'Well, let's get this started, shall we?' He took a thin cream-coloured file from a desk drawer and slid it across the vast expanse between them. As he reached, his plump wrists strained out of his stiff white cuffs and his jacket wrinkled up about his shoulders. He opened the file with his thick fingertips and turned it around to face the Major. Light finger marks now decorated the plain typed page headed 'Last Will and Testament of Robert Carroll Pettigrew.'

'As you know, Bertie has named you the executor of this will. If you are willing to serve in this capacity, I will have some forms for you to sign. As executor, you will have a couple of charitable bequests and small investment accounts to oversee. Nothing too arduous. As executor you are traditionally entitled to a small compensation, expenses and so forth, but you may wish to waive that . . .'

'I'll just read it, then, shall I?' said the Major.

'Of course, of course. Just take your time.' Mortimer sat back and laced his hands across his bulging waistcoat as if preparing to take a nap, but his eyes remained sharply focused across the desk. The Major stood up.

'I'll just take it over here and get some light on it,' he said. It was only a matter of feet to the large window overlooking the square, but the few paces created some imagined privacy.

Bertie's will was only a page and a half, with plenty of white space between the lines. His possessions were transferred to his loving wife and he asked his brother to be his executor in order to relieve her of administrative burdens during a difficult time. There was a small investment account set up for Gregory and any other grandchildren who might arrive later. There were also bequests to three charities: their old prep school got a thousand pounds and both Bertie's church and the parish church of St Mary's C of E at Edgecombe St Mary received two thousand. The Major chuckled to see Bertie, who had long ago acceded to Marjorie and become an active Presbyterian, hedging his bets with the Almighty. When he finished reading, the Major went back and read the will again, to make sure he hadn't missed a paragraph. Then he just pretended to be reading, in order to give himself time to quell his confusion.

The will made no mention of any bequests of personal items, to anyone, offering only a single line: 'My wife may dispose of any and all personal effects as she deems fit. She knows my wishes in these matters.' This bluntness was out of keeping with the rest of the document; in its few words, the Major sensed both his brother's capitulation to his wife and a coded apology to himself. 'She knows my wishes,' he read again.

'Ah, tea; thank you, Mary.' Mortimer broke his careful silence as the thin girl who worked as his secretary came in with a small gilt tray containing two cups of tea in bone china mugs and a plate with two dry biscuits. 'Is the milk fresh?' he fussed, his voice signalling that it was high time Pettigrew finished his reading and got down to business. The Major turned reluctantly from the window.

'Are there not a couple of omissions?' he enquired at last.

'I think you'll find all the required language is there,' said Mortimer. The Major could see he had no intention of helping smooth over the awkwardness of asking about the Major's own interests.

'As you know, there is the matter of my father's sporting guns,' he said. He could feel his face flushing with heat, but he was determined to be direct. 'It was understood by all, of course, that the guns were to be reunited upon the death of either one of us.'

'Ah,' said Mortimer slowly.

'I was under the impression that Bertie's will would contain explicit directions in this matter—as my own will does.' He stared hard. Mortimer put down his tea with care and pressed his fingertips together. He sighed.

'As you can see,' he said, 'no such provision was included. I did urge Bertie to be as specific as possible about any items of value that he might wish to pass on . . .' His voice trailed off.

'Those guns were passed on to us in trust by my father,' the Major said, drawing himself up as far as possible. 'It was his dying wish that we share in them during our lifetimes and that we reunite them to pass on down the generations. You know this as well as I.'

'Yes, that has always been my understanding,' agreed Mortimer. 'However, since your father gave you the guns in person, during his illness, there was no such direction in his will and therefore no obligation . . .'

'But I'm sure Bertie put it in his will,' he said, annoyed to find a begging tone creeping into his voice. Mortimer did not answer at once. He gazed up at the brass chandelier as if searching for the exact parsing of his next words.

'I can say very little,' he finally offered. 'Let us say only that, in the broadest sense possible, the leaving of any specific assets away from a spouse may become an issue of loyalty for some couples.' He grimaced in conspiratorial fashion and the Major caught the faintest echo of Marjorie's shrill voice ringing off the plain panelling of the office.

'My sister-in-law . . . ?' he began. Mortimer held up a palm to stop him.

'I cannot make any comment on client discussions or enter into any suppositions, however hypothetical,' he said. 'I can only say how sorry it makes me when my hands are so tied that I cannot even warn a good client that he should perhaps consider altering his own will.'

'Everyone knows that gun is mine,' said the Major. He was hurt and angry to the point of feeling faint. 'It should have been mine in the first place, you know—oldest son and all that. Not that I ever begrudged Bertie his share, only he never was a shooting man.'

'Well, I think you should have a friendly chat with Marjorie about it,' said Mortimer. 'I'm sure she would want to work out something. Perhaps we should hold off finalising the executor position until this is sorted out?'

'I know my duty,' said the Major. 'I will do as my brother asked of me regardless of this matter.'

'Yes, I'm sure,' said Mortimer. 'Only it might be considered a conflict of interest were you to intend any claim against the estate.'

'You mean go to court?' said the Major. 'I wouldn't dream of dragging the Pettigrew name so low.'

'I never thought you would,' said Mortimer. 'It would have been terribly awkward having to represent one side of the family against the other. Not at all in the Tewkesbury and Teale tradition.' He smiled, and the Major had the suspicion that Mortimer would love to represent Marjorie against him and would use every scrap of prior knowledge about the family to win.

'It is unthinkable,' he said.

'Well, that's settled, then,' said Mortimer. 'Just have a chat with Marjorie, will you? That way, we know there's no conflict of interest on your part. I must get the probate filed soon, so if you could get back to me . . .'

'And if she doesn't agree to give me the gun?' said the Major.

'Then, in the interest of expediting probate, I would advise you to decline the executor position.'

'I can't do that,' said the Major. 'It's my duty to Bertie.'

'I know, I know,' said Mortimer. 'You and I are men of duty, men of honour. But we live in a different world today, my dear Major, and I would be remiss as a solicitor if I did not then advise Marjorie to challenge your fitness to serve.' In an attempt to sound delicate, he squeezed the words out of his mouth like the last of the toothpaste from the tube. His face wore the glazed expression of someone calculating how much of a smile to deliver. 'We need to avoid even the semblance of any dishonourable intentions. There are liability issues, you understand?'

'Apparently, I understand nothing,' said the Major.

'Just talk to Marjorie and call me as soon as you can,' said Mortimer, rising from his chair and holding out his hand. The Major also stood up. He wished he had worn a suit now, instead of this ridiculous black sweater. It would have been more difficult for Mortimer to dismiss him like a schoolboy.

'This should not have happened this way,' said the Major. 'The Tewkesbury firm has represented my family's interests for generations. . . .'

'And it is our privilege to do so,' said Mortimer, as if the Major had complimented him. 'We may have to be a bit more bound by the rule book these days, but you can be sure that Tewkesbury and Teale will always try to do their best for you.' The Major thought that perhaps after this was all settled he would do as he should have done in the first place and find himself another solicitor.

Stepping out of the office into the square he was momentarily blinded. The fog had been pushed back from the sea, and the stucco fronts of the villas were drying to pale tones in the afternoon sunshine. He felt the sudden warmth relax his face. He breathed in and the salt water in the air seemed to wash away the smell of furniture wax and avarice that was Mortimer Teale's office.

Chapter Five

To tell Mortimer that he had never begrudged Bertie the gun had been a damn lie. Sitting on the seafront, his back pressed against the wooden slats of a park bench, the Major turned his face up to the sun. The sweater absorbed heat as efficiently as a black plastic bin liner, and it was pleasant to sit tucked away in the lee of the fishermen's black-tarred net-drying sheds, listening to the waves breaking themselves to pieces on the shingle.

There was a generous spirit about nature, he thought. The sun gave its heat and light for free. His spirit by contrast was mean, like a slug shrivelling on the bricks at midday. Here he was, alive and enjoying the autumn sunshine, while Bertie was dead. And yet even now he couldn't give up the niggling annoyance he had felt all these years that Bertie had been given that gun. Nor could he shake the unworthy thought that Bertie knew and was now paying him back for his resentment.

It had been a midsummer day when his mother called him and Bertie into the dining room, where their father lay wasting away from emphysema in his rented hospital bed. The roses were very lush that year, and perfume from the nodding heads of an old pink damask came in at the open French doors. The carved sideboard still displayed his grandmother's silver soup tureen and candlesticks, but an oxygen pump took up half the surface. He was still angry at his mother for letting the doctor dictate that his father was too frail to sit up in his wheelchair anymore. Surely there could be only good in wheeling him out to the sunny, sheltered corner of wall on the small terrace overlooking the garden? What did it matter anyway, if his father caught a chill or got tired? Though they cheerfully congratulated his father every day on how well he was doing, outside the sickroom no one pretended that these were anything other than the last days.

The Major was a second lieutenant by then, one year out of officer training, and he had been granted ten days' special leave from his base. The time had seemed to flow slowly, a quiet eternity of whispers in the dining room and thick sandwiches in the kitchen. As his father, who had sometimes failed to convey warmth but had taught him duty and honour, wheezed through the end of his life, the Major tried not to give in to the emotion that sometimes threatened him. His mother and Bertie often crept away to their rooms to wet pillows with their tears, but he preferred to read aloud at his father's bedside or help the private nurse in turning his emaciated body. His father, who was not as addled by his disease as everyone assumed, recognised the end. He sent for his two sons and his prized pair of Churchills.

'I want you to have these,' he said. He opened the brass lock and pushed back the well-oiled lid. The guns gleamed in their red velvet beds; the finely chased engraving on the silver action bore no tarnish, no smudge.

'You don't have to do this now, Father,' he said. But he had been eager; perhaps he had even stepped forward, half-obscuring his younger brother.

'I wish them to go on down through the family,' said his father, looking with anxious eyes. 'Yet how could I possibly choose between my two boys and say one of you should have them?' He looked to their mother, who took his hand and patted it gently.

'These guns mean so much to your father,' she said at last. 'We want you to each have one, to keep his memory.'

'Given to me by the Maharajah from his own hand,' whispered their father. It was an old story so rubbed with retelling that the edges were blurry. A moment of bravery; an Indian prince honourable enough to reward a British officer's courageous service in the hours when all around were howling for Britain's eviction. It was his father's brush with greatness. The old tray of medals and the uniforms might desiccate in the attic, but the guns were always kept oiled and ready.

'But to break up a pair, Father?' He could not help blurting out the question, though he read its shallowness in his mother's blanched face.

'You can leave them to each other, to be passed along as a pair to the next generation—keep it in the Pettigrew name, of course.' It was the only act of cowardice he had ever seen from his father.

The guns were not listed as part of the estate, which was passed to his mother for her lifetime use and then to him, as the eldest son. Bertie was provided for out of small family trusts. By the time their mother died some twenty years later, the trusts had eroded to an embarrassing low. However, the house was decrepit too. There was rot in some of the seventeenth-century beams, its traditional Sussex brick-and-tile-hung exterior needed extensive repairs, and their mother owed the local council money. The house still looked substantial and genteel among the smaller thatched cottages in the lane, but it was more of a liability than a grand inheritance, as he had told Bertie. He had offered his brother most of their mother's jewelry as a gesture. He had also tried to buy his brother out of the gun, both then and several other times over the years when Bertie had seemed hard up. His younger brother had always declined his generous offers.

A gull's guttural scream jolted the Major. It was waddling along the concrete path, wings spread wide, trying to bully a pigeon away from a hunk of bread roll. The pigeon tried to pick up the bread and flap aside, but the roll was too large. The Major stamped his foot.

The gull looked at him with disdain and flapped backward a few feet, while the pigeon, without so much as a glance of gratitude, scooted its bread down the path like a tiddlywink.

The Major sighed. He was a man who always tried to do his duty without regard for gratitude or even acknowledgment. Surely he could not have inspired resentment from Bertie all these years?

At no time had the Major allowed himself to feel guilty about being the eldest son. Of course the order in which one was born was random, but so was the fact that he had not been born into a family with a title and vast estates. He had never felt animosity toward those who were born into great social position. Nancy had argued with him about it when they first met. It was the sixties, and she was young and thought love meant living on baked beans and the moral directives of folk music. He had explained to her, very patiently, that keeping one's name and estate going *was* an act of love.

'If we just keep dividing things up, each generation more people demanding their share of the goodies, it just all vanishes as if it never mattered.'

'It's about redistributing the wealth,' she had argued.

'No, it's about the Pettigrew name dying out; about forgetting my father and his father before him. It's about the selfishness of the current generation destroying the remembrance of the past. No one understands stewardship anymore.'

'You are so adorable when you're being so damn conservative and uptight!' She laughed. She made him laugh too. She made him sneak off his base to see her. She made him wear improbable shirts and bright socks off duty. Once she called him from a police station after a student protest and he had to show up at the night sergeant's desk in his full dress uniform. They let her go with just a lecture.

After they were married, there were some years of heartache as children refused to gestate, but then Roger happened at the very last gasp of fertility, and at least, with only one child, there were no arguments over assets. In memory of Nancy's ideas on generosity, he had dutifully added to his own will a nice little sum of cash for his niece, Jemima. He had also specified that Jemima should receive the second-best china service from his maternal grandmother. Bertie had often hinted that he liked those plates, but the Major had been doubtful of placing vintage Minton, however faded and crazed, in the care of Marjorie. She broke dishes so often that every dinner party at Bertie's house was served on a different china pattern.

Having an updated will and precise instructions was always a priority for the Major. As a military officer (in harm's way—as he liked to put it), he had found it a great comfort to open his small iron strongbox, spread out the thick pages of his will, and read over the list of assets and distributions. It read like a list of achievements.

He would just have to be very clear with Marjorie. She was not thinking straight right now. He would have to explain again the exact nature of his own father's intention. He would have to make things clear to Roger as well. He had no intention of battling to reunite the pair of guns, only to have Roger sell them after his death.

'Ah, there you are, Major,' said a voice. He sat upright and blinked in the strong light. It was Mrs Ali, holding her large tote bag and a new library book. 'I didn't see you at the car park.'

'Oh, is that the time?' said the Major, looking in horror at his watch. 'I completely lost track. My dear lady, I am so horribly embarrassed to have kept you waiting.' Now that he had unconsciously achieved what he would never have dared to deliberately contrive, he was completely at a loss.

'It is not a problem,' she said. 'I knew you'd be along eventually and, as the day has turned out so unexpectedly nice, I thought I'd take a brief walk and maybe start my book.'

'I will, of course, pay for the car park.'

'It's really not necessary.'

'Then will you permit me to at least buy you a cup of tea?' he asked, so quickly that the words pushed and elbowed each other to get out of his mouth. She hesitated so he added: 'Unless you're in a rush to get home, which I quite understand.'

'No, there is no rush,' she said. She looked left and right along the promenade. 'Perhaps, if you think the weather will continue to hold, we could walk as far as the kiosk in the gardens?' she said. 'If you feel up to it, of course.'

'That would be lovely,' he said, though he had a suspicion that the kiosk served its tea in polystyrene cups with some kind of preserved creamer in those little tubs that were impossible to open.

❧

The promenade, when traversed from east to west as they were doing, formed a scrolling three-dimensional timeline of Hazelbourne-on-Sea's history. The net-drying sheds and the fishing boats drawn up on the shingle, where the Major had been sitting, were part of the old town, which huddled around small cobbled alleys. Lopsided Tudor shops, their oak beams worn to fossil, contained dusty heaps of cheap merchandise.

As one walked, the town grew more prosperous. In the middle, the Victorian pier's copper roofs, white wooden walls, and curlicued wrought-iron structure sat out over the Channel like a big iced cake. Beyond the pier, the mansions and hotels became imposing. Their stone porticos and dark awnings hooded over long windows implied a certain disapproval of the transient activities going on within lushly carpeted interiors. Between hotels that each occupied a full block were open squares of villas or wide streets of sweeping townhouse façades. The Major thought it such a shame that the elegance was hopelessly marred these days by the serried ranks of cars, angle-parked this way and that, like dried herring in a crate.

Beyond the appropriately named Grand Hotel, the town's march through history was abruptly interrupted by the sudden swell of the chalk cliffs into a vast headland. The Major, who often walked the entire promenade, never failed to ponder how this might represent something about the hubris of human progress and the refusal of nature to knuckle under.

Recently he had begun to worry that the walk and the hypothesis had become so inextricably linked that they looped through his mind like madness. He was quite unable to walk and think about the racing results, for example, or about repainting his living room. He tried to put it down to the fact that he had no one with whom he could discuss the idea. Perhaps, if they were at a loss for conversation over tea, he might bring it up with Mrs Ali.

Mrs Ali walked with a comfortable stride. The Major shuffled his feet trying to fall in with her rhythm. He had forgotten how to let a woman dictate the pace.

'Do you like to walk?' he asked.

'Yes, I try to get out early three or four times a week,' she said. 'I'm the crazy lady wandering the lanes in the dawn chorus.'

'We all ought to join you,' he said. 'Those birds perform a miracle every morning and the world ought to get up and listen.' He was often up at night, toward the later hours, pinned to his mattress by an insomnia that seemed equal parts wakefulness and death. He could feel his blood running in his veins, yet he could not seem to move a finger or toe. He would lie awake, eyes scratchy, watching the dim outline of the window for any sign of light. Before any hint of paleness, the birds would begin. First a few common chirpings (sparrows and such); then the warbles and peepings would become a waterfall of music, a choir sounding from the bushes and trees. The sound released his limbs to turn and stretch and expelled all sense of panic. He would look to the window, now pale with singing, and roll over into sleep.

'All the same,' she said, 'I probably should get a dog. No one thinks dog owners are crazy, even if they walk out in their pajamas.'

'What book did you pick today?' he asked.

'Kipling,' she replied. 'It's a children's book, as the librarian took pains to inform me, but the stories are set in this area.' She showed him a copy of *Puck of Pook's Hill,* which the Major had read many times. 'I only knew his Indian books, like *Kim.*'

'I used to consider myself a bit of a Kipling enthusiast,' said the Major. 'I'm afraid he's rather an unfashionable choice these days, isn't he?'

'You mean not popular among us, the angry former natives?' she asked with an arch of one eyebrow.

'No, of course not . . .' said the Major, not feeling equipped to respond to such a direct remark. His brain churned. For a moment he thought he saw Kipling, in a brown suit and bushy moustache, turning inland at the end of the promenade. He squinted ahead and prayed the conversation might wither from inattention.

'I did give him up for many decades,' she said. 'He seemed such a part of those who refuse to reconsider what the Empire meant. But as I get older, I find myself insisting on my right to be philosophically sloppy. It's so hard to maintain that rigour of youth, isn't it?'

'I applaud your logic,' said the Major, swallowing any urge to defend the Empire his father had proudly served. 'Personally, I have no patience with all this analysing of writers' politics. The man wrote some thirty-five books—let them analyse the prose.'

'Besides, it will drive my nephew crazy just to have him in the house,' Mrs Ali said with a slight smile.

The Major was not sure whether to ask more about the nephew. He was extremely curious, but it did not seem his place to enquire directly. His knowledge about the families and lives of his village friends was acquired in bits and pieces. The information was strung like beads out of casual remarks, and he often lost the earlier information as more was added, so that he never acquired a complete picture. He knew, for example, that Alma and Alec Shaw had a daughter in South Africa, but he could never remember whether the husband was a plastic surgeon in Johannesburg or a plastics importer in Cape Town. He knew that the daughter had not been home since before Nancy's death, but this information came with no explanation; it only resonated with an unspoken hurt.

'Do you have other nephews and nieces?' he said. He worried that even this vague politeness seemed to echo with questions about why she had no children, and to suggest rudely that she must of course come from a large family.

'There is only the one nephew. His parents, my husband's brother and his wife, have three daughters and six granddaughters.'

'Ah, so your nephew must be their golden boy?' said the Major.

'He was my golden boy, too, when he was little. I'm afraid that Ahmed and I spoiled him terribly.' She hugged her book a little tighter to her chest and sighed. 'We were not blessed with children of our own, and Abdul Wahid was the very image of my husband when he was small. He was a very smart boy, too, and sensitive. I thought he would be a poet one day.'

'A poet?' said the Major. He tried to picture the angry young man writing verse.

'My brother-in-law put a stop to such nonsense once Abdul Wahid was old enough to help in one of their shops. I suppose I was naïve. I wanted so much to share with him the world of books and of ideas and to pass on to him what I was given.'

'A noble impulse,' said the Major. 'But I taught English at a boarding school after the army and I can tell you it's pretty much a lost cause, getting boys over ten to read. Most of them don't own a single book, you know.'

'I cannot imagine,' she said. 'I was raised in a library of a thousand books.'

'Really?' He did not mean to sound so doubtful, but he had never heard of grocers owning large libraries.

'My father was an academic,' she said. 'He came after Partition to teach applied mathematics. My mother always said she was allowed to bring two cooking pots and a picture of her parents. All the other trunks contained books. It was very important to my father that he try to read everything.'

'Everything?'

'Yes, literature, philosophy, science—a romantic quest, of course, but he did manage to read an astonishing amount.'

'I try to manage a book a week or thereabouts,' said the Major. He was quite proud of his small collection, mostly leather editions picked up on his trips to London from the one or two good book dealers who were still in business around Charing Cross Road. 'But I must confess that these days I spend most of my time rereading old favorites—Kipling, Johnson; there's nothing to compare with the greats.'

'I can't believe you admire Samuel Johnson, Major,' she said, laughing. 'He seems to have been sorely lacking in the personal grooming department and he was always so rude to that poor Boswell.'

'Unfortunately, there is often an inverse correlation between genius and personal hygiene,' said the Major. 'We would be sorely lacking if we threw out the greats with the bathwater of social niceties.'

'If only they would take a bath once in a while,' she said. 'You are right, of course, but I tell myself that it does not matter what one reads—favourite authors, particular themes—as long as we read something. It is not even important to own the books.' She stroked the library book's yellowing plastic sleeve with a look that seemed sad.

'But your father's library?' he asked.

'Gone. When he died, my uncles came from Pakistan to settle the estate. One day I came home from school and my mother and an aunt were washing all the empty shelves. My uncles had sold them by the foot. There was an odour of smoke in the air and when I ran to the window . . .' She paused and took a slow breath.

Memories were like tomb paintings, thought the Major, the colours still vivid no matter how many layers of mud and sand time deposited. Scrape at them and they come up all red and blazing. She looked at him, her chin raised. 'I can't tell you the paralysing feeling, the shame of watching my uncles burning paperbacks in the garden incinerator. I cried out to my mother to stop them, but she just bent her head and went on pouring soapy water onto the wood.' Mrs Ali stopped and turned to look out over the sea.

The waves flopped dirty foam onto the expanse of quilted brown sand that signalled low tide. The Major breathed in the sharp tang of stranded seaweed and wondered whether he should pat her on the back.

'I'm so sorry,' he said.

'Oh, I can't believe I told you this,' she said, turning back, her hand rubbing a corner of her eye. 'I apologise. I'm getting to be such a silly old woman these days.'

'My dear Mrs Ali, I would hardly refer to you as old,' he said. 'You are in what I would call the very prime flowering of mature womanhood.' It was a little grandiose but he hoped to surprise a blush. Instead she laughed out loud at him.

'I have never heard anyone try to trowel such a thick layer of flattery on the wrinkles and fat deposits of advanced middle age, Major,' she said. 'I am fifty-eight years old and I think I have slipped beyond flowering. I can only hope now to dry out into one of those everlasting bouquets.'

'Well, I have ten years on you,' he said. 'I suppose that makes me a real fossil.'

She laughed again, and the Major felt that there was no more important and fulfilling work than to make Mrs Ali laugh. His own troubles seemed to recede as their steps took them beyond the ice cream stalls and ticket booths of the pier. Here they navigated a newly installed series of curves in the promenade. The Major withheld his usual diatribe against the stupidity of young architects who feel oppressed by the straight line. Today he felt like waltzing.

They entered the public gardens, which began as a single bed crawling with yellow chrysanthemums, and then spread along two ever widening paths to create a long thin triangular space containing several different areas and levels. A sunken rectangle contained a bandstand, set in the middle of a lawn. Empty deck chairs flapped their canvas in the breeze. The council had just planted into concrete boxes the third or fourth set of doomed palm trees. There was an unshakeable belief among the council's executive committee that the introduction of palm trees would transform the town into a Mediterranean-style paradise and attract an altogether better class of visitor. The trees died fast. The day-trippers continued to bus in, wearing their cheap T-shirts and testing their raucous voices against the gulls. At the far end of the gardens, on a small circular lawn that lay open to the sea on one side, a thin, dark-skinned boy of four or five was nudging a small red ball with his feet. He played as if doing so were a hardship. When he gave the ball a sharp tap it bounced against a low bronze sign that said 'No Ball Playing' in raised, polished letters and then rolled toward the Major. Feeling jovial, the Major attempted to chip the ball back, but it bounced sideways off his foot, struck an ornamental boulder, and rolled swiftly under a hedge of massed hydrangeas.

'Oi, there's no football allowed 'ere,' shouted a voice from a small green kiosk with a curly copper roof and shutters, which offered tea and an assortment of cakes.

'Sorry, sorry,' said the Major, waving his hands to encompass both the grey-faced, plump lady behind the kiosk counter and the small boy, who stood looking at the bushes as if they were as impenetrable as a black hole. The Major hurried over to the hedge and peered under, looking for some flash of red.

'What kind of park is it if a six-year-old can't kick a football?' said a sharp voice. The Major glanced up to see a young woman who, though obviously of Indian origin, wore the universal uniform of the young and disenchanted. She was dressed in a rumpled parka the colour of an oil spill, and long striped leggings tucked into motorcycle boots. Her short hair stuck out in a halo of stiff tufts as if she had just crawled out of bed, and her face, which might have been pretty, was twisted by a belligerent look as she faced the kiosk worker.

'There won't be no flowers left if all the kids trample about with balls all day,' said the kiosk lady. 'I don't know what it's like where you come from, but we try to keep things nice and genteel around here.'

'What d'you mean by that?' The young woman scowled. The Major recognised the abrasive northern tone he associated with Marjorie. 'What are you saying?'

'I'm not saying nothing,' replied the lady. 'Don't get all shirty with me—I don't make the rules.' The Major scooped up the somewhat muddy ball and handed it to the boy.

'Thank you,' said the boy. 'I'm George, and I don't really like football.'

'I don't really like it, either,' said the Major. 'Cricket is the only sport I really follow.'

'Tiddlywinks is a sport, too,' said George with a serious expression. 'But Mum thought I might lose the bits if I brought them to the park.'

'Now that you bring it up,' said the Major, 'I've never seen a sign saying "No Tiddlywinking" in any park, so it might not be such a bad idea.' As he straightened up, the young woman hurried over.

'George, George, I've told you a thousand times about talking to strange men,' she said in a tone that identified her as the child's mother rather than an older sister, as the Major had first thought.

'I do apologise,' he said. 'It was entirely my fault, of course. Bit of a long time since I played any football.'

'Silly old cow ought to mind her own business,' said the young woman. 'Thinks she's in a uniform instead of an apron.' This was said loud enough to carry back to the kiosk.

'Very unfortunate,' said the Major in as noncommittal a voice as possible. He wondered whether he and Mrs Ali would have to find an alternative source for tea. The kiosk lady was glaring at them.

'The world is full of small ignorances,' said a quiet voice. Mrs Ali appeared at his elbow and gave the young woman a stern look. 'We must all do our best to ignore them and thereby keep them small, don't you think?' The Major braced himself for an abusive reply but to his surprise, the young woman gave a small smile instead.

'My mum always said things like that,' she said in a low voice.

'But of course we do not like to listen to our mothers,' said Mrs Ali, smiling. 'At least, not until long after we are mothers ourselves.'

'We have to go now, George. We'll be late for tea,' said the young woman. 'Say goodbye to the nice people.'

'I'm George, goodbye,' said the boy to Mrs Ali.

'I'm Mrs Ali, how do you do?' she replied. The young woman gave a start and peered at Mrs Ali more closely. For a moment she seemed to hesitate, as if she wanted to speak, but then she appeared to decide against volunteering any further introductions. Instead, she took George by the hand and set off at a fast pace toward the town.

'What an abrupt young woman,' said the Major.

Mrs Ali sighed. 'I rather admire such refusal to bow before authority, but I fear it makes for a very uncomfortable daily existence.'

At the kiosk, the lady was still glaring and muttering something under her breath about people who thought they owned the place now. The Major tightened his upright stance and spoke in his most imposing voice, the one he had once reserved for quieting a room full of small boys.

'Do my eyes deceive me or are those real mugs you're using for tea?' he said, pointing the head of his cane toward a row of thick earthenware mugs alongside the large brown teapot.

'I don't hold with them polystyrene things,' said the woman, softening her expression just a bit. 'Makes the tea taste like furniture polish.'

'How right you are,' said the Major. 'Could we have two teas, please?'

'The lemon cake is fresh today,' she added as she slopped dark orange tea into two mugs. She was already cutting two huge slices as the Major nodded his head.

They drank their tea at a small iron table partly sheltered by an overgrown hydrangea rusty with the drying blooms of autumn. They were quiet and Mrs Ali ate her slice of cake without any trace of the self-conscious nibbling of other ladies. The Major looked at the sea and felt a small sense of contentment quite unfamiliar in his recent life. A gin-and-tonic at the golf club bar with Alec and the others did not inspire in him any of the quietude, the happiness like a closely banked fire, which now possessed him. He was struck by the thought that he was often lonely, even in the midst of many friends. He exhaled and it must have come out as a sigh, for Mrs Ali looked up from sipping her tea.

'I'm sorry, I haven't asked you how you are doing,' she said. 'It must have been difficult today, dealing with the solicitor?'

'These things have to be taken care of,' he said. 'It's always a bit of a mess, though, isn't it? People don't always take the time to leave clear instructions and then the executors have to sort it all out.'

'Ah, executors.' The dry hissing sound of the word conjured the scuttling of grey men, in ransacked rooms, looking for matches.

'Fortunately I am the executor for my brother,' he said. 'Only there are one or two things he left rather vague. I'm afraid it will require delicate negotiation on my part to make things come out right.'

'He is lucky to have an executor of your integrity,' she said.

'Nice of you to say so,' he said trying not to squirm on his seat with a sudden twinge of guilt. 'I will do my best to be absolutely fair, of course.'

'But you need to act fast,' she continued. 'Before you can take inventory, the silver is gone, the linens appear on someone else's table, and the little brass unicorn from his desk—worth next to nothing, except to you—poof! It's slipped into a pocket and no one can even remember it when you ask.'

'Oh, I don't think my sister-in-law would stoop . . .' He was seized with a sudden anxiety. 'I mean when it is a question of an item of considerable value. I don't think she'd rush to sell it or anything.'

'And everyone knows exactly what happened but no one will ever speak of it again, and the family goes on with its secrets invisible but irritating, like sand in a shoe.'

'There must be a law against it,' he said. Mrs Ali blinked at him, emerging from her own thoughts.

'Of course there is the law of the land,' she said. 'But we have talked before of the pressures of the family. One may be the most ancient of charters, Major, but the other is immutable.' The Major nodded, though he had no idea what she was talking about. Mrs Ali fiddled with her empty tea mug, tapping it almost noiselessly against the table. He thought her face had clouded over, but perhaps it was just the day. The clouds did seem to be moving back in.

'Looks like we've had the best of the weather,' he said, brushing crumbs from his lap. 'Perhaps it's time we were heading back?'

t ? J

The walk back was silent and somewhat uncomfortable, as if they had trespassed too far into personal areas. The Major would have liked to ask Mrs Ali's opinion of his situation, since he felt sure she would agree with him, but her faster stride suggested that she was still lost in her own memories. He was not about to inquire further into her life. Already there was an awkward intimacy, as if he had stumbled against her body in a crowd. This was one of the reasons he had avoided women since Nancy's death. Without the protective shield of a wife, the most casual conversations with females had a way of suddenly veering off into a mire of coy remarks and miscommunicated intentions. The Major preferred to avoid looking ridiculous.

Today, however, his usual determination to retreat was being compromised by a stubborn recklessness. As he walked his head churned with the repeating phrase 'I was wondering if you were planning to come to town next week?', but he could not bring himself to express it aloud. They reached the small blue car and a sharp sadness threatened him as Mrs Ali bent to unlock the door. He admired again her smooth brow and the brightness of her hair disappearing into its scarf. She looked up under his gaze and straightened up. He noticed her chin was hidden by the curve of the roof line. She was not a tall woman.

'Major,' she asked, 'I was wondering if it would be possible to consult you more about Mr Kipling when I've finished my book?' The sky began to spit fat drops of rain and a cold gust of wind whipped dust and litter against his legs. The sadness vanished and he thought how glorious the day was.

'My dear lady, I would be absolutely delighted,' he said. 'I am completely at your disposal.'

Chapter Six

The golf club was built on the water side of the Downs, on a low promontory that ended in a roll of grass-backed dunes. The greens ranged in quality from thick green turf, clipped to perfection, to patchy brown areas, invaded by dune grass and prone to sudden spurts of sand whipped up into the face by wind gusts. The thirteenth hole was famous for Dame Eunice, a huge Romney Marsh ewe who kept the grass cropped to the limit of her rusty chain. Visitors, especially the occasional American, might be told that it was customary to take practice swings at the large blobs of sheep droppings. A rusty shovel for cleaning up was kept in the small box on a post that also contained a manual ball-washer. Some of the newest members had been heard to complain about Eunice; in the new era of world-class golf resorts and corporate golf outings, they were worried that she made their club look like some kind of miniature golf outfit. The Major was part of the group who defended Eunice and who thought the new members' attitude reflected poor standards by the club's nomination committee. He also enjoyed referring to Eunice as 'environmentally friendly'.

The Major, feeling his spirits lift with the early morning light, and the smell of the sea and the grass, gave Eunice a surreptitious pat as he shooed her away from the green where his ball lay near the southern edge. Alec was scything dune grass with his wedge, the bald spot on his head shining in the chilly sunshine. The Major waited patiently with his putter on his shoulder, enjoying the low arc of the bay: miles of sand and ceaseless water washed with silver by the cloudy light.

'Bloody grass. Cuts you to ribbons,' said Alec, red in the face and stamping down a clump with his cleats.

'Careful there, old chap,' said the Major. 'The ladies' environmental committee'll be after you.'

'Bloody women and their bloody dune habitats,' said Alec, stamping more furiously. 'Why can't they leave well enough alone?' The ladies of the club had become recent advocates for more responsible golf course management. Posters manufactured on a home computer had begun appearing on the bulletin board urging members to keep off the dunes and advising of wildlife nestings. Alma was one of the prime agitators and the board had responded by asking Alec to head a subcommittee to explore environmental issues. It was quite obvious that the poor man was cracking under the pressure.

'How is Alma?' asked the Major.

'Won't leave me in peace,' replied Alec. He was on his hands and knees now forcing his hands into the clumps. 'What with the environmental nonsense and now the annual dance, she's just driving me crazy.'

'Ah, the annual dance.' The Major smiled and knew he was being unkind. 'And what is our theme this year?' It was a source of annoyance to the Major that what had once been a very refined black tie dance, with a simple steak menu and a good band, had been turned into a series of increasingly elaborate theme evenings.

'They haven't made the final decision,' said Alec. He stood up, defeated, and brushed off his plus fours.

'They will be hard pressed to exceed the "Last Days of Pompeii",' said the Major.

'Don't remind me,' said Alec. 'I still have nightmares of being stuck inside that gladiator costume.' Alma had rented costumes unseen from a shop in London and poor Alec had been forced to clank around all night in a close-fitting metal helmet while his neck swelled up. Alma had ordered herself a 'Lady of the Mysteries' costume, which turned out to be a courtesan's sheer and garishly painted toga. Her hasty addition of a purple turtleneck and cycling shorts had done little to improve the overall effect.

The theme, combined with an open bar until midnight, had resulted in a ridiculous loosening of standards. The usual expected and required banter, the flirtatious compliments, and the occasional pinching of bottoms had been magnified into open debaucheries. Old Mr Percy became so drunk that he threw away his cane and subsequently fell into a glass door while chasing a shrieking woman across the terrace. Hugh Whetstone and his wife had a loud row at the bar and left with different people. Even Father Christopher, in leather sandals and a hemp robe, imbibed a little too much, so that he sat mute in a chair looking for significance in a long vertical crack in the wall and Daisy had to half-drag him to the taxi at the end of the night. The Sunday sermon that weekend had been a call to more ascetic living, delivered in a hoarse whisper. The entire event was wholly unworthy of a golf club of pedigree and the Major had considered writing a letter of protest. He had composed several serious but witty versions in his mind.

'If only this year we could just go back to having an elegant dance,' he said. 'I'm tired of wearing my dinner suit and having people ask me what I'm supposed to be.'

'There's a meeting this morning to settle the issue,' said Alec. 'When we get in, you could pop your head round the door and suggest it.'

'Oh, I don't think so,' said the Major, horrified. 'Perhaps you could have a quiet word with Alma?' Alec merely snorted, took a ball out of his pocket, and dropped it over his shoulder onto the edge of the green.

'One-stroke penalty gives you four over par?' added the Major, writing in the tiny leather scorebook he kept in the breast pocket of his golfing jacket. He was a comfortable five strokes ahead at this point.

'Let's say the winner talks to my wife,' said Alec, and grinned. The Major was stricken. He put away his notebook and lined up his shot. He hit it a little fast and too low, but the ball, skipping on a budding dandelion, made a dive into the hole anyway.

'Oh, good shot,' said Alec.

On the sixteenth hole, a barren area backed by a gravel pit of steel-grey water, Alec asked him how he was feeling.

'Life goes on, you know,' he said to Alec's back. Alec concentrated on his swing. 'I have good days and bad.' Alec hit a hard drive very straight and almost to the green.

'I'm glad to hear you're doing better,' said Alec. 'Nasty business, funerals.'

'Thank you,' said the Major, stepping up to set his own ball on the tee. 'And how are you?'

'The daughter's baby, baby Angelica, is doing much better. They saved the leg.' There was a pause as the Major lined up his own shot and hit a slightly crooked drive, short and to the edge of the fairway.

'Nasty business, hospitals,' said the Major.

'Yes, thank you,' said Alec. They retrieved their bags and set off down the grassy incline.

Arriving at the clubhouse from the eighteenth hole, the Major saw that the big clock above the terrace portico stood at 11.45. Alec made a show of checking the clock against his watch.

'Ah, timed it just right for a drink and a spot of lunch,' he said, as he did every week regardless of when they finished their round. They had been at the bar as early as eleven one time. The Major was not anxious to repeat the experience. Lunch not being served before noon; they had each had several drinks and these, combined with a glass of wine to accompany the quenelles of chicken in cream sauce, had made him extremely dyspeptic.

They deposited their carts under the convenient lean-to at the side of the building and headed across the terrace toward the grill bar. As they passed the solarium, which used to be the ladies' bar before the club had opened the grill to women, a hand rapped on the glass and a shrill voice called to them.

'Yoo-hoo, Alec, in here, please!' It was Alma, rising from a circle of ladies grouped around a long table. She was waving vigorously. Daisy Green also beckoned, in commanding manner, and the other women turned behatted heads and fixed on them steely eyes.

'Shall we run for it?' whispered Alec, waving to his wife even as he continued to sidle toward the grill.

'I think we're well and truly captured,' said the Major, taking a step toward the glass doors. 'But don't worry, I'll back you up.'

'We could mime an urgent need for the gents'?'

'Good heavens, man,' said the Major. 'It's only your own wife. Come on now, stiffen up there.'

'If I stiffen up any more I'll throw my neck into spasms again,' said Alec. 'But have it your own way. Let's face the enemy.'

᚛ ᚛ ᚛

'We need a gentleman's opinion,' said Daisy Green. 'Do you know everyone?'

She waved at the assembled ladies. There were one or two unfamiliar faces, but the women in question looked too frightened of Daisy to offer any introduction.

'Will it take long?' asked Alec.

'We must settle on our theme today,' said Daisy, 'and we have one or two different ideas. While I think my suggestion has, shall we say, a large following, I believe we should explore all the options.'

'So we want you to pick your favourite,' said Grace.

'Just in a purely advisory way, of course,' said Daisy, frowning at Grace who blushed. 'To enhance our own deliberations.'

'We were actually just discussing the dance, out on the course,' said the Major. 'We were saying how lovely it might be to bring back the old dance. You know, black-tie-and-champagne sort of thing?'

'Kind of a Noël Coward theme?' asked one of the unfamiliar ladies. She was a youngish woman with red hair and thick makeup, which could not hide her freckles. The Major wondered whether there was an unspoken order from Daisy that younger women should stuff themselves into ugly bucket hats and make themselves look older in order to join her committees.

'Noël Coward is not one of the themes under discussion,' said Daisy.

'Black tie is not a theme,' said the Major. 'It's the preferred attire for people of good breeding.'

An enormous abyss of silence opened across the room. The youngish lady in the ugly hat dropped her mouth so far open that the Major could see a filling in one of her back molars. Grace appeared to be choking into a handkerchief. The Major had a fleeting suspicion that she might be laughing. Daisy seemed to consult some notes on her clipboard, but her hands grasped the piecrust edge of the table with whitened knuckles.

'What he means is . . .' Alec paused as if he had just now lost an entirely diplomatic explanation.

'Are we to take it that you disapprove of our efforts, Major?' asked Daisy in a low voice.

'Of course he doesn't,' said Alec. 'Look, best leave us out of it, ladies. As long as the bar is open, we'll be happy, won't we, Pettigrew?' The Major felt a discreet tug on his arm; Alec was signalling the retreat. The Major pulled away and looked directly at Daisy.

'What I meant to say, Mrs Green, is that while last year's theme was most creative—'

'Yes, very creative, most entertaining,' interrupted Alec.

'—not all the guests carried on in the decorous manner that I'm sure you had counted upon.'

'That's hardly the fault of the committee,' said Alma.

'Quite, quite,' said the Major. 'Yet it was most distressing to see ladies of your standing subjected to the rowdiness sometimes sparked by the perceived licence of a costume party.'

'You are absolutely right, Major,' said Daisy. 'In fact, I think the Major brings up such a good point that we should reconsider our themes.'

'Thank you,' said the Major.

'I do believe that one of our themes, and only one, calls for the appropriate decorum and elegant behaviour. I believe we can cross off "Flappers and Fops" as well as "Brigadoon".'

'Oh, but surely "Brigadoon" is beyond reproach,' said Alma. 'And the country dancing would be so much fun—'

'Men in kilts and running off into the heather?' said Daisy. 'Really, Alma, I'm surprised at you.'

'We can run off into the heather at home if you like,' said Alec, winking at his wife.

'Oh, shut up,' she said. Tears seemed imminent as two red spots burned in her cheeks.

'I think that leaves us with "An Evening at the Mughal Court"—a most elegant theme,' said Daisy.

'I thought "Mughal Madness" was the name?' said the bucket hat lady.

'A working title only,' said Daisy. '"Evening at the Court" will send an appropriate message of decorum. We must thank the Major for his contribution to our efforts.' The ladies clapped and the Major, speechless with the futility of protest, was reduced to giving them a small bow.

'The Major's an Indian. He's the one to advise you,' said Alec, clapping him on the back. It was an old joke, worn out with having been used on the Major since he was a small boy with large ears, being bullied on an unfamiliar playground.

'Are you really?' asked Miss Bucket Hat.

'I'm afraid that's Alec being amusing,' he said, through tight lips. 'My father served in India, and so I was born in Lahore.'

'But you won't find better English stock than the Pettigrews,' said Alec.

'I wonder if you might have some souvenirs of that time, Major?' said Daisy. 'Rugs or baskets—props we can borrow?'

'Any lion skin rugs?' asked the bucket head.

'No, sorry, can't say I do,' said the Major.

'I say we should talk to Mrs Ali, the lady who runs the village shop in Edgecombe,' said Alma. 'Perhaps she could cater some Indian specialties for us, or direct us to where we can buy or borrow some cheap props—like some of those statues with all the arms.'

'That would be Shiva,' said the Major. 'The Hindu deity.'

'Yes, that's the one.'

'Like the Mughals, Mrs Ali is, I believe, Muslim and might be offended at such a request,' he said, trying to bite back his irritation. It would not do to let the ladies infer any particular interest toward Mrs Ali on his part.

'Oh, well, it won't do to offend the only vaguely Indian woman we know,' said Daisy. 'I was hoping she could find us some suitably ethnic bartenders.'

'How about snake charmers?' suggested Miss Bucket Hat.

'I know Mrs Ali slightly,' said Grace. There was a general shifting of heads in her direction and she began to knot her handkerchief in her fingers under the unwelcome scrutiny. 'I'm very interested in local history and she was kind enough to show me all the old ledgers from her shop. She has records as far back as 1820.'

'How exciting,' said Alma, rolling her eyes.

'How about if I go to talk to Mrs Ali, and I could perhaps trouble the Major to help me be sure I only make suitable requests?' said Grace.

'Well . . . well, I'm sure I don't know what's suitable and what's not,' said the Major. 'Also, I don't think we should bother Mrs Ali.'

'Nonsense,' said Daisy, beaming. 'It's an excellent idea. We'll come up with a complete list of ideas. And Grace, you and the

Major can put your heads together and work out how to approach Mrs Ali.'

'If you ladies are done with us,' said Alec, 'we have people waiting for us in the bar.'

'Now let's talk about the floral arrangements,' said Daisy, dismissing them with a wave of the hand. 'I'm thinking palms and perhaps bougainvillea?'

'Good luck getting bougainvillea in November,' the lady with the bucket hat was saying as the Major and Alec slipped from the room.

'Bet you five pounds they squash her like a bug,' said the Major.

'Lord Dagenham's niece,' said Alec. 'Apparently she's living up at the manor now and assuming all kinds of social duties. Daisy's furious, so best look out. She's taking it out on everyone.'

'I'm not in the least intimidated by Daisy Green,' the Major lied.

'Let's get that drink,' said Alec. 'I think a large G and T is in order.'

❧ ❧ ❧

The Grill bar was a high-ceilinged Edwardian room, with French doors looking over the terrace and eighteenth hole toward the sea. A series of mirrored doors at the east end hid an annex with a stage, which was opened on the occasion of large tournaments as well as the annual dance. The wall of the long walnut bar to the west end was hung with arched wood panelling on which racks of bottles were ranged below portraits of past club presidents. A portrait of the Queen (an early portrait, badly reprinted and framed in cheap gilt) hung directly above some particularly vile coloured after-dinner liqueurs that no one ever drank. The Major always found this vaguely treasonable.

The room contained a few clusters of scratched and dented club chairs in brown leather and a series of tables along the windows, which could be reserved only through Tom, the barman. This prevented any monopoly of the tables by ladies who might be organised enough to telephone ahead. Instead, members with early tee times popped in first to see Tom, who would put down his mop or emerge from the cellar to add their names in the book. It was the aspiration of many members to become one of the few, very august regulars whose names were pencilled in by Tom himself. The Major was not one of these anymore. Since the creamed chicken incident, he preferred to persuade Alec to join him in a sandwich at the bar, or in one of the clusters of chairs. Not only did this protect them from a surfeit of clotted gravy and thin custards, but it freed them from the sullen charms of the waitresses who, culled from the pool of unmotivated young women being spat out by the local school, specialised in a mood of suppressed rage. Many seemed to suffer from some disease of holes in the face and it had taken the Major some time to work out that club rules required the young women to remove all jewellery and that the holes were piercings bereft of decoration.

'Good morning, gentlemen. The usual?' asked Tom, a tumbler already poised under the optic of the green gin bottle.

'Better make mine a double,' said Alec, making a great show of wiping his bare melon-shaped forehead with his pocket square. 'My goodness, we barely escaped with our lives there.'

'Make mine a half of lager instead, would you, Tom?' said the Major.

They ordered two thick ham and cheese sandwiches. Alec also put in his order for a piece of jam roly-poly since it was only offered on Fridays and tended to sell out. He topped off the order with a small salad.

Alec had an unshakeable belief that he was into fitness. He always ordered a salad at lunch, though he never ate anything but the decorative tomato. He insisted that he drank alcohol only when it was accompanied by food. Once or twice he had been caught short in an unfamiliar pub and the Major had seen him reduced to consuming a pickled egg or pork cracklings.

They had barely settled onto a couple of bar stools when a foursome came in, laughing over some incident on the final green. Father Christopher and Hugh Whetstone he recognised, and he was surprised to see Lord Dagenham, who was very rarely at the club and whose atrocious playing made for some very awkward questions of etiquette. The fourth man was a stranger, and something in his broad shoulders and unfortunate pink golf shirt suggested to the Major that he might be another American. Two Americans in as many weeks was, he reflected, approaching a nasty epidemic.

'Shaw, Major—how are you?' asked Dagenham, slapping Alec on the back and then clasping the Major firmly on the shoulder. 'Sorry to hear about your loss, Major. Damn shame to lose a good man like your brother.'

'Thank you, your lordship,' said the Major, standing up and inclining his head. 'You are very kind to say so.' It was just like Lord Dagenham to pop up from nowhere and yet to be in possession of all the latest news of the village. The Major wondered if some assistant at the Hall sent him regular faxes to London. He was very touched by his lordship's words and by the always respectful use of the Major's rank. His lordship could so easily have called him Pettigrew, and yet he never did. In return, the Major never referred to him in the familiar, even behind his back.

'Frank, allow me to present Major Ernest Pettigrew, formerly of the Royal Sussex, and Mr Alec Shaw—used to help run the Bank of England in his spare time. Gentlemen, this is Mr Frank Ferguson, who is visiting us from New Jersey.'

'How do you do,' said the Major.

'Frank is in real estate,' added Lord Dagenham. 'One of the largest resort and retail developers on the East Coast.'

'Oh, you're making too much of it, Double D,' said Ferguson. 'It's just a little family business I inherited from my dad.'

'You're in the building trade?' asked the Major.

'You got me pegged, Pettigrew,' said Ferguson, slapping him on the back. 'No use pretending to be something grand in front of you Brits. You smell a man's class like a bloodhound smells rabbit.'

'I didn't mean to imply anything . . .' the Major stumbled.

'Yep—that's the Fergusons, plain old brick-and-mortar builders.'

'Mr Ferguson can trace his lineage to the Ferguson clan of Argyll,' said Hugh Whetstone, who tried to ferret out the genealogy of everyone he met so he could use it against them later.

'Not that they were very happy to hear it,' Ferguson said. 'My ancestor faked his own death in the Crimea and ran off to Canada— gambling debts and a couple of husbands on the warpath, so I believe. Still, they were pretty happy with my offer on the castle at Loch Brae. I'm going to look into restoring the shoot up there.'

'The Major is a shooting man, too. Quite a decent shot, if I may say so,' said Lord Dagenham. 'He can drop a rabbit at a hundred yards.'

'You country people are amazing,' said Ferguson. 'I met a gamekeeper last week, shoots squirrels with a King James II ball musket. What do you shoot with, Major?'

'Just an old gun that belonged to my father,' replied the Major, so upset to be lumped with some eccentric old villager that he would not give Ferguson the satisfaction of trying to impress him.

'He's being modest as usual,' Dagenham said. 'The Major shoots with a very nice gun—a Purdey, isn't it?'

'A Churchill, actually,' said the Major, slightly annoyed that Dagenham had automatically mentioned the more famous name. 'Lesser known, perhaps,' he added to Ferguson, 'but they've made their share of exquisite guns.'

'Nothing like the workmanship in an English best gun,' said Ferguson. 'At least, that's what they say when they insist on taking a year or two to make you a pair.'

'Actually, I may be in the happy position of reuniting my pair.' The Major could not resist the opportunity to give this information directly to Lord Dagenham.

'Well, of course,' said Lord Dagenham. 'You inherit the other one from your brother, don't you? Congratulations, old man.'

'It's not all quite settled yet,' said the Major. 'My sister-in-law, you know . . .'

'Oh, quite right to take a few days. Lots of feelings after a funeral,' said Father Christopher. He hinged his long angular frame forward over the bar. 'Can we get a round, Tom? And do you have a table for Lord Dagenham?'

'A matched pair of Churchills,' said the American, smiling at the Major with slightly increased interest.

'Yes, 1946 or thereabouts. Made for the Indian market,' said the Major, not allowing even a hint of pride to show through his modesty.

'I'd love to see them in action sometime,' Ferguson said.

'The Major often comes over and has a go with us,' said Dagenham. 'Glass of cabernet please, Tom—and what'll you have, Frank?'

'Then I'm sure I'll be seeing you at Double D's shoot on the eleventh.' Ferguson stuck out his hand and the Major was forced into a ridiculous display of pumping, as if they had just made a pact to sell a horse. Dagenham stuck his own hands in his jacket pockets and looked awkward. The Major held his breath. He was aware of a certain personal humiliation, but he was equally anxious about his lordship. Lord Dagenham was now in the terrible position of having to find a gracious way to explain to his American guest that the shooting party in question was strictly for business colleagues, mostly down from London for the day. It was appalling to see a good man so trapped by the ignorance of the bad-mannered. The Major considered jumping in to explain the situation himself, but did not want to suggest that his lordship was unable to extricate himself from situations of tangled etiquette.

'Of course you must come if you can, Pettigrew,' said Dagenham at last. 'Not much of a challenge, though. We'll only be taking the ducks off the hill pond.'

Dagenham's gamekeeper raised three varieties of duck on a small pond tucked into a copse that crowned a low hill above the village. He incubated abandoned eggs, fed the ducklings by hand, and visited every day, often with delighted schoolchildren from the Hall in tow, until the ducks learned to waddle after him as he called to them. Once a year, Dagenham held a shoot at the pond. The gamekeeper, and some young helpers hired for the day, scared the ducks off the pond with yelling and thrashing about with rakes and cricket bats. The birds circled the copse once, squawking in protest, and then flew back directly into the path of the guns, urged home by the gamekeeper's welcoming whistle. The Major's disappointment at never being invited to this more elaborate shoot, with its early morning meeting on the steps of the Hall and huge breakfast party to follow, was slightly mitigated by his contempt for so-called sportsmen who needed wildfowl driven right onto the gun barrel. Nancy had often joked that Dagenham should buy the ducks frozen and have the gamekeeper toss a handful of shot in with the giblets. He had never quite been comfortable laughing with her at this, but had agreed that it was certainly not the sporting match of man and prey to which he would be proud to lend his gun.

'I'd be delighted to come,' said the Major.

'Ah, I think Tom has our table ready,' said Dagenham, ignoring the expressions of hope on the face of the Vicar and Whetstone. 'Shall we?'

'See you on the eleventh, then,' said Ferguson, pumping the Major's hand again. 'I'll be on you like a bear on honey, getting a good look at those guns of yours.'

'Thank you for the warning,' said the Major.

᠉ ᠉ ᠉

'I thought you said there was some difficulty about the gun?' Alec asked in a quiet voice as they chewed their sandwiches and refused to steal glances at Lord Dagenham's party. Whetstone was laughing more loudly than the American in order to make sure the entire room knew he was at the table. 'What are you going to do if you can't get it?' The Major now regretted mentioning Bertie's will to Alec. It had slipped out somewhere on the back nine when he was overcome again by the injustice of the situation. It was never a good idea to confide in people. They always remembered, and when they came up to you in the street, years later, you could see the information was still firmly attached to your face and present in the way they said your name and the pressure of their hand clasping yours.

'I'm sure there will be no problem when I explain the situation,' said the Major. 'She'll at least let me have it for the occasion.' Marjorie was always very impressed with titles, and she was not aware of Lord Dagenham being a reduced kind of gentry, with all but one wing of the Hall let to a small boarding school for children aged three to thirteen and most of the lands lying fallow, producing only EU subsidy payments. He was sure he could talk up his lordship to the heights of an earl and impress upon Marjorie the privilege accorded the entire family by the invitation. Once the gun was in his hands, he would be quite happy to draw out any discussion of ownership—perhaps indefinitely? He ate his sandwich more quickly. If he hurried, he might see Marjorie this afternoon and put the whole matter to rest.

'Ah, Major, I was hoping to catch you.' It was Grace, standing awkwardly by the bar, her large handbag clutched in crossed hands like a flotation cushion. 'I managed to get Mrs Ali on the telephone about the dance.'

'Very good,' said the Major in a voice as neutral as he could manage without being actively dismissive. 'So you're all set, then?' He hoped Dagenham's table was not in earshot.

'She seemed rather stiff at first,' said Grace. 'She said she didn't really do catering. I was quite disappointed, because I thought she and I were on quite good terms.'

'Can we buy you a drink, Grace?' Alec said, waving half a sandwich at her from the Major's other side. A speck of dark pickle landed dangerously close to the Major's arm.

'No, thank you,' she said. The Major frowned at Alec. It was not kind of him to make such an offer. Grace was one of those rare women who maintained a feminine distaste for being at the bar. There was also the impossibility of a lady climbing onto the high stool in any dignified manner and she would feel keenly the absence of another woman to chaperone.

'Anyway, then the strangest thing happened. I mentioned your name—that you and I were working on this together—and she suddenly changed her tune. She was most helpful.'

'Well, I'm glad you got what you needed,' said the Major, anxious to end the matter before Grace inferred anything from her own observation.

'I didn't know you knew Mrs Ali . . . ?' She was hesitant, but there was a definite question in her voice, and the Major tried not to squirm.

'I don't really,' he said. 'I mean, I buy a lot of tea from her. We discuss tea quite often, I suppose. I really don't know her well.' Grace nodded and the Major felt just a hint of guilt at denying Mrs Ali in this way. However, he comforted himself, since Grace did not seem to find it the least strange that her own friendship would count for so much less than a casual commercial exchange over tea, he had best leave well alone.

'Anyway, she said she would call up some people she knows in the town and give me some ideas and prices. I told her mostly finger food, nothing too spicy.'

'Won't do to end up with curried goat's head and roasted eyeballs,' said Alec.

Grace ignored him. 'She said she would call me next week. And perhaps set up a tasting. I told her you and I would be delighted to attend.'

'Me?' said the Major.

'I was afraid if I said just me she might go back to being stiff,' Grace explained. The Major had no answer for this.

'Looks like you're the food committee, Pettigrew,' said Alec. 'Try to slip in a plate of roast beef, will you? Something edible amongst all the vindaloo.'

'Look, I can't possibly assist you,' said the Major. 'I mean, with just losing my brother . . . I have so many things to see to . . . family and so on.'

'I understand,' said Grace. She looked at him and he read in her eyes a disappointment that he should have stooped to the dead-relative excuse. Yet he was as entitled as the next man to use it. People did it all the time; it was understood that there was a defined window of availability beginning a decent few days after a funeral and continuing for no more than a couple of months. Of course, some people took dreadful advantage and a year later were still hauling around their dead relatives on their backs, showing them off to explain late tax payments and missed dentist appointments: something he would never do.

'I will just have to do the best I can,' said Grace and her face drooped, as if defeat were inevitable. 'I was afraid I might let Daisy down again, but of course that is no excuse for me to trespass on your very great grief. Please forgive me.' She put out her hand and touched him lightly on the forearm. He was suddenly aware of a slow burn of shame.

'Oh, look here, sometime next week would probably be fine,' he said, his voice gruff. He patted her hand. 'I'll have most things straightened out with the family by then.'

'Oh, thank you, Daisy will be so pleased.'

'There's surely no need for that,' he said. 'Can't we keep it between ourselves?' Alec dug him in the ribs with an elbow and he was aware from Grace's delicate mauve blush that his words were open to interpretation. He would have liked to clarify, but she was already retreating from the room, bumping a bony hip on the corner of a table as she hurried away. The Major groaned and looked at his sandwich which seemed as appetising now as two rubber mats filled with horsehair. He pushed the plate away and signalled Tom to bring another lager.

Chapter Seven

His car was already pulled up to Marjorie's spindly fountain and a face at the double-glazed oriel window above the front door had registered his presence before the second thoughts overwhelmed him. He should have telephoned before arriving. The fiction that he was welcome to drop in at any time, because he was family, could only be maintained as long as he never took Marjorie at her word.

It had been obvious soon after Bertie's marriage that Marjorie had no intention of playing the dutiful daughter-in-law and had sought to separate the two of them from the rest of the family. In the modern style, they had formed a nucleus of two and set about filling their tiny flat with ugly new furniture and friends from Bertie's insurance office. They immediately began to defy the tradition of the family Sunday lunch at Rose Lodge and took to dropping by in the late afternoon instead, when they would decline a cup of tea in favour of a mixed cocktail. His mother would drink tea, stiff with Sunday disapproval, while Marjorie regaled them with news of her latest purchases. He would have a small sherry, a sticky and unpleasant attempt to bridge the gap. Nancy soon lost patience with them. She began to call Bertie and Marjorie the

'Pettigrubbers' and, to the Major's horror, to encourage Marjorie to elaborate on exactly how much her latest purchases had cost.

The front door remained shut. Perhaps he had only imagined a face at the window, or perhaps they didn't want to see him and were even now crouching behind the sofa hoping he would ring the bell a couple of times and then leave. He rang again. Once again the chimes played their few bars of 'Joyful, Joyful,' echoing away deep into the house. He rapped on the door knocker, a brass wreath of grapevine with a central wine bottle, and stared at the front door's aggressive oak grain. Somewhere another door closed and at last heels clicked on tile and the door was unbolted. Jemima was dressed in grey sweatpants and a black sleeveless polo neck top, with her hair pulled back under a white sweatband. She appeared, thought the Major, to be dressed as some kind of athletic nun. She gave him a glare she might have given a door-to-door vacuum salesman or an evangelical proselytiser.

'Is Mother expecting you?' she asked. 'Only I just got her to lie down for a few minutes.'

'I'm afraid I drove over on the off chance,' he said. 'I can come back later.' He looked at her carefully. Her face was devoid of the usual makeup and her hair limp. She looked like the gangly, stooped girl of fifteen she had once been; sullen but with Bertie's pale eyes and strong chin to redeem her.

'I was just doing my healing yoga,' she said. 'But I suppose you'd better come in while I'm here. I don't want people bothering Mother when I'm not around.' She turned and went in, leaving the door for him to close.

❧ ❧ ❧

'I suppose you'd like a cup of tea?' Jemima asked as they arrived in the kitchen. She put on the electric kettle and stood behind the U-shaped kitchen counter, where someone had begun to sort out a drawer full of junk. 'Mother will get up in a bit anyway. She can't seem to lie still these days.' She hung her head and picked about for bits of used pencils, which she added to a small heap in between a pile of batteries and a small arrangement of variously coloured string.

'No little Gregory today?' the Major asked, sitting himself on a wooden chair at the breakfast table in the window nook.

'One of my friends is picking him up from school,' she said. 'They've all been very good about babysitting and bringing over salads and stuff. I haven't had to cook dinner in a week.'

'Quite the welcome break, then?' said the Major. She gave him a withering look. The kettle began to boil; she produced two chunky malformed mugs in a strange olive hue and a flowery box of tea bags.

'Chamomile, Blackberry Zinger, or burdock?' she asked.

'I'll have real tea if you have it,' he said. She reached high into a cupboard and pulled out a tin of plain tea bags. She dropped one in a cup and poured boiling water up to the brim. It immediately began to give off a smell like wet laundry.

'How is your mother doing?' he asked.

'It's funny how people keep asking me that. "How's your poor mother?" they say, as if I'm just some disinterested observer.'

'How are you both doing?' he offered, feeling his jaw twitch as he bit back a more resentful retort. Her broad hint of people's insensitivity did not extend to asking how he was coping.

'She's been very agitated,' Jemima confided. 'You see, there might be an award coming—from the Royal Institute of Insurance and Actuarial Sciences. They called three days ago, but apparently they can't confirm yet. It's between Dad and some professor who created a new way of hedging life insurance premiums of Eastern European immigrants.'

'When will you know?' he said, wondering why the world always seemed to wait until death to give anyone their due.

'Well, the other man suffered a stroke and he's on a breathing machine.'

'I'm so sorry to hear that.'

'If he's still alive on the twenty-third of the month, the end of their fiscal year, then Dad's a sure thing to get the award. Posthumous is preferred, it seems.'

'What an appalling thing.'

'Yes, horrible,' she agreed. She sipped her tea, pulling the tea bag aside by its string. 'I even called the hospital in London, but they refused to give me any information on his condition. I told them they were being very inconsiderate, given my poor mother's suffering.'

The Major jiggled his own string in the cup. The swollen belly of the bag rolled in the brown water. He found himself at a loss for words.

'Ernest, how lovely to see you. You should have called and let us know you were coming.' Marjorie came in wearing a voluminous black wool skirt and a ruffled blouse of black and purple that looked as if it had been whipped up out of funeral bunting. He stood, wondering whether the circumstances required him to hug her, but she slipped behind the counter with Jemima and the two of them looked at him as if he had come to buy stamps at the post office. He decided to adopt a brisk tone of business.

'I'm sorry to just barge in like this, Marjorie,' he said. 'But Mortimer Teale and I have begun the estate work and I did want to just clarify one or two little matters with you.'

'You know, Ernest, that I have no head for these things. I'm sure you can leave most of it to Mortimer. He's such a clever man.' She picked at the tangle of string amid the junk pile but let it drop again.

'That may be, but he is not a member of the family and therefore may not be able to interpret some of the niceties—or to allow for some of the intentions, so to speak.'

'I think my father's will is very straightforward,' said Jemima, her eye beady as a gull eyeing a bag of garbage. 'We don't need anyone upsetting Mother by raising questions for the sake of it.'

'Exactly,' said the Major. He breathed slowly. 'Much better to sort it all out within the family. Keep it all away from any unpleasantness.'

'It's all unpleasant anyway,' said Marjorie, wiping her eyes on a paper towel. 'I can't believe Bertie would do this to me.' She erupted in hoarse, unpleasant sobbing.

'Mother, I can't bear it when you cry,' said Jemima. She held her mother by the shoulders, simultaneously patting her while keeping her at arm's length. Jemima's face was screwed up into an expression of distress or disgust; the Major couldn't really tell.

'I didn't mean to upset you,' he began. 'I can come back later.'

'Anything you have to say to Mother you can say now, while I'm here,' said Jemima. 'I won't have people bothering her when she's alone and vulnerable.'

'Oh, Jemima, don't be so rude to your uncle Ernest, dear,' said Marjorie. 'He is one of our only friends now. We must depend on him to look out for us.' She dabbed her eyes and gave a close approximation of a tremulous smile. The Major could see a hint of steely resolve burning under the smile, but it put him in an impossible position. He was quite unable to come up with any decent way of asking for his gun in the face of his brother's crying widow.

He saw the gun slipping away, the velvet depression in the double gun box permanently empty and his own gun never to be reunited with its partner. He felt his own loneliness, felt that he would be bereft of wife and family until claimed by the cold ground or the convenient heat of the crematorium furnace. His eyes watered and he seemed to smell ash in the potpourri scent of the kitchen. He rose again from his chair and resolved never to mention the gun again. Instead, he would slip away to his own small fireside and try to find consolation in being alone. Perhaps he would even place an order for a single gun case, something with a simple silver monogram and a lining more subdued than dark red velvet.

'I'll not trouble you any more with this,' he said, his heart full with the pleasant warmth of his sacrifice. 'Mortimer and I will file all the appropriate paperwork; nothing we can't resolve between us.' He walked over and took Marjorie's hand. She smelled of her freshly painted mauve nails and a hint of lavender hair spray. 'I will take care of everything,' he promised.

'Thank you, Ernest,' she said, her voice faint, her grip strong.

'So what about the guns?' asked Jemima.

'I'll be going along now,' he said to Marjorie.

'Do come again,' she said. 'It is such a comfort to me to have your support.'

'But let's sort out about the guns,' said Jemima again, and it was no longer possible to block out her voice.

'We don't have to go into that right now,' said Marjorie through compressed lips. 'Let's leave it until later, all right?'

'You know Anthony and I need the money right away, Mother. Private school isn't cheap, and we need to get a deposit down early for Gregory.'

The Major wondered whether the nurse at the clinic could have been wrong about his perfectly fine ECG. His chest felt constricted and liable to flower into pain at any moment. They were going to deny him even his noble sacrifice. He would not be allowed to withdraw without addressing the subject, but instead would be forced to verbalise his renunciation of his own gun. The feeling in his chest flowered not into pain but into anger. He drew himself up at attention, a move that always relaxed him, and tried to maintain a blank calm.

'We'll deal with it later,' said Marjorie again. She seemed to pat Jemima's hand, though he suspected it was really a nasty pinch.

'If we put it off, he'll only get some other idea in his head,' whispered Jemima, in a voice that would have carried to the back of the Albert Hall.

'Am I to understand that you wish to discuss my father's sporting guns?' The Major, enraged, tried to keep his voice as calm and clipped as that of a brigadier. 'I was, of course, not going to bring it up at this difficult time—'

'Yes, plenty of time later,' interjected Marjorie.

'And yet, since you bring it up, perhaps we should speak frankly on the subject—we're all family here,' he said. Jemima scowled at him. Marjorie looked back and forth at them both and pursed her lips a few times before speaking.

'Well, Ernest, Jemima has suggested that we might do very well now, selling your father's guns as a pair.' He said nothing and she rushed on. 'I mean, if we sell yours and ours together—we might make quite a bit, and I would like to help Jemima with little Gregory's education.'

'Yours and ours?' he repeated.

'Well, you have one and we have one,' she continued. 'But apparently, they're not worth nearly as much separately.' She looked at him with wide eyes, willing him to agree with her. The Major felt his vision shift in and out of focus. He scoured his mind wildly for a way out of the conversation, but the moment of confrontation was upon him and he could find no alternative but to speak his mind.

'Since you bring it up . . . I was under the impression . . . that Bertie and I had an understanding with each other as to the—to the disposition, as it were, of the guns.' He drew a breath and prepared to thrust himself even into the teeth of the frowning women before him. 'It was my understanding . . . It was our father's intention . . . that Bertie's gun should pass into my care . . . and vice versa . . . as circumstances should dictate.' There! The words had been cast at them like boulders from a catapult; now he could only stand his ground and brace for the counterattack.

'Dear me, I know you've always been very keen on having that old gun,' said Marjorie. For a moment the Major's heart leaped at her blushing confusion. Might he even prevail?

'That, Mother, is exactly why I don't want you talking to anyone without me,' said Jemima. 'You are likely to give away half your possessions to anyone who asks.'

'Oh, don't exaggerate, Jemima,' said Marjorie. 'Ernest isn't trying to take anything from us.'

'Yesterday you nearly let that Salvation Army woman talk you into giving her the living room furniture along with the bags of clothes.' She rounded on the Major. 'She's not herself, as you can see, and I won't have people try to walk all over her, no matter if they are relatives.' The Major felt his neck swell with rage. It would serve Jemima right if he popped a blood vessel and collapsed right on the kitchen floor.

'I resent your implication,' he stammered.

'We've always known you were after my father's gun,' said Jemima. 'It wasn't enough that you took the house, the china, all the money—'

'Look here, I don't know what money you're referring to, but—'

'And then all those times you tried to con my father out of the one thing his father gave him.'

'Jemima, that's enough,' said Marjorie. She had the grace to blush but would not look at him. He wanted to ask her, very quietly, whether this topic, which she had obviously chewed over many times with Jemima, had also been discussed with Bertie. Could Bertie have held on to such resentments all these years and never let it show?

'I did make monetary offers to Bertie over the years,' he conceded with a dry mouth. 'But I thought they were always fair market value.' Jemima gave an unpleasant, porcine snort.

'I'm sure they were,' said Marjorie. 'Let's just all be sensible now and work this out together. Jemima says if we sell the pair, we can get such a lot more.'

'Perhaps I might make you some suitable offer myself,' said the Major. He was not sure he sounded very convincing. The figures were already turning in his head and he failed to see immediately how he might part with a substantial cash sum. He lived very well off his army pension, a few investments, and a small annuity that had passed to him from his paternal grandmother and which, he was forced to admit, had not been discussed as part of his parents' estate. Still, dipping into principal was not a risk he cared to take in anything but an emergency. Might he contemplate some kind of small mortgage on the house? This prompted a shiver of dismay.

'I couldn't possibly take money from you,' said Marjorie. 'I won't take it.'

'In that case—'

'We'll just have to be smart and get the highest price we can,' said Marjorie.

'I think we should call the auction houses,' said Jemima. 'Get an appraisal.'

'Look here,' said the Major.

'Your grandmother once sold a teapot at Sotheby's,' said Marjorie to Jemima. 'She always hated it—too fussy—then it turned out to be Meissen and they got quite a bit.'

'Of course, you have to pay commission and everything,' said Jemima.

'My father's Churchills are not being put on the block at public auction like some bankrupt farm equipment,' said the Major firmly. 'The Pettigrew name will not be printed in a sale catalogue.'

Lord Dagenham quite cheerfully sent off pieces of the Dagenham patrimony to auction now and then. Last year a George II desk of inlaid yew had been shipped off to Christie's. At the club, he had listened politely to Lord Dagenham boasting of the record price paid by some Russian collector, but secretly he had been deeply distressed by the image of the wide desk, with its thin scrolled legs, duct-taped into an old felt blanket and upended in a rented removal van.

'What else do you suggest?' asked Marjorie. The Major suppressed a desire to suggest that they might consider removing themselves to hell. He calmed his voice to a tone suitable for placating large dogs or small, angry children.

'I would like to suggest that you give me an opportunity to look round a bit,' he said, improvising as he went. 'I actually met a very wealthy American gun collector recently. Perhaps I might let him take a look at them.'

'An American?' said Marjorie. 'Who is it?'

'I hardly think the name will be familiar to you,' said the Major. 'He is—an industrialist.' This sounded more impressive than 'builder'.

'Ooh, that sounds like it might do,' said Marjorie.

'Of course, I would have to take a look at Bertie's gun first. I'm afraid it is probably going to need some restoration work,'

'So I suppose we should just give you the gun right now?' asked Jemima.

'I think that would be best,' said the Major, ignoring her sarcasm. 'Of course, you could send it to be restored by the manufacturer, but they will charge you rather steeply. I am in a position to effect a restoration myself at no cost.'

'That's very kind of you, Ernest,' said Marjorie.

'It is the least I can do for you,' said the Major. 'Bertie would expect no less.'

'How long would this take?' asked Jemima. 'Christie's has a gun auction next month.'

'Well, if you want to pay out over fifteen per cent in commissions and accept only what the room will offer on the day . . .' said the Major. 'Personally, I cannot see myself consigning my gun to the vagaries of the market.'

'I think we should let Ernest handle it,' said Marjorie.

'As it happens, I will be attending Lord Dagenham's shoot next month,' continued the Major. 'I would have an opportunity to show my American friend how the guns perform as a pair.'

'How much will he pay?' asked Jemima, demonstrating that her mother's inclination to discuss money in public was evolving down the generations. No doubt little Gregory would grow up to leave the price tags hanging from his clothes and the manufacturer's sticker still glued to the window of his German sports car.

'That, my dear Jemima, is a delicate subject best broached after the guns have been displayed to their finest advantage.'

'We'll get more money because you shoot grouse in the mud all day long?'

'Ducks, my dear Jemima, ducks.' He tried a brief chuckle, to confirm an air of disinterest, and felt almost confident that he would win the day. There was such greed shining in both pairs of eyes. For a moment he understood the thrill of a master con artist. Perhaps he had the touch that would make old ladies believe they had won the Australian lottery, or lead them to send funds to release Nigerian bank accounts. The newspapers were full of such accounts and he had often wondered how people could be so gullible. Yet here and now, so close he could smell the gun oil, was the opportunity to load Bertie's gun into his car and drive away.

'It remains entirely up to you, dear ladies,' he said, tugging at his jacket hem in preparation for departure. 'I see no downside for you in my restoring the gun and then allowing one of the richest gun collectors in the United States to see the pair perform in the proper setting of a formal shooting party.' He saw the shoot: the other men congratulating him as he modestly denied that his was the largest bag of the day. 'I believe the dog has mistaken this fine mallard drake of yours as being mine, Lord Dagenham,' he might say, and Dagenham would take it of course, knowing full well it had fallen to Pettigrew's superior twin Churchills.

'Do you think he'd pay cash?' asked Jemima, recalling his full attention.

'I would think he might be so overwhelmed by the pageantry of the event to offer us any amount we name—in cash or gold bars. On the other hand, he may not. I make no promises.'

'Let's try it, then,' said Marjorie. 'I would like to get the most we can. I'd like to take a cruise this winter.'

'I advise you not to rush into anything, Marjorie,' he said. He was playing now; risking a prize already won just for the thrill of the game.

'No, no, you must take the gun with you and look it over, in case it does need to be sent somewhere,' said Marjorie. 'We don't want to waste any time.'

'It's in the boot cupboard with the cricket bats,' said Jemima. 'I'll run and get it.'

The Major reassured himself that he was largely telling the truth. He would be showing the guns to Ferguson, even though he had no intention of letting them be bought. Furthermore, he could hardly be expected to take the moral high road with people who would keep a fine sporting gun thrown in the back of a shoe cupboard. He was, he decided, doing the same thing as rescuing a puppy from an abusive junkyard owner.

'Here we are,' said Jemima, pointing a quilt-covered bundle at him. He took it from her, feeling for the thick stock and pointing the barrel end toward the floor.

'Thank you,' he said, as if they were handing him a gift. 'Thank you very much.'

Chapter Eight

It was just a cup of tea and a chat. As the Major mounted the step stool for a better view of the top shelf of the china cupboard, he chided himself for fussing over the arrangements like some old maid. He was determined to be completely casual about Mrs Ali's visit. Her voice on the telephone had asked in a most straightforward manner whether he might have any time on Sunday to offer her his insights on the Kipling book, which she had just finished. Sunday afternoons the shop was closed, and she implied that her nephew was used to her taking a couple of hours to herself. He had replied in a careful offhand that Sunday afternoon might suit him and that perhaps he would rustle up a cup of tea or something. She said she would come around four, if that was convenient.

Of course, the thick white earthenware teapot immediately developed an ugly chip in the spout and, despite several scourings, would not come clean inside. He realised that it must have been chipped for some time and that he had closed his eyes to its shortcomings in order to avoid the search for a new one. Twenty years ago, it had taken Nancy and him over a year to find a plain vessel that kept the heat in and did not dribble when poured. He considered running to town in the few days remaining, but he already knew it would be impossible to find anything among the florid ranks of pots that multiplied like mushrooms in stores dedicated to 'home design'. He could see them now: pots with invisible handles; pots with bird whistles; pots featuring blurry transfers of ladies on swings and curly handles awkwardly balanced. He settled instead on serving tea in his mother's silver.

The silver teapot, with a good plain belly on it and a small frill of acanthus leaves around the lid, immediately made his teacups look as thick and dull as peasants. He considered using the good china, but he did not feel he could pull off a casual image while bearing in a tray loaded with fine, gold-rimmed antiques. Then he had remembered Nancy's cups. There were only two of them, bought at a flea market before she and he were married. Nancy had admired the unusually large blue and white cups, shaped like upside-down bells, and accompanied by saucers deep enough to use as bowls. They were very old, from when people still tipped their tea into the saucer to drink. Nancy had got them cheap because they did not quite match and there were no additional pieces.

She made him tea in them one afternoon, just tea, carried carefully to the small deal table set by the window in her room. The landlady, who had been persuaded by his uniform and quiet manners that he was a gentleman, allowed him to visit Nancy's room as long as he was gone by nightfall. They were used to making love in the strong afternoon sunlight, smothering their giggles under the batik bedspread whenever the landlady deliberately creaked the floorboards outside the door. But that day the room was tidy, the usual debris of books and paints cleared away, and Nancy, hair smoothed back into a loose ponytail, had made them tea in the beautiful translucent cups, which held a scalding heat in their old porcelain and made the cheap loose tea glow like amber. She poured him milk from a shot glass, careful not to splash, her movements as slow as a ceremony. He lifted his cup and knew, with a sudden clarity that did not frighten him as much as he might have expected, that it was time to ask her to marry him.

The cups trembled in his hands. He bent down to put them carefully on the counter, where they looked suitably inert. Nancy had treated the cups lightly, sometimes serving blancmange in them because of their happy shape. She would have been the last to insist on treating them as relics. Yet as he reached for the saucers he wished he could ask her whether it was all right to use them.

He had never been one of those people who believed that the dead hung around, dispensing permissions and generally providing watchdog services. In church, when the organ swelled and the chorus of the hymn turned irritating neighbours into a brief community of raised hearts and simple voices, he accepted that she was gone. He envisaged her in the heaven he had learned about in childhood: a grassy place with blue sky and a light breeze. He could no longer picture the inhabitants with anything as ridiculous as wings. Instead he saw Nancy strolling in a simple sheath dress, her low shoes held in her hand and a shady tree beckoning her in the distance. The rest of the time, he could not hold on to this vision and she was only gone, like Bertie, and he was left to struggle on alone in the awful empty space of unbelief.

Silver teapot, old blue cups, no food. The Major surveyed his completed tea preparations with relief. The absence of food would set the right casual tone, he thought. He had the vague idea that it was not manly to fuss over the details as he had been doing and that making finger sandwiches would be dubious. He sighed. It was one of the things he had to watch out for, living alone. It was important to keep up standards, to not let things become fuzzy around the edges. And yet there was that fine line across which one might be betrayed into womanish fretting over details. He checked his watch. He had several hours before his guest arrived. He decided that perhaps he would undertake a brief, manly attempt at carpentry and fix the broken slat in the fence at the bottom of the garden and then spend some time taking his first good look at Bertie's gun.

♮ ♩ ♪

He had been sitting in the scullery, in the same fixed position, for at least ten minutes. He remembered coming in from the garden and taking Bertie's gun out of its quilt wrappings, but after that his thoughts had wandered until his eyes, focused on the old print of Windsor Castle on the wall, began to see movement in its brown water stains. The Major blinked and the spots resumed their inert positions in the pitted paper. He reminded himself that such lapses into moments of slack-jawed senility were unbecoming to his former rank. He did not want to become like Colonel Preston. He did not have the necessary interest in house plants.

On Fridays, twice a month, the Major visited his former CO, Colonel Preston, who was wheelchair-bound now with a combination of Alzheimer's and neuropathy of the legs. Colonel Preston communicated with a large potted fern named Matilda and also enjoyed watching wallpaper and apologising to house flies when they bumped into closed windows. Poor Colonel Preston could only be roused to any semblance of normality by his wife, Helena, a lovely Polish woman. Shaken on the shoulder by Helena, the Colonel would immediately turn to a visitor and say, as if in the middle of a longer conversation, 'Got out just ahead of the Russians, you know. Exchanged the dossiers for permission to marry.' Helena would shake her head in mock despair, pat the Colonel's hand, and say, 'I worked in my father's sausage shop, but he remembers me as Mata Hari.' Helena kept him freshly bathed, in clean clothes, and on his many medications. After every visit, the Major pledged to exercise more and do crossword puzzles, so as to stave off such weakening of the brain, but he also wondered with some anxiety who would wash the back of his neck so well if he were incapacitated.

In the dim light of the scullery, the Major straightened his shoulders and made a mental note to first inventory all the prints in the house for damage, and then get them looked at by a competent conservator.

He turned his attention again to Bertie's gun, lying on the counter. He would try not to waste any more time wondering why Bertie had neglected it all these years and what it meant that the gun lay unwanted in a cupboard even as Bertie rejected cash offers from his own brother. Instead, he focused his attention on a dispassionate inspection of the parts that might need repair.

There were cracks in the grain, and the wood itself was grey and dry. The ivory cap on the butt was deeply yellowed. He cracked the action open and found the chambers dull but thankfully free of rust. The barrel looked straight, though it had a small grouping of rust spots, as if it had been grasped by a sweaty hand and not wiped down. The elaborate chase work, a royal eagle entwined with persimmon flowers, was black with tarnish. He rubbed a finger under the eagle's flailing talons and sure enough, there was the trim and upright 'P' monogram, which his father had added. He hoped it was not hubris to experience a certain satisfaction that while maharajahs and their kingdoms might fade into oblivion, the Pettigrews soldiered on.

He opened the gun box, lifted out the sections of his own gun, for comparison. They slid together with well-oiled clicks. Laying the two guns side by side, he experienced a momentary lapse of faith. They looked nothing like a pair. His own gun looked fat and polished. It almost breathed as it lay on the slab. Bertie's gun looked like a sketch, or a preliminary model done in cheap materials to get the shape right and then discarded. The Major put his gun away and closed the box. He would not compare them again until he had done his best to restore Bertie's gun to its finest possible condition. He patted it as if it were a thin stray dog, found in an icy ditch.

As he lit the candle to warm the oil and took his leather case of cleaning implements out of the drawer, he felt much more cheerful. He had only to strip the gun down and work at it piece by piece until it was rebuilt just the way it was intended to be. He made a mental note to allow himself one hour a day for the project and he felt immediately the sense of calm that comes from having a well-designed routine.

When the phone rang in the early afternoon, his cheerfulness overrode his natural sense of caution at hearing Roger's voice on the other end. He was not even upset by the worse than usual quality of the connection.

'You sound as if you're calling from a submarine, Roger,' he said chuckling. 'I expect the squirrels have been chewing on the lines again.'

'Actually, it may also be that I have you on speaker,' said Roger. 'My chiropractor doesn't want me holding the phone under my chin anymore, but my barber says a headset encourages oily buildup and miniaturisation of my follicles.'

'What?'

'So I'm trying to get away with speakerphone whenever I can.' The unmistakable noise of papers being rustled on a desk, amplified by the speakerphone, sounded like one of Roger's elementary school plays in which the children made thunderstorms by rattling newspapers.

'Are you busy with something?' said the Major. 'You can always call another time, when your paperwork is finished.'

'No, no, it's just a final deal book I have to read—make sure all the decimal points are in the right place this time,' said Roger. 'I can read and chat at the same time.'

'How efficient,' said the Major. 'Perhaps I should try a few chapters of *War and Peace* while we talk?'

'Look, Dad, I just called to tell you some exciting news. Sandy and I may have found a cottage on the Internet.'

'The Internet? I think you'd better be very careful, Roger. I hear there is nothing but con games and pornography on that thing.'

Roger laughed and the Major thought of telling him about the dreadful incident of Hugh Whetstone's single entanglement with the World Wide Web but realised that Roger would only laugh all the harder. Poor Hugh's book order had resulted in six unnoticed monthly credit card charges for membership to a furry friends website that turned out not to be one of his wife's animal charities after all, but a group with distinctly more esoteric interests. It was more discreet to let the story drop anyway; it had been passed around the village as a friendly warning, but there were a few people who now called their dogs to heel when passing Whetstone in the lane.

'Dad, it's a unique opportunity. This old woman has her aunt's cottage—rent with option to buy—and she doesn't want to use an estate agent. We could save all kinds of fees.'

'Good for you,' said the Major. 'But without an estate agent, can you be sure the price is fair?'

'That's the point,' said Roger. 'We have a chance to get it locked up now, before someone makes her see what it's really worth. It sounds perfect, Dad, and it's only a few minutes away, near Little Puddleton.'

'I really don't see why you need a cottage,' said the Major. He was familiar with Little Puddleton, a village whose large contingent of weekenders had spawned several arty pottery shops and a coffeehouse selling hand-roasted beans at exorbitant prices. While the village hosted some excellent chamber music at a gazebo on the green, its pub had moved toward selling *moules frites* and little plates of dinner on which all the food was piled on top of each other and perfectly round, as if it had been moulded inside a drainpipe. Little Puddleton was the kind of place where people bought fully grown specimens of newly hybridised antique roses in all the latest shades and then, at the end of the summer, wrenched them from their glazed Italian jardinières and tossed them on the compost heap like dead petunias. Alice Pierce, his neighbour, was quite public in her annual compost heap raids and had presented him last year with a couple of bushes, including a rare black tea rose that was now flourishing against his greenhouse.

'You must know that you and your friend would be perfectly welcome here at Rose Lodge,' he added.

'We talked about that,' said Roger. 'I told Sandy there was plenty of room and I was sure you'd even consider sectioning off the back part of the house to make a separate flat.'

'A separate flat?' said the Major.

'But Sandy said it might look like we're trying to shuffle you off into a granny annex and we probably should get a place of our own for now.'

'How considerate,' said the Major. Outrage reduced his voice to a squeak.

'Look, Dad, we'd really like you to come see it with us and give us your approval,' said Roger. 'Sandy has her eye on some cow barn near Salisbury, too. I'd much rather be near you.'

'Thank you,' said the Major. He was well aware that Roger probably wanted money more than advice; but then, Roger was just as likely to ask for money for the cow barn in Salisbury, so perhaps he really did want to be close to home. The Major's heart warmed at this flicker of filial affection.

'Sussex is such an easier drive, not to mention that if I put in a few years at your golf club now, I may have a shot at membership in a serious club later on.'

'I don't quite follow you,' said the Major. The flicker of filial love went out like a pilot light in a sudden draft.

'Well, if we go to Salisbury I'll have to be on waiting lists for golf there. Your club isn't considered too prestigious, but my boss's boss plays at Henley and he said right away he'd heard of you. He called you a bunch of stubborn old farts.'

'Is that supposed to be a compliment?' said the Major, trying to catch up.

'Look, Dad, can you come and help us meet Mrs Augerspier in Little Puddleton on Thursday?' said Roger. 'We'll just give it the once-over—nose around for dry rot and that sort of thing.'

'I have no expertise in these matters,' said the Major. 'I don't know what has potential.'

'The potential's not the issue,' said Roger. 'The issue is the widowed Mrs Augerspier. She wants to sell the cottage to the "right" people. I need you to come with us and be your most distinguished and charming self.'

'So you would like me to come and kiss the hand of the poor widow like some continental gigolo until she is confused into accepting your meagre offer for a property that probably represents her entire nest egg?' asked the Major.

'Exactly,' said Roger. 'Is Thursday at two good for you?'

'Three would be better,' said the Major. 'I believe I have an appointment in town at lunchtime that may run on a bit.' There was an awkward silence. 'I really can't change it,' he added. It was true. Much as he was not looking forward to escorting Grace to meet Mrs Ali's catering friend, he had agreed to her request and could not face her disappointment if he tried to weasel out now.

'I suppose I'll have to call and see if I can change our appointment,' said Roger. The tone in his voice said he doubted that his father had any appointments of particular importance but that he would be generous and humour the old man.

❧ ❧ ❧

Mrs Ali was in the living room waiting for him to bring in the tea. He stuck his head around the door and paused to notice what a lovely picture she made as she sat in the old bay window, bent over an old book of Sussex photographs. The sun, striking in through the wobbly glass, made the dust motes shimmer and edged her profile with a light gold brushstroke. She had arrived wrapped in a shawl of deep rose, which now lay draped about the shoulders of a wool crepe outfit in a blue as dark and soft as twilight.

'Milk or lemon?' he asked. She looked up and smiled.

'Lemon and a rather embarrassing amount of sugar,' she said. 'And when I visit friends with gardens, I sometimes beg them for a mint leaf.'

'A mint leaf?' he said. 'Spearmint? Pineapple mint? I also have some kind of invasive, purple cabbage-like oddity my wife swore was mint, but I've always been afraid to eat it.'

'It sounds very intriguing,' she said. 'May I take a look at this strange plant?'

'Of course,' said the Major, grappling with the sudden change in programme. He had been saving an invitation to see the garden in case of a sudden lapse in conversation later. If they toured the garden now, the tea might become stewed and undrinkable; and what would he do later, in the event of an interminable pause?

'Just a quick peek, so the tea doesn't spoil,' she added as if she had read his mind. 'But perhaps later I might impose on you for a more complete tour?'

'I would be delighted,' he said. 'If you'd like to step through the kitchen?'

By going through the kitchen and the narrow scullery, he reasoned, they could see the side garden, which contained the herbs and a small gooseberry patch, while leaving the full vista of the back gardens to be enjoyed later, from the dining room's French doors. Of course, there was really only a low hedge separating the two parts, but as Mrs Ali viewed the low mounds of mints, the variegated sage, and the last few tall spikes of borage, she was kind enough to pretend not to look over the hedge at the roses and lawn.

'This must be your alien mint,' she said, bending to rub between her fingers the ruched and puckered surface of a sturdy purplish plant. 'It does seem a bit overwhelming for your average cup of tea.'

'Yes, I've found it too pungent for anything,' said the Major.

'Oh, but I think it would be excellent for perfuming a hot bath,' said Mrs Ali. 'Very invigorating.'

'A bath?' said the Major. He fumbled to produce some further remark that might be suited to casual discussion of perfumed bathing. He understood suddenly how one could feel naked under clothes. 'Rather like being a human tea bag, isn't it?' he said. Mrs Ali laughed and tossed the leaf aside.

'You're quite right,' she said. 'And it's also an awful bother to pick all the soggy bits of leaves out of the drain afterward.' She bent down to pick two pale leaves of peppermint.

'Shall we go in and drink our tea while it's fresh?' he asked. He waved his left arm toward the house.

'Oh, did you hurt your hand?' she asked.

'Oh, no, it's nothing.' He tucked it quickly behind his back. He had hoped she wouldn't see the ugly pink sticking plaster mashed between his thumb and forefinger. 'Just gave myself a bit of a whack with the hammer, doing a little carpentry.'

           ᘓ ᑯ ᓚ

The Major poured them each a second cup of tea and wished there were some way to stop the late afternoon light from travelling any further across the living room. Any moment now and the golden bars would reach the bookcases on the far wall and reflect back at Mrs Ali the lateness of the hour. He feared she might be prompted to stop reading.

She had a low, clear reading voice and she read with obvious appreciation of the text. He had almost forgotten to enjoy listening. During the dusty years of teaching at St Mark's preparatory school, his ears had become numb, rubbed down to nonvibrating nubs by the monotone voices of uncomprehending boys. To them, 'Et tu Brute' carried the same emotional weight as a bus conductor's 'Tickets, please'. No matter that many possessed very fine, plummy accents; they strove with equal determination to garble the most precious of texts. Sometimes, he was forced to beg them to desist, and this they saw as victory over his stuffiness. He had chosen to retire the same year that the school allowed movies to be listed in the bibliographies of literary essays.

Mrs Ali had marked many pages with tiny slips of orange paper and, after some prompting from him, she had agreed to read from the fragments that interested her. He thought that Kipling had never sounded so good. She was now quoting from one of his favourite stories, 'Old Men at Pevensey', which was set soon after the

Norman Conquest and had always seemed to the Major to express something important about the foundations of the land.

"'I do not think for myself,'" she read, quoting the knight De Aquila, master of Pevensey Castle, "'nor for our King, nor for your lands. I think for England, for whom neither King nor Baron thinks. I am not Norman, Sir Richard, nor Saxon, Sir Hugh. English am I.'"

The Major gulped at his tea making an unfortunate slurp. It was embarrassing but served to quell the 'Here, here!' that had leaped unbidden to his lips. Mrs Ali looked up from her book and smiled.

'He writes characters of such idealism,' she said. 'To be as grizzled and worldly as this knight, and yet still so clear in one's passion and duty to the land. Is it even possible?'

'Is it possible to love one's country above personal considerations?' said the Major. He looked up at the ceiling, considering his answer. He noticed a faint but alarming brown stain that had not been there last week, in the corner between the window and the front hall. Patriotism was momentarily dangled in the scale against urgent plumbing concerns.

'I know most people today would regard such love of country as ridiculously romantic and naïve,' he said. 'Patriotism itself has been hijacked by scabby youths with jackboots and bad teeth whose sole aim is to raise their own standard of living. But I do believe that there are those few who continue to believe in the England that Kipling loved. Unfortunately, we are a dusty bunch of relics.'

'My father believed in such things,' she said at last. 'Just as Saxons and Normans became one English people, he never stopped believing that England would one day accept us too. He was only waiting to be asked to saddle up and ride the beacons with De Aquila as a real Englishman.'

'Good for him,' said the Major. 'Not that there's much call for actual beacon-watching these days. Not with nuclear bombs and such.' He sighed. It was a pity, really, to see the string of beacons that ran the length of England's southern shore reduced to pretty bonfires lit for the benefit of TV cameras on the Millennium and the Queen's Jubilee.

'I was speaking metaphorically,' she said.

'Of course you were, dear lady,' he said, 'But how much more satisfying to think of him literally riding to the top of Devil's Dyke, flaming torch at the ready. The jingling of the harnesses, the thudding of hoofbeats, the cries of his fellow Englishmen, and the smell of the burning torch carried next to the banner of St George . . .'

'I think he would have settled for not being so casually forgotten when the faculty agreed to meet for a drink at the local pub.'

'Ah,' said the Major. He would have liked to be able to make some soothing reply—something to the effect of how proud he would, himself, have been to partake of a glass of beer with her father. However, this was made impossible by the awkward fact that neither he, nor anyone else he knew, had ever thought to invite her husband for a drink in the pub. Of course that was entirely a social thing, he thought, not anything to do with colour. And then, Mr Ali had never come in himself, never tried to break the ice. He was probably a teetotaller, anyway. None of these thoughts was in the least usable; the Major was mentally a hooked carp, its mouth opening and closing on the useless oxygen.

'He would have liked this room, my father.' He saw Mrs Ali's gaze taking in the inglenook fireplace, the tall bookcases on two walls, the comfortable sofa and unmatched armchairs, each with small table and good reading lamp to hand. 'I am very honoured by your graciousness in inviting me into your home.'

'No, no,' said the Major, blushing for all the times it would never have crossed his mind to do so. 'The honour is mine, and it is my great loss that I did not have the chance to host you and your husband. My very great loss.'

'You are too kind,' she said. 'I would have liked Ahmed to see this house. It was always my dream that we would buy a small house one day—a real Sussex cottage, with a white boarded front and lots of windows looking out on a garden.'

'I suppose it is very convenient, though, living directly above the shop?'

'Well, I've never minded it being a little cramped,' she said. 'But with my nephew staying . . . And then, there is really very little room for bookshelves like these.' She smiled at him and he was very happy that she shared his appreciation.

'My son thinks I should get rid of most of them,' the Major said. 'He thinks I need a wall free for an entertainment centre and a large TV.'

Roger had, on more than one occasion, suggested that he pare down his collection of books, in order to modernise the room, and had offered to buy him a room-sized television so that he 'would have something to do in the evenings'.

'It is a fact of life, I suppose, that the younger generation must try to take over and run the lives of their elders,' said Mrs Ali. 'My life is not my own since my nephew came to stay. Hence the dream of a cottage of my own has reawakened in my mind.'

'Even in your own home, they track you down with the telephone at all hours,' said the Major. 'I think my son tries to organise my life because it's easier than his own—gives him a sense of being in control of something in a world that is not quite ready to put him in charge.'

'That's very perceptive of you,' said Mrs Ali, considering a moment. 'What do we do to counteract this behaviour?'

'I'm considering running away to a quiet cottage in a secret location,' said the Major, 'and sending him news of my well-being by postcards forwarded on via Australia.'

She laughed. 'Perhaps I may join you?'

'You would be most welcome,' said the Major, and for a moment he saw a low thatched hut tucked behind a gorse-backed hill and a thin crescent of sandy beach filled with wild gulls. Smoke from the chimney indicated a fragrant stewpot left on the wood-burning stove. He and she returning slowly from a long walk, to a lamp-lit room filled with books, a glass of wine at the kitchen table . . .

Conscious that he was dreaming again, he abruptly recalled his attention to the room. Roger always became impatient when he drifted off into thinking. He seemed to view it as a sign of early-onset dementia. The Major hoped Mrs Ali had not noticed. To his surprise, she was gazing out the window as if she, too, was lost in pleasant plans. He sat and enjoyed her profile for a moment; her straight nose, her strong chin, and, he noticed now, delicate ears under the thick hair. As if feeling the pressure of his gaze, she turned her eyes back to him.

'May I offer you the full garden tour?' he said.

The flower beds were struggling against the frowziness of autumn. Chrysanthemums held themselves erect in clumps of gold and red, but most of the roses were just hips and the mats of dianthus sprawled onto the path like blue hair. The yellowing foliage of the lilies and the cut-back stalks of cone flowers had never looked so sad.

'I'm afraid the garden is not at its finest,' he said, following Mrs Ali as she walked slowly down the gravel path.

'Oh, but it's quite lovely,' she said. 'That purple flower on the wall is like an enormous jewel.' She pointed to where a late clematis spread its last five or six flowers. The stems were as unpleasant as rusty wire and the leaves curled and crisped, but the flowers, as big as tea plates, shone like claret-coloured velvet against the old brick wall.

'It was my grandmother who collected all our clematis plants,' said the Major. 'I've never been able to find out the name of this one but it's quite rare. When it grew in the front garden it generated a lot of excitement among passing gardeners. My mother was very patient about people knocking on the door asking for cuttings.' An image flickered in his mind of the long green-handled scissors kept on the hallstand and a glimpse of his mother's hand reaching for them. He tried to conjure the rest of her but she slipped away.

'Anyway, times changed,' he said. 'We had to move it round the back in the late 1970s, when we caught someone prowling in the garden at midnight, secateurs in hand.'

'Plant burglary?'

'Yes, there was quite a rash of it,' he said. 'Part of a larger crisis in the culture, of course. My mother always blamed it on decimalisation.'

'Yes. It almost invites disaster, doesn't it, when people are asked to count by ten instead of twelve?' she said, smiling at him before turning to examine the rough-skinned fruit on one of the twisted apple trees at the foot of the lawn.

'You know, my wife used to laugh at me in just the same manner,' he said. 'She said if I maintained my aversion to change I risked being reincarnated as a granite post.'

'I'm so sorry—I didn't mean to offend you,' she said.

'Not at all. I am delighted that we have progressed already to a level of . . .' He searched for the right word, recoiling from 'intimacy' as if it were sticky with lust. 'A level above mere pleasant acquaintance, perhaps?'

They were at the lower fence now, and he was aware that one of the nails he had added was bent in half and shining with evidence of his incompetence. He hoped she would see only the view beyond, where the sheep field fell away down a small fold between two hills to a copse thick with oaks. Mrs Ali leaned her arms on the flimsy top rail and considered the trees, which were now blending to a soft indigo in the fading light. The rough grass on the western hill was already dark, while on the eastern flank it was losing the gold from its tips. The ground breathed mist and the sky showed night gathering intensity in the east.

'It is so beautiful here,' she said at last, cupping her chin in one hand.

'It's just a small view,' he said, 'but for some reason I never tire of coming out in the evening to watch the sun leaving the fields.'

'I don't believe the greatest views in the world are great because they are vast or exotic,' she said. 'I think their power comes from the knowledge that they do not change. You look at them and you know they have been the same for a thousand years.'

'And yet how suddenly they can become new again when you see them through someone else's eyes,' he said. 'The eyes of a new friend, for example.' She turned to look at him, her face in shadow; the moment hung between them.

'It's funny,' she said, 'to be suddenly presented with the possibility of making new friends. One begins to accept, at a certain age, that one has already made all the friends to which one is entitled. One becomes used to them as a static set—with some attrition, of course. People move far away, they become busy with their lives . . .'

'Sometimes they leave us for good,' added the Major, feeling his throat constrict. 'Dashed inconsiderate of them, I say.' She made a small gesture, reaching out as if to lay a hand on his sleeve, but circled her hand away. He pressed the tip of his shoe into the soil of the flower bed as if he had spotted a thistle.

After a few moments, she said: 'I should be going, at least temporarily.'

'As long as you promise to come back,' he said. They began to walk back to the house, Mrs Ali drawing her shawl closer around her shoulders as the light faded from the garden.

'When Ahmed died, I realised that we had become almost alone together,' she added. 'Being busy with the shop, happy with each other's company—we had stopped making much of an effort to keep up with friends.'

'I suppose one does fall into a bit of a rut,' agreed the Major. 'Of course, I always had Bertie. He was a great comfort to me.' As he said this, he realised it was true. Incongruous as it might seem, given how little time he and Bertie had spent together in recent decades, he had always felt they remained close, as they had been when they were two grubby-kneed boys pummelling each other behind the greenhouse. It also occurred to him that perhaps this only meant that the less he saw of people, the more kindly he felt toward them, and that this might explain his current mild exasperation with his many condolence-offering acquaintances.

'You are lucky to have many friends in the village,' said Mrs Ali. 'I envy you that.'

'I suppose you could put it that way,' said the Major, opening the tall gate that led directly into the front garden. He stood aside and let Mrs Ali pass.

'And now, just when I am being asked to consider how and where I will spend the next chapter of my life,' she continued, 'I have not only had the pleasure of discussing books with you, but I have also been asked by Miss DeVere to assist her and her friends with this dance at a golf club?' She made her statement a question, but he could not begin to think quite what it was or what answer she expected. He felt a strong inclination to warn her away from any such social entanglements.

'The ladies are tireless,' he said. It didn't sound much of a compliment. 'Many, many good works and all that sort of thing.' Mrs Ali's smile indicated that she understood him.

'I was told you suggested my name,' she said. 'And Grace DeVere has always been very polite. I suppose I am wondering whether this might be a small opening for me to participate in the community. A way to spread some more roots.' They were at the front gate already, and the garden and lane were almost dark. Down the hill, a single band of tangerine light hung low in a gap between the trees. The Major sensed that Mrs Ali was tethered to the village by only the slightest of connections. A little more pressure from her husband's family, another slight from an ungrateful villager, and she might be ripped away. Most people would not even take the time to notice. If they did, it would be only to enjoy complaining that her nephew's morose proprietorship was yet another sign of what the world was coming to. To persuade her to stay, just for the pleasure of having her nearby, seemed utterly selfish. He could not, in good conscience, promote any association with Daisy Green and her band of ladies. He could more easily recommend gang membership or fence-hopping into the polar bear enclosure at the Regents Park zoo. She looked at him and he knew she would give his opinion weight. He fiddled with the latch of the gate.

'I may have inadvertently pledged my cooperation, too,' said the Major at last. 'There is a food tasting I appear to have agreed to attend.' He was aware of a slight constriction in his voice. Mrs Ali looked amused. 'It is a great help to Grace that you have been willing to put your expertise at her disposal,' he continued. 'However, I must warn you that the committee's overabundance of enthusiasm, combined with a complete absence of knowledge, may produce some rather theatrical effects. I would hate for you to be offended in any way.'

'In that case, I shall tell Grace to count on us,' she said. 'Between the three of us, perhaps we can save the Mughal Empire from once again being destroyed.' The Major bit his tongue. As they shook hands and promised to meet again, he did not express his conviction that Daisy Green might represent a greater menace to the Mughal Empire than the conquering Rajput princes and the East India Company combined.

Chapter Nine

The Taj Mahal Palace occupied a former police station in the middle of a long stretch of Myrtle Street. The redbrick building still bore the word 'Police' carved into the stone lintel of the front door but it had been partially covered by a neon sign that flashed in succession the words 'Late Nite—Take Out—Drinks.' A blue martini glass adorned with a yellow umbrella promised a sophistication the Major found quite implausible. A large painted sign bore the restaurant name and offered Sunday buffet lunches, halal meat, and weddings. In order to back the car into a narrow space between a plumbing truck and a motor scooter, the Major put his arm across the back of the passenger seat, a manoeuvre that caused Grace to shrink and blush as if he had dropped a hand on her thigh. Mrs Ali smiled at him from the back, where she had chosen to sit after Grace's long and flustered monologue as to who should sit where and why it didn't matter to her if she sat in the back, only the Major should not sit alone up front like a taxi driver. The Major had tried to suggest they drive separately, since he had to meet Roger right after, but Grace had expressed an immediate need to visit Little Puddleton's famous yarn shop, the Ginger Nook, and had insisted on making an outing of it. The Major prayed he might now fit the car into the space in a single move.

A well-upholstered woman with a wide, smiling face and a flowing mustard-coloured shawl stood waiting for them in the glass doorway. Her feet in high-heeled shoes were so tiny that the Major wondered how she managed to balance, but as she tripped forward to meet them she carried herself with the lightness of a helium balloon. She waved a plump hand full of heavy rings and smiled.

'Ah and here is my friend Mrs Rasool to greet us,' said Mrs Ali. She waved back and prepared to get out of the car. 'She and her husband own two restaurants and a travel agency. They are quite the business tycoons.'

'Really?' Grace seemed overwhelmed by the woman now bobbing on tiptoes in front of her door. 'I suppose that requires a lot of energy.'

'Oh yes, Najwa is very enthusiastic.' Mrs Ali laughed. 'She is also the toughest businessperson I know—but don't let her know I told you. She always pretends that her husband is in complete charge.' Mrs Ali got out of the car and immediately disappeared into a vast mustard-coloured hug.

'Najwa, I'd like you to meet Major Pettigrew and Miss Grace DeVere,' said Mrs Ali, her arm still tucked in that of her friend.

'My husband, Mr Rasool, and I are delighted to have you grace our humble restaurant and catering hall,' said Mrs Rasool, greeting them with an enthusiastic grasping of both hands. 'We are quite the small operation—all hands-on and homemade, you know—but we do silver service for five hundred people here and everything piping hot and fresh. You must come in and see for yourself . . .' And she was already sweeping into the restaurant waving for them to follow. The Major held the door for the ladies and followed them in.

Several tables in the cavernous restaurant were occupied. Two women lunching by the window nodded at Mrs Ali, but only one of them smiled. The Major felt other patrons taking surreptitious looks. He concentrated on examining the tiled floor and tried not to feel out of place.

The tiles bore scars of the former police station. The outline of a booking desk ran across the middle of the room like a blueprint and in the back several large booths were built into cubicles that might once have been cells or interrogation rooms. Raising his gaze, he noted the walls were a cheerful orange—no doubt the paint cans had been labelled 'Mango' or 'Persimmon'—and bright saffron silk curtains swagged the large iron-framed windows, which still had bars on the lower portions. To the Major's eye, the effect of the grand room was marred only by the effusive use of obviously plastic flowers in jarring chemical shades. They swooped in swags of pink and mauve roses across the ceiling and crammed cement floor urns. Orange water lilies floated in the central tiled fountain, collecting by the overflow valve like dead koi.

'How cheerful it is in here,' said Grace, craning her neck to view the giant iron chandeliers with their collars of ivy and stiff lilies. Her genuine delight in all the colour seemed incongruous, thought the Major, in a woman who preferred mushroom-brown tweeds. Today's dull burgundy and black blouse and dark green stockings would have rendered her invisible in any mildly wet woodland.

'Yes, I'm afraid my husband is very adamant about being generous with the floral displays,' said Mrs Rasool. 'Please come this way and let me introduce you.'

She led the way back to a large booth, partially screened by a carved wood panel and another huge silk curtain. As they approached, a thin man with sparse hair and a shirt starched as stiff as a shell stood up from where he was sitting with an elderly couple. He gave them a reserved bow.

'Mr Rasool, these are our guests, Major Pettigrew and Ms DeVere,' said Mrs Rasool.

'Most welcome,' said Mr Rasool. 'And may I introduce to you my parents and the founders of our business, Mr and Mrs Rasool.' The old couple stood up and bowed.

'Pleased to meet you,' said the Major, leaning with difficulty across the wide table to shake hands. The Rasools bobbed their heads and mumbled a greeting. The Major thought they resembled two halves of a walnut, charming in their wrinkled symmetry.

'Please sit down with us,' said Mr Rasool.

'Do we need to tire your mother and father with a long meeting?' said Mrs Rasool to her husband. Her clipped tone and raised eyebrow gave the Major the impression that the old people had not been invited.

'My parents are honoured to assist with such important clients,' said Mr Rasool, addressing himself to the Major and refusing to meet his wife's eyes. He slid onto the banquette next to his mother and waved them to the other side of the booth. 'Do join us.'

'Now, I hope Mrs Ali has explained that we are on a strict budget?' said Grace, inching along the banquette as if it were made of Velcro. The Major tried to allow Mrs Ali to slide in, both to be polite and because he hated to be confined, but Mrs Rasool indicated that he should sit next to Grace. She and Mrs Ali took the outside chairs.

'Oh, please, please,' said Mr Rasool. 'No need to talk of business. First we must hope you enjoy our humble offerings. My wife has ordered a few small samples of food for you, and my mother has ordered a few more.' He clapped his hands together and two waiters came through the kitchen doors bearing silver trays covered with domed silver lids. They were followed by a pair of musicians, one with a hand drum and one with some kind of sitar, who sat down on low stools near the booth and began a spirited atonal song.

'We have musicians for you,' said Mrs Rasool. 'And I think you will be very happy with the decorations we have sourced.' She seemed resigned now to the presence of her in-laws. The Major felt sure that negotiations between the generations were a feature of all family businesses, but he thought that Mrs Rasool's obvious competence must add an extra measure of irritation. The old woman wagged her finger and spoke rapidly at Mrs Rasool.

'My mother insists that first our guests must eat,' said Mr Rasool. 'It is an offence to talk business without offering hospitality.' The mother frowned at the Major and Grace as if they had already committed some breach of decorum.

'Well, perhaps just a little taste,' said Grace, pulling from her bag a small notebook and a thin silver pen. 'I really don't eat much at lunchtime.'

The dishes came quickly, small bowls of steaming food, blurry with colour and fragrant with spices that were familiar and yet could not be readily named. Grace nibbled her way through them all, pursing her lips in determination at some of the more dark and pungent offerings. The Major watched with amusement as she wrote them all down, her writing becoming more laboured as the food and several servings of punch made her sleepy.

'How do you spell "gosht"?' she asked for the third time. 'And this one is what meat?'

'Goat,' said Mr Rasool. 'It is the most traditional of ingredients.'

'Goat gosht?' Grace manoeuvred her jaw around the words with difficulty. She blinked several times, as if she had just been told she was eating horse.

'But the chicken is very popular, too,' said Mrs Rasool. 'May we pour you another glass of lunch punch?'

The Major had detected the merest scent of juniper in the first glass of punch, which Mrs Rasool had presented to them as a lightly alcoholic lunchtime refresher. It came in an elaborately scrolled glass pitcher garnished with cucumber slices, pineapple chunks, and pomegranate seeds. But a crook of her finger when she ordered the second round must have been a signal to lubricate the proceedings with a healthy dumping of gin. The cucumbers were positively translucent with shock and the Major himself felt a desire to fall asleep, bathed in the fragrance of the food and the iridescent light of the silk curtains. The Rasools and Mrs Ali drank only water.

'My parents' tradition is to serve this dish family style or buffet,' said Mr Rasool. 'A large clay platter with all the trimmings in little silver bowls around it—sunflower seeds, persimmon slices, and tamarind chutney.'

'I wonder if it might be a little spicy for the main course,' said Grace, cupping her hand around her mouth as if making a small megaphone. 'What do you think, Major?'

'Anyone who doesn't find this delicious is a fool,' said the Major. He nodded his head fiercely at Mrs Rasool and Mrs Ali. 'However . . .' He was not sure how to express his firm conviction that the golf club crowd would throw a fit if served a rice-based main course instead of a hearty slab of congealing meat. Mrs Rasool raised an eyebrow at him.

'However, it is perhaps not foolproof, so to speak?' she asked. The Major could only smile in vague apology.

'I understand perfectly,' said Mrs Rasool. She waved her hand and a waiter hurried into the kitchen. The band stopped abruptly as if the wave included them. They followed the waiters out of the room.

'It's certainly a very interesting flavour,' said Grace. 'We don't want to be difficult.'

'Of course not,' said Mrs Rasool. 'I'm sure you will approve of our more popular alternative.' The waiter returned at a run, with a silver salver that held a perfectly shaped individual Yorkshire pudding containing a fragrant slice of pinkish beef. It sat on a pool of burgundy gravy and was accompanied by a dollop of cumin-scented yellow potatoes and a lettuce leaf holding slices of tomato, red onion, and star fruit. A wisp of steam rose from the beef as they contemplated it in astonished silence.

'It's quite perfect,' breathed Grace. 'Are the potatoes spicy?' The elder Mr Rasool muttered something to his son. Mrs Rasool gave a sharp laugh that was almost a hiss.

'Not at all. I will give you pictures to take back with you,' she said. 'I think we have agreed on the chicken skewers, samosas, and chicken wings as passed hors d'oeuvres, and then the beef, and I suggest trifle for dessert.'

'Trifle?' said the Major. He had been hoping for some samples of dessert.

'One of the more agreeable traditions that you left us,' said Mrs Rasool. 'We spice ours with tamarind jam.'

'Roast beef and trifle,' said Grace in a daze of food and punch. 'And all authentically Mughal, you say?'

'Of course,' said Mrs Rasool. 'Everyone will be very happy to dine like the Emperor Shah Jehan and no one will find it too spicy.'

The Major could detect no hint of derision in Mrs Rasool's tone. She seemed completely happy to accommodate. Mr Rasool also nodded and made a few calculations in his black book. Only the old couple looked rather stern.

'Now, what about the music?' asked Mrs Rasool. 'Do you need to hear more from the sitar or would you prefer to arrange a dance band?'

'Oh, no more sitar, please,' said Grace. The Major breathed a sigh of relief as Mrs Rasool and Grace began to discuss the difficulty of finding a quiet band that knew all the standards and yet could impart an exotic air to the evening.

The Major felt he was not obliged to participate in the discussion. Instead, he took the opportunity of the relative quiet to lean across to talk to Mrs Ali.

'When I was a small boy in Lahore, we always had rasmalai for our special dessert,' he whispered. It was the only local dish he remembered his mother allowing in the cool white villa. Mostly they had jam puddings and meat pies and thick gravy like the rest of their friends. 'Our cook always used rose petals and saffron in the syrup and there was a goat in the service yard to get the milk for cheese.' He saw a brief image of the goat, a grumpy animal with a crooked back leg and pieces of dung always caught in its stringy tail. He seemed to remember that there was also a boy, around his own age, who lived in the yard and took care of the goat. The Major decided not to share this recollection with Mrs Ali. 'Whenever I order it now, it never seems to taste quite as I remember.'

'Ah, the foods of childhood,' said Mrs Ali, breaking into a smile. 'I believe the impossibility of recreating such dishes may be due more to an unfortunate stubbornness of memory than any inherent failure of preparation, but still we pursue them.' She turned to Mrs Rasool and touched her sleeve. 'Najwa, could the Major try some of your mother-in-law's famous homemade rasmalai?' she asked.

Over the Major's protestations that he could not eat another thing, the waiters brought bowls of cheese curds floating in bright pink syrup.

'My mother-in-law makes this herself,' said Mrs Rasool. 'She likes to keep a small presence in the kitchen.'

'You must be very talented,' said Grace to the old woman, speaking loud and slow as if to a deaf person. 'I always wish I had the time to cook.' The old woman glared at her.

'It is mostly a matter of watching cheese drip dry,' said Mrs Rasool. 'But it allows her to keep an eye on everything else in the kitchen, doesn't it, Mummy?'

'My parents are a big help to us,' added Mr Rasool, patting his wife on the arm in a tentative way.

The Major took a spoonful of dessert and felt the pleasure of the smooth cheese and the light syrup: a thrill of recognition in the lightness, the taste more scent than flavour.

'This is almost it,' he said quietly to Mrs Ali. 'Very close.'

'Lovely,' said Grace puckering her lips around the tiniest spoonful of cheese. 'But I do think the trifle is a better idea.' She pushed away her dish and drank from her glass of punch. 'Now, what can you suggest about decorations?'

'I was looking into it, as Mrs Ali asked,' said Mrs Rasool, 'and I was afraid it would all be very expensive.'

'But then we struck on a lucky coincidence,' added Mr Rasool. 'A distinguished friend offered to help.'

'Oh, really?' said Grace. 'Because our budget, as you know . . .'

'I know, I know,' said Mr Rasool. 'So let me introduce you to my friend Mrs Khan. She is the wife of Dr Khan, a specialist at Hill Hospital. One of our most prominent families. She has her own decorating business.' He waved his hand and the Major looked to see the two ladies from the window table getting up. The older one waved back and spoke to her companion, who hurried out of the restaurant.

'Saadia Khan?' asked Mrs Ali quietly. 'Are you sure that's a good idea, Najwa?' Najwa Rasool gave a pained smile.

'My husband insists that she is very keen to help.'

'Oh, yes, Mrs Khan implied she might even help out on a complimentary basis,' said Mr Rasool. 'I believe her husband has many friends among the membership of your respected club.'

'Really?' said Grace. 'I haven't heard the name. Dr Khan, is it?'

'Yes, very prominent man. His wife is involved in many charitable efforts. She is very concerned with the welfare of our young women.'

Mrs Khan loomed impressively over the table. She wore a tweed suit with a heavy gold brooch on the lapel and a single ring on each hand, one a plain gold band and the other an enormous sapphire in a heavy gold setting. She carried a large, stiff handbag and a tightly rolled umbrella. The Major thought her face seemed rather smooth for her age; her hair, in lacquered layers, reminded him of Britain's former lady Prime Minister. He tried to stand up and caught his thigh painfully on the edge of the table as he struggled out of the banquette to stand by Mrs Ali's chair. He blinked several times. The Rasools also stood and introductions were made.

'How do you do, Major? Do call me Sadie, everyone does,' said Mrs Khan with a big smile that did not wrinkle any other part of her face. 'And Miss DeVere, I believe we met at that awful Chamber of Commerce garden party last year?'

'Yes, yes of course,' said Grace in a voice that telegraphed her complete lack of such a recollection. Mrs Khan leaned completely across Mrs Ali to shake Grace's hand.

'Such a crush of people, but my husband and I feel we must support such basic institutions,' added Mrs Khan. She stepped back and seemed to see Mrs Ali for the first time.

'Why, Jasmina, you are here, too?' she asked. The Major recognised the use of Mrs Ali's first name as a deliberate slight but he was very grateful to finally hear it. It sounded enchanting even from such a raw and ill-intentioned source.

'Saadia,' said Mrs Ali, inclining her head again.

'Why, what a treat it must be for you to be liberated from the shop counter,' added Mrs Khan. 'A small break from the frozen peas and newspapers?'

'I think you have some fabric samples to show us?' said Mrs Rasool.

'Yes,' said Mrs Khan. 'My assistant Noreen and her niece are bringing them now.' They watched Mrs Khan's lunch companion and a younger woman struggle through the heavy restaurant door with several armfuls of sample books and a small box of fabrics. A small boy followed, carrying a large book precariously in both arms. The Major recognised him immediately as the young boy from the Promenade. He felt a schoolboy flush of panic rise into his face at the possibility that he and Mrs Ali would be exposed. Of course, there had been only public tea drinking, not some kind of debauchery. Still, as the small group came slowly across the expanse of the restaurant, running the gauntlet of curious faces, he felt miserable that he was to be discovered in his private friendship. The Major could not move. He could only clutch the back of Mrs Ali's chair and guess the feelings in the glossy head beside him.

'Oh, my goodness, the niece has brought her boy,' said Mrs Khan in a loud whisper to Mrs Rasool. 'I'll get rid of him right away—what was she thinking?'

'Don't be silly,' said Mrs Rasool. She laid a hand on Mrs Khan's sleeve. 'It will be perfectly all right.'

'I'm trying to help, if only for Noreen's sake,' said Mrs Khan. 'But the young woman is very difficult.' She gave the Major and Grace an uncomfortable glance.

'What a darling little boy,' exclaimed Grace as the women dropped their heavy load onto a nearby table and the boy struggled to do the same. 'What's his name?' There was the briefest of pauses, as if introductions had not been expected. The woman named Noreen looked quite frightened. She patted her thin grey hair with a nervous hand and darted her eyes at Mrs Khan, whose lips were pressed to a thin line.

'I couldn't just leave him in the car,' said the young woman, also looking at Saadia Khan, but with a face as fierce as her aunt's was meek.

'I believe his name is George,' said Mrs Ali, dispelling the tension. She got up and went over to shake the small boy by the hand again. 'We had the pleasure of meeting in the park. Did you manage to get your ball all the way home?'

The young woman frowned and swung George up onto her hip. 'He managed that day, but he lost it down a drain on the way to the shops the next day.' She said nothing to the Major, giving him only a brief nod. Today she wore a long, shapeless black dress over leggings; the tone was spoiled only by violently crimson sneakers that laced up over the ankle. Her hair was partially hidden under a stretchy bandana. She had made an obvious effort to dress more conservatively, but it seemed to the Major that she had just as deliberately measured out a stubborn resistance. She looked as out of place at the restaurant as she had done on the Promenade, when she had screamed at the tea lady.

'Jasmina, I believe Amina and George are from your home turf up north,' said Mrs Khan with a silky smile. 'Perhaps your families are acquainted?'

The Major couldn't tell whether Mrs Ali was amused or angry. She compressed her lips as if suppressing a chuckle, but her eyes flashed.

'I don't think so, Saadia,' she replied. The Major detected a deliberate avoidance of the name Sadie. 'It's a big place.'

'Actually, I think you might have a nephew my age who used to live there,' Amina put in. Her aunt Noreen trembled like a leaf in a sudden squall and fiddled with the books of fabrics. 'Maybe I went to school with him?'

'Well, perhaps, but he left a while ago,' said Mrs Ali. There was a hint of caution in her voice that the Major had not heard before. 'He has been in Pakistan studying for some time.'

'And now I hear he is living with you,' said Mrs Khan. 'How fortunate to be given the chance to move to Sussex. My charity does a lot of work in these northern cities, and there are many, many problems.' She patted Amina on the arm as if Amina constituted most of them. The young woman opened her mouth and looked from one to the other as if torn between saying something more to Mrs Ali and delivering a stinging retort to Sadie Khan. Before she could speak, her aunt gave a savage tug to her arm and she clamped her mouth shut again and turned away to help unfold a length of heavy fabric. The Major watched them tussle over it in silent argument.

'Shall we talk about decorations?' said Mrs Rasool, clearly uncomfortable with the conversation. 'Why don't you show us the table runner fabrics first, Mrs Khan?'

Mrs Khan, Mrs Rasool, and Grace were soon arguing over the relative merits of the iridescent sorbet sheers and the heavy damasks resplendent with rioting paisleys. Amina and her aunt Noreen unfolded fabrics and turned sample book pages in silence, the former with pressed lips. The Major regained his seat and the waiters brought glasses of hot tea. Ignoring the elderly Rasools, the Major watched Mrs Ali invite George to climb up on her lap.

She handed him the teaspoon dipped in honey and he gave it a cautious lick. 'George likes honey,' he said with a perfectly serious face. 'Is it organic?' Mrs Ali laughed.

'Well, George, I've never seen anyone injecting bees with antibiotics,' said the Major, who was generally in favour of medicating sick livestock and saw nothing wrong in a healthy application of properly aged manure. George frowned at him, and for a moment the Major was reminded of Mrs Ali's dour nephew.

'Organic is better, my mum says.' He ran the spoon down the entire length of his tongue. 'My nanni puts honey in her tea, but she died,' he added.

Mrs Ali bent her head to the top of his and gave his hair a brief kiss. 'That must make you and your mother sad,' she said.

'It makes us lonely,' said George. 'We're lonely in the world now.'

'You mean "alone"?' asked the Major, aware that he was being pedantic. He resisted the urge to ask about a father. These days it was better not to; and somehow, it seemed unlikely that there was one.

'Can I have more honey?' asked George, closing the subject with a child's honest abruptness.

'Of course you can,' said Mrs Ali.

'I like you,' said George.

'Young man, you have very good taste,' said the Major.

Grace came back to the booth beaming and informed the Major of the good news that Mrs Khan would lend them wall hangings and draperies and charge them at cost for lengths of fabric used as table runners, which were almost certain to get stained.

'It is such an old and important institution in the area,' said Mrs Khan. 'And my husband has so many friends who are members. We are glad to help in any way.'

'I'm sure it will be appreciated,' said the Major. He raised his eyebrows at Grace who gave him a blank smile in return. 'Perhaps Grace, you'd like to get a final approval from your committee chairwoman?'

'What? Oh, yes, of course I should,' said Grace. 'Though I'm sure they'll be thrilled with everything.'

'My husband and I would be pleased to come and meet with your colleagues if necessary,' said Mrs Khan. 'Since we know so many of them already, we would be delighted to help make them comfortable with the Rasools' wonderful catering. I can tell you I've used Mrs Rasool on many occasions for my own functions.' The Major caught sight of Mrs Rasool rolling her eyes at Mrs Ali. Mrs Ali smothered a giggle and put down George, who ran back to his mother.

'That sounds lovely,' said Grace in a vague manner. As the Major shook hands with Mrs Khan, he couldn't help feeling sorry for her. Regardless of her husband's prominence, or their generosity, he thought it quite unlikely that Daisy or the membership committee would have any interest in entertaining the question of their joining the club. He could only hope they would have the decency to refuse the Khans' generous offer and keep things properly separated with cash instead. He made a note to have a quiet word with Grace later on.

Chapter Ten

On the way to Little Puddleton, Grace elected to sit in the back of the car, where she sprawled at a strange angle and, after a few moments of heavy traffic out of the town, declared herself to be feeling just the tiniest bit green.

'Would you like me to stop the car?' asked the Major, though he could only manage a half-hearted attempt at sincerity. It was getting close to three and he did not want to disappoint Roger by being late. He accelerated as the road became clear and ran the heavy car effortlessly up over the crest of the hill.

'No, no, I'll just rest my eyes,' said Grace in a faint whisper. 'I'll be fine.'

'I have some eau de cologne wipes in my bag,' said Mrs Ali. She rummaged in her tote and handed back to Grace a small jewelled bag. The light scent of flowers in alcohol invaded the car.

'These are wonderful,' said Grace. 'I'll feel right as rain in just a jiffy, and then I can't wait to show you the new alpaca yarns, Mrs Ali. It'll be the highlight of our afternoon.'

'I am to be converted to the joys of knitting,' said Mrs Ali, smiling at the Major.

'My condolences,' he said.

As they made the long slow swoop downhill into Little Puddleton, the Major tried to keep up a good speed and ignore the stifled groans from the backseat. He was sure Grace would feel much better once he dropped them both off at the craft shop. Just the sight of all that coloured yarn would no doubt cheer her up.

The village green was as obsessively manicured as the Major remembered. Wooden posts with a fresh coat of whitewash held up a knee-high chain all around the edges of the cropped grass. Bronze signs warned people to keep off except for concert afternoons. Gravel paths curved this way and that like some strange Venn diagram. The gazebo at one end looked across the elliptical duck pond, on which floated three bleached-looking swans. There were always just three and it fascinated the Major to try to work out which was the odd one out and why it stuck around. The cottages and houses of the village huddled together companionably. An army of topiaries in terracotta pots guarded pastel front doors. Window boxes foamed with painterly foliage. Windows twinkled with custom double glazing.

The shops occupied a small street running away from the green. The Major pulled the car up in front of the Ginger Nook. Its brimming windows offered a cornucopia of cushion covers waiting to be cross-stitched; dolls' houses awaiting paint and furniture, and baskets of wool skeins in a rainbow of colours.

'Here we are,' said the Major in what he hoped was a jolly, rallying tone. 'Shall we say I'll come back for you in one hour?' There was only a groan from the backseat. In the mirror, he caught a glimpse of a grey face in which Grace's pink lipstick stood out like new bricks.

'Or I can try to be quicker,' he said. 'My son just wants me to have a look at a cottage with him. Seems to think I could help make a good impression.'

'Grace, I think you'll feel much better in the fresh air,' added Mrs Ali, who had turned around in her seat and was staring with concern. 'I'll come around and help you out.'

'No, no,' whispered Grace. 'I can't get out here, not in front of everybody.' To the Major, the road appeared largely deserted. The Ginger Nook itself seemed to have only a couple of ladies browsing.

'What should we do?' he asked Mrs Ali. The clock on the church steeple was pointing to three and he was beginning to panic. 'I am already expected at Apple Cottage.'

'Why don't we go there?' said Mrs Ali. 'You can go in, and I'll walk with Grace in the lane. Would that be all right, Grace?' There was another indistinct groan from the backseat.

'Wouldn't you be happier sitting on the Green?' asked the Major, horrified. 'There are some lovely benches by the pond.'

'She might get cold,' said Mrs Ali. 'It would be better if we stay near the car, I think.' She looked at him rather sternly. 'If our presence in the vicinity won't spoil your good impression, of course?'

'Not at all,' said the Major, who could already imagine Roger's raised eyebrows. Perhaps, he hoped, he could park a little away from the cottage and walk there.

᠃ ᠂ ᠉

Apple Cottage was at the end of a small lane, which ended in a five-bar gate and a field. The Major was already upon the place before he had time to stop and park. Sandy's Jaguar was parked by the field, leaving room for another car directly in front of the cottage's front gate. The Major had no choice but to pull up there. He could see Roger's brown head over the hedge next to Sandy's shiny blonde hair. The top of a brown felt hat indicated the presence of a third person: the widow Augerspier, he assumed. His son was looking up at the cottage roof and nodding as if he had some expertise in the evaluation of rotting thatch.

'Here we are,' said the Major. 'I don't expect to be too long. I'll leave the car unlocked for you.'

'Yes, please go ahead,' said Mrs Ali. 'Grace will feel much better after a walk, I'm sure.' As the Major got out of the car, Grace was still groaning. He hurried through the gate of the cottage and hoped her groans wouldn't carry too far on the still afternoon air.

Mrs Augerspier was from Bournemouth. She had a long face set in a slight frown, and lips that seemed thinned by sourness. She wore a stiff suit of black wool. Her hat boasted black feathers sweeping in serried rows across her sunken forehead.

'Ah, my father was a colonel in the military,' she said when introduced. She did not specify which military. 'But he made his money in hats,' she added. 'After the war, there was much demand for European hats. My husband took over the business when my father died.'

'From military to millinery,' said the Major. Roger glared at him as if he had flung an insult and then turned a wide smile toward the dead crow on the widow's brow.

'They certainly don't make hats the way they used to,' he said. He held the smile as if waiting for a photo to be taken. His teeth seemed larger and whiter than the Major remembered, but perhaps it was just an illusion caused by the artificial stretch of the lips.

'You are so right, young man,' said the widow. 'When I was married I had a hat covered entirely in swan's feathers. But of course, you can't get the wings now. It's a great pity.' The Major thought of amputee swans paddling on the Little Puddleton pond.

'Is that a real vintage hat?' asked Sandy. 'I just have to send a picture to my editor friend at *Vogue* magazine.'

'Yes, yes, I suppose it is now,' said the widow, tipping her head at a coquettish angle while Sandy snapped pictures with her diminutive mobile phone. 'My father made it for my mother's funeral. She looked so beautiful. And after, he gave it to me to remember her by. Last month I wore it to my aunt's funeral.' She took out a small, lace-edged handkerchief and wiped her nose.

'We're very sorry for your loss,' said Roger.

'She could never wear a hat properly,' said the widow. 'She was not a lady in the same way as my mother. My mother would never use the telephone, you know. And she would chase away a tradesman with a broom if he came to the front door instead of the service door.'

'Isn't hat-making a trade?' asked Sandy. 'Did she make her husband come in the back door too?'

'Of course not,' said the widow. The feathers quivered and Roger looked slightly sick. 'Why, my father made hats for the nobility.'

'May we see the inside of the cottage now?' asked Roger, trying to glare at Sandy without the widow seeing. 'I'm sure Sandy would love to talk hats with you for hours, Mrs Augerspier, but we would like to see it in the afternoon light.'

As far as the Major could determine, the cottage was a damp and unsuitable mess. The plaster bubbled suspiciously in several corners. The beams looked wormy and the floors downstairs seemed to be made of uneven garden pavers. An inglenook fireplace had more soot on the outside of the oak Bessemer than in the flue. The windows were original, but the panes were buckled and twisted as if the handmade glass might pop from the heavy leading with the slightest rattle of wind.

'It might be possible that I will sell some of the furnishings to the new tenants,' said Mrs Augerspier, smoothing a lace doily over the back of a tattered armchair. 'If I get the right sort of people, of course.' The Major wondered why Roger nodded with such enthusiasm. The dead aunt's possessions ran to cheap pine furniture, seaside knickknacks, and a collection of plates featuring scenes from famous movies. There did not seem to be a single item that would suit Roger and Sandy's taste, yet his son examined everything.

In the large empty kitchen, a boxy extension from the 1950s with cheap beams added to a textured plaster ceiling, the Major peered around an open door into a mousy larder and counted eleven boxes of dried chicken soup on the otherwise empty shelves. It seemed very sad that life should have gradually thinned out until so little remained. He shut the door quietly on the evidence.

'Oh, I wouldn't change a thing,' Sandy was saying loudly to Mrs Augerspier. 'Only maybe I could fit a regular US-sized refrigerator into that back corner.'

'My aunt always found the refrigerator perfectly adequate,' said Mrs Augerspier pulling aside the check curtains under the counter to show a small green fridge with a fringe of rust. 'But then young people today will insist on all that convenience food.'

'Oh, we're going to shop all the local farm shops,' said Roger. 'There's nothing quite like fresh vegetables, is there?'

'Horribly overpriced, of course,' said the widow. 'Designed to rob the weekenders from London. I refuse to shop in them.'

'Oh,' said Roger. He flung a hopeless glance at the Major, who could only stifle a laugh.

'This is a very good table,' continued Mrs Augerspier, knocking on the plastic. It was still covered with a checked oilcloth. 'I would be willing to sell the table.'

'I think we're going to commission a handmade oak table and a couple of traditional English settles,' said Sandy, turning the dull sink taps and examining the trickle of brown water that was produced. 'An art director friend of mine knows this great craftsman.'

'I would like to think of the table remaining here,' said the widow, as if she had not heard. 'I think it fits here.'

'Absolutely,' said Roger. 'We could have an oak table in the dining room instead, couldn't we, Sandy?'

'I will show you the dining room,' said the widow. 'But it already has a very nice modern dining set.' She unlatched a door and waved them to follow her. Roger followed; as the Major stepped back to allow Sandy to pass, they heard the widow saying, 'I would be willing to consider selling the dining set.'

'Do you think the aunt died in her bed here?' whispered Sandy, grinning, as she went by. 'And do you think she'll let us buy the mattress?' The Major could not suppress a laugh.

As they prepared to mount the crooked stairs to the upper floor, Roger shot him a look like a Jack Russell terrier with urgent business. The Major recognised an appeal and was pleased to find he could still read his son's facial communications.

'My dear Mrs Augerspier,' said the Major, 'I was wondering whether you might consent to show me the garden. I'm sure these young people can manage to look around upstairs by themselves.' The widow looked suspicious.

'That would be so great,' said Sandy, warmly. 'We'd love the chance to talk things over as we go.'

'I don't usually let people go unaccompanied,' Mrs Augerspier said. 'You can't be certain of anyone these days.'

'If I might vouch for the complete integrity of these particular young people,' said the Major. 'It would be so kind of you to indulge me with your companionship.' He extended an arm and resisted the urge to stroke his moustache. He was afraid his deliberately charming smile might look more like a leer.

'I suppose it would be acceptable,' said the widow, taking his arm. 'One gets so few opportunities for refined conversation these days.'

'After you,' said the Major.

⸙

Coming from the musty cottage, the air smelled like pure oxygen. The Major took a grateful breath and was rewarded with the scent of box and hawthorn underlaid with a hint of damp oak leaves. Mrs Augerspier turned right along the mossy flagstones and led the way to the main stretch of garden, which rose gently to one side of the cottage. Under a small arbour at the far end, Mrs Ali sat with Grace who, the Major noticed with alarm, was slumped with closed eyes against the lichen-covered teak seat. Mrs Ali seemed to be taking her pulse.

'People are so rude to keep coming without an appointment,' said Mrs Augerspier, hurrying over the grass. 'And always they are not suitable,' she added.

'Oh, they're not here about the house,' said the Major, but the widow wasn't listening.

'The house is not available,' she called flapping her hands as if to shoo away recalcitrant chickens. 'I must ask you to go now.' Grace opened her eyes and shrank back against the seat. Mrs Ali patted her hand and stood up, stepping forward as if to shield her from the angry bobbing figure rushing across the grass.

'It's all right, Mrs Augerspier,' said the Major, catching up at last. 'They're with me.' Grace threw him a grateful look, but Mrs Ali continued to look at the widow.

'My friend Grace needed to sit down,' she said. 'We didn't think anyone would mind.' Grace hiccupped loudly and sank her face in her handkerchief.

'Well,' said the widow. 'Only I get the strangest people wandering in from the road. One couple walked right into the kitchen and then said they thought the house was empty.'

'Now that we have established our credentials, perhaps a glass of water?' asked Mrs Ali.

'Certainly,' said Mrs Augerspier. 'Wait here and I will bring it to you.' She hurried back toward the house, leaving an awkward silence.

'Dreadful woman,' said the Major at last. 'I'm so sorry. I should have driven you both straight home.'

'Oh, no, please, I'm feeling very much better,' whispered Grace. 'I think I just had a bit of a reaction to some of the spices.'

'I'm afraid we're not contributing to the good impression your son was anxious to make,' said Mrs Ali.

'Oh, not at all, not at all,' said the Major. 'Don't even think about it. Roger will be delighted to see you both.' He swung his cane absently and had taken the heads off three late dahlias before he realised it. He looked up to see Roger jogging up the lawn with a glass of water slopping over his hand. His son wore a look of concern that closely resembled a scowl.

'Mrs Augerspier said one of your friends needed a glass of water,' said Roger. In a quieter voice he added, 'You invited people along?'

'You remember Miss DeVere, Roger,' said the Major, passing the glass of water to Grace. 'And this is Mrs Ali from the village shop.'

'How do you do,' said Mrs Ali. 'We are so sorry to intrude.'

'Not at all,' said Roger in an indifferent tone. 'Only I do need to borrow my father for a few minutes.'

'I remember when you were just a little boy, Roger . . .' said Grace, wiping her eyes. 'Such a lovely little boy with all that unruly hair.'

'Is she drunk?' whispered Roger to the Major. 'Did you bring a drunken woman here?'

'Certainly not,' said the Major. 'Just a little touch of something from our rather large Indian luncheon.'

'Do you remember that time you boys stayed out smoking cheroots in the woods?' asked Grace. 'Your poor mother was convinced that you were trapped in an abandoned refrigerator in some ravine.'

'Sorry, got to run, ladies,' said Roger already turning away. As the Major found himself being hustled along back to the house, he heard Grace's voice ramble on.

'Stole them from the Vicar's coat during services and made themselves sick as dogs . . .'

'Roger, you were very rude,' he said.

'Rude?' said Roger. 'How could you bring them here? Mrs Augerspier is all nervous now. She keeps peering out the window.'

'What on earth for?' said the Major.

'I don't know. But we've gone from being the right sort of people to being a strange bunch with a circus of hangers-on. For God's sake, one's Pakistani and one's tipsy—what were you thinking?'

'You're being ridiculous,' said the Major. 'I won't have my friends subjected to such rudeness.'

'You promised to help me,' said Roger. 'I suppose I'm not as important as your friends? And since when did you count shopkeepers as friends? Are you best friends with the milkman now?'

'As you know perfectly well, there hasn't been a milkman in Edgecombe St Mary for twenty years,' said the Major.

'Hardly the point, Dad, hardly the point,' said Roger. He opened the cottage door and stood aside as if waiting to shepherd in a troublesome child. The Major fumed as he was marched in.

Sandy was sitting on the rickety sofa with a fixed smile on her face. Mrs Augerspier was once again peering from the window.

'It's just that I've been so nervous since that couple last week,' she said, holding her hand to her heart. Sandy nodded in apparent sympathy.

'Mrs Augerspier was just explaining to me about a very rude couple who came to see the cottage last week.'

'I only told them that since they were used to a warmer climate, I thought they would find the cottage much too damp. They were quite unreasonable about it.'

'Where were they from?' asked Roger.

'I think you said from Birmingham, Mrs A?' asked Sandy, her eyes stretched to wide innocence.

'But they were from the islands originally; the West Indies,' said Mrs Augerspier. 'Such rudeness—and from doctors, too. I told them I'd report them to the medical board.'

'So naturally Mrs Augerspier is feeling a little intimidated around strangers,' said Sandy. 'But only until she knows them.'

'A lady is comfortable around all persons once properly introduced,' opined Mrs Augerspier. 'I am proud to say that I have not a bone of bias in me.'

The Major looked at Roger whose mouth was open, making slight movements but no sound. Sandy looked unperturbed. She even seemed to be enjoying herself.

'Mrs Augerspier, you are an unvarnished original,' said Sandy. 'I can't wait to hear your opinions on—oh, on everything.'

'I must say, for an American you are very civil,' said Mrs Augerspier. 'Are your family originally from Europe?'

'Roger, are you finished looking around?' asked the Major. He hoped his tone was abrupt enough to register his disapproval of the widow without creating a direct confrontation. Mrs Augerspier gave him a vague smile which indicated that while he had avoided any rudeness, he had failed miserably to deliver a snub.

'We really shouldn't take up too much of your time,' said Roger. He walked over to pat Sandy on the shoulder. 'Are you done, darling?' The Major flinched at the casually delivered endearment, the verbal equivalent of tossing a stranger the keys to the family house.

'I could move in right now,' said Sandy. 'What's it going to be, Mrs A? Are we suitable, do you think?'

Mrs Augerspier smiled, but her eyes narrowed in an unpleasant fashion. 'It is important that I find just the right people . . .' she began.

Sandy turned to look at Roger and patted his hand like a mother to a small boy who has forgotten his manners.

'Oh, yes, I forgot,' said Roger. He dug in his coat pocket and flourished a brown envelope. 'My fiancée and I took the liberty of bringing a cashier's check for six months' rent just in case you could let us have it right away.' He opened the envelope and handed a check to Mrs Augerspier, who appeared fascinated.

'Roger, are you sure you're not being too spontaneous?' asked the Major, his mind struggling to process the word 'fiancée'. He focused instead on watching the widow examine both back and front of the check. Her eyes wobbled in delight. She pursed her lips and gave him a frown.

'Well, I believe I could agree to six months—on a strictly trial basis,' she said. 'But I won't have time to effect any repairs, you know. It will take all my strength just to pack up my dear aunt's personal effects.'

'We'll be happy with it just as it is,' said Sandy.

The widow put the check in her jacket pocket, being careful to push it all the way down. 'It will take me a few days to sort out which of the personal effects I might be able to part with.'

'Take all the time you need,' said Roger, shaking her hand. 'Now, what say we all go and have a cup of tea somewhere to seal the deal?'

'That sounds very lovely,' said Mrs Augerspier. 'I believe there's a local hotel that offers a wonderful afternoon tea—now where did I put my rental form?' The Major personally thought chewing stinging nettles and washing them down with a pint of ditch water might be more pleasant than watching the widow bob her feathers over a mountain of whipped cream.

'Major, you look as if you have some pressing engagement,' said Sandy, winking at him. Roger looked up and gave the Major a pleading glance.

'I rather think I must get the ladies home,' said the Major. 'Grace is quite unwell.'

The door opened and Mrs Ali put her head around it.

'I'm so sorry to interrupt you,' she said. 'I wanted to let you know that Grace is feeling much better.' The Major experienced a sense of panic. It was all he could do to keep from shaking his head at Mrs Ali. He must have made some small involuntary spasm because she smoothly changed her emphasis.

'However, I do think it would be preferable to get her home as soon as possible, Major.' She held out the empty water glass, which the widow hurried over to take from her.

'We're just finished, just finished,' said Mrs Augerspier. She hovered by the doorway as Sandy and Roger signed the form and took the carbon copy. 'Of course you must get your friend home. We would not dream of dragging you to tea with us.'

ٹ ؟ ڡ

Out in the lane, waiting for the widow to lock up, Roger's enthusiasm reduced him to babble. 'Isn't it great? I mean, isn't it the greatest cottage? I can't believe we got it—'

'Honey, it's a dump,' said Sandy, 'but it's our dump and I can make something of it.'

'She preferred this other place,' said Roger. 'But I told her I just knew this would be the one.'

'Will you come back to the house afterward?' asked the Major. 'Perhaps we could discuss your engagement?' He hoped Roger caught the acid note in his voice, but Roger just grinned at him.

'Sorry, Dad, we've got to get back,' he said. 'But we'll come over one weekend really soon.'

'Splendid,' said the Major.

'Yeah, there are one or two things—like my old desk and the oak trunk in the attic—I thought would go great in the cottage.'

'I get veto power on all items of furniture,' said Sandy. 'I'm not getting stuck with ugly furniture just because you carved your schoolboy fantasies into it.'

'Of course,' said Roger. 'Over here, Mrs A.' The widow came down the path wrapped in a voluminous tweed coat topped with what looked like a very antique dead fox.

'Nice to meet you ladies,' called Sandy, waving at Mrs Ali and Grace, who were already in the Major's car. With Mrs Augerspier ceremoniously installed in the confines of the front seat and Sandy tucked in the back, Roger revved the engine until the birds flew from the hedge.

The Major was glad that the ladies were quiet on the drive home. He felt tired and his jaw ached. He realised it was clamped shut.

'Is something the matter, Major?' asked Mrs Ali. 'You seem upset.'

'Oh, no, I'm fine. Long day, though.'

'Your son rented the cottage, did he not?' she said. 'He seemed so full of cheer.'

'Oh, yes, yes, all signed and sealed,' said the Major. 'He's very happy about it.'

'How lovely for you,' she said.

'It was all just a bit hasty,' said the Major, taking a fast right turn in front of a tractor to dive the car into the single-track shortcut back to Edgecombe St Mary. 'Apparently they're engaged.' He looked back at Grace, hoping she would not start groaning again. The sound made it so difficult to drive. 'Feeling better?'

'Much better, thank you,' said Grace, whose face still looked grey and sunken. 'I offer you my congratulations, Major.'

'I just hope they know what they're getting into,' said the Major. 'All this renting cottages together. It seems so premature.'

'It seems to be the way they all go on today, even in the best families,' said Grace. 'You mustn't let anyone make you feel bad about it.' He was immediately annoyed, both by the suggestion and by the way her handkerchief fluttered like a trapped dove in his rearview mirror as she fanned herself.

'They should be able to buy the place eventually,' said the Major. 'Roger tells me it will be rather a smart investment.'

'When true love combines with clear financial motive,' said Mrs Ali, 'all objections must be swept away.'

'Is that a saying in your culture?' asked Grace. 'It seems very apt.'

'No, I'm just teasing the Major,' said Mrs Ali. 'I think the circumstances may prove to be less important than the fact that life has made a turn and brought your son and a future daughter-in-law closer, Major. It is an opportunity to be seized, is it not, Miss DeVere?'

'Oh, certainly,' said Grace. 'I wish I had children to come and live near me.' Her voice held a hint of a pain unconnected with digestive problems.

'I have tried to see my nephew's presence in such a light,' said Mrs Ali. 'Though the young do not always make it easy.'

'I will follow your advice and try to seize on my son's new proximity,' said the Major as he sped up to escape the outer limits of Little Puddleton. 'And I live in hope that he will want more from the relationship than a good deal of my old furniture.'

'You must bring your son and his fiancée to the dance, Major,' said Grace. 'Introduce them to everyone. Everyone is always so relaxed and approachable when they're in costume, don't you think?'

'Yes, but they often don't remember you the next day, I find,' said the Major. Mrs Ali laughed.

'I suppose I'll wear my Victorian tea dress again,' said Grace. 'Maybe I can borrow a pith helmet or something.'

'If you would be interested, I would be more than happy to lend you a sari or a tunic set and shawl,' said Mrs Ali. 'I have several very formal pieces, packed away in the attic somewhere, that I never use.'

'Do you really?' said Grace. 'Why, that would surprise the ladies at the club, wouldn't it—little me in full maharani splendour.'

'I think you would carry a sari very well with your height,' added Mrs Ali. 'I will look out a few things and drop them off for you to try.'

'You are very kind,' said Grace. 'You must come and have tea with me and that way you can tell me what you think—I may look like a complete fool.'

'That would be lovely,' said Mrs Ali. 'I'm usually free on Tuesday or Sunday afternoons.' The Major felt his jaw compress again as the vision of another Sunday discussing Kipling faded. He told himself to be happy that Mrs Ali was making other friends in the village, but in his heart, he cried out at the thought of her crossing someone else's threshold.

Chapter Eleven

If there was one trait the Major despised in men, it was inconstancy. The habit of changing one's mind on a whim, or at the faintest breath of opposition; the taking up and putting down of hobbies, with the attendant bags of unused golf clubs in the garage and rusting weed trimmers leaning against sheds; the manoeuvrings of politicians in ways that sent uneven ripples of bother through the country. Such flailing about was anathema to the Major's sense of order. Yet in the days following his excursion with Mrs Ali and Grace, he found himself tempted to switch directions himself. Not only had he allowed himself to be drawn into a ridiculous situation with regard to the dance, but perhaps he was behaving like a fool with regard to Mrs Ali as well. He had thought of their friendship as being set apart from the rest of the village, and yet now here she was, plunging into the ordinary activities of the other village ladies. Of course, one tea did not signal a complete assimilation by the female social machine; but it made him depressed anyway.

As Sunday afternoon dragged its weary hours, he sat alone with Kipling's masterpiece, *Kim*, unopened on his knee and tried not to imagine her laughing over her teacup as Grace twirled and paraded in a froth of sequined and embroidered costumes. On

Tuesday, when he ran out of milk, he avoided the shop and drove instead to the filling station for petrol and bought his milk from the refrigerator next to a display of oil cans. When Alec called about golf on Thursday, he tried to beg off by complaining of a mild backache.

'If you sit about, it'll only knot up worse,' said Alec. 'A leisurely round is just the thing to get the kinks out. How about just nine holes and lunch?'

'Truth is, I'm not feeling very sociable,' said the Major. Alec gave a loud snort of laughter.

'If you're worried about running into the ladies' dance committee, I shouldn't worry. Daisy has whisked Alma off to London to look at costumes. I told Alma if she gets me anything more than a pith helmet I'm calling in the solicitors.'

The Major allowed himself to be persuaded. To hell with women, anyway, he thought as he went to find his golf bag. How much better it was to focus on the manly friendships that were the foundation of a quiet life.

༄ ༅ ༆

Preparations for 'An Evening at the Mughal Court' were in full vulgar display as the Major arrived early for his game. In the annex beyond the Grill, where tea and coffee urns were usually set out for morning golfers, there was no urn in sight. Instead, all the tables had been pushed aside to create rehearsal space in front of the stage. The girls of the luncheon staff, their scowls deepened with concentration, were engaged in flinging scarves about with their arms and stamping their feet as if to crush earwigs. They wore anklets of tiny bells whose seamless jarring wash of sound gave away the fact that not a single dancer was moving in time with any other. Amina, the young woman from the Taj Mahal restaurant, seemed to be teaching the group. George was ensconced on top of a steep pile of chairs, drawing with a fat coloured pencil in a thick sketchbook.

'Five, six, seven . . . hold the eight for two beats . . . stamp, stamp!' called Amina, leading with graceful steps from the front while the women lumbered behind her. The Major thought she might be better off turning around to watch them, but then perhaps it was too painful to look at the sweating faces and assorted large feet for an extended period. As he scanned the entire room in vain for a tea urn, trying to remain invisible, a cry went up from a large girl in the back row.

'I'm not doing this if people keep coming in looking at us. They told us it would be private.'

'Yeah, we're in bare feet here,' said another girl. The entire troupe glared as if the Major had invaded the ladies' locker room. George looked up from his book and waved. His stack of chairs wobbled.

'Sorry, just looking for some tea,' said the Major. The girls continued to glare. Having been relieved of their other duties in order to do whatever it was they were actually doing, they had no intention of helping a club member.

'Girls, we only have a couple of weeks to do this,' said Amina, clapping her hands together. 'Let's take a five-minute tea break and then we'll talk about feeling the rhythm.' The Major had not expected to hear such a tone of authority coming from someone so scruffy and odd. Even more surprising was how the girls shuffled obediently through the swing doors to the kitchen with scarcely a mutter. The Major tried not to think of so many sweaty footprints on the kitchen floor.

'Major Pettigrew, right?' said Amina. 'You were at the Taj Mahal with Miss DeVere and that Mrs Ali?'

'Nice to see you and George again,' said the Major, waving at the boy and not answering the particulars of her question. 'May I ask what you are attempting to do with our lovely ladies of the luncheon service?'

'I'm trying to teach them some basic folk dance routines to perform at the big dance,' said Amina with a sour laugh. 'Sadie Khan told Miss DeVere that I dance, and they asked me to help.'

'Oh, dear, I'm truly sorry,' said the Major. 'I can't believe she roped you in to something so impossible.'

'If it was easy, I wouldn't have done it,' said Amina, an ugly frown flickering across her face. 'I don't take charity.'

'No, of course not,' he said.

'Oh, who am I kidding? I really needed the money,' said Amina. 'They're not so bad if you don't ask them to do more than three different steps. So we'll be shaking a lot of hips, and I'm thinking of bringing bigger scarves.'

'Yes, the more veils the better, I think,' said the Major. 'The naked feet will be quite alarming enough.'

'So, how well do you know Mrs Ali?' she asked abruptly.

'Mrs Ali runs a very nice shop,' said the Major, responding to the direct question with automatic evasiveness. 'So many of our village shops are being lost today.' There was a brief pause. 'May I assume you are a dancer by profession?' he added by way of turning the conversation.

'Dance, yoga, aerobics. Dance doesn't pay very well, so I teach whatever,' she said. 'Do you think she's nice, then, Mrs Ali?'

'You are obviously very good at what you do,' said the Major. The lunch girls were filing back into the room and he felt multiple ears listening to the conversation.

'I was hoping you could tell me more about her,' said Amina. 'I was thinking of going over to see her. I heard she wants some part-time help in the shop.'

'You did?' said the Major who couldn't quite see her in a shop apron, stacking tins of spaghetti rings and being polite to old ladies. On the other hand, she could hardly be worse than the grumpy nephew. 'I can tell you Mrs Ali's a lovely woman. Very nice shop,' he said again.

'Of course, it's not what I want to do long term—shop work.' She seemed to be talking to herself, the Major thought. 'And it'd have to be school hours or I'd have to bring George with me.'

'I hope you get the job,' said the Major. He looked away toward the door and raised an eyebrow to acknowledge an imaginary passing acquaintance—an invisible Alec to help him escape the room. 'I must be getting along to find my partner.'

'D'you think you could give us a lift after your game?' said the young woman. The Major knew he should answer, but he found he had no idea how to parry such a bold request from a stranger. He simply stared at her. 'Only it's two different buses from here to Edgecombe,' she added. 'We'll probably have to hitchhike.'

'Oh, I couldn't let you do that,' said the Major. 'Not safe at all, hitchhiking, especially with the boy.'

'Thank you, then,' she said. 'I'll wait and go with you.'

'I may be some time,' he began.

'Oh, I've got plenty of work here,' she said as the slack-postured lunch girls filed back from the kitchen. 'They've offered us lunch and then we can just wait for you in the lobby.' Several faces perked up as she said this and the Major had the horrible sensation of being caught making an assignation. He fled as fast as possible, determined to retrieve his golf bag and wait discreetly somewhere outside until Alec arrived.

↻ ⟩ ↺

'Ah, there you are,' said Alec. 'Is there a reason you're loitering in a hedge, and do you realise that ancient bag of yours rather gives the whole thing away?'

'I am not loitering,' said the Major. 'I am simply indulging in a few moments of pastoral solitude—together with my very distinguished bag, which you covet and of which you therefore feel compelled to make fun.' They both looked at the bag, a well-oiled leather bag that had belonged to the Major's father and that bore a small embossed leather patch from the Lahore Gymkhana Club. It reclined on a vintage wooden-wheeled carrier with a bamboo handle and was a source of some pride to the Major.

'I thought maybe you were trying to avoid the secretary. I hear he's looking for you.'

'Why would he be looking for me?' said the Major as they set off toward the first tee.

'Probably wants to sort out about your son,' Alec said. 'I hear there was some mix-up when he came in the other day?'

'My son?' asked the Major with surprise.

'Didn't you know he was here?' asked Alec, his eyebrows stretching like two rabbits getting up from a nap.

'Well, yes, no, of course—I mean we talked about his taking out a membership,' said the Major.

'He stopped by on Sunday. I happened to be here. I think the secretary was just a little surprised. You hadn't mentioned it to him and then . . .' Alec paused, fiddling with the heads of his clubs as he chose his driver. The Major detected a small discomfort in his face. 'Well, look, Pettigrew, he's your son, so perhaps you should have a word with him.'

'What do you mean?' asked the Major. He felt a sensation in his stomach as if he were descending in a slow lift. 'Was this last Sunday?' Roger had called to apologise for not visiting, but they had been tied up all day getting the widow Augerspier moved out of the cottage. They were too exhausted, he had said, to do anything but drive straight back to London.

'Yes, Sunday afternoon. The fact is, he seemed to think he could just sign something and be done,' said Alec. 'Rather got the secretary's back up, I'd say.'

'Oh, dear,' said the Major, sighting away down the fairway with his club. 'I suppose I forgot to mention anything. I'll have to smooth things over.'

'I think it got smoothed over,' said Alec. 'Lord Dagenham's niece, Gertrude, came in and it was all kissy-kissy and so on. Secretary seemed quite mollified.'

'That was very nice of her,' said the Major. 'I mean, I hardly know the woman. I suppose my help with the dance is appreciated after all.'

'At the same time, you might want to mention to Roger that we don't allow those newfangled club heads.'

'He brought clubs with him?' asked the Major, unable to hide the dismay in his voice.

'Oh, I'm sure he wasn't expecting to be able to play,' said Alec diplomatically. 'Probably thought of running his kit by the pro, only since it was Sunday the pro shop was closed.'

'I'm sure that's so,' said the Major, miserably wondering if there was a limit to Roger's self-absorption. 'I'll have a chat with him.' He savaged his ball with a clout that sent it arcing high and into the rough on the right of the fairway.

'Oh, rotten luck,' said Alec and the Major wondered if he meant unlucky in golf or unlucky with offspring. Both, the Major felt, were accurate today.

~ ~ ~

Amina and George were not in the Grill when the Major finished his round. He made a halfhearted effort to look around the tables and thought he might be able to avoid all obligation with a quick dash through the lobby.

Her voice reached him through the lobby doors and caused several members to raise their heads from their chocolate sponge puddings.

'No chinless flunky in a bow tie tells my son to wait by the servants' entrance.'

'It's not "servants", it's "service" entrance,' corrected the diminutive club secretary, a piggy-eyed man who wore his green club blazer like holy vestments and was now hopping from foot to foot in unseemly anger. 'The main entrance is for members and their guests only, not workers.'

'No one tells my son he's a servant, or a "worker" neither!' Amina was holding George behind her and now dropped her heavy gym bag on the floor right at the secretary's feet. He leaped back in shock. 'We were asked to help out and no one is going to treat us like dirt.'

'Young woman, you are an employee,' stuttered the secretary. 'You will not speak to me with such insolence, or you will be terminated with cause.'

'Bloody terminate me, then, you old git,' said Amina. 'Better do it fast. From the colour of your face, you're going to drop dead any second.' The secretary's face had indeed flushed an unusual purple, which extended up to the scalp under his thin sandy hair. It clashed with his tie. The Major was frozen to the spot with horror at the argument. Roger's gaffe was enough to earn him a stern lecture from the secretary, and now his name was linked with this young woman's rudeness. He had not suffered such a confrontation in thirty years.

'I demand that you leave the premises immediately,' said the secretary to Amina. Puffed up to his maximum chest capacity, the Major thought he looked like a plump squirrel.

'Suits me fine,' said Amina. She picked up her bag and swung it onto her shoulder. 'Come on, George, we're out of here.' She held George's hand and stalked out of the front door.

'But that door's for members . . .' came the secretary's feeble cry.

The Major, who had been frozen to the spot, now became aware that to the diners behind him, he might seem to be cowering behind the Grill door. He feigned peering at his watch and then patted his pockets as if he might be looking for some forgotten item and turned on his heel to go back through the Grill and out onto the terrace. His only hope was to bundle the girl and her son into his car and leave without anyone seeing.

Amina was waiting for him in the car park, leaning on a concrete post with her arms wrapped across her chest. He noticed that she was not wearing a warm enough coat and her hair had begun to wilt in the chill drizzle. George was squatting at her feet, trying to protect his book from the rain. There was no avoiding her, so the Major waved as if nothing had happened. Amina hoisted the huge gym bag onto her thin shoulder and joined him at his car.

'I thought you had gone,' he said as he unlocked the car. 'I looked all over for you.'

'Got kicked out,' she said, tossing her heavy, clinking bag in the boot on top of his clubs. 'Some flunky in a bow tie suggested we wait by the servants' entrance.'

'Oh dear, I'm sure he wasn't trying to be offensive,' said the Major, who was sure of no such thing. 'I'm so sorry you felt . . .' He searched for the right word; 'excluded' and 'unwelcome' were too accurate to provide the comfortable vagueness he sought. '. . . bad.'

'Don't worry about it. I don't have space in my head to put up with harmless old gits trying to make me feel bad,' said Amina, folding her arms. 'I've learned to tell the difference between the people who can really hurt you and those who just want to look down their noses.'

'If they're harmless, why confront them?' asked the Major, thinking again of the seething tea lady on the seafront.

'Because they're bullies, and I'm teaching George not to put up with bullies—right, George?' she said.

'Bullies have no brains,' repeated George from the backseat. The scribble of pencil against paper indicated that he was still drawing.

'They expect you to slink away or tip your cap or something,' said Amina. 'When you spit back at them, they get all flustered. Bet you've never tried it, have you?'

'No, I suppose I was raised to believe in politeness above all,' said the Major.

'You ought to try it sometime,' she said. 'It can be really funny.' There was a weary tone to her voice that made the Major doubt she found it as amusing as she claimed. They drove in silence for a while and then she shifted in her seat to look at him. 'You're not going to ask me about George, are you?' she asked in a low voice.

'None of my business, young lady.' He tried to keep any judgment out of his tone.

'Women always ask,' she said. 'My aunt Noreen is having migraine attacks from all the scandalised ladies dropping by to ask her about me.'

'Nasty things, migraines,' said the Major.

'Men never ask, but you can see they've made up a whole story about me and George in their heads.' She turned away and placed her fingers where the rain ran sideways along the glass of her window. The Major's first impulse was to claim he had never given it a thought, but she was very observant. He wondered what truthful comment he could make.

'I'm not going to answer for men, or women, in general,' he said after a moment. 'But in my own case, I believe there is a great deal too much mutual confession going on today, as if sharing one's problems somehow makes them go away. All it really does, of course, is increase the number of people who have to worry about a particular issue.' He paused while he negotiated a particularly tricky, right-hand turn across the busy road and into the shortcut of a narrow back lane. 'Personally, I have never sought to burden other people with my life history and I have no intention of meddling in theirs,' he added.

'But you're making judgments about people all the time—and if you don't know the whole story . . .'

'My dear young woman, we are complete strangers, are we not?' he said. 'Of course we will make shallow and quite possibly erroneous judgments about each other. I'm sure, for example, that you already have me pegged as an old git too, do you not?' She said nothing and he thought he detected a guilty smirk.

'But we have no right to demand more of each other, do we?' he continued. 'I mean, I'm sure your life is very complicated, but I'm equally sure that I have no incentive to give it any thought and you have no right to demand it of me.'

'I think everyone has the right to be shown respect,' she said.

'Ah well, there you go.' He shook his head. 'Young people are always demanding respect instead of trying to earn it. In my day, respect was something to strive for. Something to be given, not taken.'

'You know, you should be an old git,' she said with a faint smile, 'but for some reason I like you.'

'Thank you,' he said, surprised. He was equally surprised to find that he felt pleased. There was something about this prickly young person that he also liked. He was not about to tell her so, however, in case she took it as an invitation to tell him more about her life. It was with a feeling of relief that he pulled up the car in front of Mrs Ali's shop and let his passengers out.

'Do they have comics?' asked George.

'I've got no money, so just be a good boy and maybe when we get home I'll make you a cake,' said Amina.

'Good luck,' the Major called though the window as Amina paused in front of the shop, holding George by the hand. The face she turned to him was quite grey and frightened. He felt a dawning of suspicion that she was not going to the shop for a mere job interview. Whatever she was up to, she seemed more frightened of Mrs Ali than she had been of the club secretary.

‹ ? ›

He had returned home and had put the tea in the pot but not yet poured a cup, when his uneasiness about dropping the strange young woman and her son on Mrs Ali's doorstep was compounded by the horrible sensation that it was the third Thursday of the month. He went to the calendar to check and his fears were realised. On the third Thursday in every month, the bus company shifted all the afternoon buses to some mysterious other duties. Even the Parish Council had been unable to get a clear answer as to where they went. The company would only say it was a 'rationalisation' of service to allow 'increased presence in underserved markets'. Since buses came to Edgecombe only every two hours on a normal day, the Major and others had voiced the opinion that the village was itself underserved, but the matter had not been resolved. While his neighbour Alice had suggested protests on the steps of the county hall, he and most of the other village leaders had been content to retreat to the comfort of their cars. Alec had even gone out and bought a four-wheel drive, claiming that he would regard it as a vital community resource now that buses could not be counted upon in an emergency.

The Major was sure that Amina had told George the truth when she said she had no money. He was certain she could not afford a taxi. With great reluctance, tinged with curiosity, he put the cosy on the pot and fetched his coat. He would have to at least offer to drive the pair back to town.

۱ ۱ ۶

Through the distortion of the plate glass window he could see Mrs Ali leaning against the counter as if she were slightly faint. Her nephew stood rigid, which was hardly unusual, but he was staring past the Major's shoulder at some distant point outside the window. Amina looked down at her bright crimson boots, her shoulders sunk into an old woman's hunch that telegraphed defeat. This was no job interview. The Major was just thinking about sneaking away again when he was accosted by a loud voice.

'Major, yoo-hoo!' He turned around and was greeted with the sight of Daisy, Alma, Grace, and Lord Dagenham's niece, Gertrude, crammed into Daisy's Mercedes with so many overstuffed and billowing bags and packages that they looked like four china figurines packed in a gift box. 'So happy to have spotted you, you're just the man we wanted to see,' added Daisy, as the four ladies did their best to emerge from the car without spilling their purchases into the street. It was not the most dignified scene. The Major held the car door for Alma and tried not to look at her plump knees as he bent to rescue a large yellow satin turban that had almost tumbled into a puddle.

'I see Alec is all taken care of,' he said.

'I'm so glad we spotted you,' repeated Daisy. 'We couldn't wait to tell you all about the exciting new plan we came up with,'

'It involves you!' said Alma, as if the Major should feel pleased.

'Major, we have been debating whether our folk dancing was enough to set the theme of our evening,' said Daisy. 'Then this morning, while we were breakfasting at Lord Dagenham's, we came up with a delightful proposition.'

'It was a lovely breakfast, Gertrude,' said Alma to the niece. 'Such a delightful start to the day.'

'Thank you,' said Gertrude. 'I'm more used to grabbing a bacon sandwich in the stables than entertaining other ladies. I'm so sorry about the kippers.'

'Nonsense,' said Alma. 'Quite my own fault for gobbling them up so fast.'

'I was standing by to attempt the Heimlich, but I'm more experienced with horse choke.'

'Ladies, ladies,' said Daisy. 'If we could stay on point?' She paused for effect. 'We've settled on a series of scenes—very tasteful—and we were discussing how to make them relevant.'

'Oh, you tell him, Grace—it was partly your idea,' added Alma.

'Oh, no, no,' said Grace. She stood a little apart, shifting slightly from foot to foot. The Major found this nervous fretting irritating in an otherwise sensible woman. 'We were just talking about local connections to India and I happened to mention your father. I didn't mean to suggest anything.'

'My father?' asked the Major.

'If I might explain,' said Daisy, quelling Grace with a lifted eyebrow. 'We were reminded of the story of your father and his brave service to the Maharajah. We've decided to do it in three or four scenes. It'll be the perfect core of our entertainment.'

'No, no, no,' the Major said. He felt quite faint at the idea. 'My father was in India in the thirties and early forties.'

'Yes?' said Daisy.

'The Mughal Empire died out around 1750,' said the Major, his exasperation overcoming his politeness. 'So you see it doesn't go at all.'

'Well, it's all the same thing,' said Daisy. 'It's all India, isn't it?'

'But it's not the same at all,' said the Major. 'The Mughals—that's Shah Jehan and the Taj Mahal. My father served at Partition. That's the end of the English in India.'

'So much the better,' said Daisy. 'We'll just change "Mughal" to "Maharajah" and celebrate how we gave India and Pakistan their independence. Dawn of a new era and all that. I think it's the only sensitive option.'

'That would solve the costume problem for a lot of people,' said Alma. 'I was trying to tell Hugh Whetstone that pith helmets weren't fully developed until the nineteenth century, but he didn't want to hear it. If we add an element of "Last Days", they can wear their "Charles Dickens" summer dresses if they prefer.'

'Though "Last Days" is what got us in trouble last year,' ventured Grace.

'We needn't be so specific,' snapped Alma.

'Partition was 1947,' said the Major. 'People wore uniforms and short frocks.'

'We're not trying to be rigidly historical, Major,' said Daisy. 'Now I understand you do have possession of your father's guns? And what about some kind of dress uniform? I understand he was at least a colonel, wasn't he?'

'We'll need to find someone younger than you, Major, to play him, of course,' said Alma. 'And we'll need some men to play the murderous mob.'

'Maybe Roger, your son, would do it?' said Gertrude. 'That would be very appropriate.'

'To be a murderous mob?' asked the Major.

'No, to be the Colonel, of course,' said Gertrude.

'I'm sure the lunch girls have a few murderous-looking boyfriends between them to be our mob,' said Daisy.

'My father was a very private man,' said the Major. He almost stammered under the sense that all around him were losing their reason. That the ladies could imagine that he or Roger would consent to appear in any sort of theatrical was beyond comprehension.

'My father thinks it's a wonderful story,' added Gertrude. 'He wants to present you with some kind of silver plate at the end of the evening's speeches. Recognition of the Pettigrews' proud history, and so on. He'll be so disappointed if I have to tell him you declined his honour.' She looked at him with wide eyes and he noticed she held her mobile phone ready as if to call on a moment's notice. The Major fumbled for words.

'Perhaps we should give the Major some time to absorb the idea,' said Grace, speaking up. Her feet ceased to move and became planted as she defended him. 'It's rather a big honour, after all.'

'Quite right, quite right,' said Daisy. 'We'll say no more right now, Major.' She looked at the windows of the shop and waved at Mrs Ali inside. 'Let's go in and secure Mrs Ali's help for the dance, shall we, ladies?'

'Why, that's Amina, the girl who's teaching our waitresses to dance,' said Gertrude also looking in the window. 'I wonder what on earth she's doing here in Edgecombe.'

'Oh, it's a small community,' said Alma with the sweeping certainty reserved for the ignorant. 'They're all related in some way or another.'

'Perhaps now is not the best time,' said the Major, anxious to spare Mrs Ali an assault by the ladies. 'I believe they have business together.'

'It's the perfect opportunity to speak to both of them,' said Daisy. 'Everybody in, in, in!' The Major was obliged to hold the door open and found himself herded inside the shop along with the ladies. It was a tight squeeze around the counter area, and the Major found himself standing so close to Mrs Ali that it was difficult to raise his hat.

'I'm sorry,' he whispered. 'I could not dissuade them from coming in.'

'Those that will come, will come,' she said in a tired voice. 'It is not in our power to prevent them.' She looked at Amina, to whom Daisy was talking.

'What luck that you are here as well,' said Daisy. 'How is the dancing coming along?'

'Considering they all have two left feet and no sense of rhythm, it was going quite well,' said Amina. 'But I don't think your club manager will be letting me back in anytime soon.'

165

'You mean the secretary?' said Gertrude. 'Yes, he was quite apoplectic on the phone.' She stopped to chuckle. 'But don't you worry about the little man. I told him he must have more patience, considering your unfortunate circumstances and our pressing need for your talent.'

'My circumstances?' said Amina.

'You know, single mother and all that,' said Gertrude. 'Afraid I laid it on a bit thick but we do hope you'll carry on. I think we can approve a little more money, given the bigger scope of the project.'

'You're dancing for money?' asked Mrs Ali's nephew.

'I'm only teaching a few routines,' she said. 'You mustn't think of it as dancing.' He said no more, but his scowl deepened, and the Major marvelled anew at the way so many people were willing to spend time and energy on the adverse judgment of others.

'Oh, she's teaching all our girls how to shake those hips,' said Alma. 'Such a wonderful display of your culture.' She smiled at Mrs Ali and her nephew. The nephew turned an ugly copper colour and rage flickered under his skin.

'Now, Mrs Ali, we were wondering whether we could prevail on you to attend the dance.'

'Well, I don't know,' said Mrs Ali. A sudden, shy pleasure lit her face.

'My aunt will not engage in public dancing,' said Abdul Wahid. The Major could tell that his voice bubbled with rage, but Daisy only peered at him with condescension suitable for shop assistants who might unwittingly forget their manners.

'We were not expecting her to dance,' she said.

'We wanted kind of a welcoming goddess, stationed in the niche where we keep the hat stand,' said Alma. 'And Mrs Ali is so quintessentially Indian, or at least quintessentially Pakistani, in the best sense.'

'Actually, I'm from Cambridge,' said Mrs Ali in a mild voice. 'The municipal hospital, ward three. Never been further abroad than the Isle of Wight.'

'But no one would know that,' said Alma.

'Mrs Khan feels we need someone to welcome and to take the hats and coats,' said Daisy. 'She and her husband, Dr Khan, are coming as guests, so they can't do it. She suggested you, Mrs Ali.' Mrs Ali's face grew pale and the Major felt a rage climbing into his own throat.

'My aunt does not work at parties—' began the nephew, but the Major cleared his throat loudly enough that the young man stopped in surprise.

'She won't be available,' he said, feeling his face redden. They all looked at him, and he felt torn between a desire to run for the door and the urgent need to stand up for his friend.

'I have already asked Mrs Ali to attend as my guest,' he said.

'How extraordinary,' said Daisy, and she paused as if fully expecting him to reconsider. Mrs Ali's nephew looked at the Major as if he were a strange bug discovered in the bathtub. Alma could not disguise a look of shock; Grace turned away and appeared suddenly struck by some important headline in the rack of local newspapers. Mrs Ali blushed but held her chin in the air and looked straight at Daisy.

'I'm sure Mrs Ali will add a decorative note to the room anyway,' said Gertrude, stepping blunt but welcome into the awkward silence. 'We will be happy to have her as an ambassador at large, representing both Pakistan and Cambridge.' She smiled, and the Major thought perhaps he had underestimated the redheaded young woman's character. She seemed to have a certain authority and an edge of diplomacy that might drive Daisy insane eventually. He could only look forward to that day.

'Then there's no more to be done here,' said Daisy in a huffy voice. 'We must go over the plans and we must call the Major and arrange to search his house for uniforms and so on.'

'I will call Roger; he and I can work on the Major,' said Gertrude, giving him a conspiratorial smile. 'It's my job to get more young people involved in the entertainment and, as a new member, I'm sure he'll be itching to help.'

'I never understand why it's so hard to get the men involved,' said Alma as the ladies left, talking loud plans all the way to the car.

'Thank you for your quick thinking, Major,' said Mrs Ali. To his surprise, she seemed to be herding him toward the door also. 'Did you need anything before you go? I'm going to shut the shop for a little while.'

'I just came to see if Amina needed a lift back to town,' the Major said. 'There are no buses in the afternoon today.'

'I didn't know that,' said Amina. She looked at Mrs Ali. 'I had better go if the Major is willing to drive us home.'

'No, you must stay and we will talk some more,' said Mrs Ali.

'She should leave and go back to her mother,' said Abdul Wahid in a fierce, low voice.

'My mother died two months ago,' said Amina, speaking just to him. 'Thirty years in the same street, Abdul Wahid, and only six people came to the funeral. Why do you think that was?' Her voice cracked, but she refused to look away from him. To break the painful silence, the Major asked, 'Where is George?'

'George is upstairs, out of the way,' said Mrs Ali. 'I found him some books to look at.'

'I am sorry that your mother had to bear that shame,' said the nephew. 'But it was none of my doing.'

'That's what your family would say,' said the girl, tears now making tracks down her thin cheeks. She picked up her backpack. 'George and I will go now and you will never have to be bothered by us again.'

'Why did you have to come here at all?' he asked.

'I had to come and see for myself that you don't love me.' She wiped at her face with the cuff of her shirt and a streak of dirt made her look like a small child. 'I never believed them when they said you left of your own accord, but I see now that you are the product of your family, Abdul Wahid.'

'You should go,' said Abdul Wahid, but his voice cracked as he turned his head away.

'No, no, you will stay and we will go upstairs with George and have something to eat,' said Mrs Ali. 'We will not leave things like this.' She looked flustered. She chewed her bottom lip and then projected toward him a smile that was painfully false. 'Thank you for your offer, Major, but everything is fine here. We will make our own arrangements.'

'If you're sure,' said the Major. He felt an unseemly fascination, like a driver who has slowed down to peer at a road accident. Mrs Ali moved toward the door and he had no choice but to follow. He added, in a whisper, 'Did I do wrong in bringing her here?'

'No, no, we are delighted to have them,' she said loudly. 'It turns out that they may be related to us.' A last puzzle piece slipped into place and the Major saw in his mind an image of little George frowning and looking so much like Abdul Wahid. He opened his mouth to speak, but Mrs Ali's face was a mask of exhausted politeness and he did not want to say something that might break the fragile veneer.

'Extra relatives are useful, I suppose—additional bridge player at family parties, or another kidney donor,' he babbled. 'I congratulate you.' A small smile lifted her weary face for a moment. He wished he could hold her hand and ask her to unburden herself to him, but the nephew was still glowering.

'Thank you also for your chivalrous deception about the dance, Major,' added Mrs Ali. 'I'm sure the ladies meant well, but I am glad to decline their request.'

'I am hoping you will not prove me a liar, Mrs Ali,' he replied, trying to speak quietly. 'It would be my honour and pleasure to escort you to the dance.'

'My aunt would not dream of attending,' said Abdul Wahid loudly. His jaw quivered. 'It is not appropriate.'

'Abdul Wahid, you will not attempt to lecture me on what is appropriate,' said Mrs Ali sharply. 'I will rule my own life, thank you.' She turned to the Major and extended her hand. 'Major, I accept your kind invitation.'

'I'm much honoured,' said the Major.

'And I'm hoping we can continue to discuss literature,' she said in a clear voice. 'I missed our Sunday appointment very much.' She did not smile as she said it and the Major felt a sting of disappointment that she was using him to wound her nephew. As he raised his hat to say goodbye, he noticed that the tension had returned. Or perhaps tension was the wrong word; as he walked away he thought that it was more like a low-grade despair. He paused at the corner and looked back. He was sure the three people in the shop had many hours of painful discussion ahead of them. The shop window revealed nothing but patchy, glittering reflections of street and sky.

Chapter Twelve

It was not cricket season, so the Major was confused for a moment by the muffled sound of wickets being hammered into turf. The sound shivered along the grassy rise of the field at the bottom of the garden and flushed a few pigeons from the copse on the hill. The Major, carrying a mug of tea and the morning paper, went down to the fence to investigate.

There was not much to see, only a tall man in rubber boots and a yellow waterproof coat consulting a theodolite and a clipboard while two others, following his directions, paced out lengths and hammered bits of orange-tipped wood into the rough grass.

'Major, don't let them see you,' said a disembodied voice in a loud stage whisper. The Major looked around.

'I'm keeping my head down,' said the voice, which he now recognised as belonging to Alice from next door. He walked toward the hedge, peering to see where she was.

'Don't look at me,' she said in an exasperated tone. 'They've probably spotted you, so just keep looking about as if you're alone.'

'Good morning to you, Alice,' said the Major, swallowing some tea and 'looking about' as well as he could. 'Is there some reason we're being so covert?'

'If we're going to take direct action, it won't do for them to see our faces,' she explained, as if to a small child. She was crouched on a folding camp stool in the tiny space between her own compost box and the hedge that divided her garden from the field. She did not seem bothered by the slight tang of rotting vegetables. Risking a quick glance, the Major saw a tripod and telescope poked into the greenery. He also noticed that Alice's attempts at discretion did not extend to clothing, which included a magenta sweater and orange pants in some kind of baggy hemp.

'Direct action?' asked the Major. 'What kind of—'

'Major, they're surveying for houses,' said Alice. 'They want to concrete over this entire field.'

'But that can't be true,' said the Major. 'This is Lord Dagenham's land.'

'And Lord Dagenham intends to make a pretty penny from selling his land and building houses on it,' said Alice.

'Perhaps he's just putting in new drains.' The Major always found he became deliberately more cautious and rational around Alice, as if her woolly enthusiasms might seep into his own consciousness. He liked Alice, despite the handmade posters for various causes that she taped in her windows and the overblown appearance of both her garden and her person. Both seemed to suffer from a surfeit of competing ideas and a commitment to the organic movement.

'Drains, my arse,' said Alice. 'Our intelligence suggests there's an American connection.' The Major felt a shift again in his gut. He was miserably sure she was right. There was a slow murder going on all over England these days as great swathes of fields were divided into small, rectangular pieces, like sheep pens, and stuffed with identical houses of bright red brick. The Major blinked hard, but the men would not disappear. He felt a sudden desire to go back to bed and pull the covers up over his head.

'Since they've seen your face, you might as well go and interrogate them,' said Alice. 'See if they crack under direct confrontation.'

The Major walked around into the field and asked to speak to the man in charge. He was directed to the tall man, in glasses and a neat shirt and tie under his yellow coat, who seemed perfectly pleasant as he shook hands but politely refused to explain his presence.

'I'm afraid it's all quite confidential,' he said. 'Client's all hush-hush.'

'I quite understand,' said the Major. 'Most people round here have a quite ridiculous dislike of any kind of change and can make themselves a nuisance.'

'Well, exactly,' said the man.

'When I shoot with Dagenham on the eleventh, I'll have to ask him for a private peek at the plans,' said the Major. 'I'm quite interested in architecture—in an amateur capacity, of course.'

'I can't promise they'll have all the architectural plans by then,' said the man. 'I'm just the engineer. We have to do all the top fields, and then there's the traffic studies for the commercial area, which takes time.'

'Yes, of course the commercial will take some months, I imagine.' The Major felt quite faint. Behind him, he could feel Alice's eye at the telescope watching. 'What should I tell people if they ask?'

'If they're persistent, I tell 'em it's drains,' said the man. 'Everyone's in favour of drains.'

'Thanks very much,' said the Major, turning away. 'I'll tell Lord Dagenham you're on top of things.'

'And tell 'em not to try pulling out my stakes,' said the man. He cocked his head at the buzz of a small plane approaching and jabbed his thumb skyward. 'Aerial photos of every completed site. Usually beats the local vandals.'

༄ ༄ ༄

Back behind his own gate, the Major felt a small spasm of grief. He had been feeling better in recent days and it was a surprise to find that his sorrow over his brother had not gone away but had been merely hiding somewhere waiting to ambush him on just such an occasion. He felt his eyes water and he pressed the fingernails of his free hand into his palm to stop it. He was keenly aware of Alice, crouched behind the hedge.

'My informant is back,' said Alice into a mobile phone. The Major was sure she would have preferred a two-way radio. 'I'll debrief right away.'

'I'm afraid you may be right,' said the Major, being careful not to look down at her. He gazed instead at the sunlit rear façades of the houses camped out like so many sleeping cows along the edge of the field. 'It's houses for sure—and some commercial component.'

'Good God, it's a whole new town,' said Alice into the phone. 'Not a moment to lose, of course. We must take action right away.'

'If anyone asks you, please tell them I said it was drains,' said the Major, preparing to retire to the house for a second cup of tea. He felt quite ill.

'You can't just walk away from this,' said Alice. She stood up, phone still pressed to the ear. He wondered who was on the end of the phone and pictured a group of faded hippies, with ripped jeans and balding heads. 'You must join us, Major.'

'I'm as upset as you are,' said the Major. 'But we don't have all the facts. We should contact the council and find out where we stand regarding planning permission and so on.'

'Okay, the Major will head up communications,' said Alice into the phone.

'No, really . . .' began the Major.

'Jim wants to know if you could whip up a few posters,' Alice said.

'That would be rather too arty for me,' said the Major, wondering who Jim was. 'Not one for the Magic Markers.'

'The Major is reluctant to join us, officially,' said Alice into her phone. 'With his connections, maybe he can be our unofficial man on the inside?' There was some excited chatter from the other end of the phone. Alice looked the Major up and down. 'No, no, he's completely reliable.'

She turned away and the Major could barely hear what she was saying behind the broad curtain of her curly hair. He leaned toward her. 'I'm prepared to vouch for him,' he heard her say.

The Major found it slightly preposterous but touching that Alice Pierce should be vouching for him. He could not be sure that he would be able to do the same for her if called upon. He perched on the side arm of the bench that sheltered under the dividing hedge and let his head flop onto his chest with a sigh. Alice shut her mobile phone and he could feel her looking at him.

'I know you love this village more than anyone,' she said. 'And I know how much Rose Lodge means to you and your family.' She spoke with an unusual gentleness. He swivelled to look at her and was touched to see it was entirely genuine.

'Thank you,' he said. 'You've been quite a while in your house, too.'

'I've been able to be very happy here,' she said. 'But it's only been twenty years, which hardly counts in this village.'

'It makes me feel old and foolish—I assumed progress couldn't touch our little corner of the world,' he said.

'It's not about progress,' she said. 'It's about greed.'

'I refuse to believe Lord Dagenham would give up his lands like this,' said the Major. 'He's always supported the countryside. He's a shooting man, for heaven's sake.' Alice shook her head as if at his naïveté.

'We're all in favour of preserving the countryside until we see how much money we can make by adding on, adding up, or building down the back of the garden. Everyone's green except for their one little project, which they assure us won't make much difference—and suddenly whole villages are sprouting attic windows and two-car garages and mum-in-law extensions.' She rubbed her hands through her hair, shaking out the curly mass and smoothing it backward. 'We're all as guilty as Dagenham—he's just on a bigger scale.'

'There is his obligation to stewardship,' said the Major. 'I'm sure he will realise and change his mind.'

'When that fails, we fight,' she said. 'It's never over until you've charged the bulldozers and been thrown in jail.'

'I admire your enthusiasm,' said the Major. He stood up and threw the dregs of his tea over a dead dahlia. 'But I cannot, in good conscience, assist you with any civic unrest.'

'Civic unrest? This is war, Major,' said Alice, chuckling at him. 'Man the barricades and break out the Molotov cocktails!'

'You do what you must,' said the Major. 'I shall write a stern letter to the planning officer.'

That afternoon, the Major walked down to the postbox with his letter and stood for some time, envelope in hand. Perhaps he had been too blunt in his request. He had excised the words 'we demand' from several places and replaced them with 'we request' but still he felt he was putting the planning officer on the spot. At the same time, he had feared Alice would not look kindly on his being overly polite, so he had added a phrase or two about the need for transparency and the council's responsibility for the stewardship of the land. He had toyed with 'sacred land' but to avoid confusion with fields owned by the church had made it 'ancient' at the last minute. He had also debated copying the letter directly to Lord Dagenham but decided that this might be put off, perhaps until a date after the duck shoot, without any serious moral compromise. The insertion of a crisp folded letter into a fresh envelope always gave him pleasure, and as he looked at the envelope now, he decided his words were adequately composed and the letter suitably concise and grave. He popped the envelope into the box with satisfaction and looked forward to the entire matter being resolved in an amicable manner between reasonable men. The letter posted, he was free to look at the village shop and decide, as if hit by a sudden idea, to go in and inquire after Mrs Ali and her nephew.

Inside the shop, Mrs Ali was seated at the counter pushing small squares of silk into the raffia baskets that she usually filled with sandalwood candles and packets of tuberose and eucalyptus bath salts. Wrapped in cellophane and a silk bow, they were popular gifts. The Major had bought two the year before to give to Marjorie and Jemima for Christmas.

'Those sell quite well, I believe,' he said, by way of greeting. Mrs Ali looked startled, as if she had not paid attention to the doorbell. Perhaps, he thought, she had not expected to see him.

'Yes, they are the favourite last-minute purchase of people who have entirely forgotten the person for whom they must buy,' said Mrs Ali. She appeared agitated, twirling a completed basket at the end of her long slender fingers. 'There is profit in panic, I suppose.'

'You appeared to be somewhat in distress yesterday,' he said. 'I came to see whether everything was all right.'

'Things are . . . difficult,' she said at last. 'Difficult, but possibly also very good.' He waited for her to elaborate, finding himself curious in a way that was entirely unfamiliar. He did not change the conversation, as he would have done if Alec or some other friend had ventured to hint at some personal difficulty. He waited and hoped that she would continue.

'I've finished polishing the apples,' said a small voice. The boy, George, came from the back of the store holding a clean duster in one hand and a small green apple in the other. 'This one is much smaller than the others,' he added.

'That is just much too small to sell, then,' said Mrs Ali. 'Would you like to eat it up for me?'

'Yes, please,' said George, his facing breaking into a large grin. 'I'll go and wash it.' He walked to the back of the shop. Mrs Ali watched him all the way and the Major watched her as her face relaxed into a smile.

'I would say you have a special touch with children,' said the Major. 'However, in the case of straight bribery one should reserve judgment.' He had meant to make her laugh, but when she looked up at him her face was grave. She smoothed her hands along her skirt and he noticed that her hand trembled.

'I have to tell you something,' she began. 'I'm not supposed to tell anyone, but if I do, perhaps it will help make things real. . . .' Her voice died away and she examined the backs of her hands as if searching for her lost thought among the faint blue veins.

'You don't have to tell me anything,' he said. 'But be assured anything you choose to tell me will be kept in complete confidence.'

'I am in some confusion, as you can see,' she said, looking at him again with just a hint of her usual smile. He waited. 'Amina and George stayed with us last night,' she began. 'It turns out that George is my great-nephew. He is Abdul Wahid's son.'

'Is he indeed?' said the Major, feigning ignorance.

'How could I not have guessed, not have felt it?' she said. 'And yet now, with a word from Amina, I am welded to this small boy by a deep love.'

'Are you sure it's the truth?' said the Major. 'Only there are cases, you know—people do take advantage and so on.'

'Little George has my husband's nose.' She blinked, but a tear escaped and rolled down her left cheek. 'It was right there but I couldn't see it.'

'So you are to be congratulated?' asked the Major. He had not meant to phrase it as a question.

'I thank you, Major,' she said. 'But I cannot escape the fact that this brings shame on my family, and I would understand if you preferred not to continue our acquaintance.'

'Nonsense; such a thought never crossed my mind,' said the Major. He could feel himself blushing at this small lie. He was doing his best to squelch the uncomfortable desire to slide out of the shop and free himself from what was, however you looked at it, a slightly sordid business.

'Such humiliations should not happen in good families,' she said.

'Oh, it's been going on for a thousand years,' interrupted the Major, feeling the need to bluff himself as well as her. 'The Victorians were worse than the rest, of course.'

'But the shame does seem so trivial compared to that beautiful child.'

'People are always complaining about the loosening of moral standards,' the Major went on. 'But my wife always insisted that prior generations were just as lax—they were merely more furtive.'

'I knew Abdul Wahid was sent away because he was in love with some girl,' she said. 'But I never knew there was to be a child.'

'Did he know?' asked the Major.

'He says not.' Her face darkened. 'A family will do many things to protect their children, and I fear life has been made very difficult for this young woman.' There was silence as the Major searched in vain for some useful words of comfort. 'Anyway, they are here now, Amina and George, and I must make things right.'

'What will you do?' asked the Major. 'I mean, you hardly know anything about this young woman.'

'I know I must keep them here, while we find out,' Mrs Ali said, her chin lifted in an attractive arc of decisiveness. He recognised a woman on a mission. 'They will stay with me for at least a week, and if Abdul wants to continue sleeping in the car, that is what he will have to do.'

'Sleeping in the car?'

'My nephew insists he cannot sleep under my roof with an unmarried woman, so he slept in the car,' said Mrs Ali. 'I pointed out the obvious, inconsistency in his thinking, but his new religiosity permits him to be stubborn.'

'But why have them stay at all?' asked the Major. 'Can't they just visit?'

'I fear if they go back to town, they may disappear again,' she said. 'Amina seems very highly strung and she says her aunt is practically hysterical with people asking questions about her.'

'I suppose renting a room at the pub is not allowed,' said the Major. The landlord of the Royal Oak offered two flowery bedrooms under the eaves and a hearty full breakfast served in the slightly sticky bar area.

'Abdul Wahid has threatened to go to town and ask the Imam for a bed, which would mean our business would be the gossip of the entire community.' She covered her face with her hands and said softly, 'Why must he be so stubborn?'

'Look here, if it's really important to you to keep them all here, how about your nephew coming to stay with me for a few days?' The Major surprised himself with the offer, which seemed to emerge of its own accord. 'I have a spare room—he wouldn't be in my way.'

'Oh, Major, it is too much to expect,' said Mrs Ali. 'I could not trespass this way on your kindness.' Her face, however, had lit up with anticipation. The Major was already deciding to put the young man in Roger's old room. The spare room was rather cold, as it was north facing, and the bed had a few suspicious holes in one leg that he had been meaning to investigate. It wouldn't do to have a guest fall out of bed because of woodworm.

'Look, it's really no trouble,' he said. 'And if it helps you resolve this problem, I'm glad to be of service.'

'I will be entirely in your debt, Major.' She stood up from her stool, came close and laid her hand on his arm. 'I cannot express my gratitude.' The Major felt warmth spreading up his arm. He kept still, as if a butterfly had alighted on his elbow. For a moment nothing existed but the feel of her breath and the sight of his own face on her dark eyes.

'Well, it's quite all right.' He gave her hand a quick squeeze.

'You are a most astonishing man,' she said, and he realised he had inspired a sense of trust and indebtedness that would make it entirely impossible for an honourable man to attempt to kiss her anytime soon. He cursed himself for a fool.

⟍ ⟍ ⟋

It was dark when Abdul Wahid knocked at the door of Rose Lodge. He was carrying a few belongings rolled tightly in a small prayer rug tied with a canvas strap. He looked as if he were used to rolling his life up in this simple bundle.

'Do come in,' said the Major.

'You are very kind,' said the young man, who wore the same frown as usual. He carefully removed his battered brown slip-on shoes and placed them under the hallstand. The Major knew this was a sign of respect for his home, but he felt embarrassed by the intimacy of a stranger's feet in damp socks. He had a sudden vision of the village ladies leaving imprints of their stockings in coven circles on his polished boards. He was glad his own feet were encased in stout wool slippers.

Leading the way upstairs, he decided to show the nephew to the north-facing spare room after all. Roger's room, with its old blue rug and the good desk with the writing lamp, seemed suddenly too luxurious and soft for this hard-faced young man.

'Will this do?' he asked, surreptitiously kicking the weak bed leg to make sure it was sturdy and no dust fell from the wormholes. The thin mattress, the pine chest of drawers, and the single print of flowers on one wall seemed suitably monastic.

'You are too kind.' Abdul Wahid deposited his few belongings gently on the bed.

'I'll get you some sheets and let you settle in,' said the Major.

'Thank you,' said Abdul Wahid.

When the Major came back with the linens, and a thin wool blanket that he had selected instead of a silk eiderdown, Abdul Wahid had already settled in. On the chest were laid out a comb, a soap dish, and a copy of the Qur'an. A large cotton dishtowel, printed with calligraphy, had been hung over the picture. The prayer rug lay on the floor, looking small against the expanse of worn floorboard. Abdul Wahid sat on the edge of the bed, his hands on his knees, staring into thin air.

'I hope you'll be warm enough,' the Major said, placing his bundle on the bed.

'She was always so beautiful,' whispered Abdul Wahid. 'I could never think straight in her presence.'

'The window rattles a bit if the wind gets round this corner of the house,' the Major added, and went over to tighten the catch. He found himself slightly unnerved at having the intense young man in his home and, for fear of saying something wrong, he decided to play the jovial, disinterested host.

'They promised me I would forget her, and I did,' said the young man. 'But now she is here and my brain has been spinning all day.'

'Maybe it's a low-pressure system.' The Major peered out through the glass for signs of storm clouds. 'My wife always got headaches when the barometer dropped.'

'It is a great relief to be in your home, Major,' said Abdul Wahid. The Major turned in surprise. The young man had stood up and now made him a short bow. 'To be once again in a sanctuary far from the voices of women is balm to the anguished soul.'

'I can't promise it will last,' said the Major. 'My neighbour Alice Pierce is rather fond of singing folk music to her garden plants. Thinks it makes them grow or something.' The Major had often wondered how a wailing rendition of 'Greensleeves' would encourage greater raspberry production but Alice insisted that it worked far better than chemical fertilisers, and she did produce several kinds of fruit in pie-worthy quantities. 'No sense of pitch, but plenty of enthusiasm,' he added.

'Then I will add a prayer for rain to my devotions,' said Abdul Wahid. The Major could not determine whether this was intended as a humorous remark.

'I'll see you in the morning,' he said. 'I usually put on a pot of tea around six.' As he left his guest and proceeded down to the kitchen, he felt in his bones the exhaustion of such a strange turn of events. And yet he could not help but register a certain sense of exhilaration at having thrust himself into the heart of Mrs Ali's life in such an extraordinary manner. He had acted spontaneously.

He had asserted his own wishes. He was tempted to celebrate his own boldness with a large glass of Scotch, but as he reached the kitchen he decided that a large glass of sodium bicarbonate would be more prudent.

Chapter Thirteen

Saturday morning was sunny and the Major was in the back garden, forking a pile of leaves into a wheelbarrow, when his son's raised voice from the house snapped him to attention and caused him to drop the entire load with a half-formed oath. Having no idea that Roger would follow through on his threat to visit, the Major had not told him that there would be a guest in the house. From the continued shouts inside, accompanied by what sounded like a chair being overturned, the Major surmised that he might need to run if he were to save both Roger and his houseguest from a skirmish.

As he hurried toward the door, he cursed Roger for never bothering to phone but always turning up unannounced whenever he felt like it. The Major would have liked to institute some rational system of pre-visit notification, but he never seemed to find the right words to tell Roger that his childhood home was no longer available to him at all hours. He was unaware of any established etiquette as to when a child should be stripped of family privilege, but he knew the time had long since passed in this case.

Now he would be stuck with Roger pouting as if he owned the place and the Major and his guest were the interlopers. As he reached the back door, Roger came panting through, his face red and furious and his fingers poised over his mobile phone. 'There's a man in the house claims he's staying here,' said Roger. 'Sandy's keeping him talking but I've got the police on speed dial.'

'Oh, good heavens, don't call the police,' said the Major. 'That's just Abdul Wahid.'

'Abdul what?' said Roger. 'Who the hell is he? I almost hit him with a dining chair.'

'Are you quite mad?' asked the Major. 'Why would you assume my guest is some kind of intruder?'

'Is that any more absurd than assuming my father has suddenly become friendly with half the population of Pakistan?'

'And you left Sandy alone with my "intruder"?' asked the Major.

'Yes, she's keeping him occupied, talking to him about handmade clothing,' said Roger. 'Spotted that his scarf was some vintage tribal piece and quite calmed him down. I ducked out just to check he was on the up and up.'

'So much for chivalry,' said the Major.

'Well, you said yourself, he isn't dangerous,' said Roger. 'Who the hell is he and what's he doing here?'

'I don't see that it is any of your concern,' said the Major. 'I am simply helping out a friend by putting up her nephew for a couple of days, a couple of weeks at most. She wanted to invite the fiancée to move in and— It's a bit complicated.'

He felt himself on shaky ground. It was hard to defend his invitation when he himself did not fully understand what Mrs Ali was trying to accomplish in immediately moving Amina and George into the flat above the shop. She had stared hungrily at little George, and the Major had not recognised the look until later. It was the same look Nancy had sometimes given Roger, when she thought no one was looking. She had looked that way on the day of his birth and she had looked at him just the same as she lay wasting away in the hospital. In that bleach-scented room with its flickering fluorescent light and its ridiculous new wallpaper border bursting with purple hollyhocks, Roger had chattered on about his own concerns as usual, as if a cheery recitation of his promotion prospects would wipe out the reality of her dying, and she had gazed at him as if to burn his face into her fading mind.

'It sounds quite ridiculous,' said Roger, speaking in such an imperious tone that the Major wondered how he would react to a swift butt on the shins with a rake handle. 'Anyway, Sandy and I are here now, so you can use us as an excuse to get rid of him.'

'It would be entirely rude to "get rid" of him,' said the Major. 'He has accepted my invitation—an invitation I might not have made had I known you were coming down this weekend.'

'I did say we'd be down to visit soon,' said Roger. 'I told you at the cottage.'

'Alas, if I planned my weekends around the hope that you would carry through on a promise to visit, I would be a lonely old man sitting amid a growing tower of clean bed linen and uneaten cake,' said the Major. 'At least Abdul Wahid showed up when invited.'

'Look, I'm sure he's a perfectly nice chap, but you can't be too careful at your age,' said Roger. He stopped and looked around as if to detect eavesdroppers. 'There have been many cases of elderly people taken in by scam artists.'

'What do you mean, "elderly people"?'

'You have to be especially careful about foreigners.'

'Would that apply equally to Americans?' asked the Major. 'Because I spot one of them now.' Sandy was standing in the doorway. She appeared to be examining the long curtains and the Major wished that the pattern of poppies had not faded to rust all along the edges.

'Don't be ridiculous,' said Roger. 'Americans are just like us.'

As his son greeted Sandy with a kiss on the lips and an arm around the waist, the Major was left to gape at such a peremptory dismissal of any distinction of national character between Great Britain and the giant striving nation across the Atlantic. The Major found much to admire in America but also felt that the nation was still in its infancy, its birth predating Queen Victoria's reign by a mere sixty years or so. Generous to a fault—he still remembered the tins of chocolate powder and waxy crayons handed out in his school even several years after the war—America wielded her huge power in the world with a brash confidence that reminded him of a toddler who has got hold of a hammer.

He was prepared to admit that he might be prejudiced, but what was one supposed to think of a country where history was either preserved in theme parks by employees wearing mob caps and long skirts over their sneakers, or was torn down—taken apart for the wide-plank lumber?

'Are you all right, darling?' asked Roger. 'Turns out Abdul is here at my father's invitation.'

'Of course he is,' said Sandy. She turned to the Major. 'Ernest, you have a lovely home.' She held out her long hand and the Major took it, noting that her nails were now pink with broad white tips. It took him a moment to realise that they had been painted to look like fingernails, and he sighed over the extraordinary range of female vanities. His wife, Nancy, had had lovely oval nails, like filbert nuts, and had never done anything more than buff them with a small manicure tool. She had kept them short, the better to thrust them into the garden soil or to play the piano.

'Thank you,' said the Major.

'You can almost smell the centuries,' said Sandy, who was perfectly dressed for a literary version of the countryside, or perhaps an afternoon in Tunbridge Wells. She wore high-heeled brown shoes, pale, well-pressed slacks, a shirt with autumn leaves printed on it, and a cashmere sweater tied around her shoulders. She did not look ready to climb over a stile and walk through soggy sheep fields to the pub for lunch. A happy maliciousness prompted the Major to suggest just that immediately.

'Let's celebrate the lovely surprise of your visit, shall we?' he said. 'I thought we'd walk down for lunch at the Royal Oak.'

'Actually we brought lunch with us,' said Roger. 'Picked up supplies at this great new place in Putney. Everything is flown in from France by overnight mail.'

'I hope you like truffle dust.' Sandy laughed. 'Roger had them powder everything but the madeleines.'

'Perhaps you'd like to invite that Abdul chap to join us, by way of apology,' added Roger, as if it were the Major who had created an offence.

'It's not polite to call him Abdul. It means servant,' said the Major. 'Formally, you should use the entire Abdul Wahid. It means Servant of God.'

'Touchy about it, is he?' said Roger. 'And his aunt would be Mrs What's-Her-Name from the village shop? The one you brought to the cottage to freak out Mrs Augerspier?'

'Your Mrs Augerspier is an objectionable woman—'

'That goes without saying, Dad.'

'Just because it goes without saying doesn't mean one shouldn't speak up, you know. Or at least refuse to do business with such a person.'

'There's no point in being confrontational and losing out on something lucrative, is there?' asked Roger. 'I mean, it is much more satisfying to beat them by getting the better end of the bargain.'

'On what philosophical basis does that idea rest?' asked the Major. Roger gave a vague wave of the hand and the Major saw him roll his eyes for Sandy's benefit.

'Oh, it's simple pragmatism, Dad. It's called the real world. If we refused to do business with the morally questionable, the deal volume would drop in half and the good guys like us would end up poor. Then where would we all be?'

'On a nice dry spit of land known as the moral high ground?' suggested the Major.

Roger and Sandy went to fetch their hamper and as the Major tried not to think of truffles, which he had always avoided because they stank like sweaty groins, Abdul Wahid came out of the house. As usual he was carrying a couple of dusty religious texts tucked tightly under his armpit partly and was wearing the dour frown which the

Major now understood was the result of excessive thinking rather than mere unpleasantness. The Major wished young men wouldn't think so much. It always seemed to result in absurd revolutionary movements or, as in the case of several of his former pupils, the production of very bad poetry.

'Your son has come to stay,' said Abdul Wahid. 'I should leave your home.'

'Oh, no, no,' said the Major, who was growing used to Abdul Wahid's abrupt style of speaking and no longer found it offensive. 'There is no need for you to rush off. I told you, the room is yours as long as you want.'

'He has brought his fiancée with him,' said Abdul Wahid. 'I must congratulate you. She is very beautiful.'

'Yes, but on the other hand, she's an American. There's surely no reason for you to leave.' He thought it quite ridiculous that this young man should career away from every unmarried woman he met.

'You will need the guest room,' said Abdul Wahid. 'Your son was very clear that they will be staying with you for several weekends, until their cottage is made habitable.'

'Ah, will they?' said the Major. He could think of no immediate response. He doubted that the spare room would be required in this case, but he realised that this information would only hasten Abdul Wahid's departure while placing himself in the awkward position of having to make direct reference to his son's sleeping arrangements.

'I should return to the shop, and Amina and George should go back to her auntie in town,' said Abdul Wahid in a firm voice. 'This whole idea that we can be together again is just foolish.'

'Many a fool has later been labelled a genius,' said the Major. 'There is no hurry to make decisions, is there? Your aunt seems to think the family will come around. And she dotes on little George.'

'My aunt has discussed the matter with you?' asked Abdul Wahid.

'I knew your uncle,' said the Major, but he felt the lie in this and could not look at Abdul Wahid.

'My aunt has always defied the normal and necessary limits of real life. She sees it as a duty, almost,' he said. 'But I see only indulgence and if I do not put an end to this confusion, I fear my aunt will break her heart this time.'

'Look, why don't you stay to lunch and we could walk down together?' asked the Major. He was worried that Abdul Wahid might be right. If Mrs Ali persisted in investing in George all her dreams of children and grandchildren, she might well get her heart broken. However, he was reluctant to let the young man precipitate some crisis. Moreover he found himself eager to inflict his guest upon Roger—or perhaps to inflict them on each other, in the hope of jolting both out of their moral complacency. 'I would really like you to meet my son properly.'

Abdul Wahid gave a strange bleating sound and the Major realised he was actually laughing.

'Major, your son and his fiancée have brought you an entire feast of pâtés, hams, and other pig-related products. I barely escaped the kitchen with my faith.'

'I'm sure we can make you a cheese sandwich or something,' said the Major. Abdul Wahid shuffled his feet and the Major pressed his invitation home. 'I do wish you'd sit around the table with us.'

'I will of course defer to your wishes,' he said. 'I will drink a glass of tea if you will allow.'

੮ ੭ ੮

In the kitchen an unfamiliar cloth of blue-striped burlap had been laid across the table. His best wineglasses, the ones the Major brought out at Christmas, were laid out next to plastic plates in a lurid lime green. A wine bucket he had never used held a bottle of fizzy water chilling in what looked like every last ice cube from the plastic trays. Strange mustards had been decanted into his china finger bowls while an unfamiliar vase like a tree root held a bunch of yellow calla lilies, which had sunk to the tabletop in a low bow. Sandy was tucking more wilting lilies among the bric-a-brac on the mantelpiece. They had kindled an unnecessary but attractive fire in the grate and the Major wondered whether they had purchased firewood in Putney as well. Roger was frying something on the stove.

'Is your jacket smouldering, Roger,' asked the Major, 'or are you just cooking something made of tweed?'

'Just a few truffle slices sautéed with foie gras and sorrel,' said Roger. 'We had it in a restaurant last week and it was so fabulous I thought I'd try it myself.' He poked at the pan, which was beginning to blacken. 'It doesn't smell quite like the chef made it, though. Perhaps I should have used goose fat instead of lard.'

'How many of us are there for lunch?' asked the Major. 'Is there a coach tour about to turn up?'

'Well, Dad, I planned for leftovers,' said Roger. 'That way you'll have some food for the week.' He tipped the contents of the frying pan into a shallow bowl and dumped the black, hissing pan into the sink, where it continued to smoke.

'Ernest, do you have a corkscrew?' asked Sandy and the Major's indignation at the suggestion that he needed to be provided food was displaced by the need to head off a cultural misunderstanding.

'Abdul Wahid has consented to sit at the table with us, so perhaps I'll put on the kettle for tea and get us all a nice jug of lemon water,' said the Major. Sandy paused, cradling a bottle of wine against one hip.

'Oh, I say, do we have to—' began Roger.

'Please do not mind my presence,' said Abdul Wahid. 'You must drink as you wish.'

'Good show, old man,' said Roger. 'If everyone would just show such good manners, we could solve the Middle East crisis tomorrow.' He bent his lips into a vacant smile and displayed teeth too white to be natural.

'Do come and sit down by me, Abdul Wahid,' said Sandy. 'I want to ask you more about traditional weaving in Pakistan.'

'I won't be much help,' said Abdul Wahid. 'I was raised in England. I was considered a tourist and an Englishman in Pakistan. I bought my scarf in Lahore, in a department store.'

'Nothing beats a plain glass of cold clear water,' said the Major, who was still rummaging for a corkscrew in the small drawer by the stove. Sandy handed him her wine bottle as she sat down by Abdul Wahid.

'Now, Father, you surely aren't going to pass up a nice '75 Margaux,' said Roger. 'I picked it out especially for you.'

Two large glasses of decent claret in the middle of the day were not part of the Major's usual schedule. He had to admit that they imparted a rosy air to a luncheon that would otherwise have been stilted. Sandy's impeccably made-up face seemed soft in the haze of firelight and wine. Roger's brash commands—he had compelled them to swirl their wine around the glass and stick their noses in as if they had never tasted a decent vintage before—seemed almost endearing. The Major wondered whether his son acted in this eager way in front of his friends in London and whether they were indulgent of his enthusiasms or just laughed at him behind his back for his feeble attempts to order everyone around. Abdul Wahid gave no sign of derision. He seemed less dour than usual—perhaps dazzled, thought the Major, by the sight of the blonde and highly groomed Sandy. He alternated sips of his lemon water and his tea and answered Sandy's few questions with the politest of replies.

Roger was pointed in ignoring their guest and chattered on about the new cottage. In one week he and Sandy had apparently managed to engage the services of a carpenter and a team of painters.

'Not just any old painters, either,' said Roger. 'They're so in demand, doing galleries and restaurants. Sandy knows them through a friend at work.' He paused and took Sandy's hand with a loving smile. 'She's the queen of the right connections.'

'Lots of connections, very few close friends,' said Sandy. The Major caught a hint of regret that sounded genuine. 'It's so refreshing just to sit around with family and friends, like we're doing now.'

'Where is your family?' asked Abdul Wahid. His abrupt question startled the Major from his growing sleepiness.

'We're scattered all over,' she said. 'My father lives in Florida, my mother moved to Rhode Island. I have a brother in Texas, and my sister moved with her husband to Chicago last year.'

'And what, may I ask, is your religion?'

'Good heavens, Sandy's family is staunch Anglican,' said Roger in a clipped voice. 'Tell my father about the time your mother got her picture taken with the Archbishop of Canterbury.'

'Yes, my mother did once stake out a men's room to get a photo with the Archbishop,' said Sandy. She rolled her eyes. 'I believe she thought it might make up for the rest of the family. I think we're now one Buddhist, two agnostics, and the rest are plain old atheist.'

'Nonpractising Anglicans,' said Roger.

'The word "atheist" does rather give that impression, Roger,' replied the Major.

'Roger doesn't like to talk about religion, do you?' said Sandy. She started to tick subjects off on her fingers: 'No religion, no politics, sex only through innuendo—it's no wonder you British obsess about the weather, darling.' The Major winced again at the endearment. He supposed he would have to become accustomed to it.

'I feel it is important to discuss our different religions,' said Abdul Wahid. 'But in Britain, we keep it all behind closed doors and swept under the wall-to-wall carpet. I have not found anyone to sit down and discuss this topic.'

'Oh, my God—an ecumenical Muslim,' said Roger. 'Are you sure you're talking about the right religion?'

'Roger!' said Sandy.

'It is all right,' said Abdul Wahid. 'I prefer such directness. I cannot defend my religion against evasion and the politeness which hides disdain.'

The Major felt an urgent need to change the subject. 'Have you two set a wedding date, or were you going to make that a surprise as well?' he asked. Roger looked down and crumbled bread on the side of his plate. Sandy took a long swallow of wine, which the Major observed with pleasure as a possible crack in her façade of perfection. There was a moment's pause.

'Oh, goodness no,' said Roger finally. 'We have no plans to get married anytime soon, or I would have told you.'

'No plans?' asked the Major. 'I'm not sure I understand.'

'I mean, once you're married people start thinking "family man", and before you know it your whole career smells of impending nappies,' said Roger, twirling the wine cork in his fingers. He used it to mash the pile of bread crumbs into a tiny patty. 'I've seen it nail people to their current job title.'

Sandy paid close attention to her wineglass and said nothing.

'Marriage is a wonderful part of life,' said the Major.

'Yes, so's retirement,' said Roger. 'But you might as well put them both off as long as possible.'

'Are you not afraid it will suggest dilettantism and lack of moral fibre?' said the Major, doing his best to contain his outrage. 'All this lack of commitment these days—doesn't it smack of weakness of character?'

'As one who has been weak,' said Abdul Wahid in a quiet voice, 'I can attest to you that it is not a path to happiness.'

'Oh, I didn't mean you, Abdul Wahid,' said the Major, horrified that he had unintentionally offended his guest. 'Not at all.'

'Look, Sandy's her own boss, and she has no problem with it,' said Roger. 'Tell them, Sandy.'

'It was my idea, actually,' said Sandy. 'My firm kept the whole visa thing dangling over my head, so getting engaged to a Brit seemed the ideal answer. I don't mean to offend you, Abdul Wahid.'

'I am not offended,' said Abdul Wahid. He blinked several times and took a deep breath. 'Only sometimes when we pick and choose among the rules we discover later that we have set aside something precious in the process.'

'But everyone puts off marriage if they can,' said Roger. 'I mean, just look at the royal family.'

'I won't stand for you being disrespectful, Roger,' the Major responded. The current fashion for bandying about stories and jokes, as if the royal family were the cast of a TV soap opera, was deeply distasteful to him.

'I must get back to the shop now.' Abdul Wahid stood up from the table and inclined his head to the Major and to Sandy. The Major rose to see him out of the room.

'I hope we see you again,' said Sandy.

'What's his problem?' said Roger when the Major returned.

'Abdul Wahid has just discovered he has a son,' said the Major. 'It is a warning to all of us that unorthodox romantic arrangements are not without consequences.'

'I agree you're right, at least when it comes to the working classes and foreigners,' said Roger. 'Totally oblivious about birth control and things. But we're not like them, Sandy and I.'

'The human race is all the same when it comes to romantic relations,' said the Major. 'A startling absence of impulse control combined with complete myopia.'

'Look, we'll see how it goes with the cottage, Dad,' said Roger. 'Who knows, maybe in six months we'll be ready to commit.'

'To marriage?'

'Or at least to buying a place together,' said Roger. Sandy drained her wineglass and said nothing.

❧ ❧ ❧

After lunch, Roger wanted to smoke a cigar in the garden. The Major made a pot of tea and tried to dissuade Sandy from washing dishes.

'Please don't clear up,' he said. He still found all offers of help in the kitchen to be an embarrassment and a sign of pity.

'Oh, I love doing dishes,' said Sandy. 'I know you probably consider me a dreadful Yank but I'm so in love with the fact that people here are able to live in tiny houses and do chores without complicated appliances.'

'I should point out that Rose Lodge is considered rather spacious,' said the Major. 'And I'll have you know I own a rather top-of-the-line steam iron.'

'You don't send out your ironing?'

'I used to have a woman come in,' said the Major, 'when my wife was ill. But she ironed my trouser seams until they were shiny. I looked like a damn band captain.' Sandy laughed and the Major did not wince quite so much. Either he was getting used to her, or the claret had not yet worn off.

'Maybe I won't bother getting a dishwasher for the cottage,' said Sandy. 'Maybe we'll keep things authentic.'

'The way my son uses saucepans, I think you need one,' said the Major chipping at the burnt frying pan with a fork and speaking loudly so that Roger, coming in from the garden, would register the remark.

'I went down to the club last week,' said Roger taking the dry tea towel the Major offered him but then sitting down at the table instead of helping.

'I heard,' said the Major. 'Why on earth didn't you call me so I could take you down and introduce you properly?'

'Sorry. I was just passing, really, and I thought since I'd spent all those years as a junior member that I might as well just pop in and check out what's what,' said Roger.

'And what exactly was what?' asked the Major.

'That old secretary is a damn idiot,' said Roger, 'But I ran into Gertrude Dagenham-Smythe and she fixed everything. I told Sandy it was quite funny to see the club secretary fawning all over her. He couldn't have whipped me out a membership application any faster.'

'I'll need to fill out a sponsorship document, of course,' said the Major. 'You shouldn't have upset the secretary.'

'Actually, Gertrude said she'd have her uncle sponsor me,' said Roger indulging in a wide yawn.

'Lord Dagenham?'

'When she offered, I thought I might as well get sponsored by someone as high up the food chain as possible.'

'But you don't even know her,' said the Major, who still thought of Gertrude as the lady in the bucket hat.

'We've met Gertrude a few times in town,' said Sandy. 'She remembered Roger right away—joked about how she had a crush on him one summer when she visited.'

The Major had a sudden vision of a tall, thin girl with a blunt chin and green glasses who had haunted the lane one summer. He remembered Nancy inviting her in a couple of times.

'I remember Roger being very rude to her,' said the Major. 'Anyway, it's out of the question. It simply wouldn't do not to be sponsored by your own family.'

'If you insist,' said Roger, and the Major could only fume as he realised he had been put in the position of begging not to be cut out of Roger's social progress. 'Do you remember how she was always popping out of the hedge and presenting me with gifts?' continued Roger. 'She was as plain as the back of a bus and I had to drive her off with a pea-shooter.'

'Roger!' said the Major. The young lady's status as Lord Dagenham's niece was enough to grant her a certain distinction if not beauty.

'Oh, he's very attentive to her now,' said Sandy. 'She asked his help with this golf club dance and he agreed right away. Good thing I'm not the jealous type.'

'I'm not at all happy with the dance,' said the Major. 'There are some ridiculous ideas floating about that you must help me quash.'

'I'm your man,' said Roger. 'I don't want anything silly detracting from the central theme—the glory of the Pettigrew name.'

'But that's precisely the piece we need to quash,' said the Major. 'I don't like our name being bandied about as cheap entertainment.'

'But how else would we get our name bandied about so fast?' asked Roger. 'They've asked me to play Grandfather Pettigrew. It's unbelievably good luck.' He yawned again.

'It's an outrage,' said the Major.

'It's a boost to my social career and it won't cost you a penny,' said Roger. 'Would you deny me that chance?'

'We'll look ridiculous,' said the Major.

'Everyone looks ridiculous in the country,' said Roger. 'The point is to join in so they don't suspect you.' The Major was tempted to reward his son's self-absorption with a box on the ear with the freshly scrubbed frying pan.

❧

'Your father is just wonderful,' said Sandy as they sat over tea in the living room. 'It's so nice to meet someone real for a change.'

'We met one of the biggest art collectors in Europe this week,' said Roger. 'Russian guy—he has an entire house on the edge of Regents Park.'

'I don't think your father would have liked it much,' said Sandy.

'He has six Picassos and amethyst handles on all the taps in the toilets,' said Roger. 'Ten minutes of chatting with him, and Sandy had an order for an entire new wardrobe of clothes for his girlfriend.'

'I do admire a man who doesn't do things by halves,' said Sandy.

'You should call her, darling, and see if we can wangle a lunch invitation,' said Roger.

'Oh, God, Roger, not lunch,' said Sandy. 'Lunch requires conversation. I don't think I can sustain a whole hour of listening to her catalogue her handbags.'

'It'd be worth it if we get on the list of people invited to their private tent at the art fair,' said Roger. 'If we work 'em right, we could be yachting in the Black Sea next summer, or at least invited down to Poole for the weekend.'

'In my day I don't think we ever felt the need to "work" our social contacts in such a manner,' said the Major. 'It seems a bit gauche.'

'Oh come on, it's always been the way of the world,' said Roger. 'You're either in the game, making the connections, or you're left in the social backwoods, reduced to making friends with—well, with shopkeepers.'

'You're very rude,' said the Major. He felt his face flushing.

'I think your father has the right idea,' said Sandy. 'To be interesting, you have to make contacts in all sorts of worlds. That way you keep people off guard.'

'Sandy is a real master at making friends with people,' said Roger. 'She has everyone convinced she really likes them.'

'I do like them all,' said Sandy, blushing. 'Okay, maybe I don't like the Russian. We may have to rent a canoe if you want a boating holiday.'

'She has my boss's wife eating out of her hand. One minute I can't get a cup of coffee with my boss, and the next, he's asking me to go shooting with him and a client,' said Roger. 'Never underestimate the power of the female Mafia.'

'I seem to remember a small boy blubbering over a dead woodpecker and vowing never to pick up a gun again,' said the Major. 'Are you really going shooting?' He leaned toward Sandy and poured her more tea. 'Could never get him to come out with me after that,' he added.

'Yeah—like "bring Woody" is a great invitation,' said Roger. 'It was my first shoot and I potted an endangered bird. They never let me forget it.'

'Oh, you have to learn to shrug these things off, my boy,' said the Major. 'Nicknames only stick to people who let them.'

'My father.' Roger rolled his eyes. 'A great believer in the cold-baths-and-blistering-rebuke school of compassion.'

'Roger is going shooting now,' said Sandy. 'We had to spend three hours in a store on Jermyn Street, getting him the proper outfit.'

'An outfit?' asked the Major. 'I could have lent you a pair of breeches and a jacket.'

'I got everything I needed, thanks,' said Roger. 'Except a gun, of course. I was hoping I could borrow yours and Uncle Bertie's.' The request was smoothly made. The Major set down his cup and saucer and considered his son's placid face with equal parts curiosity and rage.

Roger betrayed no hint that he understood the effrontery of the request. It was of no more significance to him than asking to borrow some spare wellies during a rainstorm. The Major pondered how to produce a response that would be blunt enough to make an impression on Roger.

'No.'

'I'm sorry?' said Roger.

'No, you may not borrow the guns,' said the Major.

'Why ever not?' asked Roger with round eyes. The Major was about to answer when he recognised that his son was tempting him into explanations. Explaining would then simply open negotiations.

'Let's not discuss it in front of our guest,' said the Major. 'It is out of the question.' Roger stood up so quickly that he slopped tea into his saucer.

'How come you always have to undermine me?' he asked. 'How come you can never just put yourself out to support me? This is my career we're talking about.' He banged down his teacup and turned away to look into the fireplace, clenching his hands together behind his back.

'I'm sure your host has arranged some perfectly adequate extra guns,' said the Major. 'Besides, as a novice, you would look ridiculous banging away with such a valuable pair. You would look absurd.'

'Thank you, Father,' said Roger. 'Nice of you to be as frank as usual about my limitations.'

'I'm sure your father didn't mean it that way,' said Sandy, looking as if she had suddenly remembered why business acquaintances were, after all, preferable to family.

'I'm just trying to keep you from looking foolish,' said the Major. 'What kind of shoot is this, anyway? If it's clay shooting, they often have just the right equipment.'

'No, actually it's a local country thing,' said Roger. He paused as if reluctant to say more, and a horrible premonition came over the Major. He debated stuffing his fingers in his ears so he would not have to hear Roger's next words.

'I told Roger you'd be happy for him,' said Sandy. 'But he's been concerned all week that you might feel offended that after all these years he gets an invitation instead of you.'

'I'm shooting with Lord Dagenham next week,' said Roger. 'Sorry, Dad, but it just came about and I couldn't exactly say no.'

'Of course not,' said the Major. He was stalling for time as he counted up his options. He wondered briefly whether Roger and he could get through the day without having to acknowledge each other. He then considered the advantages of saying nothing now and then acting surprised to meet Roger on the day, but dismissed the idea since Roger could not be relied upon to supply a dignified response to such a fiction.

'I wanted to ask Gertrude about adding another person, but I believe only a certain number of guns can be accommodated,' said Roger. 'I thought it wasn't polite to press them.' He blushed and the Major saw with some wonder that embarrassment about one's relations went both up and down the generations. He was mortified at the thought of Roger waving a shotgun around, and for just an instant he saw himself explaining a dead peacock on the lawn. However, the Major accepted the futility of trying to hide his connection with Roger. He would just have to keep an eye on him.

'Oh, no need to worry about me,' said the Major finally. 'My old friend Dagenham asked me some time ago to come and help him beef up the line.' He paused for greatest effect. 'Said we needed some old hands to show you London chaps how it's done.'

'That's wonderful,' said Sandy. 'I'm so glad it all worked out.' She stood up, adding, 'Excuse me,' and gave the vague wave which seemed to the Major to be the universal female signal that a moment will be taken to freshen up.

'I'm looking forward to giving the old Churchills a good day's work,' said the Major, also standing as Sandy left the room. 'You should stick with me, Roger, and that way I can toss a few extra birds in your bag if you need them.' Roger, as he closed the door behind Sandy, looked sick to his stomach, and the Major felt he might have gone too far. His son had never been able to stand up to much of a ribbing.

'Actually, there's an American chap who's interested in buying them and I'm going to show them off as best I can,' he said.

'Are you really going to sell them?' asked Roger, looking instantly more cheerful. 'That's excellent news. Jemima was starting to get worried that you'd run off with them.'

'You've been talking to Jemima behind my back?'

'Oh, it's not like that,' said Roger. 'It's more—since the funeral, you know, we thought it might be useful to keep in touch since we both have parents to take care of. She has her mother to worry about, and I—well, you seem all right now, but then so did Uncle Bertie. You never know when I might have to jump in and take care of things.'

'I am rendered speechless with gratitude by your concern,' said the Major.

'You're being sarcastic,' said Roger.

'You're being mercenary,' said the Major.

'Dad, that's not fair,' said Roger. 'I'm not like Jemima.'

'Oh, really?' said the Major.

'Look, all I'm asking for is that when you sell the guns, you consider giving me a bit of a windfall you don't even need,' continued Roger. 'You have no idea how expensive it is to be a success in the city. The clothes, the restaurants, the weekend house parties—you have to invest to get ahead these days, and quite frankly it's embarrassing just to try and keep up with Sandy.' He sat down and his shoulders slumped. For a moment he looked like a rumpled teenager.

'Perhaps you need to moderate your expectations a little,' said the Major, genuinely concerned. 'Life isn't all about flashy parties and meeting rich people.'

'That's what they tell the people they don't invite,' said Roger, sunk in gloom.

'I would never attend a function to which I had found it necessary to inveigle an invitation,' said the Major. As he said this, he reassured himself that he had done nothing to precipitate his own invitation. It had been, he remembered, an entirely spontaneous gesture from Lord Dagenham.

Sandy came back down the stairs and they ceased speaking. A hint of fresh cologne and lipstick brightened the air in the room and the Major made a note to open the windows more often. He worked hard at keeping the place clean and polished but perhaps, he thought, a certain stale quality was inevitable when one lived alone.

'We should be going if we want to speak to the painters before they leave,' said Sandy.

'You're right,' said Roger.

'You told Abdul Wahid you would probably be staying here?' said the Major. Roger and Sandy traded a guarded look. The Major felt like a small boy whose parents are trying to shield him from grown-up conversation.

'I did explain to him that we would need a place to stay while the cottage is under renovation,' said Roger. 'He quite understood that it wouldn't be convenient having us all here, what with the shared bathrooms and so on.'

'You are completely right,' said the Major. 'As I told Abdul Wahid, you and Sandy will be much happier staying down at the pub.'

'Hang on a minute,' said Roger.

'You must ask the landlord for the blue room, my dear,' said the Major to Sandy. 'It has a four-poster and, I believe, one of those whirlpool tubs of which you Americans are so fond.'

'I'm not staying at the damn pub,' said Roger, his face a picture of outrage. It was not noble, of course, to take pleasure in the discomfort of one's own flesh and blood, but Roger had been altogether too forward and needed a firm check.

'It is true that the whirlpool tub does reverberate through the public end of the bar,' said the Major, as if pondering the subject deeply. He noticed that Sandy was having a hard time keeping a straight face. Laughter tweaked at her lips, and her eyes had taken his measure.

'You can't expect my fiancée to share this house with some strange shopkeeper's assistant from Pakistan,' Roger spluttered.

'I quite understand,' the Major said. 'Unfortunately, I had already invited him to stay and I'm afraid it's not possible to throw him out because my son does not approve,'

'For all we know, he could be a terrorist,' said Roger.

'Oh, for God's sake, Roger, go and see your painters before they have to rush off to touch up the Vatican or whatever,' said the Major, in a harsher tone than he had intended.

He took the tea tray back to the kitchen. There was a muffled argument in the living room and then Roger stuck his head around the kitchen door to say that he and Sandy were off but would indeed be back to stay the night. The Major only nodded in reply.

He was sad at his own outburst. He wanted to feel the kind of close bond with Roger that Nancy had enjoyed. The truth was that now, without his wife to negotiate the space that they occupied as a family, he and Roger seemed to have little common ground. If there had been no bond of blood, the Major felt now, he and Roger would have little reason to continue to know each other at all. He sat at the table and felt the weight of this admission hang about his shoulders like a heavy, wet coat. In the shrunken world, without Nancy, without Bertie, it seemed very sad to be indifferent to one's own son.

Chapter Fourteen

What's this plastic thing for?' asked George, handing the Major an intricately die-cut disc that had come with the kite purchased especially for the afternoon's expedition.

'Probably just part of the packaging,' said the Major, who had improvised as well as he could, given that the assembly instructions were in Chinese. The cheap purple and green kite fluttered against his hand. He released the rudimentary catch on the spool and handed it to George. 'Ready to take it up?'

George took the spool and began to walk backward, away from the Major, across the rabbit-cropped grass. The park, busy with families on this fine Sunday, occupied the whole top of the broad headland to the west of the town. It was good for kites but not so good for balls, many of which were at that very moment careening downhill where the land tilted sharply, on one side dipping to the weald and on the other to the edge of the high cliff. Signs warned people that the white chalk face was always being slivered away by the action of the sea and the weather. Small crosses and bunches of dead flowers made cryptic reference to the many people every year who chose this spot to plunge to their deaths on the jagged rocks below. Every mother in the park seemed to feel the need to call to her children to stay away from danger. It formed a background chorus louder than the sea.

'Eddie, come away from the edge!' shouted a woman from a neighbouring bench. Her son was spinning his arms like a windmill as he ran about after a small dog. 'Eddie, I'm warning you.' Yet she did not bother to get up from the bench, where she was engaged in eating a very large sandwich.

'If they are so afraid for their children, why did they insist on coming?' asked the Major, handing Mrs Ali the kite to launch. 'Are you ready, George?'

'Ready!' said George. Mrs Ali tossed the kite into the air, where it hovered for a fluttering moment and then, to the Major's immense satisfaction, soared into the sky.

'That's the ticket,' called the Major as George ran backward, unspooling more line. 'More line, George, more line.'

'Don't go too far, George,' called Mrs Ali in a sudden anxiety. Then she clapped a hand over her mouth and turned wide eyes of apology to the Major.

'Not you as well?' he said.

'I'm afraid it must be a trick of nature,' she said, laughing. 'The universal bond between all women and the children in their care.'

'More like a universal hysteria,' said the Major. 'It's hundreds of yards to the edge.'

'Do you not find it even the slightest bit disorienting?' asked Mrs Ali, surveying the smooth grass running away to the abrupt drop-off. 'I can almost feel the earth spinning beneath my feet.'

'That's the power of it,' said the Major. 'Draws people here.' He looked out at the green cliff and the enormous bowl of sky and sea and reached for the appropriate quotation.

'Clean of officious fence or hedge,
Half-wild and wholly tame,
The wise turf cloaks the white cliff-edge
As when the Romans came.'

'I expect Roman women also cried out to their children to be careful,' said Mrs Ali. 'Is that Kipling?'

'It is,' said the Major, pulling a small red volume of poetry from his pocket. 'It's called "Sussex" and I was hoping to share it with you over our tea today.' She had called to cancel their planned reading, explaining that she had volunteered to take little George out for the afternoon. The Major, refusing to be disappointed for a second Sunday, found himself asking if he might come along.

'How amazing it is that we ever planned to read it indoors,' said Mrs Ali. 'It has so much more power out here where it was made.'

'Then perhaps we should walk about after Master George, and I might read you the rest of it?' said the Major.

When the poetry had been read, the kite had been tossed several dozen times into the air, and George had run until his small legs were exhausted, the Major suggested that they get some tea. They settled, with tea and a plate of cakes, at a sheltered table on the terrace of the pub that was absurdly built right on the headland. Mrs Ali's cheeks were warm from the walking, but she looked a little drawn. George swallowed a bun almost whole and drank a rather flat glass of lemonade before wandering off to view a puppy being walked nearby.

'My nephew suggested we come here,' said Mrs Ali. 'He says he walks up here all the time after mosque because here he can imagine that Mecca is just over the horizon.'

'I think France might be in the way,' said the Major, squinting at the horizon and trying to imagine the correct bearing for Saudi Arabia. 'But on a spiritual level, there is something about the edge of the land that does make one feel closer to God. A sobering sense of one's own smallness, I think.'

'I was very glad he wanted George to see it,' she said. 'I think it is a good sign, don't you?' The Major thought it might have been a better sign had the young man shown George the place himself, but he did not want to spoil Mrs Ali's afternoon.

'I must thank you again for putting up my nephew,' she said. 'It has allowed George and Amina to be with us and has allowed Abdul Wahid to get to know his son.'

The Major tested the colour of the tea and gave the pot a dissatisfied stir. 'I am glad he doesn't object to Amina being in the shop.'

'A shop is a curious thing,' said Mrs Ali. 'I have always found it to be a tiny free space in a world with many limits.'

'More complicated, then, than just selling eggs and working through the important holidays?'

'A place of compromise,' she added. 'It's very hard to put into words.'

'Compromises are often built on their being unspoken,' said the Major. 'I think I understand you perfectly.'

'I could never talk to my nephew about it,' she said. 'Yet I will whisper to you that I pin my hopes on the space of the shop allowing Abdul Wahid to see where his real duty lies.'

'You believe he loves her?' asked the Major.

'I know that they were very much in love before,' she said. 'I also know that the family has gone to many lengths to separate them.'

'He seems to believe that despite your good offices, your late husband's family will never accept Amina,' he said as he poured the tea. Mrs Ali accepted a cup of tea, her fingertips meeting his on the edge of the saucer. The Major felt a skip in his veins that could only be happiness. She seemed anxious at his question and hesitated, drinking some tea and carefully placing her cup back on the tea tray before answering.

'I am afraid that I have been very selfish,' she said.

'I cannot allow you to suggest such a thing,' said the Major.

'It is true,' she said. 'I have told Abdul Wahid that I have written to the family—and I have written.' Here she paused again. She wrapped her arms around her chest and gazed out at the vista. She did not look at the Major as she continued. 'But each day I have been somehow too busy to post the letter.' She fumbled in a small handbag and withdrew a thin envelope, very creased and folded. Turning to him, she held it out. The Major took it gently from her fingers.

'A letter unposted is a heavy burden,' he said.

'Each day that passes I feel heavier,' she said. 'I feel the weight of knowing things cannot go on as they are. But at the same time, each day I feel a lightness I had almost forgotten.' She gazed at George, who was crouched on the grass, talking to the boy with the puppy while the puppy jumped at both their knees.

'How long can you continue to postpone the necessary conversation?'

'I was hoping you might reassure me that I can postpone it forever,' she said. 'I am afraid that the letter will undo all.' She turned to him, a wistful smile hovering on her lips.

'My dear Mrs Ali . . .'

'I am afraid everything will be taken from me,' she said in a quiet voice. The Major felt a desire to throw the offending letter into the nearby rubbish bin along with the paper plates and sticky ice cream wrappers.

'If only it were possible to ignore them entirely,' he said.

'That will not do,' said Mrs Ali. 'I know my nephew, who has his own doubts to overcome, will not be able to proceed without his father's blessing.' She took the envelope back and pushed it into her handbag again. 'Perhaps we will see a postbox on our way home.'

'I hope your letter will meet with a more friendly reaction than you imagine,' said the Major.

'My faith does permit the occasional miracle,' said Mrs Ali. 'My hope is that they will see they have been unjust. Of course, if that fails to work, I am prepared to bargain on a more temporal level.'

'One really shouldn't have to bargain with one's family like a used-car salesman.' The Major sighed. With acknowledged cowardice, he had ignored two phone calls from Marjorie, finally finding a use for the incoming number display on his phone. He felt that he could no more hold off an inevitable confrontation about the guns than frail Mrs Ali could hope to hold back the fury of her family.

'Someone must stand up for George,' she said. 'It is not permitted in Islam to let a child carry the weight of a parent's shame on his shoulders. He had to witness his grandmother's funeral shunned by all but a handful of people. It was a great dishonour.'

'Terrible,' said the Major.

'I am afraid my husband's family may have increased the shame by spreading certain untruths,' said Mrs Ali. 'I know Abdul Wahid understands this, and I believe it will help him decide to put things right.'

'He does seem fond of her and the boy,' said the Major.

'I am glad that you say that,' said Mrs Ali. 'I was hoping you might talk to him for me. I think he needs a man's perspective on this.'

'It's not really my place,' began the Major, horrified at the thought of talking about such intimate matters. He would not have been able to broach such a subject with his own son, let alone the stubborn and reticent young man currently using his guest room.

'With your military background, you understand better than most men the concept of honour and pride,' said Mrs Ali. 'In the end, I am a woman and I would throw away every shred of pride to keep this little boy with me. Abdul Wahid knows this and therefore mistrusts my ability to see his point of view.'

'I'm not an expert on the faith behind his sense of duty,' said the Major. 'I could not instruct him.' Yet he felt his opposition melting under the warm satisfaction of hearing Mrs Ali's compliment.

'I ask you only to talk to him as one honourable man to another,' said Mrs Ali. 'Abdul Wahid is still exploring his relationship to his faith. We all pick and choose and make our religion our own, do we not?'

'I can't imagine the various ayatollahs or the Archbishop of Canterbury agreeing with you,' said the Major. 'I believe you are being unorthodox.'

'I am being realistic,' said Mrs Ali.

'I had no idea shopkeepers were so heretical,' said the Major. 'I am quite astonished.'

'Will you talk to him for me?' she asked, her brown eyes unwavering.

'I will do anything you ask,' he said. He read gratitude in her face. He wondered if he might also be seeing some happiness. He turned away and made himself busy poking at a large weed with the tip of his stick as he added, 'You must know that I am entirely yours to command.'

'I see chivalry lives on,' she said.

'As long as there's no jousting involved, I'm your knight,' he said.

Just as the Major was thinking that he could not remember, in recent years, a more satisfying Sunday afternoon, a woman walked across the grass below them and pulled the small boy and his puppy away from George. They moved off toward the car park as if to leave, but a couple of hundred feet away she stopped and shook the boy by the arm, her angry face close to his as she spoke to him. The boy was then released again to run with his dog. George, who had stood up and watched as they walked away, now came slowly back to the table with his shoulders hunched.

'What happened, George?' said Mrs Ali. 'Was that woman rude to you?' George shrugged.

'Speak up, now,' said the Major, trying to keep his voice from being too gruff. 'What's the matter?'

'Nothing,' said George. He sighed. 'His mum just said he wasn't allowed to play with me.'

'The ignorance of some people,' said the Major, half-rising from his seat. He saw now that it was the woman who had been screaming earlier, the mother of Eddie. He would have bounded after her only she was very large and, though a slow and lumbering woman, was likely to be belligerent.

'I'm sorry, George,' said Mrs Ali. She placed a hand on the Major's arm as if to restrain him and the Major sank back onto his seat.

'Back home no one plays with me, either.'

'Surely you must have many friends,' said the Major. 'Fine young men just like you?'

George gave him a pitying glance, as if he himself were the old man, and the Major an ignorant child. 'If you have a mum but not a dad, they don't play with you,' he explained. 'Can I have another bun?' The Major was so stunned he passed the plate without thinking. It was only as George sank his face into the icing that the Major remembered how he had never allowed his own son more than a single treat at tea and had sometimes, at suitably random intervals, made him do with no treats at all in order to avoid spoiling him. In this case, another cake seemed the only remedy to hand.

'Oh, George, your mother and your aunt Noreen love you so much, and your nanni loved you very much,' said Mrs Ali, running around the table and falling to her knees on the slightly dirty concrete to wrap her arms around the boy. 'And I love you very much as well.' She kissed his face and stroked his hair while George squirmed and tried to keep the bun from tangling in her long hair. 'You mustn't lose sight of that when people are cruel.'

'You seem like a very intelligent little chap,' said the Major as Mrs Ali released George from her hugs. The boy looked with some suspicion at the Major, who decided not to offer the 'sticks and stones' advice he had intended but instead reached toward George's dirty, sticky hand and said, 'I would be honoured if you would consider counting me as a friend.'

'Okay,' said George, shaking hands. 'But what else can you play besides kites?' Mrs Ali laughed while the Major did his best to maintain a grave and thoughtful expression.

'Have you ever played chess?' he asked. 'I could teach you, I suppose.'

❧ ❧ ❧

On the way home, George slept in the backseat, tired from all the running and filled with cake. The Major drove as scenic a route as possible; Mrs Ali seemed entranced by the high banks and snug cottages of the less-travelled lanes. She spotted an old round postbox at a crossroads and he stopped the car so she could post her letter. He held his breath as she stood for a moment, letter in hand, her head curved in thought. He had never imagined so clearly the consequences of mailing a letter—the impossibility of retrieving it from the iron mouth of the box; the inevitability of its steady progress through the postal system; the passing from bag to bag and postman to postman until a lone man in a van pulls up to the door and pushes a small pile through the letterbox. It seemed suddenly horrible that one's words could not be taken back, one's thoughts allowed none of the remediation of speaking face to face. As she dropped the letter in the box, all the sun seemed to drain out of the afternoon.

ᘈ ᘉ ᘊ

The question of how to begin a casual conversation designed to persuade a young man to accept a stranger's guidance on life-altering decisions plagued the Major for several days. There seemed to be few opportunities, even if one could find the appropriate words. Abdul Wahid rose very early and left without so much as a cup of tea. He returned late most days, having already had his dinner at the shop, and slipped up at once to his room where he read from his small stack of religious books. His arrival home was often signalled only by a small token of thanks left on the kitchen table: a parchment paper twist of some new tea blend, a package of plain shortbread, a bag of apples. The only strangeness was the sight of his empty shoes lined up at night by the back door and the faint hint of a lime-based aftershave lingering in the bathroom, which Abdul Wahid left wiped and spotless each morning. The Major despaired of finding an opening and in order to fulfil his promise to Mrs Ali, he began to keep the teapot primed and a kettle warm on the stove, while he lurked about in his own scullery hoping to waylay his guest coming through the back door.

One evening when it was raining heavily, the Major found his chance. Abdul Wahid was delayed in the back hall by the need to shake out and hang up his dripping rain jacket. His shoes must have been soaked through, for the Major heard him stuffing them with crumpled newspaper from the recycling basket. Transferring the kettle to a hotter plate on the Aga, the Major set the teapot in the middle of the table and put out two large mugs.

'Won't you join me in a mug of hot tea?' he asked as Abdul Wahid entered the kitchen. 'It's a rough night out there.'

'I do not want to give you any trouble, Major,' said Abdul Wahid, hesitating. He seemed to be shivering from the cold. The thin sweater he wore over his shirt was hardly adequate, thought the Major. 'Your hospitality is already more than I deserve.'

'You would be doing me a great favour, sitting down for a while,' said the Major. 'I've been by myself all day today and I could use the company.' He poked up the fire as if the matter were already settled. As he bent over the smoking logs, he realised that his suggestion of loneliness was true. Despite his attempts to maintain a vigorous structure of errands, golf games, visits, and meetings, there were sometimes days like this one, filled with rain and touched with a gnawing sense of parts missing from life. When the slick mud ran in the flower beds and the clouds smothered the light, he missed his wife. He even missed Roger and how the house used to ring to the kicking shoes of grubby boys playing up and down the stairs. He was sorry now for the many times he had rebuked Roger and his friends—he had underrated the joy in their rowdiness.

Abdul Wahid took a seat at the kitchen table and accepted a cup of tea. 'Thanks. It's pretty damp out tonight.'

'Yes, not too nice,' agreed the Major, wondering if they would be stuck for long in the inevitable loop of weather talk.

'It is funny that you are tired of spending the day alone,' said Abdul Wahid. 'While I am tired of being around a busy shop filled with chattering people all day. I would love to trade with you and have time to myself for reading and for thinking.'

'Don't rush to trade places with an old man,' said the Major. 'Youth is a wonderful time of vigour and action. For possibilities, and for collecting friends and experiences.'

'I miss being a student,' said Abdul Wahid. 'I miss the passionate discussions with my friends, and most of all the hours among the books.'

'Life does often get in the way of one's reading,' agreed the Major. They drank their tea in silence as the logs cracked and spat in the flames of the fireplace.

'I am sorry to leave you to your solitary days, Major, but I have decided to move back to the shop,' said Abdul Wahid at length. 'I have burdened you with my presence too long.'

'Are you sure?' asked the Major. 'You really are welcome to stay on here. Roger and Sandy have no real intention of visiting more than a few nights, I guarantee, and you are welcome to any books on my shelves.'

'Thank you, Major, but I have decided to live in a small outbuilding we have behind the store,' said Abdul Wahid. 'It has a toilet and a small window. Once I have moved out what appears to be a dead tractor and several chicken coops, I believe a fresh coat of paint will transform it into a room just like the one I had at university. It will be a sanctuary until things are decided.'

'You haven't yet heard from your family, then,' said the Major.

'A letter has come,' replied Abdul Wahid.

'Ah,' said the Major. Abdul Wahid stared into the fire and said nothing, so, after an interminable pause, the Major added: 'Good news, I hope?'

'It appears the moral objections may be overcome,' said Abdul Wahid. He screwed his face up, as if tasting something sour.

'Well, that's wonderful,' said the Major. 'Isn't it?' He was puzzled by the fact that the young man seemed so unhappy. 'Soon you can be with your son, and maybe even live in the same house instead of the chicken shed.'

Abdul Wahid got up and walked over to the mantelpiece, where he squatted on his heels and held his palms close to the flames.

'I do not think you would be so quick to approve if it was your son,' he said. The Major frowned as he tried to quell the immediate recognition that the young man was right. He fumbled for a reply that would be true but also helpful. 'I do not mean to offend you,' added Abdul Wahid.

'Not at all,' said the Major. 'You are not wrong—at least, in the abstract. I would be unhappy to think of my son becoming entangled in such a way and many people, including myself, may be guilty of a certain smug feeling that it would never happen in our families.'

'I thought so,' said Abdul Wahid with a grimace.

'Now, don't you get offended, either,' said the Major. 'What I'm trying to say is that I think that is how everyone feels in the abstract. But then life hands you something concrete—something concrete like little George—and abstracts have to go out the window.'

'I did not expect them to agree with anything my aunt proposed,' he said. 'I expected them to make my decision easy.'

'I had no idea that you didn't want to marry Amina,' said the Major. He put down his tea mug, the better to emphasise his attention to the conversation. 'I seem to have jumped to a conclusion that was not there.'

'It's not that I don't want to marry her,' said Abdul Wahid, returning to his chair. He tented his fingertips and blew on them softly. 'In her presence, I'm lost to her. She has such eyes. And then she was always so funny and wild. She is like a streak of light, or maybe a blow to the head.' He smiled, as if remembering a particular blow.

'That sounds suspiciously like love to me,' said the Major.

'We are not expected to marry for love, Major,' said Abdul Wahid. 'I do not wish to be one of those men who bends and shapes the rules of his religion like a cheap basket to justify his comfortable life and to satisfy every bodily desire.'

'But your family has given permission?' said the Major. 'You have been given a chance.' Abdul Wahid looked at him, and the Major was concerned to see a gaunt misery in his face.

'I do not want to be the cause of my family stooping to hypocrisy,' he said. 'They took me away from her because of faith. I didn't like it, but I understood and I forgave them. Now I fear they withdraw their objection in order to secure financial advantage.'

'Your aunt has offered to support the union,' said the Major.

'If faith is worth no more than the price of a small shop in an ugly village, what is the purpose of my life—of any life?' said Abdul Wahid. He slumped in his chair.

'She will give up the shop,' said the Major. He did not phrase it as a question, because he already knew the answer. That Abdul Wahid should slight, in one sentence, both the sacrifice of his aunt and the pastoral beauty of Edgecombe St Mary incensed the Major to the point of stuttering. He peered for a long time at Abdul Wahid and saw him once more as a sour-faced, objectionable young man.

'She will give up the shop, which is a huge and generous gift from her,' added Abdul Wahid, spreading his hands in a gesture of conciliation. 'There is only the question of where she will live that is to be determined.' He sighed. 'But what will I give up in accepting?'

'Your absolute arrogance might be a welcome start,' said the Major. He could not prevent the caustic anger in his words. Abdul Wahid widened his eyes and the Major was maliciously happy to have shocked him.

'I don't understand,' he said, frowning.

'Look here, it's all very tidy and convenient to see the world in black and white,' said the Major, trying to soften his tone slightly. 'It's a particular passion of young men eager to sweep away their dusty elders.' He stopped to organise his thoughts into some statement short enough for a youthful attention span. 'However, philosophical rigidity is usually combined with a complete lack of education or real-world experience, and it is often augmented with strange haircuts and an aversion to bathing. Not in your case, of course—you are very neat.' Abdul Wahid looked confused, which was an improvement over the frown.

'You are very strange,' he said. 'Are you saying it is wrong, stupid, to try to live a life of faith?'

'No, I think it is admirable,' said the Major. 'But I think a life of faith must start with remembering that humility is the first virtue before God.'

'I live as simply as I can,' said Abdul Wahid.

'I have admired that about you, and it has been refreshing to my own spirit to see a young man who is not consumed by material wants.' As he said this, the thought of Roger and his shiny ambition made a bitter taste in his mouth. 'I am just asking you to consider, and only to consider, whether your ideas come from as humble a place as your daily routine.'

Abdul Wahid looked at the Major with some amusement now dancing in his eyes. He gave another of his short, barking laughs.

'Major, how many centuries must we listen to the British telling us to be humble?'

'That's not what I meant at all,' said the Major, horrified.

'I'm only joking,' said Abdul Wahid. 'You are a wise man, Major, and I will consider your advice with great care—and humility.' He finished his tea and rose from the table to go to his room. 'But I must ask you, do you really understand what it means to be in love with an unsuitable woman?'

'My dear boy,' said the Major. 'Is there really any other kind?'

Chapter Fifteen

The sun was red, haloed in mist and barely showing over the hedgerows as the Major crunched across the frost-stiffened grass. He had elected to walk up through the fields to the manor house, intending to arrive before the rest of the shooting party. In a dark holly bush a robin was tweedling a solo to the watercolour hills.

The Major had waited too long for the occasion to hurry its beginning or to arrive in a noisy clatter of smoking exhaust and splattered gravel. It was not that he feared that his Rover would make an inadequate impression among the glittering luxury vehicles and four-by-fours of a London crowd. He felt no shallow envy. He simply preferred to enjoy the ritual of the walk. He felt the balance of his guns, cracked open and cradled in the crook of his elbow. Bertie's gun was now oiled to a deep shine, almost a match for his own gun's patina. He enjoyed the creaking seams of his old shooting coat and the weight of his pockets. The waxed cotton bulged with brass cartridges laden with steel shot. An old game bag draped its strap and buckle across his chest and flopped on one hip. It would probably not hold game today—Dagenham would doubtless have the ducks retrieved and carried for the guns by the beaters—but it was satisfying to buckle it on, and the bag was a useful place to stash a new foil-wrapped bar of Kendal Mint Cake, his trademark snack at all the shoots he attended. The bar of mint-oil-flavoured compressed sugar, which he ordered by mail from the original company in Cumbria, was a tidy food and ideal for offering around, unlike the squashed ham sandwiches some of the farmers pulled from their bags and offered to tear apart with powder-stained fingers. He was sure there would be no squashed sandwiches or lukewarm tea today.

As he swung his boots over a stile and jumped a mud patch, he was sorry that Mrs Ali could not see him now, decked out as a hunter-gatherer. Kipling would have dressed in much the same manner, he thought, to hunt big game with Cecil Rhodes. He could almost see them, waiting ahead for him to catch up so they might gauge his opinion on Cecil's most recent difficulties in organising a new nation.

The Major immediately scolded himself for this momentary fancy. The age of great men, when a single mind of intelligence and vision might change the destiny of the world, was long gone. He had been born into a much smaller age, and no amount of daydreaming would change the facts. Neither would a pair of fine guns make anyone a bigger man, he reminded himself, resolving to remain humble all day despite the compliments he was bound to receive.

On the edge of what remained of the manor house parkland, he entered a short allée of elms, fuzzy with tangled branches, which constituted the truncated remains of what had once been a mile-long ride. It was clear they had not seen the services of an arborist in a decade. Underfoot, the grass was worn from sheep hooves and smelled of dung and moss. Between the trees, crude wire cages and a plastic contraption attached to a small generator bore evidence of the gamekeeper's duck-raising. The cages were empty now. They would be refilled with hand-raised eggs and chicks in the spring. The gamekeeper, who was also a general maintenance man for the house and grounds, was not to be seen. The Major was disappointed. He had hoped for a discussion about the state of this year's flock and the layout of the line today. He had entertained a mild thought that after such a talk, he might approach the main gravel courtyard with the gamekeeper in tow and so show the London types immediately that he was a local expert. A rustle in an overgrown wall of rhododendron revived his hopes, but as he assembled a smile and appropriate words of casual greeting, a small pale boy popped out of the hedge and stood staring transfixed at the Major's guns.

'Hullo, who are you then?' said the Major. He tried not to look pained by the boy's sloppy school uniform, which featured a frayed shirt collar, stringy tie, and a sweatshirt instead of a proper jumper or blazer. The boy looked about five or six and the Major remembered arguing with Nancy about sending Roger away to school at eleven. She would have had much to say, he thought, about this school and its tiny pupils. He spoke carefully to the boy. 'Not a good idea to be playing hide and seek when there's a shoot about to happen,' he said. 'Are you lost?'

The boy screamed. It was a scream like a power saw through corrugated iron. The Major almost dropped his guns in fright.

'I say, there's no call to go on so,' he said. The boy could not hear him over the roiling of his own howls. The Major stepped back but could not seem to get himself to walk away. The screaming boy seemed to skewer him on sound waves. Overhead, a cloud of ducks flew up like a feathered elevator straight into the sky. The pond was close and the boy's scream had launched the entire duck brigade aloft.

'Quiet, now,' said the Major, trying for a raised tone of calm authority. 'Let's not frighten the ducks.' The boy's face began to turn purple. The Major wondered whether he should make a run for the house but he feared the boy would follow.

'What's going on?' asked a familiar female voice from the other side of the hedge. After some rustling, Alice Pierce pushed her way through, a few twigs catching at the knobby orange and purple yarn flowers that made up an enormous woolly poncho. Alice's hair was partly controlled by a rolled scarf of brilliant green, and beneath the poncho the Major caught a glimpse of wide green trousers over scuffed black sheepskin boots. 'What are you doing here, Thomas?' she asked the boy as she took him gently by the arm. The boy clapped shut his mouth and pointed at the Major. Alice frowned.

'Thank goodness you're here, Alice,' said the Major. 'He just started screaming for no reason.'

'You don't think a strange man with a pair of huge shotguns might constitute a reason, then?' She raised an eyebrow in mock surprise, hugging the boy hard to her ample poncho. The boy whimpered under his breath and the Major hoped he was being comforted rather than suffocated. The Major was not about to argue with Alice. 'Why aren't you on the bus, Thomas?' she asked, and stroked his hair.

'I'm so very sorry, young man,' said the Major. 'I had no intention of frightening you.'

'I didn't know you'd be here, Major,' said Alice. She looked worried.

'You mean shooting?' asked the Major. 'I expect you don't approve?' Alice said nothing. She just frowned as if thinking something through.

'What are you doing here?' asked the Major. 'Are you chaperoning the children?'

'Not really,' said Alice, with an obvious vagueness. 'That is to say, I had better get Thomas back to Matron right away.'

There was a further rustling in the hedge and Lord Dagenham and the keeper popped out.

'What the hell was all the racket?' asked Dagenham.

'The Major here frightened Thomas with his guns,' said Alice. 'But it's all right now—we've made friends, haven't we, Thomas?' The boy peeked at the Major from under Alice's arm and stuck out his tongue.

'They were all supposed to be on the bus ten minutes ago,' said Dagenham. 'My guests are arriving now.'

'No harm done,' offered the Major.

'I'm sure it's not as easy as all that,' said Alice, drawing herself up. 'The children are all understandably upset this morning.'

'Good God, I'm giving them a trip to the bowling alley and an ice cream party on the pier,' said Dagenham. 'What on earth do they have to be upset about?' Alice narrowed her eyes in a way the Major recognised as being dangerous.

'They know about the ducks,' she whispered, leading the boy away. He went with her but the whimpering started again. 'They're young, but they're not stupid, you know,' she added in a louder voice.

'There'll be duck soup for dinner,' said Dagenham under his breath. Alice gave him a look of pure poison as she and the boy disappeared through the hedge again. 'Thank God it was only you, Major. Could have been rather embarrassing otherwise.'

'Glad to have headed them off, then,' said the Major, deciding to take Dagenham's remark as a compliment.

'Thought it might be protesters from the damn "Save Our Village" picket line, down the road,' said Dagenham. 'Height of bad manners, throwing themselves in front of my guests' cars like that. I was afraid they were infiltrating the grounds.'

'I hope no one is getting hurt,' said the Major.

'Oh, no, quite a solid front grill on those limousines,' said Dagenham. 'Hardly a scratch.'

'Glad to hear it,' said the Major absently as he worried about whether Alice had been 'infiltrating' and what else she might be up to.

'Shall we get along up to the house?' said Dagenham. 'I'm hoping Morris's wife has it all aired out by now.' The gamekeeper, Morris, nodded his head.

'We started opening windows about five a.m.,' he said. 'Matron weren't too pleased but I told her, no one was never 'armed by a bit of fresh air'.

As they strode up toward the house, Dagenham added, 'I had no idea that fee-paying pupils would smell bad. I really thought the school would be preferable to a nursing home, but I was wrong.'

He sighed and stuffed his hands in his pockets. 'At least with the old dears you can keep them all sedated and no one cares. The kids are so awake. That art teacher is the worst. She encourages them. Always sticking up their pictures in the hallways. Sticky tape and drawing-pin holes all over the plaster. I told the Matron they ought to be learning something useful like Greek or Latin. I don't care if they're only five or six, it's never too early.' He paused and straightened his shoulders to take a deep breath of chill morning air. The Major felt queasy, thinking that he ought to say something in Alice's defence—at least to let it be known that she was a friend and neighbour. However, he could not think how to do this without offending Lord Dagenham. So he said nothing.

త ఆ ల

As the three men emerged into the courtyard of the mellow stone Georgian manor house, the Major realised he had obtained his wish. There was a small group of men, drinking coffee and munching on plates of food, and the last of the luxury cars were pulling in at the driveway just in time to see him arriving with both the keeper and the master of the house. The moment would have been perfect, but for two incongruities. One was the old green bus pulling away through the same gates, the windows filled with the glass-squashed faces of small, angry children. Alice Pierce strode along behind them, waving as she went. The other was the sight of Roger, emerging from someone's car dressed in a stiff new shooting jacket with a small tag still swinging from the hem. Roger did not appear to see his own father but busied himself greeting a second car full of guests. The Major gratefully decided not to see Roger, either; he had a vague hope that in the next half hour Roger's coat and moleskin breeches might at least develop a few respectable creases around the elbows and knees.

'Good morning, Major. You will step in and get a cup of tea and a bacon roll before we start, won't you?' The Major found Dagenham's niece at his elbow, looking slightly anxious. 'I'm afraid I rather overdid the light breakfast.' She pulled him into the lofty entrance hall, where a fire burning in the white marble fireplace could only lay an illusion of heat over the cold that rose from the black-and-white stone floor and travelled unimpeded in and out of the old thin panes of the vast windows. The room was empty of furniture save two immense carved wooden chairs, too heavy, or maybe just too tastelessly overwrought, to bother removing.

A buffet table to one side held a tray, which overflowed with pyramids of bacon rolls. A large oval platter of sausages and a basket of tumescent American-style muffins rounded out the 'light' fare. A huge tea samovar and several thermos jugs of coffee were arrayed as if waiting a crowd several times the size of the gathering party, which looked to number about twenty in all. The smell of damp tweed mingled with the not quite vanished smells of institutional cabbage and bleach. 'My uncle seems to think it's a bit lavish, given that there'll be a full breakfast after the shooting,' said Gertrude.

'They seem to be tucking in,' said the Major. Indeed, the remaining London bankers were filling up their plates as if they had not eaten in recent days. The Major wondered how they intended to swing a heavy gun barrel on such a full stomach; he accepted only a cup of tea and the smallest bacon roll he could find. As he savoured his roll, a cream-coloured Bentley pulled up at the open door and disgorged Ferguson, the American.

The Major ceased to chew as he took in the sight of Ferguson shaking hands with some people on the steps. The American was dressed in a shooting jacket of a tartan with which the Major was unfamiliar. Blinding puce, crossed with lines of green and orange, the wool fabric itself was of a thickness more akin to an army blanket than to single tweed. With this the American wore reddish breeches and cream stockings tucked into shiny new boots. He wore a flat shooting cap in too bright a green and a yellow cravat tucked into a cream silk shirt. He resembled a circus barker, thought the Major, or a down-at-heels actor playing a country squire in a summer stock revival of an Oscar Wilde play. He was shadowed by a pale young chap in impeccably rumpled clothes but overly shiny boots who wore a fedora instead of a cap. There was a momentary hush as they swept into the room; even the bankers paused in their foraging to stare. Ferguson took off his cap and gave a general wave.

'Good morning, all,' he said. He spotted Dagenham and shook the cap at him like a dog showing off with a rabbit. 'I say, Double D, I hope that wasn't our ducks I just saw taking off over the Downs toward France?' There was a general murmur of laughter around the room as the assembled men seemed to make a group decision to ignore Ferguson's outlandish getup. There was a palpable easing of tension and a deliberate turning away, back into small groups of conversation. Dagenham was slightly slower than the rest to wipe the look of astonishment from his face as he shook Ferguson's hand and was loudly introduced to the young associate, a Mr Sterling. The Major took this to be a sign that good breeding still ran in Lord Dagenham's veins.

'So how d'you like the new duds?' Ferguson gave a half turn to allow a better view of his outfit. 'I'm reviving the old family tartan.'

'Very sporting,' said Dagenham. He had the grace to look a little sick.

'I know it's a bit much for a day of blasting duck in the south, but I wanted to check out the feel. I'm thinking of starting a whole line of technical shooting clothes.' He raised his arms to show stretchy green side panels that resembled a medical corset; the Major swallowed his tea the wrong way and began to choke.

'Ah, there's the Major,' said Ferguson, taking two large strides and sticking out his hand. The Major was forced to control his coughing, move the bacon roll to his saucer, and shake hands all in one move. 'You're old school, Major. Say, how do you like my neoprene sweat panels?' He smacked the Major on the back with his free hand.

'Do those assist one in swimming after the ducks, perhaps?' asked the Major.

'That's what I love about this guy, Sterling,' said Ferguson. 'His dry sense of humour. Major, you're an original.'

'Thank you,' said the Major, who could not help but be aware that there were many ears tuned in to the conversation. He felt himself being sized up and there was a vibration of approval in the room. He noticed Roger frowning at an inquiry from an older man. He hoped his son was being asked about the very distinguished gentleman who was laughing with Dagenham and Ferguson.

'Speaking of originals, how about giving me a look at those Churchills of yours?' said Ferguson.

'Oh, yes, we're all dying to get a look at the famous Pettigrew Churchills—gift of the grateful Maharajah,' said Dagenham. 'Shall we get started, gentlemen?'

The Major, who had dreamed of such a moment for years, found himself surrounded by the small crowd following him out to the temporary rack where they had left their guns. He was offered many hands to shake, not that he had any hope of distinguishing one wax-coated banker from the next, and at one point found himself shaking hands with his own son.

'Father, if you have a minute I want you to come and meet my boss, Norman Swithers,' said Roger, indicating a well-fed barrel of a man in rumpled shooting attire and promotional bank-logo socks who waved and managed to raise his pendulous jowls into a brief smile. Roger's usual air of condescension seemed to have been replaced by an attitude of genuine respect and the Major felt a moment of triumph as he allowed himself to be led over to meet the man. The moment was swiftly curtailed as Roger added, 'Why didn't you tell me you were so friendly with Frank Ferguson?'

꒰ ꒱ ꒱

A line had been established behind a waist-high hedge that ran along a narrow field to the east of the pond's edge. Thick woods shaded the opposite side of the field. The field itself provided an open flightway for the ducks to the small dewpond, which was almost circular and fringed on the western side by a straggly copse of trees and some dense, untended undergrowth. Behind this showed the tops of the elm allée where the ducklings were bred. As they walked down to the hedge, the Major could see that both the pond and the copse were thick with ducks. Green ropes divided the stands and, in what the Major considered rather a departure from the usual rules, the pulling of pegs from a bag had been forgone and instead names had been drawn in marker on wooden stakes to show each man his position. A folding stool and a crate for dead game were provided and young men, drawn from local farms, stood ready to act as loaders. As etiquette demanded, conversation ceased as the men came toward their spots.

'Good luck,' whispered a nervous Roger, from his own spot near the pond. The Major continued down the line toward the more favoured end. He was both gratified and annoyed to find his own name on a prime spot next to Ferguson's. He was not altogether pleased by the prospect of having Ferguson's beady eyes fixed on his Churchills all morning. He feared the American might be so crass as to ask to borrow them. The Major nodded at his red-haired young loader and silently passed him one gun and a box of cartridges.

'Comfy there, are you, Pettigrew?' asked Lord Dagenham in a low voice, clapping him on the back as he went by. 'Show our American friend how it's done, will you?'

As the assembled guns waited quietly, the Major inhaled cold air and felt his spirits soar. The grass of the field had begun to steam in the strengthening sunlight and the adrenaline of the impending sport began to sing in his extremities. He thought of Mrs Ali still tucked up in bed, dreaming behind her flowered curtains. She would awaken soon to the sound of the guns popping above the valley. He allowed himself to imagine striding into her shop at the end of the day, smelling of gunpowder and rain-misted leather, a magnificent rainbow-hued drake spilling from his game bag. It would be a primal offering of food from man to woman and a satisfyingly primitive declaration of intent. However, he mused, one could never be sure these days who would be offended by being handed a dead mallard bleeding from a breast full of tooth-breaking shot and sticky about the neck with dog saliva.

A loud rattling sound from behind the pond launched the ducks, almost vertically. It was Morris the keeper, thrashing the inside of an old oil barrel with a cricket bat—an alarm to which all the ducks had been trained to fly away. South behind the wood they disappeared, their cries, like old hinges, growing faint. The Major loaded cartridges in his gun. As he raised the gun to his shoulder, he felt as if the whole world were holding its breath. He took deliberate care to breathe out and in slowly, relaxing his shoulders and his fingers.

The sound of ducks began again in the distance and grew until a chorus of calls came in waves down the field, followed by the urgent flapping of wings. The whole squadron curved over the wood and began their descent along the field, heading for their home pond. The first gun barked and soon the entire line was popping at the blur of wings. The smell of powder hung over the line and small bundles began to thud into the rough grass. The Major lost his shot at a fat drake as Ferguson, having missed it, took an extra shot well out of his own line. The Major waited a fraction of a second for the next duck to come by. Sighting at the target he moved his gun smoothly into the lead, squeezed the trigger, absorbed the hard recoil into the shoulder as he followed through, and watched with satisfaction as the bird fell dead. Ferguson potted a second duck flying at the lowest limit of what any man would consider a sporting height. The Major swung his own gun high and squeezed off a difficult shot at a bird soaring up and slightly away. The bird fell on the far side of the field and the Major marked it before reaching back to hand his empty weapon to his loader and retrieve his second gun, Bertie's gun. His third shot missed but the gun worked smoothly and felt perfectly balanced and solid in his hands. He thought of how much these guns had meant to his father. He thought of Bertie and how the two of them had perhaps been as separated as these two guns in the last, wasted years. He tracked another duck but did not fire; whether because the flock was thinning out or because he was overcome with strong emotion, he could not say. Ferguson shot a straggler, who was flapping in slowly at the end of the line as if resigned to his own death.

A great splashing on the pond indicated that many ducks had made it through the barrage and were quarrelling over their options like politicians. In a matter of a few minutes, Morris would bang the oil can again and send them all aloft to repeat their suicidal mission. Meanwhile the hired youths went out to comb the field, enthusiastically competing to collect the small green and blue bodies and toss them over the hedge to the right gun. The red-haired youth gave the Major a wink as he tossed Ferguson's drake at the Major's feet.

'I think this was actually your kill,' he said, picking it up by the neck and handing it to the American.

'Afraid I poached your airspace on that one,' said Ferguson, his face alight with cheer as he took the dead bundle and tossed it in a crate. 'Couldn't bear to let him get the better of me.'

'Not a problem. We keep things fairly informal down here,' said the Major, who wished to be polite while also delivering a clear rebuke.

'You'll have to come shoot with me in Scotland and show them how to keep it loose,' said Ferguson. 'I've had my own ghillie scream at me in front of my guests for shooting over the line.'

'My father is very knowledgeable about shooting,' said Roger, appearing out of nowhere and sticking out his hand. 'Roger Pettigrew. Pleased to meet you.'

'Oh my God, there are multiple generations of you,' said Ferguson, shaking hands. 'How does anybody survive the onslaught of humour?'

'Oh, Roger claims he doesn't have any,' said the Major, checking and reloading his gun. He wiped his hands on the special rag he kept in the pocket of his shooting jacket. 'He thinks it detracts from a man's sense of importance.'

'I'm with Chelsea Equity Partners,' said Roger. 'We did an underwrite for you on the Thames effluent plant deal.'

'Oh, one of Crazy Norm's boys,' said Ferguson. The Major could not imagine what Roger's imposing and taciturn boss could possibly have done to be tagged with such an offensive nickname—unless, perhaps, he wore ridiculous socks every day. 'Didn't I meet you at the closing dinner?' continued Ferguson. 'You had a broken arm from your diving accident on the Great Barrier Reef.' The Major watched with miserable fascination as his son's face worked through several contortions that indicated he was inclined to accept Ferguson's suggestion.

'No, I wasn't actually at the dinner,' said Roger, honesty or fear of discovery winning out. 'But I'm hoping we get to do another one soon.' The Major breathed a sigh of relief.

'Well, I may have a deal for you sooner than you expect,' said Ferguson. He put an arm around Roger's shoulders. 'I think you're just the man to negotiate my next acquisition for me.'

'I am? I mean, whatever you need,' said Roger, beaming.

'The seller's pretty stubborn,' said Ferguson, grinning at the Major. 'I don't think it's just gonna be about the price with this one.' Roger beamed as if he was being put in charge of buying a small country and the Major was irritated by the both of them.

'I think Mr Ferguson is hoping you can persuade me to sell him my guns,' said the Major. 'I can assure you, Mr Ferguson, you'll have Roger's full cooperation on that score.'

'What—oh, of course.' Roger blushed. 'You're the American buyer.'

'I sure hope to be,' said Ferguson. 'Bring me home that deal, son, and I'll make sure Crazy Norm puts you in charge of his entire deal team.'

The cricket bat resounded in the barrel again and in the cacophony of fleeing ducks, men all along the line dropped their conversations abruptly.

'Of course, I would be delighted to help you with anything you need,' said Roger, hovering as Ferguson struggled to stuff cartridges into his gun.

'Roger, get to your position,' said the Major in a terse whisper. 'Talk later.'

'Oh, right, must bag another couple of ducks,' said Roger. The Major felt sure by his tone that he had failed to hit anything so far.

'Don't forget to get a lead on them,' said the Major and his son nodded, looking momentarily grateful for the advice as he hurried away.

'Eager youngster,' said Ferguson. 'Is he any kind of shot?'

'Bagged a prime bird on his first ever outing,' said the Major, mentally asking pardon of the long-dead woodpecker.

'My first shoot, I shot the guide in the butt,' said Ferguson. 'Cost my dad a fortune to shut the guy up and he took out every dime on my hide. My aim got much better real quick after that.'

'Here they come,' said the Major, privately wondering whether further spanking might have kept the American from potting other people's birds.

As the guns were raised and the squawking cloud of ducks wheeled in over the far trees, the Major caught sight of movement at the lower edge of his vision. Refocusing he saw, with horror, that small figures were emerging all along the woods and beginning to run, in stumbling fashion, across the field.

'Hold your fire, hold your fire!' shouted the Major. 'Children on the field!' Ferguson pulled his trigger and blasted a duck from the sky. One or two other shots rang out and there were screams from the field as uniformed children ducked and zigzagged. A separate group of people, some carrying signs that could not be read at such a distance, came marching, in a flanking action, from the direction of the copse. Alice Pierce, in all her orange and green glory, dropped her sign, broke from the group and began shouting and waving her hands as she ran toward the children.

'Hold your fire!' bellowed the Major, dropping his own gun and moving to push up Ferguson's gun barrel.

'What the hell!' said Ferguson, removing a large orange earplug.

'Children on the field!' shouted the Major.

233

'Hold fire,' called Morris the gamekeeper. He sent his dogs racing along the hedge, which seemed to catch the attention of the shooting party better than the mass of crying and running children.

'What the devil is going on?' asked Dagenham, from his place in the line. 'Morris, what on earth are they doing?' Morris gave a signal and the farmhands ran out and began trying to corral the children like unruly sheep. The Major saw a beefy young man tackle a skinny boy to the ground in none too gentle a fashion. Alice Pierce gave a cry of rage and threw herself on the young man like a woolly boulder. There was a general cry of outrage from the adults on the field who began chasing the farm youths, jabbing about with their signs like pitchforks. The dogs barked and dodged, snapping at ankles until Morris's piercing whistle called them away. The Major recognised the landlord from the pub, running closer to the hedge. He carried a sign that read 'Don't Destroy Us'. A woman the Major now recognised with horror as Grace, in a sensible coat and neat brown leather gloves, flapped at a young man with her sign, which read 'Peace, Not Progress'. Hanging back by the pond, removed from the general mêlée, stood two figures who the Major was almost sure were the Vicar and Daisy. They did not carry signs and they seemed to be arguing with each other.

'Goddamnit, the protesters are rioting,' said Ferguson. 'I'll call the security people.' He fumbled in his pocket and stuck an earpiece in his ear.

'Morris, tell those people they're trespassing,' cried Dagenham. 'I want them all arrested.'

'Maybe we should just shoot them,' said a banker somewhere down the line. A chorus of approval followed and one or two men levelled their guns at the field.

'Steady there, gentlemen,' said Morris, walking the hedge.

'Too many idiots wanting to shut down our way of life these days!' shouted a loud voice. Someone fired both barrels of his shotgun into the air. There were screams from the field as farm workers and protesters ceased battling to throw themselves to the ground.

The Major heard cheers and jeers from along the line of guns. The children continued to wander about, most of them crying. Thomas stood in the middle of the field. His continuous scream, like a siren, seemed to play havoc with the ducks' central nervous systems and they flapped up and down the field in haphazard, spiky loops.

'Are you quite mad?' shouted the Major. He laid down his gun and began to cross the green ropes, waving his hands and grabbing by the arm men who had not uncocked their guns. 'Put up your guns. Put up your guns.' He was dimly aware of Morris doing the same thing from the opposite side of the hedge.

'Watch who you're shoving,' said Swithers. The Major understood that it was he who had fired into the air. He gave him a withering look of contempt and Swithers had the grace to look slightly ashamed and lower his gun.

'For God's sake, man, there are women and children out there,' said the Major. 'Stand down, everyone.'

'No one's shooting at anybody,' said Roger with a faint derision designed to let everyone know he was not responsible for his father's actions. 'Only trying to put the wind up them a little bit. No need to be upset.'

'Morris, I want those trespassers arrested now,' said Dagenham, red in the face with anger and embarrassment. 'Don't just stand there waving, man, get it done.'

'Until these gentlemen put away their guns, I can't hardly be calling the constable,' said Morris. He turned to the field and gave a piercing whistle that caused the farm workers to lift their heads from the dirt. 'Come away, boys, leave them children alone now.'

'May I suggest a prompt retreat to the house,' said Ferguson, coming up to Lord Dagenham. 'Cool tempers and so on.'

'I'll be damned if I'll be forced to retreat from my own land,' said Dagenham. 'What the hell is Morris doing?' he added as the gamekeeper headed off to meet his men. The protesters sent up a feeble cheer and began to pick themselves up from the ground. The bankers gathered in a huddle, guns broken over their arms. There was a low murmur of discussion.

Helen Simonson

'If I may agree with Mr Ferguson, returning to the house would not be a question of retreat,' said the Major. 'Completely the moral high ground—keeping the peace and ensuring the safety of women and children and so on.'

'They killed our duckies,' came a wail from a child holding up a bloody carcass. The protesters abandoned their signs and set about trying to gather the children into a loose group. From the woods, the figure of their matron hurried into view, followed by a man who was quite possibly a bus driver.

'I really think your guests would be happier back at the house,' said the Major.

'He's right,' said Ferguson.

'Oh, very well,' said Lord Dagenham. 'Everybody down to the house, please. Breakfast is served.' The bankers trotted away, looking grateful for the excuse. The Major saw Roger was at the front of the departing crowd.

'Major Pettigrew, are you there?' came the distinct cry of Alice Pierce, who was resolutely advancing on the hedge waving a large and rather grubby white handkerchief. As she came closer the Major could see she was shivering.

'I'm here, Alice, and so is Lord Dagenham,' said the Major. 'You're quite safe.' Lord Dagenham gave a snort but did not contradict him.

'Oh, Major, the poor children,' she said. 'The matron says they escaped from the bus and she had no idea they were going to come here.'

'Oh, please,' said Lord Dagenham. 'I'll have you all brought up on negligence charges for letting innocent children join in such a riot.'

'Negligence?' said Alice. 'You shot at them.'

'We did not shoot at them,' said Dagenham. 'For God's sake, woman, they ran into the guns. Besides, you're all trespassing.'

'The children are not trespassing; they live here,' said Alice. Matron hurried up to say that they needed to get the children home right away and perhaps have the doctor in.

'We only stopped a moment for the picket line,' she said. 'Then Thomas started being sick and he threw up on the bus driver, so we got out for a minute and before we knew it, they just all ran from the bus and scattered and we didn't know where to find them.' She paused to breathe, holding a bony hand against her narrow chest. 'They always get attached to the ducks, what with feeding them every day and keeping the ducklings in the classroom under heat lamps, but we've never had a problem like this before.' Alice looked carefully neutral. The Major had no doubt as to who had used her art lessons to impart a few lessons in truth to the children.

'Someone put the little beggars up to it,' said the bus driver. 'Who's going to pay for my dry cleaning?'

'I'll help you get them back in the school,' said Alice to the matron.

'Can't have them back in the house. I'm hosting a breakfast for my guests,' said Dagenham, stepping between the matron and the path to the house. 'Put them back on the bus.'

The Major cleared his throat and caught Dagenham's eye. 'Might I suggest, Lord Dagenham, that you allow the children, under the good care of their matron, to take some food in their rooms and have a rest?'

'Oh, very well,' said Lord Dagenham. 'But for goodness' sake, Matron, take them in the back door and keep them quiet.'

'Let's go,' said Alice, and she and the matron went off to escort the children away down the lane to the house.

Dagenham was surveying the field, where the protesters had reorganised themselves into lines. They now began to advance on the hedge, chanting 'Down with Dagenham' and 'Don't pillage our village'. The Major found the latter rather interesting and wondered who had come up with it.

'Where are the damn police?' said Dagenham. 'I want these people arrested.'

'If it's all the same to you, Double D, better to keep the cops out of it,' said Ferguson. 'We don't need that kind of attention. Not that we're in the wrong, mind you, but the publicity isn't what the project needs right now.' He clapped Dagenham on the back. 'You gave us a dash of excitement. Now come and give us a good breakfast.'

'What do I do about them?' said Dagenham, nodding to where the protesters were slowly advancing on the hedge.

'Oh, let 'em protest and get it out of their system,' said Ferguson. 'My guys'll keep 'em away from the house and take plenty of pictures. Generally I find it best to let people think they're making a difference.'

'You sound as if you've had plenty of experience,' said the Major.

'Can't build a billion square feet these days without riling up the local hornets' nest,' said Ferguson, quite oblivious to the slight distaste in the Major's voice. 'I have a whole system of control, containment, and just-plain-make-it-go-away.'

'Major, you're a good man to have around,' said Dagenham. 'I think, Ferguson, that we should invite the Major to the private briefing after breakfast. You'll stay behind, won't you, Major?'

'I'd be more than happy to,' said the Major, puzzled as to what might be worthy of a briefing but enjoying a small expansion of pride in his chest at being invited.

'I'm with you on that,' said Ferguson. 'And maybe the Major'd like to have that bright son of his sit in, too?'

As they walked back to the house for breakfast, the cries of the protesters growing dim behind them, the Major's pleasure was diminished only by a small nagging worry that Alice Pierce would not approve. He did not usually seek Alice's approval for anything, so the feeling was new and entirely unexpected. They passed two security guards dressed in black and sitting in a large black four-by-four. Ferguson nodded and the idling car pulled across to block the path behind them. Containment of the locals had obviously begun.

The breakfast, eaten in an elegant parlour overlooking the terrace, was hearty and fuelled by large quantities of Bloody Marys and hot punch. On the long buffet table in the hall, the bacon rolls had been replaced with steaming globes containing bacon, sausage, and scrambled eggs, along with an entire side of smoked salmon and a marble board of cold meats and pungent cheeses. A giant baron of beef, surrounded by roast potatoes and individual Yorkshire puddings, sat in unapologetic dinner-menu magnificence under a heat lamp, being sliced in thick bloody pieces by a white-gloved server. A tower of cut fruit and an iced bowl of yogurt were going all but untouched.

Gertrude did not sit down to breakfast but stomped in and out checking on the service from the temporary waiters and shaking hands here and there; she whispered an apology to the Major for the beef being a bit pink. Only Lord Dagenham, however, complained, sending his underdone slice to the kitchen to be microwaved to a deep muddy brown. The bankers were so loud, outstripping each other in the length and ribaldry of their anecdotes, that there was no disturbance to the party at all from the presence of children overhead.

'Don't know why I bothered all these years, sending them off to the seaside at my expense,' said Dagenham over the trifle and chocolate éclairs that followed the breakfast buffet. 'Never knew I could just as well lock 'em in with a ham sandwich and a few crayons.' He laughed. 'Not that one minds being generous, of course. Only one's funds get so eroded by the government's constant demands these days.' Gertrude came in again and said, 'The villagers in the lane said thank you very much for the ham sandwiches and hot toddies, Uncle.'

'What the devil do you mean sending them food?' asked Dagenham.

'It was Roger Pettigrew, actually, who mentioned that it might be a nice gesture given the earlier confrontation,' she said, smiling down the table toward Roger. Roger raised a glass in her direction.

'Very shrewd operators those Pettigrews,' said Ferguson, winking at the Major.

'The constable thought it was a sign of great consideration,' added Gertrude. 'He's down there having a sandwich, and whoever called him is too polite to make any complaints while eating.'

'I told you Gertrude was a smart girl, Ferguson,' said Dagenham. 'Her mother, my sister, was a wonderful woman. No one loved her like I did.' He dabbed the corner of his eye with his napkin. The Major found this claim unexpected: it was well known in the village that May Dagenham had run off with a singer at a young age and had been largely disowned by the family. Gertrude displayed no obvious response to her uncle's remark, but her lips pressed together more firmly and the Major saw some flicker of expression in her eyes that might, he thought, be anger. In that expression, he saw again the gawky young girl who had hung around the lane, in her shapeless smock and leggings, waiting to bump into Roger. He looked down the table at his own son, who was regaling his colleagues with some exaggerated tale of how Swithers had pushed an insolent golf caddy into a water hazard. The Major found for once that he was more understanding of his son. He might be obnoxious, but his ambition demonstrated some spark of life; some refusal to bow before adversity. He thought it was preferable to Gertrude's quiet pain.

'Family is everything to you Brits,' said Ferguson. 'I'm still hoping to pick one up one of these days.' This occasioned more laughter around the table, and the breakfast party moved on to coffee and cigars.

After breakfast, which went so long as to bleed imperceptibly into lunch, most of the bankers left. Roger was saying goodbye to Gertrude when Swithers tapped him on the shoulder and indicated with a certain gruffness that he was to stay. Roger looked delighted and came over directly to the Major.

'I'm to stay for some hush-hush business with Ferguson,' he said. 'Just us senior bankers. I think he's going to unveil his next project.' His chest seemed to puff up and the Major thought he might pop with delight. 'Do you have a lift home?' added Roger.

'I'm invited to stay myself, thank you,' said the Major, careful to keep a neutral tone and not to claim credit for Roger's invitation in case it spoiled his son's obvious pleasure.

'Really? I can't imagine you'll understand much of it,' said Roger. 'Stay close to me and I'll try to explain some of the technical terms to you if you like.'

'That's exactly what I told Lord Dagenham and his American colleague when they asked me if you should be invited,' said the Major. He was slightly ashamed that his good intentions had been so quickly abandoned, but he told himself that the fleeting glance of dismay on his son's face was for Roger's own good. 'Shall we join the others?'

❧

The table in the middle of the old stone dairy wore a lumpy nylon cover, concealing something large and horizontal. There was barely room for the remaining guests to squeeze along the edges where, noticed the Major, one's backside immediately radiated with numbing cold from the stone walls. A smelly heater of indeterminate age burned fiercely in one corner but failed to do more than take off the chill.

'Sorry about the accommodations, gentlemen, but this is more private than the house,' said Lord Dagenham. 'With Mr Ferguson's approval—or should I say with the approval of Lord Ferguson, Laird of Loch Brae'—here Ferguson winked, and waved away the honour with a modesty that did not conceal his delight—'I will reveal to you at once the greatest advance in appropriate English countryside development since his Royal Highness's fully planned village at Poundbury.' He and Ferguson gripped the fabric cover and drew it gently off the table. 'I give you the Twenty-first Century Enclave at Edgecombe.'

What was revealed was a model of the village. The Major could see at once the folds and creases of the familiar landscape.

On one side, the model ended in an upsweep of downland, on the other it spread out into flat farm country. He could see the village green and the pub, which seemed to have been painted pale green and to have developed some carbuncular buildings on one side. He could see the lane leading up to Rose Lodge and even pick out his own garden, edged with fuzzy miniature hedges and furnished with a single architect's model tree. The village, however, seemed to have sprouted a few too many versions of Dagenham Manor. They produced a strange mirror effect, with almost identical manor houses, each sporting a long carriage drive, squares of formal gardens, stable blocks set round with miniature cars, and even a round pond, complete with silver paint surface and three mallards each. There was one such manor in the field behind his own house and another where the bus stop should have been. The bus stop and the main road seemed to have disappeared, removed to the edge of the model, where they disappeared into the farmland. The Major peered closer at the village green, looking for the shop. The plate glass window was gone and the shop, faintly recognisable behind a new bowed window and shutters of teal blue said, 'Harris Jones and Sons, Purveyors of Fine Comestibles and Patisserie'. A wicker basket of apples and an old iron dog cart containing pots of flowers stood at the new bubbled-glass door. A tea shop, a milliner's, and a tack and gun shop had been added. The Major felt frozen to the spot.

'In looking to the future of the Dagenham estate,' said Ferguson, 'my good friend Lord Dagenham asked me how he could possibly develop the site, in order to shore up the financial foundation of the estate, while also preserving the best of the English countryside.'

'I told him no shopping centres!' said Dagenham. The small cadre of bankers laughed.

'I could not answer that question until I had the chance to purchase Loch Brae Castle and experience for myself what it means to be a steward of the countryside.' Here Ferguson stopped to place a hand over his heart as if pledging allegiance. 'To be responsible for the lives of all those crofters and the land itself calling out for our protection.' Now the bankers seem puzzled, as if he had started speaking another language. 'So together we came up with a vision of the highest-end luxury development, unparalleled in the UK. Taking advantage of the availability of planning permission for new, architecturally significant country estates, my company, St James Homes, will build an entire village of prestigious manor homes and redevelop the village to service those estates.' As he paused to draw breath, the bankers bobbed and squatted to view the tabletop village from closer angles. This was not the easiest of gymnastic exercises after so large a meal, and there was much huffing and panting between questions. 'Where's the retail corridor?' 'Is there a motorway connection?' 'How's the cost per square foot compared to Tunbridge Wells?'

'Gentlemen, gentlemen—my colleague Mr Sterling and I will be glad to take all your questions.' He was smiling, as if the deal were already completed. 'I have info packets for all back in the house. May I suggest you finish looking at the model and we'll gather back in the house to talk numbers where it's warm?'

⟨ ⟩ ⟨

The Major lingered around the model after the last of the bankers had left. Alone with his village, he kept his hands inside his jacket pockets in order to resist the temptation to pluck off all the little manor houses and cover the empty spots by moving around some of the wire brush trees.

'Cigar?' He turned to find Dagenham at his side.

'Thank you,' he said, accepting a cigar and a light.

'You are, of course, appalled by all this,' said Dagenham squinting at the model like an architect's apprentice. He was so matter-of-fact that the Major was unable to say otherwise.

'I would say I did not expect it,' said the Major in a careful tone. 'It is quite—unexpected.'

'I saw your letter to the planning chappie,' said Dagenham. 'I told Ferguson, the Major will be appalled. If we can't convince him of what we're doing, we might as well give up.' The Major flushed, confused at being confronted with this evidence of his disloyalty.

'Fact is, I'm appalled myself,' said Dagenham. He bent down and touched a fingertip to a manor house, moving it slightly deeper into a stand of trees. He squinted again and stood back up, looking at the Major with a wry smile. 'Trouble is, even if I were prepared to bury myself here all year round I couldn't save the old place, not long term.' He walked to a window and opened it slightly, blowing smoke into the stable yard.

'I'm sorry,' said the Major.

'Estates like mine are in crisis all over the country,' said Dagenham. His sigh seemed to contain genuine defeat and the Major, watching his profile, saw his jaw tighten and his face grow sad. 'Can't keep up the places on the agricultural subsidies, can't even cut down one's own timber without permission, hunting is banned, and shooting is under attack from all sides as you just saw. We're forced to open tea shops or theme parks, to offer weekend tours to day-trippers or host rock festivals on the lawn. It's all sticky ice cream wrappers and car parking in the lower fields.'

'What about the National Trust?' asked the Major.

'Oh, yes, they used to be there, didn't they? Always hovering, waiting to take one's house away and leave one's heirs with a staff flat in the attic,' said Dagenham, with malice in his voice. 'Only now they want a cash endowment, too.' He paused and then added, 'I tell you, Major, we're in the final decades now of this war of attrition by the tax man. One day very soon the great country families will be wiped out—extinct as the dodo.'

'Britain will be the poorer for it,' said the Major.

'You are a man of great understanding, Major.' Dagenham clapped a hand on the Major's shoulder and looked more animated. 'You can't imagine how few people I can actually talk to about this.' He moved his hands to the edge of the model, where he set them wide apart and squinted down, like Churchill over a war map of Europe. 'You may be the only one who can help me explain this to the village.'

'I understand the difficulties, but I'm not sure I can explain how all this luxury development saves what you and I love,' said the Major. He looked over the model again and could not keep disdain from giving a curl to his lip. 'Won't people be tempted to insist that this is similar to the kind of new-money brashness that is killing England?' He wondered if he had managed to express himself politely enough.

'Ah, that's the beauty of my plan,' said Dagenham. 'This village will be available only to old money. I'm building a refuge for all the country families who are being forced out of their estates by the tax man and the politicians and the EU bureaucrats.'

'They're all coming to Edgecombe St Mary?' asked the Major. 'Why?'

'Because they have nowhere else left to go, don't you see?' said Dagenham. 'They are being driven off their own estates, and here I am offering them a place to call their own. A house and land where they will have other families to contribute to the upkeep, and a group of neighbours with shared values.' He pointed at a large new barn on the edge of one of the village farms. 'We'll have enough people to maintain a proper hunt kennel and a shared stables here,' he said. 'And over here, behind the existing school, we're going to found a small technical college where we'll teach the locals all the useful skills like masonry and plasterwork, stable management, hedging, butlering, and estate work. We'll train them for service jobs around the estates and have a ready pool of labour. Can you see it?' He straightened a tree by the village green. 'We'll get the kind of shops we really want in the village, and we'll set up an architectural committee to oversee all the exteriors. Get rid of that dreadful mini-mart-style shop frontage and add a proper chef at the pub—maybe get a Michelin star eventually.'

'What about the people who already live in the village?' asked the Major.

'We'll keep them all, of course,' said Dagenham. 'We want the authenticity.'

'What about Mrs Ali at the shop?' asked the Major. His face felt hot as he asked; he looked very hard at the model to disguise his feelings. Dagenham gave him a considering stare. The Major struggled to remain neutral but feared his eyes were crossed with the effort.

'You see, this is just where you might advise me, Major. You are closer to the people than I am and you could help me work out such nuances,' said Dagenham. 'We were looking for the right multicultural element, anyway, and I'm sure we could be flexible wherever you have—shall we say—an interest?' The Major recognised, with a lurch of disappointment, the universal suggestion of a quid pro quo. It was more subtle than some bribes he had refused in a career of overseas postings to places where such things were considered normal business, but there it lay nonetheless, like a pale viper. He wondered how much influence he might barter for his support and he could not help looking long and hard at the house squatting in the field behind Rose Lodge. 'I assure you none of this is set in stone yet,' continued Dagenham. He laughed and flipped one of the model houses onto its roof with a fingertip. 'Though when it is, it'll be the best white limestone from Lincolnshire.'

A clatter outside drew their attention to the doorway. A figure in green was just disappearing around the corner of the house. 'Who the devil was that, I wonder?' said Dagenham.

'Maybe one of Morris's farm lads cleaning up,' suggested the Major, who was fairly sure it had been Alice Pierce, minus the loud poncho. He had to control a chuckle at the thought that Alice's louder than usual getup had been a deliberate distraction and that underneath it she had worn drab green clothes suitable for slinking about like a commando in a foreign jungle.

'Damn hard trying to keep this huge model to ourselves.' Dagenham picked up the cover from the floor. 'Ferguson doesn't want to reveal anything before we have to.' The Major helped him and was grateful to watch the ruined village being swallowed in the tide of grey fabric.

'Is there really no other way?' asked the Major. Dagenham sighed.

'Maybe if Gertrude weren't so stubbornly plain, we might have tempted our American friend to the more old-fashioned solution.'

'You mean marriage?' asked the Major.

'Her mother was such a great beauty, you know,' he said. 'But she's happiest in the stables shovelling manure. In my day that would have sufficed, but these days, men expect their wives to be as dazzling as their mistresses.'

'That's shocking,' said the Major. 'How on earth will they tell them apart?'

'My point exactly,' said Dagenham, missing the Major's hint of irony. 'Shall we march on over to the house and see if Ferguson has nailed down any offers of financing?'

'They're probably securing houses for themselves,' said the Major as they left. He felt gloomy at the prospect.

'Oh, good God, no banker is going to be approved to live here,' said Dagenham. 'Though I'm afraid we will have to swallow Ferguson.' He laughed and put an arm around the Major's shoulder. 'If you support me in this, Major, I'll make sure Ferguson doesn't end up in the house behind yours!'

As they crossed the courtyard toward the house, Roger came out looking for Dagenham. The bankers were apparently impatient to talk to him. After shaking hands, Dagenham hurried in and the Major was left alone with his son.

'This project is going to make my career, Dad,' said Roger. He clutched a navy blue cardboard folder emblazoned with a Dagenham crest and the words 'Edgecombe St Mary, England's Enclave'. 'Ferguson's being so attentive to me, my boss is going to have to put me in charge of our team on this.'

'This project is going to destroy your home,' said the Major.

'Oh, come on, we'll be able to sell Rose Lodge for a fortune once it's built,' said Roger. 'Think of all that money.'

'There is nothing more corrosive to character than money,' said the Major, incensed. 'And remember, Ferguson is only being nice because he wants to buy my guns.'

'That's quite true,' said Roger. From the frown over his eyebrows, he seemed to be thinking hard. 'Look, he mentioned inviting us both to Scotland in January to shoot pheasant. You must absolutely promise me not to sell your guns to him before then.'

'I thought you were anxious to sell,' said the Major.

'Oh, I am,' said Roger, already turning on his heel to go. 'But as soon as you sell them, Ferguson will drop us like a hot potato. We must hold him off as long as we can.'

'And what about Marjorie and Jemima?' asked the Major as his son trotted away from him toward the house.

'If necessary, we'll file a complaint in probate court just to hold things up,' called Roger, waving a hand. 'After all, Father, everyone knows Uncle Bertie's gun was supposed to be yours.' With this extraordinary remark, Roger disappeared and the Major, feeling quite dizzy with surprise, thought it best to collect his guns and retreat to home.

Chapter Sixteen

He had planned to bring Mrs Ali a dozen long-stemmed roses, swathed in tissue and a satin bow and carried casually in the crook of his arm. But now that he was to pick her up with Grace, at Grace's cottage, the roses seemed inappropriate. He settled for bringing each of them a single rose of an apricot colour on a long spidery brown stem.

He had dashed for his car in order to avoid being seen by Alice Pierce, whose protest at the shoot had been followed by a door-to-door petition drive against St James Homes, and rallies of protest at every public appearance by either Lord Dagenham or Ferguson. The effort was not going well. The Vicar, who had been seen suddenly consulting an architect on the long overdue restoration of the steeple, had declined to speak from the pulpit, citing the church's need to provide love and spiritual comfort to all sides in the dispute. Many people, including the Major, had been glad to accept posters that urged 'Save Our Village', but only about half thought it polite to display them. The Major put his in the side window, where it screamed its message at the garage and not at the street. Alice continued to rush about the village with her band of followers, mostly strangers who seemed to favour hand-crocheted coats. She seemed unaware that even where she was supported locally, she was also studiously avoided by anyone who was planning on attending the Golf Club dance.

Straightening his bow tie and giving a final tug to his dinner jacket, the Major knocked on the insubstantial plywood of Grace's mock Georgian front door. It was Mrs Ali who opened it, the light spilling out onto the step around her and her face in partial shadow. She smiled and he thought he detected the shine of lipstick.

'Major, won't you come in,' she said and turned away in a breathless, hurried manner. Her back, receding toward the front room, was partly revealed against the deep swoop of an evening dress. Under a loosely tied chiffon wrap, her shoulder blades were sharply delineated and her bronze skin glowed between the dark stuff of the dress and the low bun at the nape of her neck. In the front room, she half pirouetted on the hearth rug and the folds of the dress billowed around her ankles and came to rest on the tips of her shoes. It was a dark blue dress of silk velvet. The deeply cut décolletage was partially hidden by the sweep of the chiffon wrap, but Mrs Ali's collarbones were exquisitely visible several inches above the neckline. The material fell over a swell of bosom to a loosely gathered midriff where an antique diamond brooch sparkled.

'Is Grace still getting ready, then?' he asked, unable to trust himself to comment on her dress and yet unwilling to look away.

'No, Grace had to go early and help with the setup. Mrs Green picked her up a short while ago. I'm afraid it's just me.' Mrs Ali almost stammered and a blush crept into her cheekbones. The Major thought she looked like a young girl. He wished he were still a boy, with a boy's impetuous nature. A boy could be forgiven a clumsy attempt to launch a kiss but not, he feared, a man of thinning hair and faded vigour.

'I could not be happier,' said the Major. Being also stuck on the problem of how to handle the two drooping roses in his hand, he held them out.

'Is one of those for Grace? I could put it in a vase for her.' He opened his mouth to say that she looked extremely beautiful and deserved armfuls of roses, but the words were lost in committee somewhere, shuffled aside by the parts of his head that worked full-time on avoiding ridicule.

'Wilted a bit, I'm afraid,' he said. 'Colour's all wrong for the dress anyway.'

'Do you like it?' she said, turning her eyes down to the fabric. 'I lent Grace an outfit and she insisted that I borrow something of hers in fair trade.'

'Very beautiful,' he said.

'It belonged to Grace's great-aunt, who was considered quite fast and who lived alone in Baden Baden, she says, with two blind terriers and a succession of lovers.' She looked up again, her eyes anxious. 'I hope the shawl is enough.'

'You look perfect.'

'I feel quite naked. But Grace told me you always wear a dinner jacket, so I just wanted to wear something to—to go with what you're wearing.' She smiled, and the Major felt more years melt away from him. The boy's desire to kiss her welled up again. 'Besides,' she added, 'A shalwar kameez isn't exactly a costume for me.'

The Major reached a spontaneous compromise with himself and reached for her hand. He raised it to his lips and closed his eyes while kissing her knuckles. She smelled of rose water and some spicy clean scent that might, he thought, be lime blossom. When he opened his eyes, her head was turned away, but she did not try to pull her hand from his grasp.

'I hope I have not offended you,' he said. 'Man is rash in the face of beauty.'

'I am not offended,' she said. 'But perhaps we had better go to the dance?'

'If we must,' said the Major, giving a stubborn push past the fear of ridicule. 'Though anyone would be just as content to sit and gaze at you across this empty room all evening.'

'If you insist on paying me such lavish compliments, Major,' said Mrs Ali, blushing again, 'my conscience will force me to change into a large black jumper and perhaps a wool hat.'

'In that case, let us leave immediately so we can put that horrible option out of reach,' he said.

❧ ❧ ❧

Sandy was waiting for them under the tiny porch by the front door of the Augerspier cottage. As they pulled up, she came down the path, a large wool coat hugged tightly around her. Her face, in the dim light of the car as she slid into the back, seemed more ivory than usual and her blood-red lipstick was stark. Her shiny hair was pulled into a series of lacquered ripples and finished with a narrow ribbon under one ear. A frill of silver chiffon peeked from the turned-up collar of her thick coat. She looked, thought the Major, like a porcelain doll.

'I'm so sorry you had to come out of your way,' she said. 'I told Roger I'd take a cab.'

'Not at all,' said the Major, who had been extremely put out by Roger's request. 'It is inconceivable that you should have to arrive unescorted.' His son had pleaded a need to arrive early for a dress rehearsal. He insisted that Gertrude felt his assistance was crucial in directing the troupe of male friends of the staff who had agreed to appear in the performance in exchange for a free supper of sandwiches and beer.

'I'm doing this for you, Dad,' he had pleaded. 'And Gertrude needs me if we're to make anything at all of the production.'

'I'd be happier if the "thing" were cancelled,' the Major had replied. 'I still can't believe you agreed to participate.'

'Look, if it's a problem, Sandy'll just have to take a taxi,' said Roger. The Major was appalled that his son would allow his fiancée to be transported to the dance in one of the local taxis with their tobacco-stained, torn interiors and their rough drivers, who could not be relied upon to be more sober than the passengers. He had agreed to pick her up.

'Sorry Roger dumped me on you,' she said now. She closed her eyes and leaned back into the seat. 'I thought about staying home, but that would be too easy.' The acid in her voice painted a broad stroke of awkwardness between them.

'I hope you and your fiancé are happy with the cottage?' asked Mrs Ali. The Major, who had successfully tamped down any anxiety about the evening, was suddenly worried about Roger and his capacity for thinly disguised rudeness.

'It turned out beautifully,' said Sandy. 'Of course, it's just a rental—we're not planning on getting too attached.' The Major saw her, in the mirror, settling further into the folds of her coat. She looked intently at the window, where only the darkness pressed in on the glass. They drove the rest of the way in silence.

ᔆ ᔆ ᔆ

The golf club had abandoned its usual discreet demeanour and now, like a blowsy dowager on a cheap holiday in Tenerife, it blazed and sparkled on its small hill. Lights filled every door and window; floodlights bathed the plain stucco façade and strings of fairy lights danced in trees and bushes.

'Looks like a cruise ship,' said Sandy. 'I warned them to go easy on the floods.'

'I hope the fuse box holds,' said the Major as they walked up the gravel driveway, which was outlined in flaming torches. Rounding a corner, they were startled by a half-naked man in an eye mask wearing a large python around his neck. A second man capered at the edge of the drive, blowing enthusiastically into a wooden flute. Tucked between two fifty-year-old rhododendron bushes, a third man swallowed small sticks of fire with all the concern of a taxi driver eating chips.

'Good God, it's a circus,' said the Major as they approached the fountain, which was lit with orange floodlights and filled with violently coloured water lilies.

'I believe Mr Rasool loaned the lilies,' said Mrs Ali. She choked back a giggle.

'I think I went to a wedding in New Jersey that looked just like this,' said Sandy. 'I did warn Roger about the line between opulence and bad taste.'

'That was your mistake,' said the Major. 'They are the same thing, my dear.'

'Touché,' said Sandy. 'Look, I'm going to run ahead and find Roger. You two should make your fabulous entrance together.'

'No really,' began the Major, but Sandy was already hurrying up the steps and into the blazing interior.

'She seems like a nice young lady,' said Mrs Ali in a small voice. 'Is she always so pale?'

'I don't know her well enough to say,' said the Major, a little embarrassed that his son had kept him at arm's length from both of them. 'Shall we throw ourselves into the festivities?'

'I suppose that is what comes next,' she said. She did not move, however, but hung back just on the edge of where the lights pooled on the gravel. The Major, feeling her slight pressure on his arm, paused too. Her body telegraphed inertia, feet planted at rest on the driveway.

'I suppose one can make the case that this is the most wonderful part of any party,' he said. 'The moment just before one is swallowed up?' He heard a waltz strike up in the Grill and was relieved that there was to be real music.

'I didn't know I would be so anxious,' she said.

'My dear lady, what is there to fear?' he said. 'Except putting the other ladies quite in the shade.' A murmur like the sea swelled from the open doors of the club, where a hundred men were no doubt already jostling for champagne at the long bar, a hundred women discussing costumes and kissing cheeks. 'It does sound like it's a bit of a crush in there,' he added. 'I'm a little frightened myself.'

'You're making fun of me,' said Mrs Ali. 'But you must know that it will not be the same as sharing books or walking by the sea.'

'I'm not quite sure what you mean.' The Major took her by the hand and pulled her to one side, nodding at a couple who passed them. The couple gave them an odd stare and then bobbed their heads in reply as they went up the steps. The Major was quite sure that this was exactly what she had meant.

'I don't even dance,' she said. 'Not in public.' She was trembling, he noticed. She was like a bird under a cat's paw, completely still but singing in every sinew with the need to escape. He dared not let go of her hand.

'Look, it's slightly gaudy and horribly crowded, but there's nothing to be nervous about,' he said. 'Personally I'd be happy to skip it, but Grace will be looking for you and I've promised to be there to accept the silly award thing as part of the entertainment.' He stopped, feeling that these were stupid ways to encourage her.

'I don't want to burden you,' she said.

'Then don't make me go in there alone, like a spare part,' he said. 'When they hand me my silver plate, I want to walk back and sit with the most elegant woman in the room.' She gave him a small smile and straightened her back.

'I'm sorry,' she said. 'I don't know why I'm being such a fool.' He tucked his arm under her elbow and she allowed him to lead her up the steps, moving fast enough that she would not have time to change her mind.

༄ ༅ ༆

The doors to the Grill had been pinned back by two large brass planters containing palm trees. Scarlet fabric looped from the door surround, caught up in swags by gold braid, fat tassels, and strings of bamboo beads. In an alcove, a large, fully decorated Christmas tree, complete with fairy on the top, attempted to disguise its incongruity with lots of tiny Indian slipper ornaments and presents wrapped in Taj Mahal wrapping paper.

In the centre of the vestibule, Grace was handing out dinner cards and programmes. She was dressed in a long embroidered coat and pyjama pants in a deep lilac hue, and her feet were tucked into jewelled sandals. Her hair seemed softer around her jaw than usual, and for once she seemed to have left off the creased caking of face powder.

'Grace, you really look enchanting this evening,' said the Major and he felt the joy of being able to offer a compliment he actually meant.

'Daisy tried to ruin it with a garland of paper flowers.' Grace appeared to be speaking more to Mrs Ali than him. 'I had to dump them in a flower pot.'

'Good move,' said Mrs Ali. 'You look perfect.'

'So do you,' said Grace. 'I wasn't sure about adding a shawl, but you've made the dress even more seductive, my dear. You look like a queen.'

'Are you coming in with us?' asked the Major, looking at the heaving Technicolor mass that was the crowd in the Grill.

'Daisy has me on duty here another half hour,' said Grace. 'Do go in and let our Grand Vizier announce you.'

Mrs Ali gripped his arm as if she were afraid of tripping and gave him a smile that was more determination than happiness. As they crossed the Rubicon of the short crimson entrance carpet he whispered, 'Grand Vizier—good God, what have they done?'

At the end of the carpet Alec Shaw stood waiting for them, frowning in a large yellow turban. An embroidered silk dressing gown and curly slippers, from which his heels hung out the back, were complemented by a long braided beard. He looked unhappy.

'Don't even speak,' he said, raising an arm. 'You're the last bloody people I'm doing. Daisy can get some other idiot to stand around looking ridiculous.'

'I think you're rather convincing,' said the Major. 'You're sort of Fu Manchu on an exotic holiday.'

'I told Alma the beard was all wrong,' said Alec. 'But she's been saving it ever since they did *The Mikado* and she glued it on so tight I may have to shave it off.'

'Perhaps if you soak it in a large glass of gin, the glue will soften,' said Mrs Ali.

'Your companion is obviously a lady of intelligence as well as beauty.'

'Mrs Ali, I believe you know Mr Shaw,' said the Major. Mrs Ali nodded, but Alec peered from under the slipping turban as if unsure.

'Good heavens,' he said, and turned a red that clashed with the mustard-yellow collar of his gown. 'I mean, Alma said you were coming, but I would never have recognised you—I mean, out of context.'

'Look, can we skip the announcements and just all go and find a drink?' said the Major.

'Certainly not,' said Alec. 'I haven't had anyone interesting to announce in half an hour. Watch me turn their heads with this one.' Taking up a small brass megaphone wrapped in paper flowers, Alec bellowed over the sound of the orchestra.

'Major Ernest Pettigrew, costumed as the rare Indian subcontinental penguin, accompanied by the exquisite queen of comestibles from Edgecombe St Mary, Mrs Ali.' The orchestra embarked on a choppy segue into its next tune and, as the dancers paused to pick up the new rhythm, many turned their heads to peer at the new arrivals.

The Major nodded and smiled as he scanned the blur of faces. He acknowledged a wave from Old Mr Percy, who winked as he danced with a tanned woman in a strapless gown. Two couples he knew from the club nodded at him, but then whispered to each other from the sides of their mouths and the Major felt his face flush. In the thick of the dancing crowd he caught a glimpse of a familiar hairdo and wondered whether it was some trick of the psyche that he should see his sister-in-law, Marjorie. He had always found excuses not to invite her and Bertie, fearing that she would unleash her loud voice and money questions on all his friends. It seemed unimaginable that she would be here now. He blinked, however, and there she was, twirling under the arm of a portly member who was known at the club for his lively temper and who held the record for most golf clubs thrown into the sea. As the dancers turned away into a fast swing, Alec said, 'I'll be off now,' and took off his turban to run a hand over his sweaty head. 'If he's not good company, just come and find me and I'll take care of you,' he added, holding out his damp hand. Mrs Ali took it without shrinking and the Major wondered where she found such reserves.

'Let's plunge in, shall we?' he said over the rising exuberance of the music. 'This way, I think.'

The room was uncomfortably full. To the east, the folding doors had been flung back and the small orchestra sawed away on the stage set against the far wall. Around the edge of the dance floor, people were packed in tight conversational clumps between the dancers and the crowded rows of round tables, each decorated with a centrepiece of yellow flowers and a candle lantern in the shape of a minaret. Groups of people jostled in every available aisle. Waiters squeezed in and out of the crowd, carrying tilting trays of hors d'oeuvres high above everyone's head as if competing to make it the length of the room and back without dispensing a single puff pastry. The room was redolent with a smell like orchids, and slightly humid, either from perspiration or from the tropical ferns that dripped from many sizes and shapes of Styrofoam column.

Mrs Ali waved to Mrs Rasool, who could be seen dispensing waiters from the kitchen door as if she were sending messengers to and from a battlefield. As they watched, she dispensed Mr Rasool the elder; he wobbled out with a tray held dangerously low and made it no farther than the first set of tables before being picked clean. Mrs Rasool hurried forward and, with practised discretion, pulled him back to the safety of the kitchen.

The Major steered Mrs Ali into a slow circle around the dance floor. As the main bar, next to the kitchen, was invisible behind the battalion of thirsty guests waving for drinks, he had decided to steer for a secondary bar, set up in the lee of the stage, hoping that he might then navigate them into the relative quiet of the enclosed sun porch. The Major had forgotten how difficult it was to navigate such a crush while protecting a lady from both the indifferent backs of the chatting groups and the jousting elbows of enthusiastic dancers. The benefit however, of needing to keep Mrs

Ali's arm tucked close against his side was almost compensation enough. He had a fleeting hope that someone might knock her over into his arms.

❧ ❧ ❧

Costumes ran the full array from the expensively rented to the quickly improvised. Near a tall column decked in trailing vines, they met Hugh Whetstone wearing a safari jacket and a coolie hat.

'Is that also from *The Mikado*?' asked the Major, shouting to be heard.

'Souvenir from our cruise to Hong Kong,' said Whetstone. 'I refused to spend another penny on costumes after what the wife went out and spent on full maharani rig.' Together they looked around the room. The Major spotted Mrs Whetstone in a lime-green sari talking to Mortimer Teale, who had traded his usual sober solicitor's suit for a blazer and yellow cravat, worn over cricket pants and riding boots. He seemed to be enjoying a good leer at Mrs Whetstone's flesh, which emerged in doughy rolls from a brief satin blouse. She seemed to be happily explaining to Mortimer all about the temporary tattooed snake that rose out of her cleavage and over her collar bone.

'I mean, where is she ever going to wear it again?' complained Hugh. The Major shook his head, which Hugh took to be agreement but which was really the Major dismissing both Hugh, who didn't care enough to even notice other men paying attention to his wife, and Mortimer, who never brought his wife anywhere with him if he could help it.

'Perhaps you could use it as a bedspread,' suggested Mrs Ali.

'I'm sorry! Mrs Ali, you know Hugh Whetstone?' The Major had hoped to avoid introductions; Hugh was already listing to one side and breathing fumes.

'Don't think I've had the pleasure,' said Hugh, obviously not recognising her either.

'I'm usually wrapping you half a pound of streaky bacon, three ounces of Gorgonzola, and a half dozen slim panatelas,' said Mrs Ali, raising an eyebrow.

'Good God, you're the shop lady,' he said, leering openly now. 'Remind me to up my order from now on.'

'Got to go. Must get a drink,' said the Major, making sure to put his body between Mrs Ali and Hugh's notorious bottom-pinching hands as he led her away. He realised with some pain that all evening he was going to have to introduce Mrs Ali to people who had been buying their milk and newspapers from her for years. Whetstone bellowed after them: 'Renting a native princess is pretty excessive, I'd say.'

Before the Major could formulate a retort, the music ended; in the rearrangement of the crowd, Daisy Green was suddenly upon them like a beagle on a fox cub. She was dressed as some kind of lady ambassador in a white gown and blue sash with many strange medals and pins. A large feathered brooch decorated one side of her head and a single peacock feather trailed backward, catching people in the face as they walked by.

'Mrs Ali, you're not in costume?' she said, as if pointing out a trailing petticoat or a trace of spinach on the teeth.

'Grace and I swapped costumes,' said Mrs Ali, smiling. 'She has my antique shalwar kameez, and I have her aunt's gown.'

'How disappointing,' said Daisy. 'We were so looking forward to seeing you in your beautiful national costume, weren't we, Christopher?'

'Who?' said the Vicar, appearing from a nearby knot of people. He looked slightly dishevelled in riding boots, rumpled military jacket, and safari hat. He wore a cravat made from a scrap of brightly patterned madras and looked, the Major thought, like the ambassador's wife's illicit drunken lover. He smiled at a stray image of Daisy and Christopher carrying on such a game at home, after the party.

'Ah, Pettigrew!' The Major shook the proffered hand. He did not attempt to have a conversation: the Vicar was notoriously unable to hear in noisy crowds. This had proved hilarious to several generations of choirboys, who delighted in all talking at once and seeing who could slip the most offensive words past the Vicar's ears during singing practice.

'Of course, with your wonderful complexion you can wear the wildest of colours.' Daisy was still talking. 'Poor Grace, on the other hand—well, lilac is such a difficult colour to carry off.'

'I think Grace looks quite wonderful,' said the Major. 'Mrs Ali, too, of course—Mrs Ali, I believe you know Father Christopher?'

'Of course,' said the Vicar, while his eyes crossed slightly, a clear indication that he had no idea who she was.

'Grace's aunt was quite legendary for her expensive tastes,' said Daisy, looking up and down Mrs Ali's dress as if measuring out a few alterations. 'Grace told me she could never get up the nerve to wear any of the dresses. She is so sensitive to even the suggestion of impropriety. But you, my dear, carry it off so well. Do enjoy yourself as much as you can, won't you.' She was already sweeping away. 'Come along Christopher.'

'Who are all these people?' asked the Vicar.

༺ ༃ ༻

'It is a good thing I don't drink,' said Mrs Ali as they pushed on around the crowd.

'Yes, Daisy has that effect on many people,' said the Major. 'I'm so sorry.'

'Oh, please don't apologise.'

'Sorry,' said the Major before he could stop himself. 'Look, I think the bar is just beyond that palm tree.'

There was almost a small opening in the crowd at the bar, but the space between the Major and a welcome gin-and-tonic was occupied by a rather unhappy-looking Sadie Khan and her husband, the doctor. The doctor looked stiff to the point of rigor mortis, thought the Major. He was a handsome man with thick short hair and large brown eyes, but his head was slightly small and was stuck well into the air as if the man were afraid of his own shirt collar. He wore a white military uniform with a short scarlet cloak and a close-fitting hat adorned with medals. The Major could immediately see him as a photo in the newspaper of some minor royalty recently executed during a coup. Mrs Khan wore an elaborately embroidered coat as thick as a carpet and several strands of pearls.

'Jasmina,' said Mrs Khan.

'Saadia,' said Mrs Ali.

'My goodness, Mrs Ali, you look quite ravishing,' said the doctor, giving a low bow.

'Thank you.' Mrs Ali gathered an end of her wrap and tossed a second layer across her neck under the pressure of the doctor's admiring gaze. Sadie Khan pursed her lips.

'Major Pettigrew, may I present my husband, Dr Khan.'

'Delighted,' said the Major, and leaned across to shake Dr Khan's hand.

'Major Pettigrew, I believe we are all to be seated together this evening,' said Sadie. 'Are you at table six?'

'I can't say I know.' He fumbled in his pocket for the card that Grace had handed to him in the foyer and peered with disappointment at the curly 'Six' written on it in green ink.

'And your friend Grace DeVere is also going to be joining us this evening, I believe,' said Sadie, leaning past Mrs Ali to read his card. 'Such a lovely lady.' The emphasis on the word 'lady' was almost undetectable, but the Major saw Mrs Ali flush, and a small twitch along her jaw line betrayed her tension.

'Would anyone care for champagne?' said one of Mrs Rasool's catering waiters, who had glided up with a tray of assorted glasses. 'Or the pink stuff is fruit punch,' he added in a quiet voice to Mrs Ali.

'Fruit punch all round, then, and keep 'em coming?' asked the Major. He assumed none of them drank and wanted to be polite, though he wondered how he was to get through the evening on a child's beverage.

'Actually, I'll get another gin-and-tonic,' said Dr Khan. 'Care to join me, Major?'

'Oh, you naughty men must have your little drink, I know,' said Sadie, smacking her husband's arm lightly with a large alligator clutch bag. 'Do go ahead, Major.' There was an uncomfortable pause in conversation as they all watched the drinks being poured.

'You must be very excited about the "dance divertissement" before dessert,' said Sadie Khan at last, waving the thick white programme labelled 'A Night at the Maharajah's Palace Souvenir Journal'. She held it open with a thick thumb adorned with a citrine ring and the Major read over her long thumbnail:

COLONEL PETTIGREW SAVES THE DAY

An interpretive dance performance incorporating historic Mughal folk dance traditions, which tells the true story of the brave stand in which local hero Colonel Arthur Pettigrew, of the British army in India, held off a train full of murderous thugs to rescue a local Maharajah's youngest wife. For his heroism, the Colonel was awarded a British Order of Merit and personally presented with a pair of fine English sporting guns by the grateful Maharajah. After partition, the Maharajah was forced to give up his province but was happily resettled in Geneva with his wives and extended family. After the dance, a Silver Tea Tray of recognition will be awarded to the family of the late Colonel by our distinguished Honorary Event Chair, Lord Daniel Dagenham.

'Relative of yours?' asked Dr Khan.

'My father,' said the Major.

'Such an honour,' said Mrs Khan. 'You must be very thrilled.'

'The whole thing's a bit embarrassing,' said the Major, who could not quell a small bubble of satisfaction. He looked at Mrs Ali to see whether she was at all impressed. She smiled, but she seemed to be biting her lip to keep from chuckling.

'It is absurd the fuss they make,' said Mrs Khan. 'My husband is quite appalled at the way they've splashed the sponsors all over the cover.' They all looked at the front cover, where the sponsors were listed in descending type size, beginning with 'St James Executive Homes' in a bold headline and finishing up, behind 'Jakes and Sons Commercial Lawn Supplies', with a tiny italic reference to 'Premiere League Plastic Surgery'. This last was Dr Khan's practice, the Major surmised.

'Who on earth is "St James Executive Homes"?' said Dr Khan. The Major did not feel like enlightening him. However, the mystery of the decorative extravagance was now clear: Ferguson had made another shrewd move toward controlling the locals.

'They want to build big houses all over Edgecombe St Mary,' said Mrs Ali. 'Only the rich and the well-connected will be allowed to buy.'

'What a clever idea,' said Mrs Khan to her husband. 'We should look into how big a house is permitted.'

'It's Lord Dagenham's doing,' added Mrs Ali.

'I understand Lord Dagenham is to present the award to you himself tonight,' said Mrs Khan to the Major. 'My husband was so relieved not to be asked. He loves to contribute, but he hates the limelight.'

'Of course, when you're a lord, you don't have to come up with any cash,' said Dr Khan. He took a long drink from his small glass of gin and tried in vain to signal for another round.

'My husband is very generous,' added Mrs Khan.

A small drumroll interrupted their conversation. Alec Shaw, turban once again quivering on his head, announced the arrival of the Maharajah himself, accompanied by his royal court. The orchestra broke into a vaguely recognisable processional piece.

'Is that Elgar?' asked the Major.

'I think it's from *The King and I* or something similar,' said Mrs Ali. She was actively chuckling now.

The crowd pressed to the sides of the dance floor. The Major found himself pinned uncomfortably between the doctor's sword hilt and Mrs Khan's upholstered hip. He stood as tall as possible so as to shrink away from any contact. Mrs Ali looked equally uncomfortable trapped on the other side of the doctor.

From the lobby, down the crimson carpet, there came two waiters carrying long banners, followed by Lord Dagenham and his niece dressed in sumptuous costumes. Dagenham, in purple tunic and turban, seemed to be having some difficulty in not snagging his scimitar on his spurred boots, while Gertrude, who had obviously been instructed to wave her arms about to display her flowing sleeves, held them at a stiff thirty degrees from her body and clumped down the length of the room as if still wearing wellies instead of satin slippers. Two lines of dancing girls—the lunch ladies—trudged after them, led by the light-footed Amina in a peacock blue pyjama costume. She had hidden her hair under a tight satin wrap and though her face, below kohl-ringed eyes, was obscured behind a voluminous chiffon veil, she looked surprisingly beautiful. There was a distinct symmetry to her troupe: and as they passed, it came to the Major that they had been arranged in order of their willingness to participate, the lead girls wriggling their arms with abandon while those in the back trudged with sullen embarrassment.

Two drummers and a silent sitar player followed the girls, then two more waiters with flags, the fire-eater, and finally a tumbling acrobat, who did a few spins in place to give the procession time to exit. The flag bearers had some difficulty getting through the door stage left and the Major noticed a faint singed smell that suggested the fire-eater had been impatient. Lord Dagenham and his niece mounted the stage from opposite sides and came together behind Alec, who gave them a low bow and almost tumbled the microphone stand. Lord Dagenham made a small leap to steady it.

'I declare this wonderful evening officially open,' he said. 'Dinner is served!'

Chapter Seventeen

Table six was placed in a very visible spot along the window side of the dance floor, and toward the middle of the room; the Khans seemed satisfied with their prominence.

'So happy to meet another sponsor,' said Mrs Khan to the couple already there, who had proved to be Mr and Mrs Jakes. They were already tucking into the bread basket.

'We always give them a good discount on the weed killer come spring, so they invite us. The wife likes a bit of a dance now and then,' said Mr Jakes. He was wearing a plain beige shalwar kameez with dark socks and a pair of wingtip shoes. His wife wore a matching outfit but with gold wedge sandals and a large gold headband. The Major thought they looked as if they were wearing surgical scrubs.

'Ooh, they're playing the mambo,' said Mrs Jakes, jumping up in a way that made the silverware tinkle. The Major hurried to stand up. 'Excuse us, won't you?' The couple scurried off to dance. The Major sat down again, wishing it were possible to ask Mrs Ali to dance.

Grace arrived at the table and introduced Sterling, who was wearing a long antique military coat in yellow with black lace and frogging and a black cap with a yellow-and-black scarf hanging down the back.

'Oh, you're American,' said Mrs Khan, holding out her hand. 'What a charming costume.'

'The Bengal Lancers were apparently a famous Anglo-Indian regiment,' said the young man. He pulled at his thighs to display the full ballooning of the white jodhpurs. 'Though how the Brits conquered the empire wearing clown pants is beyond me.'

'From the nation that conquered the West wearing leather chaps and hats made of dead squirrel,' said the Major.

'So nice to see you again, Major,' said the young man, extending a hand. 'Always a hoot.'

'And where is Mr Ferguson?' asked Grace.

'He likes to come late for security reasons,' said Sterling. 'Keep things low key.' Just then, Ferguson appeared at the door. He was dressed in a military uniform so sumptuous as to look almost real. It was topped with a scarlet cloak trimmed and lined with ermine. Under his left arm he carried a tall cocked hat and with his right hand he was checking text on his phone. Sandy, in a column of dove-grey chiffon and pink gloves, was holding his elbow.

'Oh, look, Major, isn't that Roger coming in with Mr Ferguson?' asked Grace. Indeed he was: buttoned too tight into his grandfather's army jacket and conversing in an eager terrier manner with Ferguson's broad back. He almost bumped into Ferguson as the American paused to look for his table. Sandy seemed to be struggling to keep her pale, diplomatic smile.

'Mr Ferguson has quite outdone even our Maharajah in magnificence,' said Mrs Khan.

'Where on earth did he get such a rig?' said Dr Khan. His face showed quite clearly that he was no longer as happy with his own costume.

'Isn't it fabulous?' said Grace. 'It's Lord Mountbatten's viceroy uniform.'

'How historically appropriate.' A slight stiffness crept into Mrs Ali's voice. 'You are joking, I hope.'

'Not the real thing, of course,' said Sterling. 'Borrowed it from some BBC production, I think.'

'Major, is that your son playing Mountbatten's man?' asked Dr Khan.

'My son—' began the Major, making a serious attempt to control the urge to splutter. 'My son is dressed as Colonel Arthur Pettigrew, whom he will portray in tonight's entertainment.' There was a small silence around the table. Across the room, Roger continued to shuffle behind Ferguson in a way that did suggest an orderly more than a leader of men. Roger was by no means a bulky man and the way he filled the uniform so tightly gave the Major the unpleasant sensation that his own father must have been more slight and insubstantial than he remembered.

'Roger looks so handsome in uniform,' said Grace. 'You must be so proud.' She caught Roger's eye and waved. Roger, with a smile that expressed more reluctance than pleasure, started across the dance floor toward them. As he approached, the Major tried to focus on pride as a primary emotion. A certain embarrassment attached to seeing his son wearing a uniform to which he was not entitled. Roger had been so adamant in his refusal to join the army: the Major remembered the discussion they had had one blustery Easter weekend. Roger, home from college with a box full of economics textbooks and a new dream to become a financier, had cut a sharp slice through the Major's discreet inquiries.

'The army is for bureaucrats and blockheads,' said Roger. 'Careers grow about as fast as moss and there's no room for breakout success.'

'It's a matter of serving one's country,' the Major had said.

'It's a recipe for getting stuck in the same box as one's father.' Roger's face had been pale but there was no hint of shame or apology in his eyes. The Major felt the pain of the words expand on impact, like a blow from a lead cosh in a wool sock.

'So your grandfather was a colonel?' asked Mrs Khan as Roger was introduced. 'And how wonderful that you are following the family tradition.'

'Tradition is so important,' added the doctor, shaking hands.

'Actually, Roger works in the City,' said the Major. 'Banking.'

'Though it often feels like we're down in the trenches,' said Roger. 'Earning our scars in the fight against the markets.'

'Banking is so important nowadays,' said Dr Khan, switching gears with the poise of a politician. 'You certainly have the opportunity to make important connections.' They watched as Lord Dagenham's table assembled in the centre of the room, mounting the low dais.

'I saw Marjorie,' said the Major, pulling Roger aside. 'Did you invite her?'

'Heavens, no,' said Roger. 'Ferguson did. She said she got a lovely note, inviting her to be his guest.'

'Why would he do such a thing?'

'I expect he's looking to pressure us over the guns,' Roger said. 'Stand firm, Dad.'

'I intend to,' said the Major.

                    ᴗ ♪ ♪

Dinner proceeded as an exercise in barely contained chaos. Waiters forced their way through the aisles as guests refused to remain seated. There was a full complement on the dance floor, but many people merely pretended to be going to or fro; they wandered from table to table greeting friends and promoting their own self-importance. Even the Khans, who excused themselves for a cha-cha, were to be seen hovering in the small group around Lord Dagenham. The crowd was so thick that the Major could see Sandy, sitting between Dagenham and Ferguson, signal a waiter to hand her dinner across the expanse of table rather than try to serve over her shoulder. During the main course, it became clear that the waiters were far too busy pouring wine to bother fetching fruit punch for Mrs Ali.

'I'll make a quick dash for the bar, if you'll be all right?' he asked.

'I'll be fine,' said Mrs Ali. 'Grace and I will sit and gossip about all the flesh on display.'

'Nothing for me,' said Grace. 'I'll stick to my single glass of wine.' She then gathered her evening bag and hastily excused herself to visit the ladies' lounge.

'Perhaps we should tell her that every time she looks away, the waiter manages to top up her Chardonnay,' said the Major.

❧ ❧ ❧

Forcing his way back from the bar, the Major paused in a quiet spot behind a palm fern and took a moment to observe Mrs Ali, who sat quite alone, dwarfed by the large expanse of the table. Her face was a polite blank, her eyes fixed on the dancing. The Major felt she did not look as confident in this warm room as she did on a blustery promenade in the rain and he had to admit that, as he had noticed many times before, people who were alone and ignored often appeared less attractive than when surrounded by admiring companions. As he peered harder, Mrs Ali's face broke into a wide smile that restored all her beauty. Alec Shaw had leaned in to talk to her and, to the Major's surprise, she then rose from her chair, accepting an invitation to a rather fast foxtrot. As Alec took her hand and passed his arm about her slender waist, someone slapped the Major's shoulder and demanded his attention.

'Having a good time, Major?' Ferguson was carrying a glass of Scotch and chewing on an unlit cigar. 'I was on my way out for a smoke.'

'Very good, thank you,' said the Major, who was trying to follow Alec's head through the crowd as he twirled Mrs Ali around the room with rather an excessive number of spins.

'I was glad your sister-in-law could make it,' said Ferguson.

'I'm sorry—what?' asked the Major still looking at the dancers. She was as light on her feet as he had dreamed, and her dress flew around her ankles like blue waves.

'She told me all about her plans to take a cruise when she has the money,' he said.

'What money?' asked the Major. He was torn between a sudden urge to throttle Alec and a small voice that told him to pay attention to Ferguson. With great difficulty, he dragged his eyes from the dance floor.

'Not to worry.' Ferguson now also seemed to be watching Mrs Ali spinning through the crowd of dancers like a brilliant blue flame. 'I'm ready to deal square with you if you're square with me.' The cigar moved up and down like an insult. Ferguson turned to face him and added. 'As I told Sterling, sure I could just pay the widow a big premium for her gun now, then take it out of Pettigrew's hide later, but why would I do that? I respect the Major too much as a gentleman and a sport to pull a fast one.' He smiled, but it did not reach his eyes.

'You invited her to the dance,' said the Major.

'Least I could do, old chap,' said Ferguson, slapping him again on the back. 'Got to have the whole Pettigrew family to witness your receiving this award.'

'Of course,' said the Major, feeling sick.

'You might want to grab those guns quick after the show,' Ferguson added as he moved away. 'She did seem very interested to know they were here.'

The Major was so dazed by the implied threat that he sank back into the shadow of the door's curtain to recover his composure. He was just in time to escape the notice of Daisy Green, who promenaded by with Alma. She, too, had noticed Alec and Mrs Ali dancing, for she paused and took Alma by the arm.

'I see she's ensnared your husband.'

'Oh, doesn't she look pretty,' said Alma. 'I asked Alec to make sure she wasn't left out.'

'I'm just saying that maybe if Grace showed a bit more cleavage, he wouldn't have been led on by more exotic charms.'

'You mean Alec?' asked Alma.

'No, of course I don't mean Alec, you ninny.'

'I think Grace is worried about neck wrinkles,' said Alma, smoothing her own neck, which was swathed in a purple satin scarf with orange glass balls clicking on the fringed ends. She wore a Victorian high-buttoned blouse set over a voluminous and crumpled velvet skirt that seemed to have sustained many a moth.

'She'll have more to worry about when her so-called friend snaps him up and rubs all our noses in it,' hissed Daisy.

'If she marries him, I suppose we should invite her into the garden club?' asked Alma.

'We must all do our Christian duty, of course,' said Daisy.

'His wife wasn't much of a joiner,' said Alma. 'Maybe she won't be, either.'

'Unfortunately, it wouldn't be appropriate to ask her to join in activity related to the church.' Daisy gave an unpleasant smile. 'I think that keeps her off most of the committees.'

'Maybe she'll convert.' Alma giggled.

'Don't even joke like that,' said Daisy. 'Let's just hope it's just a last fling.'

'One last small bag of wild oats found in the back of the shed, so to speak?' said Alma. The two women laughed and moved away deeper into the hot, crowded room.

It was a moment before the Major could move his body, which seemed to have stuck itself to the cold glass of the French door and was strangely numb. A brief thought that perhaps he should not have invited Mrs Ali to the dance made him ashamed of himself and he instantly changed to being angry at Daisy and Alma. It was astonishing that they would consider making up such stories about Mrs Ali and him.

He had always assumed gossip to be the malicious whispering of uncomfortable truths, not the fabrication of absurdities. How was one to protect oneself against people making up things? Was a life of careful, impeccable behaviour not enough in a world where inventions were passed around as fact? He looked around at the high-ceilinged room filled with people he considered to be his friends and neighbours. For a moment he saw them as complete strangers; drunk strangers, in fact. He stared into the palm tree but found only a label that identified it as plastic and made in China.

Returning to the table, he was in time to see Alec depositing Mrs Ali in her seat with a flourish.

'Now, remember what I told you,' said Alec. 'Don't you pay them any attention.' With that he added, 'Your lady is a wonderful dancer, Ernest,' and disappeared to find his dinner.

'What was he talking about?' asked the Major as he set down their drinks and took his seat at her side.

'I think he was trying to be reassuring,' she said, laughing. 'He told me not to worry if some of your friends seemed a bit stiff at first.'

'What friends?' asked the Major.

'Don't you have any?' she asked. 'Then who are all these people?'

'Blessed if I know,' he said and added: 'I didn't think you danced, or I would have asked you myself.'

'Will you ask me now?' she said. 'Or are you going to have seconds on the roast beef?' Mrs Rasool's waiters were circling with vast platters.

'Will you please do me the honour?' He led her to the floor as the dance band struck up a slow waltz.

Dancing, the Major thought, was a strange thing. He had forgotten how this vaguely pleasant exercise and social obligation could become something electric when the right woman stepped into one's arms. Now he could understand why the waltz had once been as frowned upon as the wild gyrations that today's young people called dance. He felt that he existed only in the gliding circle they made, parting the other dancers like water. There was no room beyond her smiling eyes; there were no people beyond the two of them. He felt the small of her back and her smooth palm under his hands and his body felt a charge that made him stand taller and spin faster than he would have ever thought possible.

He did not see the two men who gossiped at his back as he swung past the stage and the bar but he heard, in a brief silence between cascades of melody, a man ask, 'Do you really think they'll ask him to resign from the club?' and then a second voice, speaking a little loud over the sound of the music: 'Of course I wouldn't, but the club secretary says it does seem like George Tobin all over again.'

The Major's face burned; by the time he risked a glance at the bar, the men had turned away and he could not be sure whom they had been talking about. As the Major looked around for any other impropriety that might suggest censure, Old Mr Percy swept by with his lady companion in his stiff arms. Her strapless dress had turned quite around so that her ample bosom threatened to burst from the top of the zipper, while on her back two boned protuberances suggested the buds of undeveloped wings. The Major sighed with relief and thought that perhaps the club would benefit from certain tighter standards.

The case of George Tobin, who had married a black actress from a popular television series, still made him uneasy, though it had been considered merely a question of privacy. They had all agreed that Tobin had gone beyond the pale in exposing the club to the possible attention of paparazzi and a celebrity-hungry public by marrying a TV star. As the Major had reassured a very upset Nancy, the membership committee had vigorously denied any suggestion that colour was an issue. After all, Tobin's family had been members for several generations and had been very well accepted despite their being both Catholic and of Irish heritage. Tobin was happy to resign quietly on the understanding that his son from his previous marriage would be allowed his own membership, so the whole thing had been handled with the utmost discretion. Nancy, however, had refused to set foot in the club again, and the Major had been left feeling vaguely uncomfortable.

As the music began to reach its crescendo, the Major shook all thoughts of the club from his mind and refocused on Mrs Ali. She looked slightly puzzled, as if his slipping away into thought had registered in his expression. Cursing himself for wasting any moment of the dance, he gave her a big smile and spun them around until the floor threatened to come away from their feet.

A drumroll at the end of the dance and an enthusiastic flashing then dowsing of the main chandeliers announced the after-dinner entertainment. In the sudden dark, the room roiled with squeals, muttered oaths, and a small crash of glassware in a distant corner as people struggled to their seats. Old Mr Percy continued to spin his partner around and had to be urged off the floor by one of the waiters. The Major did his best to navigate Mrs Ali smoothly back to their table.

❧ ❧ ❧

A crash of cymbals from the band gave way to the flat squeal of recorded music and the whistle of a train. In the darkness, a single slide projector lit up a white scrim with sepia-toned images of India flickering and cascading almost too fast to register actual scenes. The Major felt a horrible sense of familiarity build until a brief image of himself as a boy, sitting on a small painted elephant, told him that Roger had indeed raided the tin box in the attic and put the family photographs on public display.

A scatter of applause hid the muffled jingling of ankle bells; as the lights came up again a lurid green spotlight revealed the dancers, swaying in time to a train's motion and waving about an assortment of props including baskets, boxes, and a number of stuffed chickens. Roger sat on a trunk smoking an absurdly curly pipe as he perused a newspaper, apparently oblivious to the colourful chaos around him. At one end of the ensemble, Amina made flowing gestures toward some wide and distant horizon. With the music, the train whistle, and the flickering scrim, the Major thought it looked much more effective than he would have imagined. He decided to forgive Roger for using the photographs.

'It's not as bad as I feared,' he said to Mrs Ali, conscious of a small, nervous pride in his voice.

'Very lifelike, isn't it?' said Mrs Jakes. 'Just like being in India.'

'Yes, personally I never travel by train without a chicken,' said Mrs Ali, looking with great intent at the dancers.

'It is the End of Empire, end of the line . . .' As Daisy Green's shrill voice narrated the story of the young, unsuspecting British officer returning to his barracks in Lahore on the same train as the beautiful new bride of the Maharajah, Amina danced a brief solo, her flowing veils creating arcs of light and movement.

'She's really good, isn't she?' said Grace as a round of applause greeted the end of the solo. 'Like a real ballerina.'

'Of course, only courtesans would have danced,' said Sadie Khan to the table. 'A maharajah's wife would never have so displayed herself.'

'The line is blocked! The line is blocked!' shrieked Daisy. As the dancers stamped their jingling feet and swirled their chickens and baskets with more urgent energy, Roger continued to peruse his newspaper, oblivious to the action around him. The Major began to feel impatient. He was sure his father would have been quicker to pick up on the change of mood on the train. He was tempted to cough, to attract Roger's attention.

'A murderous mob rains terror on the innocent train,' cried Daisy. From all the doorways of the Grill room staggered the hastily recruited boyfriends, dressed in black and flailing large sticks.

'Oh, dear,' said Grace. 'Perhaps it wasn't a good idea to give them the beer and sandwiches before the performance.'

'I probably would have thought twice about the cudgels,' joked the Major. He looked to Mrs Ali, but she did not smile at his comment. Her face, fixed on the scene, was as still as alabaster.

As the images flickered ever faster on the scrim, the men set about a series of exaggerated slow-motion attacks on the writhing women. The Major frowned at the muffled shrieking and laughter from the dancers which was not entirely covered by the wailing music. Amina engaged in a frantic dance with two attackers, who did their best to lift her and throw her away whenever she grabbed their arms. Their movements were more enthusiastic than pretty to look at, though the Major thought Amina made it look passably threatening. At last she broke free and, leaping away, spun right into Roger's lap. Roger raised his head from the newspaper and mimed suitable astonishment.

'The Maharajah's wife throws herself upon the protection of the British officer,' said Daisy's voice again. 'He is only one man, but by God he is an Englishman.' A round of cheers broke out in the audience.

'Isn't it exciting?' said Mrs Jakes. 'I've got goose bumps.'

'Perhaps it's an allergic reaction,' said Mrs Ali in a mild voice. 'The British Empire may cause that.'

'Disguising the Maharani as his own subaltern . . .' continued Daisy. The Major did not want to be critical, but he could not approve of Roger's performance. To begin with, he had assumed a stance more James Bond than British military; furthermore, he was using a pistol, having handed Amina his trench coat and rifle. The Major thought this an unforgivable tactical error.

The sound of gunshots mingled with the music and the squealing. The spotlights flashed red and the scrim went dark.

'When help arrived, the brave Colonel, down to his last bullet, still stood guard over the Princess,' said Daisy. The lights rose on a mass of inert bodies, both male and female. Only Roger still stood, pistol in hand, the Maharani fainting in his arms. Though one or two girls could be seen to be giggling—probably the fault of the young men lying across their legs—the Major felt the whole room go quiet, as if everyone were holding their breath. The momentary hush gave way to a burst of applause as the lights went down.

When the lights rose again, a glittering final tableau featured Lord Dagenham and Gertrude on thrones, Amina at their feet. On the steps of the stage and the floor, the dancers were arrayed, now wearing gaudy necklaces and sparkling headscarves. Alec Shaw, as Vizier, was holding out an open box containing the shotguns; Roger, standing at attention, saluted the royal court. On the scrim behind them, a sepia photo showed the same scene. The Major recognised, with a sting of emotion that was equal parts pride and pain, the photo his mother had hung in a dark corner of the upstairs hallway, not wishing to appear showy.

A series of photo flashes exploded in the room, loud Asian pop music with a wailing vocalist blared over the loudspeakers, and, as the audience clapped along, the female dancers broke into a Bollywood-style routine and spread up and down the edges of the dance floor, picking men from the audience to join them in their gyrations. As he blinked his dazzled eyes, the Major became dimly aware of a small man climbing onto the stage, shouting in Urdu and reaching for Daisy Green's microphone.

'Get away from me, you horrible little man,' cried Daisy.

'Isn't that Rasool's father?' shouted Dr Khan. 'What on earth is he doing?'

'I have no idea,' said Mrs Khan. 'This could be a disaster for Najwa.' She sounded very happy.

'Ooh, let's go and dance,' said Mrs Jakes, dragging away her husband.

The doctor got to his feet. 'Someone should get the old fool out of there. He will make us all look bad.'

'Please don't get involved,' said Mrs Khan. She did not place a hand on her husband's sleeve to stop him but merely gestured in that direction. The Major had often noted this kind of shorthand between married people. The doctor sat down again.

'My husband is always so compassionate,' said Mrs Khan to the table.

'Bit of an occupational hazard, I'm afraid,' said Dr Khan.

Mr Rasool Senior had the microphone now and was wagging his finger in the face of a shocked Daisy Green. He was shouting now in English, so loudly it hurt the ears to hear his voice cracking and sputtering at the limits of the sound system.

'You make a great insult to us,' they heard. 'You make a mock of a people's suffering.'

'What is he doing?' asked Grace.

'Maybe he is upset that the atrocities of Partition should be reduced to a dinner show,' said Mrs Ali. 'Or maybe he just doesn't like bhangra music.'

'Why would anyone be insulted?' asked Grace. 'It's the Major's family's proudest achievement.'

'I'm so sorry,' said Mrs Ali. She pressed the Major's hand and he flushed with a sudden shame that perhaps she was not apologising to him but for him. 'I must help Najwa's father-in-law—he is not a well man.'

'I can't see why it should be your responsibility,' said Sadie Khan in a malicious voice. 'I think you really should leave it to the staff.' But Mrs Ali had already risen from the table. She did not look at the Major again. He hesitated, but then hurried after her.

'Let go of him before I break your arm,' said a voice from the stage as the Major thrust through the crowd. He was in time to see Abdul Wahid at the front of a small group of waiters, advancing on a couple of the male dancers, and some band players, who were holding the senior Mr Rasool by the arms. 'Show some respect for an old man.' The men grouped themselves like a defensive wall.

'What are you doing here?' the Major thought he heard Amina ask as she tried to grab Abdul Wahid by the arm but maybe, he thought, he was only lip-reading over the continuous crashing of the music. 'You were supposed to meet me outside.'

'Do not speak to me now,' said Abdul Wahid. 'You have done enough damage.' Dancing couples, taking notice of the commotion, began to back away into tables.

'The old man is crazy,' said Daisy Green in a faint voice. 'Someone call the police.'

'Oh, please, no need to call the police,' said Mrs Rasool, collecting her father-in-law's arm from a scowling trombonist. 'My father-in-law is only a little confused. His own mother and sister died on such a train. Please forgive him.'

'He's a lot less confused than most people here,' said Abdul Wahid in a voice that carried. 'He wants you to know that your entertainment is a great insult to him.'

'Who the hell does he think he is?' said Roger. 'It's a true story.'

'Yeah, who asked him?' jeered a voice in the crowd. 'Bloody Pakis.' The waiters swivelled their heads and a pale, thin man ducked behind his wife.

'I say, that's not on,' called out Alec Shaw from underneath his teetering turban.

The Major knew, even as he witnessed the event, that he would be hard pressed later to relay the details of the fight that now erupted. He saw a short man with large feet shove Abdul Wahid, who fell against one of the waiters. He saw another waiter slap a male dancer across the face with his white arm towel, as if to challenge him to a duel. He heard Daisy Green call out, somewhat hoarsely, 'People, please remain civilised,' as a riot erupted in the middle of the dance floor. Things became a blur as women screamed, men shouted, and bodies hurled themselves at one another only to crash to the ground. There was much ineffectual thumping of backs and indiscriminate kicking.

As the music segued into an even more raucous tune, the Major was astonished to see a large drunken guest whip off his turban, hand his hookah pipe to his girlfriend, and throw himself across the heaving mass of assailants as if it were all a game. The Vicar waded in to grab him by the trousers but was kicked backward and fell on Alma. He became tangled in her green sari in a way that made Mortimer Teale look quite jealous, and was rescued by Alec Shaw; he dragged them behind the bar, which Lord Dagenham and Ferguson seemed to have commandeered as if for a siege.

'Oh, please, there is no need for violence,' cried Daisy as two combatants spun out from the crowd and landed on a table which collapsed in a heap of gravy-soaked plates. Several of the fighters, already looking winded, seemed to find it more effective to kick someone else's opponent while clutching their own with their arms to prevent being punched.

Most of the guests had been pressed into the corners of the room and the Major wondered why those nearest the door did not just run out into the night. He guessed that they had not yet been served dessert and were reluctant to leave before parting gifts had made an appearance in the vestibule.

The fight might have organised itself into something actually dangerous had not someone found the appropriate switch backstage and killed the music. In the sudden quiet, heads popped up from the heaving mass of bodies and punches hesitated in midair. Old Mr Percy, who had been staggering around the perimeter of the mêlée, whacking indiscriminately with a stuffed chicken, now gave one final blow. The chicken burst in a wave of polystyrene beads. Combatants soaked in gravy and now covered in white polystyrene seemed to realise that perhaps they looked foolish and the fight began to lose steam.

'I am terribly sorry,' said Mrs Rasool to Daisy as she and her husband held up the elder Mr Rasool. 'My father-in-law was only six years old when his mother and sister were killed. He didn't mean to cause a fuss.' The old man swayed and looked as faint and translucent as parchment paper.

'He's ruined everything!' shrieked Daisy.

'He's obviously quite ill,' said Mrs Ali. 'He needs to get out of here.' The Major cast around for an easy exit, but combatants were still being pulled apart and the crowd, no longer held in the corners, had swelled into all the spaces not covered with gravy.

'Mrs Rasool, why don't we squeeze through and bring him to the porch?' said Grace, taking charge. 'It's quieter out there.'

'Is there something wrong with the kitchen?' shrieked Daisy as he was led away.

'It's probably dementia, wouldn't you say?' Mrs Khan asked her husband loudly.

'Oh no, Daisy is always that way,' said the Major without thinking.

❧ ❧ ❧

'I guess we call it a night and get a cleaning crew in here,' said Lord Dagenham, surveying the damage. Five or six overturned tables complete with broken dishes, a palm tree cut in half, and curtains down in the entranceway seemed to be the only major damage. There were spots of blood on the dance floor from some bruised noses, and several sets of dirty footprints.

'I'll get the parting gifts and send people home,' said Gertrude.

'Nonsense! No one's leaving until we have dessert and then make our presentation to Major Pettigrew,' said Daisy. 'Where is that caterer? Where is the band?'

'I am here and ready to get my team back to work,' said Mrs Rasool, appearing at Daisy's side. 'We will finish the job in the same professional manner we began.' She turned to the waiters. 'Do you hear me, boys? Get straightened up and start resetting those tables. No more nonsense now, please. Ladies—please let your young men go backstage and have a good drink and we'll start the dessert procession.'

The band gathered and began a particularly objectionable polka; to the Major's surprise, the waiters began to move. There were some muttered words among them, but they obeyed Mrs Rasool, some picking up tables and the rest disappearing out into the kitchen. The lunch girls, more truculent and louder in their comments, were disinclined to leave their injured friends, but half of them complied while the others led away their aggrieved warriors to be comforted in the backstage room. The guests began to filter toward the bars, and a few club members helped to pick up tables. A groundskeeper two-stepped his way across the dance floor with a huge wet mop and disappeared through a French door into the night.

'Mrs Rasool, you should have been a general,' said the Major, deeply impressed as the room began to assume normality and a parade of lunch ladies entered bearing tiered stands of petits fours.

'Major Pettigrew, my apologies for the disturbance,' said Mrs Rasool, drawing him aside. 'My father-in-law has been very frail lately and the sight of all the dead bodies came as a shock to him.'

'Why do you apologise?' said Abdul Wahid, startling the Major, who had not seen him approach. 'Your father-in-law spoke nothing but the truth. They should be apologising to him for making a mockery of our land's deepest tragedy.'

'You have no right to call it a mockery,' said Amina, her voice wobbling from exhaustion and anger. 'I worked like crazy to make a real story out of this piece.'

'Abdul Wahid, I think you should take Amina home now,' said Mrs Ali. Abdul Wahid looked as if he had plenty more to say, and Amina hesitated. 'Both of you will leave now. We will not discuss this further,' added Mrs Ali, and some steel in her tone, which the Major had never heard before, caused them to do as she said.

'Look here, normally I'd say the show must go on,' said Lord Dagenham. 'But maybe we just drop it and avoid any further controversy? Give the Major his tray on the quiet.'

'That would be fine with me,' said the Major.

'Nonsense!' said Daisy. 'You can't let some old man's aspersions drive you from the stage, Major.'

'If you do, people may think there is some kind of truth to his view,' said Ferguson.

'Well, I don't see how anyone could be insulted,' said Roger. 'My grandfather was a hero.'

'I'm sure you can understand that many people still grieve for those who were murdered during this time,' said Mrs Ali in a conciliatory tone. 'Thousands died, including most on your grandfather's train, it seems.'

'Well, you can't expect one man to have defended a whole train, can you?' said Roger.

'Certainly not,' said Dagenham, clapping the Major on the back. 'Personally I think he would have been quite justified in jumping out a window and saving his own skin.'

'Pity he didn't have more warning,' said Ferguson. 'He could have organised the passengers to tear up the seats and use them to barricade the windows. Maybe made some crude weapons or something.'

'You must be American,' said Mrs Ali. She looked angry now. 'I think you'll find that works a lot better in the movies than in a real war.'

'Look, the truth belongs to the guy who's best at sticking to his story,' said Ferguson. 'We see a picture of all of us in the paper with that silver tray, Double D, then this dance was a big success and this little contretemps never happened.'

'So let's get the tray and the guns and round up the dancers,' agreed Dagenham. 'Then we make sure we include the doctor and his wife here, and Mrs Ali who looks so lovely, and we'll have a fine story.'

As they walked away, taking Roger with them to fetch the guns from backstage, Mrs Khan touched up her hair with her hands and sidled toward Daisy.

'Oh, we don't want to be in the limelight,' she simpered. 'Perhaps just in the back row?'

'Where your presence will no doubt still radiate,' said Mrs Ali.

'I am surprised you didn't know the old man was unstable,' said Sadie Khan in an icy voice. 'You are so intimate with the Rasools.' She leaned closer to Daisy to add: 'It's so hard to be sure about one's suppliers these days.'

'The photographer's almost ready,' said Roger, coming up to them, bearing the box of guns in his arms. 'We're getting set up for the presentation and pictures.'

'I will not appear in the picture,' said Mrs Ali.

'Is that for religious reasons?' asked Roger. 'Understandable, of course.'

'No, I am disinclined to be paraded for authenticity,' said Mrs Ali. 'You will have to rely on Saadia for that.'

'Oh, how very tiresome,' said Daisy Green. 'It really isn't polite to come to our party and then complain about everything.'

'Daisy, there's no need to be rude,' said Grace. 'Mrs Ali is my good friend.'

'Well, Grace, that should tell you that you need to get out more,' said Daisy. 'Next you'll be having the gardener in for tea.' There was an instant of stunned silence and the Major felt compelled to interject a rebuke.

'I think Grace is entitled to have anyone she likes to tea,' he said. 'And it's no business of yours to tell her otherwise.'

'Of course you do,' said Daisy with an unpleasant smile. 'We are all aware of your proclivities.'

The Major felt despair strike him like a blow to the ear. He had defended the wrong woman. Moreover, he had encouraged Daisy to further insult.

'Major, I wish to go home,' said Mrs Ali in an unsteady voice. She looked at him with the smallest of painful smiles. 'My nephew can drive me, of course. You must stay for your award.'

'Oh no, I insist,' he said. He knew it was imperative to persuade her, but he could not avoid a quick glance toward Roger. He was not about to abandon his gun box to Roger while both Marjorie and Ferguson were still in the building.

'You must stay with your friends and I must run and catch up with Abdul Wahid,' she said. 'I need to be with my family.'

'You really can't leave now, Dad,' said Roger, in a urgent whisper. 'It would be the height of rudeness to Dagenham.'

'At least let me walk you out,' said the Major as Mrs Ali walked away.

As he hurried after her, he heard Sadie Khan speaking. Daisy's response, in a crystal voice, carried over the music and voices: 'Yes, of course, you would be so much more suitable, my dear, only we are quite oversubscribed in the medical professions and the club works so hard to promote diversity in the membership.'

∽ ❦ ∾

Out in the cold night, the stars were abundant in a way that increased the pain of the moment. Mrs Ali paused on the top step and the Major stood at her shoulder, mute with humiliation at his own foolishness.

'We are always talking outside like this,' she said at last. Her breath steamed in the cold and her eyes shone, perhaps with tears.

'I made a mess of everything, didn't I?' he said. Below them, Amina and Abdul were arguing as they walked down the driveway. Mrs Ali sighed.

'I was in danger of doing the same,' she said. 'Now I see what I must do. I must put an end to the family squabbling and see those two settled.'

'They are so different,' he said. 'Do you think they can live together?'

'It is funny, isn't it?' she said in a quiet voice. 'A couple may have nothing in common but the colour of their skin and the country of their ancestors, but the whole world would see them as compatible.'

'It's not fair,' he said. 'But it doesn't have to be that way, does it?'

'Maybe, while they disagree about some big issues, they share the small pieces of their culture without thinking. Perhaps I do not give that enough weight.'

'May I come and see you tomorrow?' he asked.

'I think not,' she said. 'I think I shall be busy, preparing to go to my husband's family.'

'You can't be serious. Just like that? What about our Sunday readings?'

'I will think of you whenever I read Mr Kipling, Major,' she said, with a sad smile. 'Thank you for trying to be my friend.' She offered her hand and he again put it to his lips. After a few moments, she tugged it gently away and stepped down to the driveway. He wanted so much to run down after her but he found himself fixed where he was, standing in the light of the doorway with the music spilling around him and the crowd waiting for him inside.

'I could come down early,' he called after her. 'We could talk.'

'Go back to your party, Major,' she said. 'You'll catch cold standing in the dark.' She hurried down the driveway and as she disappeared, blue dress into deep night, he knew he was a fool. Yet at that moment, he could not find a way to be a different man.

Chapter Eighteen

Mrs Ali left the village. The Major did not see her go. He had meant to go down to the shop and visit her, but his anger and despair at having made such a mess of the evening seemed to help bring on the full-blown cold she had so carelessly predicted and he lay in bed for three days. As he dozed in rumpled pyjamas and furred teeth, ignoring the shrill rings of the telephone and the torturing tick of his bedroom clock, Mrs Ali went north to her husband's family and, by the time he was well enough to walk down to the village, it was too late.

The Major put his head down and prepared to battle through the tinsel storm that passed for Christmas now in an England that he remembered had once been grateful for a few pairs of wool socks and a hot pudding with more raisins than carrots. He woke each day hoping to feel fully recovered from his illness but could not shake a dry cough and a persistent lassitude. He felt buffeted to the point of collapse by the tinny music in the stores and streets. The more the crowds in the town carolled and laughed and loaded themselves, and their credit cards, with bags of presents, cases of beer, and hampers containing jars of indigestibles from many nations, the more he felt the whole world become hollow.

Holiday preparations in Edgecombe St Mary seemed to elbow aside all other concerns. Even the campaign against St James Homes seemed to be muted. The 'Save our Village' posters that had sprung up right after the shooting party were hardly noticeable in windows amid all the flashing fairy lights, the lurid lawn displays of inflatable Santas, and the electric-twig reindeer with endlessly grazing heads. Even Alice Pierce had taken down one of her three posters and replaced it with a painting on wood of a dove carrying a ribbon that read 'Joy to the World'. It was illuminated at night by the pinkish glow of two bare compact fluorescent bulbs, mounted on a board below together with a timer that turned them on and off at excruciatingly slow intervals.

At the village shop, which the Major avoided as long as possible, Christmas decorations helped obliterate any trace of Mrs Ali. A forest of foil dangly things and paper chains and large crêpe-paper balls promoting a beer had transformed the shop into a festive horror. There were none of Mrs Ali's handmade samosas next to the packaged meat pies in the cold case. The large caddies of loose tea behind the counter had been replaced by a display of chocolate assortment boxes of a size guaranteed to cause acute happiness followed by acute gastric distress in small children. The modest, hand-wrapped gift baskets, which the Major had decided to stock up on for the holidays, had been replaced by large cheap commercial baskets painted in garish colours and crowned with yellow cellophane; each was skewered by a bamboo stick adorned with a plastic teddy bear made furry with what appeared to be wallpaper flocking. Who would possibly take pleasure in a bear-on-a-stick was a mystery the Major could not comprehend. He stood staring through his glasses at the poor things until a hard-featured old woman who was knitting behind the counter asked him if he wanted to buy one.

'Good heavens no, no, thank you,' he said. The old woman glared at him. She was evidently able to knit and glare at the same time, as there was no pause in the furious clicking of her needles. Abdul Wahid, appearing from the back, greeted him rather coldly and introduced the woman as one of his great-aunts.

'Pleased to meet you,' lied the Major. She inclined her head, but her smile retracted itself almost at once into a pursing of the lips that seemed her usual expression.

'She doesn't speak much English,' said Abdul Wahid. 'We have only just persuaded her to retire here from Pakistan.' He retrieved a plastic bag from under the counter. 'I am glad you came in. I have been asked to return something to you.' The Major looked in the bag and saw the little volume of Kipling poetry that he had given Mrs Ali.

'How is she?' asked the Major, hoping not to betray any urgency in his voice. The aunt released a torrent of language at Abdul Wahid, who nodded and then smiled apologetically.

'We are all very nicely settled, thank you,' he said and his voice continued to brick up a barrier of cold and indifference between them. The Major could find no crack of warmth on which to turn the conversation. 'My auntie wants to know what we can get for you this morning.'

'Oh I don't need anything, thank you,' said the Major. 'I just popped in to—er—see the decorations.' He waved his hand toward an extra-large round paper ball topped with the flat outline of a winking girl with fat lips and an elf hat. Abdul Wahid blushed, and the Major added: 'Of course, there can be no question of excess where there is commercial imperative.'

'I will not forget your hospitality this autumn, Major,' said Abdul Wahid. His voice at last offered some hint of recognition, but it was combined with an unanswerable finality, as if the Major were also planning on leaving the village forever. 'You were very kind to extend your assistance to my family and we hope you will continue to be a valued customer.' The Major felt his sinuses contract and tears begin to well at the loss of connection even to this strange and intense young man. A lesser man might have grabbed for his sleeve or uttered a plea for—he supposed he had become used to Abdul Wahid's presence, if not his friendship. He dove in his pocket for a handkerchief and blew his nose loudly, apologising for his lingering cold. The auntie and Abdul Wahid both drew back from the invisible menace of his germs and he was able to escape the shop without embarrassing himself.

Christmas was still present, he hoped, in the church, where he went one morning to lend some carved wooden camels for the crèche by the altar, as his father had begun doing many years ago. It was a ritual to unpack them from their tea chest in the attic, to unwind their linen wrappings, and to give the cedar a light rub with beeswax.

The church was blissfully bare of any manufactured decoration. The simple crèche was supplemented by two brass urns of holly flanking the altar and an arrangement of white roses draping the font. Handmade cards from the church school hung from wooden pegs on a line strung across the aisle. Still tired from his cold, the Major dropped into the front pew for a few moments of quiet reflection.

The Vicar, emerging from the sacristy with a handful of leaflets, gave a small start—almost a hesitation—and then walked over to shake hands.

'Brought the dromedaries, I see,' he said and sat down. The Major said nothing but watched the sunlight pour across the ancient flagstone floor and light up the dust motes. 'Glad to see you out and about,' the Vicar went on. 'We heard you were laid up after the dance, and Daisy kept meaning to check on you.'

'Entirely unnecessary and so no apologies required, Vicar,' said the Major.

'Bit of a shambles, that dance,' said the Vicar at last. 'Daisy was very upset.'

'Was she?' said the Major in a dry tone.

'Oh, she worries about everyone so much, you know,' said the Vicar. 'She has such a big heart.' The Major looked at him, astonished.

Such touching delusion must underlie many otherwise inexplicable marriages, he thought, and liked Christopher all the better for loving his wife. The Vicar took an obvious deep breath.

'We heard that Mrs Ali has moved away to be with family?' His eyes were nervous and probing.

'That's what I'm told.' The Major felt a choke of misery rise into his voice. 'There was nothing to keep her here.'

'It's good to be with family,' said the Vicar. 'Among your own people. She's very lucky.'

'We could have been her people,' said the Major in a low voice. There was a silence as the Vicar shifted his bottom on the hard pew. He opened his mouth a few times, to no effect. The Major watched him struggle like a fly with one leg in a cobweb.

'Look, I'm as ecumenical as the best of them.' The Vicar set his hands in his lap and looked at the Major directly. 'I've done my share of blessings for mixed-faith couples and you've attended our interfaith festival yourself, Major.'

'The Jamaican steel band was a nice touch,' said the Major in an acid tone. The parish had seemed, for many years, oblivious to the fact that hymn singing in the village hall with the local Catholic church might not encompass the full range of world faiths. More recently the Vicar had tried to broaden the welcome, against some stiff opposition. Alec Shaw had suggested adding a Hindu speaker this past year. They had been led in a couple of chants and basic arm stretches by a lady yoga instructor who was a friend of Alma's and who had learned all about Hinduism while staying in India with the Beatles in the 1960s. The world's major faiths had also been represented by paintings of foreign children done by the Sunday school and the aforementioned reggae entertainment.

'Don't laugh,' said the Vicar. 'People loved those chaps. We're inviting them back for the fête next summer.'

'Perhaps you could have invited Mrs Ali,' said the Major. 'Put her in charge of the tombola.'

'I know you feel you've lost—a friend,' said the Vicar, hesitating over the word, as if the Major had been engaged in a steamy affair. 'But it's for the best, believe me.'

'What are you saying?'

'Nothing, really. All I'm trying to tell you is that I see people get into these relationships—different backgrounds, different faiths, and so on—as if it's not a big issue. They want the church's blessing and off they go into the sunset as if everything will be easy.'

'Perhaps they're willing to endure the hostility of the uninformed,' said the Major.

'Oh they are,' said the Vicar. 'Until it turns out the hostility is from Mother, or Granny cuts them out of the will, or friends forget to invite them to some event. Then they come crying to me.' He looked anguished. 'And they want me to promise that God loves them equally.'

'I take it he does not?' said the Major.

'Of course he does,' said the Vicar. 'But that doesn't mean they'll both be saved, does it? They want me to promise they'll be together in heaven, when the truth is I can't even offer both a plot in the cemetery. They expect me to soft-pedal Jesus as if he's just one of many possible options.'

'Sort of like a cosmic pick-and-mix?' said the Major.

'Exactly.' The Vicar looked at his watch, and the Major got the distinct impression that he was wondering whether it was too early for a drink. 'Often, I think, they don't believe in anything at all and they just want to prove to themselves that I don't really believe anything either.'

'I've never heard you talk like this, Christopher,' said the Major. The Vicar looked a little sick, as if he might already be regretting the outburst.

'Might as well get it all on the table, then, Ernest,' he said. 'My wife was in tears after that stupid dance. She feels that she may have been unkind.' He stopped and they both understood that this admission, while pathetically short of the mark, was nonetheless extraordinary coming from Daisy.

'I am not the one to whom any apology is owed,' said the Major at last.

'That will be the burden my wife will have to bear,' said the Vicar. 'But as I told her, the best way to prove our remorse is not to compound the injustice with a lie.' He looked at the Major with a determination in his tightened jaw that the Major had never seen. 'Therefore I will not sit here and pretend that I wish things had turned out differently.'

The silence seemed to reach to the very walls of the sanctuary and hum against the rose window. Neither man moved. The Major supposed he should feel angry, but he only felt drained, realising that people had been discussing him and Mrs Ali and that they had evoked such a strong response that the Vicar would state his opinion, even though the subject was moot.

'I've upset you,' said the Vicar at last, rising from the pew.

'I will not pretend that you haven't,' said the Major. 'I appreciate your candour.'

'I thought you deserved honesty,' said the Vicar. 'People never speak of it directly, but you know that these things are difficult in a small community like ours.'

'I take it, then, that you won't be giving a sermon on this subject of theological incompatibility?' asked the Major. He felt no rage, only a calm and icy distance, as if this man, who had been both a friend and an adviser, was now talking to him on a bad phone line from an ice floe in the Arctic.

'Of course not,' said the Vicar. 'Since the Bishop's office did market research on the devastating impact of negative or unduly stern sermons on the collection plate, we're all under orders to stick with the positive.' He patted the Major on the shoulder. 'I hope we'll see you back in church this Sunday?'

'I expect so,' said the Major. 'Though, since we're being candid, I'd rather welcome a stern sermon, since what you usually read puts me to sleep.' He was gratified to see the Vicar flush even as he kept a smile fixed on his face. 'I thought your honesty deserved reciprocity,' he added.

Upon leaving the church, the Major found himself walking toward the lane in which Grace lived. He felt an urgent need to talk over his immediate sense of permanent estrangement from the Vicar, and he felt cautiously optimistic that Grace would share his sense of outrage. He was also certain he could bully her into telling him what people were really saying. At her front door, he paused, remembering the night of the dance and how everything had seemed possible in the sparkling hours of anticipation. After he rang the bell, he placed his fingertips on the door and closed his eyes as if he might conjure Jasmina in her midnight-blue dress, but the door stayed stubbornly real and the hall behind it now sounded with Grace's footsteps. He was grateful to hear her coming. She would give him tea and agree with him that the Vicar was being absurd and she would talk to him about Jasmina and be sorry that she was gone. In return, he now decided, he would invite her to join him at Roger's cottage for Christmas dinner. 'What a nice surprise, Major,' she said as she opened the door. 'I hope you're feeling better?'

'I feel as if the entire village is against me,' he burst out. 'Everyone is a complete idiot.'

'Well, you had better come in and have a cup of tea,' she said. She did not bother to pretend she did not understand what he meant, nor did she ask to be reassured that she herself was not included in his sweeping denunciation of his neighbours. As he stepped into her narrow hallway, he was very glad that England still created her particular brand of sensible woman.

The Major, with Grace's complete agreement, had decided he would look ridiculous, and be more talked about, if he avoided the village shop, so he continued to pop in though every visit was painful, like picking at a scab. Amina, who worked during school hours and in the evenings, had lost the spiky tufts from her hair and no longer wore any bright colours or wild footwear. She maintained a subdued, noncommittal tone when Abdul Wahid's ancient auntie was around.

'How's little George?' he asked during a moment when she was alone. 'I never see him.'

'He's fine,' she said, ringing up his bag of cakes and two navel oranges as if she had always worked a till. 'Two kids were mean to him his first day of school and there was a rumour that one family was taking their kids out. But the headmistress told them they wouldn't get a free bus pass to the school they wanted, so that told them.'

'You seem very accepting.' Where had her usual prickliness gone? She looked at him squarely, and for a moment her eyes flashed with the old anger.

'Look, we all make our own beds,' she said in a low voice. 'George lives here now, and he has a father who makes a solid living in his own business.' She looked around to check the shop was empty. 'If that means biting my tongue and not chewing the heads off the customers, well, I know what I have to do.'

'I'm sorry,' he said, feeling a little nibbled.

'And if it means giving up dancing, and having to wear old-lady shoes, well . . .' Here she paused and gave him a conspiratorial grin. 'I can stand it while I need to.'

A few days later, on Christmas Eve, he met her in the lane by his house. She was pressed into the hedge shivering and smoking a cigarette. She looked nervous when he smiled at her.

'I don't smoke anymore,' she said. She ground the stub beneath her sensible shoe and then kicked it away. 'Soon as I'm married, I'm going to make Abdul Wahid send that old bat home. She gives me the creeps.'

'You don't get along?' asked the Major, hoping for a dizzy moment that Mrs Ali might return.

'They say she was a midwife in her village.' Amina spoke as if talking to herself. 'If you ask me, I think that's code for some kind of witch.' She looked at him and anger burned in her dark eyes. 'If she pinches George one more time, I'm going to slap her silly.'

'Do you hear from Mrs Ali—Jasmina?' he asked, desperate to bring her name into the conversation. 'Perhaps she might return to help you.' Amina hesitated, as if unwilling to say anything, but then added in a rush, 'They say if Jasmina doesn't like where she is, she'll go to Pakistan and live with her sister.'

'But she never wanted to go to Pakistan,' said the Major, appalled.

'I can't say for sure. It's not really my place to get involved.' Here she looked away with what the Major took to be a consciousness of guilt. 'She'll have to work it out herself.'

'Your happiness was important to her,' said the Major, hoping to suggest a similar responsibility in Amina.

'You can't reduce life to something as simple as happiness,' she said. 'There's always some bloody compromise to be made—like having to work in a godawful shop for the rest of your life.'

'I was supposed to teach George chess,' said the Major. He realised he was clutching for some last continued filament of connection to Jasmina, however tenuous.

'He has a lot going on right now,' she said too quickly. 'And he's spending his free time with his father.'

'Of course,' said the Major. Hope melted in the soft cold of the lane.

He held out his hand and, though she looked surprised, Amina shook it. 'I admire your tenacity, young lady,' he said. 'You are the kind of person who will succeed in making your own happiness. George is a lucky boy.'

'Thank you,' she said, turning away down the hill. As she left, she turned her head and grimaced at him. 'George may not agree with you tomorrow. Now that we live with his father, I've told him Christmas is strictly a store decoration. He won't be getting any of the gifts his nanni and I used to slip under his pillow.'

As she disappeared from sight, the Major found himself wondering whether it was too late to rush to town to buy George a solid but not overly expensive chess set. He quashed this idea with a sigh, refusing to give in to the foolish human tendency toward butting in where one was not wanted. He reminded himself that when he got home, he really should put away the little book of Kipling poems, which he had left on the mantelpiece. There had been no note tucked inside (he had shaken out the pages in hope of some brief parting message) and it was foolish to keep it out as if it were a talisman. He would put it away, and then later he would pop over to Little Puddleton to pick up a Christmas gift for Grace; something plain and tasteful that would suggest a depth of friendship without implying any nonsense. Fifty pounds should cover it. Then he would call in on Roger and let him know he would be bringing a guest for Christmas dinner.

Chapter Nineteen

He thought for a moment that they were not home. A single lamp burned in the window of the cottage, as people like to leave who have gone out and who wish to deter burglars and also not stumble about in the dark when they return. The front hall and bedroom floor were dark and no flicker of television or sound of a stereo gave any sign of life.

The Major knocked anyway and was surprised to hear the scraping of a chair and feet in the passage. Several bolts were drawn and the door opened to reveal Sandy, dressed in jeans and a white sweater, carrying in her hand a large, professional-looking packing tape dispenser. She seemed pale and unhappy. Her skin was scrubbed bare of makeup, and her hair escaped in wisps from the rolled-up scarf she wore as a headband.

'Don't shoot,' he said, raising his hands a little.

'Sorry, come on in,' she said, laying the dispenser down on a small console table and letting him into the warm hallway. 'Roger didn't tell me you were coming over.' She gave him a hug, which he found disconcerting but not unpleasant.

'He didn't know,' said the Major, hanging up his coat on a hook made from some bleached animal bone. 'Spur-of-the-moment visit.

I was just shopping in the neighbourhood and thought I'd drop off a couple of gifts and wish you happy Christmas Eve.'

'He's not here,' she said. 'But you and I can have a drink, can't we?'

'A dry sherry would be welcome,' he said advancing into a very sparsely furnished living room where he stopped in his tracks to peer at a giant black bottle brush that he supposed must be a Christmas tree. It reached the ceiling and was decorated only with silver balls in graduated sizes. It glowed in waves of blue light from the fibre-optic tips of its many branches. 'Good heavens, is it Christmas in Hades?' he asked.

'Roger insisted. It's considered very chic,' said Sandy, busy aiming a remote control at the chimney, where flames lit up in a fire basket of white pebbles. 'I was prepared to go more traditional down here, but since it cost a fortune and it'll be out of fashion by next year, I threw it in the car and brought it down with me.'

'I am usually all in favour of domestic economy,' he said doubtfully as she poured a large sherry over so much ice he would have to drink fast or face complete dilution.

'Yeah, yeah, it's hideous.'

'Perhaps you can rent it out in the spring to clean chimneys?'

'I'm sorry we didn't get the chance to have you over before.' She waved him to the low white leather couch. It had a short, rounded back and no arms, like a banquette in a ladies' shoe store. 'Roger wanted everything to be done before he showed it off, and then we got stuck with a whole lot of banker dinner parties and such.' Her voice was low and uninflected and the Major worried about whether she was feeling unwell, which might have unknown ramifications for Christmas Day's dinner effort. She poured herself a large glass of red wine and curled her long legs onto a metal chaise that seemed to be covered in horse skin. She waved her hand around the room and the Major tried to take in the white cropped fur of the rug and the wood-rimmed glass coffee table and the coloured metal shades of a standing lamp that bristled like a temporary traffic light.

'Saves on the dusting I suppose, keeping things minimal,' he said. 'The floors look very clean.'

'We scraped off seven layers of linoleum and sanded off so much varnish, I thought we were going right through the boards,' she said looking at the pale honey of the wide planks. 'Our contractor says they'll be good now for another lifetime.'

'It's a lot of effort for a rented place.' The Major had wanted to say something more complimentary and was annoyed that the same old critical language had come from his lips unchecked. 'I mean, I hope you get to keep it.'

'Well, that was the plan,' she said. 'Now I suppose Roger will try to buy it and flip it.'

'I'm sorry?'

To his surprise, she started crying. The tears ran down her cheeks in silence as she cupped one hand over her face and turned away toward the fire. The wine trembling in the glass in her other hand was the only visible movement. The Major could see misery in the hunch of her back and the shadowed edge of her frail collarbones. He swallowed down some sherry and put his glass very quietly on the coffee table before speaking.

'Something is the matter,' he said. 'Where is Roger?'

'He's gone to the party at the manor house.' Bitterness clipped her words short. 'I told him he should go if that's what he wanted, and he went.'

The Major considered this as he shifted his weight on the uncomfortable leather. It was never wise to get in the middle of a couple who were having a domestic squabble: one inevitably got sucked into taking sides and, just as inevitably, the couple worked things out and then turned on all who had dared to criticise either party. He feared, however, that his son must be at fault if such a self-possessed woman had been reduced to the fragility of glass.

'What can I do to help you?' he asked, removing a clean handkerchief from his breast pocket and offering it to her. 'Can I get you some water?'

'Thank you.' She took the handkerchief to wipe her face with slow measured strokes. 'I'll be fine in a minute. Sorry to act so stupid.'

When he came back from the kitchen, which was a sort of space-age farmhouse look with wooden cabinets with no visible legs, she looked strained but controlled. She drank as if she had been thirsty for a while.

'Feeling any better?' he asked.

'Yes, thank you. Sorry to put you in such a position. I promise not to start telling you everything that's wrong with your son.'

'Whatever he's done, I'm sure he'll be sorry directly,' said the Major. 'I mean, it's Christmas Eve.'

'It won't matter, anyway. I won't be here when he gets back,' she said. 'I was just taping up a couple of boxes of my stuff to be sent on later.'

'You're leaving?' he said.

'I'm driving back to London tonight and flying home to the States tomorrow.'

'But you can't leave now,' he said. 'It's Christmas.' She smiled at him and he saw that her eyeliner had run. It was probably now all over his handkerchief.

'Funny, isn't it, how people insist on hanging on through the holidays,' she said. 'Can't have an empty seat at the dinner table—think of the kids. Can't dump him before New Year's because you must have someone to kiss at midnight?'

'It's hard to be alone during Christmas,' he said. 'Can't you stay and work things out?'

'It's not so hard,' she said and he saw, as a flicker across her face, that there had been other Christmases alone. 'There will always be a fabulous party to go to and fabulous important people to mingle with.'

'I thought you were—fond of each other,' he said, choosing to tread lightly over any mention of love or marriage.

'We are.' She looked around her, not at the stylish furnishings but at the heavy beams and the smooth floor and the old slats of the kitchen door. 'I just forgot what we started out to do, and I got kinda carried away with the thought of this place.' She turned away again and her voice trembled. 'You have no idea, Major, how hard it is to keep up with the world sometimes—just to keep up with ourselves. I guess I let myself dream I could get out for a while.' She wiped her eyes again and stood up and smoothed her sweater. 'A cottage in the country is a dangerous dream, Major. Now, if you don't mind, I'd better finish my packing.'

'Is there nothing I can do to fix this?' asked the Major. 'Can I go and fetch him home? My son is an idiot in many respects, but I know he cares for you and—well, if you let him go, then we have to let you go and that's three of us made all the lonelier.' He felt as if he were being left behind on the dock while all around him others chose to embark on journeys without him. It felt not like loss but like an injustice that he should always remain behind.

'No, don't go after him,' she said. 'It's all decided. We both need to get back to doing what we do.' She held out her hand and as he took it, she leaned in to kiss him on both cheeks. Her face was damp and her hands cold. 'If I make my connection in New York, I might be able to join our Russian friends in Las Vegas for a few days. I think it's about time we moved the centre of the fashion world to Moscow, don't you?' She laughed and the Major saw that with a new application of makeup, a fresh suit, and the ministrations of the crew in the first-class cabin she expected to cement over any crack in her heart and move on.

'I envy you your youth,' he said. 'I hope you find a way to be happy in the world one day.'

'I hope you find someone to cook your turkey,' she said. 'You do know not to rely on Roger, right?'

‿ ❧ ‿

The Major awoke Christmas morning with a feeling that today was to be the low point of his world, an Antarctic of the spirit. Getting out of bed, he went to the window and leaned his head against the cold glass to look at the dark drizzle over the garden. There were holes in the back field now, and a large digging machine with a tall arm, some kind of core testing drill, was parked against his hedge as if the driver had tried to arrange for its massive rusting bulk some shred of protection. The trees hung their heads under the constant dripping, and mud ran thick in the gaps between paving stones as if the earth were melting. It did not seem like a day to rejoice in a birth that had promised the world a new path to the Lord.

The morning began with the awkward question of how early to telephone Roger. It had to be done soon, yet who among the bravest of men would relish calling a drunkard out of his slumber to remind him, in the agonies of the hangover and the anguish of a lost love, that the turkey has to go in at 200 Celsius, and not to let the giblets boil dry? He was tempted not to call at all, but he did not want to parade Roger's humiliations before Grace and besides, he wanted his Christmas dinner. Compounding the difficulty was that he had no idea how large a bird Roger and Sandy might have purchased. Hazarding a guess that they would have been intimidated by anything over fifteen pounds, he waited until the last possible moment, eight thirty, to pick up the phone. He had to redial two more times before a hoarse voice answered.

'Hurro,' whispered the ghost of Roger, voice desiccated and distant.

'Roger, have you put the turkey in yet?'

'Hurro,' came the voice again. 'Who, who the . . . what day is it?'

'It's the fourteenth of January,' said the Major. 'I think you've overslept.'

'What the . . .'

'It's Christmas Day and it's already past eight thirty,' said the Major. 'You must get up and put on the turkey, Roger.'

'I think it's in the garden,' said Roger. The Major heard a faint retching and held the phone away from his ear in disgust.

'Roger?'

'I think I threw the turkey out the window,' said Roger. 'Or maybe I threw it through the window. There's a big draft in here.'

'So go and fetch it,' said the Major.

'She left me, Dad.' Roger's voice was now a thin wail. 'She wasn't here when I got home.' The Major heard a sniffling sound from the phone and was annoyed to feel rising in his chest a sense of compassion for his son.

'I know all about it,' said the Major. 'Take a hot bath and some aspirin and get into clean clothes. I'll come and take over.'

༄ ༈ ༉

He called Grace, just to let her know he would be out for the morning and that he would drive over and pick her up at noon as arranged. He found himself sketching quickly what had happened, mostly in case she would like to withdraw from the festivities.

'I can't promise what shape dinner will be in,' he said.

'Can I come and help you with dinner, or would that be too embarrassing for your son?' she asked.

'Any embarrassment on his part is entirely self-induced and therefore not to be encouraged,' said the Major who, to tell the truth, was not sure whether he remembered how to make gravy or when to put in the pudding. Come to think of it, he wasn't sure there was to be a pudding. He was clutched by a sudden horror that Roger and Sandy might have commissioned a *bûche de Noël* to match their hideous tree, or planned to serve something strange, like mango. 'But I wouldn't want to put you out,' he added.

'Major, I am up for the challenge,' she said. 'I will confess that I've been dressed for hours and I'm sitting about here with my bag and my gloves doing absolutely nothing. Do let me help you in this time of need.'

'I'll pick you up directly,' said the Major. 'We'd better bring our own aprons.'

༄ ༈ ༉

Can the bleakest of circumstances be pushed aside for a few hours by the redeeming warmth of a fire and the smell of a dinner roasting in the oven? This was the question the Major pondered as he sipped a glass of champagne and stared out the window of Roger's kitchen at the wilting garden. Behind him, a large saucepan jiggled its lid as the pudding simmered; Grace was straining gravy through a sieve. The turkey, rescued from under the hedge, had proved to be organic, which meant it was expensive and skinny. It was also missing a wing but, well washed and stuffed lightly with brown bread and chestnuts, it was now turning a satisfying caramel colour atop a pan of roasting vegetables. Roger was still sleeping; the Major had peeked in and seen him, wet hair sticking up all over and mouth open on the pillow.

'It was lucky you had a spare pudding.' The Major had searched Roger's cupboards but found only assorted nuts and a large brown bag of biscotti.

'Thank my niece for always sending me a hamper instead of visiting,' said Grace, lifting her glass of champagne in response. She had brought a large tote bag filled with the pick of the hamper and had already spread crackers with smoked oysters, tipped cranberry sauce with spiced orange into a cut-glass dish, and set the Cornish cream to chill on the scullery windowsill. There would be Turkish delight and shortbread for later, and a half bottle of port to aid digestion. The Major had even managed to work out how to use Roger's stereo system, which had no visible buttons and was controlled from the same remote control as the fireplace. After a few false starts—a moment of loud rock music and leaping pyrotechnics in the pebble basket being the worst—he had managed to arrange both a low fire and a quiet Christmas concert from the Vienna Boys' Choir.

The Major did not have to go and wake his son: the phone rang and he heard Roger pick it up. He was putting the finishing touches to the table and knocking about Grace's carefully placed sprigs of holly, when Roger appeared, neatly dressed in a navy sweater and slacks and smoothing down his hair.

'Thought I heard you earlier,' said Roger, looking with some queasiness at the table. 'You didn't make dinner, did you?'

'Grace and I made it together,' said the Major. 'Are you up for champagne, or would you like a plain club soda?'

'Nothing for me just yet,' said Roger. 'I can't really face it.' He shifted from foot to foot in the manner of a hovering waiter. 'Grace is here, too?'

'She's done most of the cooking and supplied the pudding,' said the Major. 'Why don't you just sit down and I'll ask her to join us.'

'Only the thing is, I didn't realise you'd be going to all this trouble,' said Roger. He was looking out the window now and the Major felt a slow but familiar sinking feeling. 'I thought it was all cancelled.'

'Look, if you can't manage to eat, that's perfectly understandable,' said the Major. 'You'll just sit and relax and maybe later you'll feel like having a turkey sandwich or something.' Even as he said this, he felt as if Roger were slipping away from him somehow. There was a look of absence in the eyes and the way he stood, balanced on the balls of his feet, suggested that either Roger or the room was about to shift sideways. In the absence of any imminent earthquake, the Major could only assume that Roger was about to move. A small car pulled up outside, the top of its roof only just visible over the gate.

'It's just that Gertrude is here to pick me up,' said Roger. 'I was awfully cut up about the row with Sandy, you see, and Gertrude was so understanding . . .' He trailed off. The Major, feeling rage stiffen the sinews of his neck and choke his speech, said, in the quietest of voices, 'Grace DeVere has made you Christmas dinner.' At that moment, Grace came in from the kitchen, wiping her hands on a tea towel.

'Oh, hello, Roger, how do you feel?' she asked.

'Not too bad,' said Roger. 'I'm very grateful about the dinner, Grace, only I don't think I can eat a thing right now.' He looked out of the window and waved at Gertrude, whose head was now smiling above the gate. She waved back and the Major raised a hand in automatic greeting. 'And my father didn't tell me you were here, you see, and I promised Gertrude I'd go to the manor and play bridge.' A faint redness about the ears told the Major that Roger knew he was behaving badly. He pulled out his mobile phone as if it were evidence. 'She's being so good calling me and trying to take care of me.'

'You can't go,' said the Major. 'Out of the question.'

'Oh, he mustn't stay because of me,' said Grace. 'I'm quite the interloper.'

'You are no such thing,' said the Major. 'You are a very true friend and—we consider you to be quite family, don't we, Roger?' Roger gave him a look of such crafty blandness that the Major itched to slap him.

'Absolutely,' said Roger with enthusiasm. 'I wouldn't go if Grace wasn't here to keep you company.' He went around the couch, took Grace's hand, and gave her a loud kiss on the cheek. 'You and Grace deserve to enjoy a nice dinner together without me groaning on the couch.' He dropped her hand and sidled toward the hallway. 'I wouldn't go at all, but I promised Gertrude and her uncle that I'd make up the numbers,' he said. 'I'll be back in a few hours, tops.' With that, he disappeared into the hall and the Major heard the front door open.

'Roger, you're being an ass,' said the Major, hurrying after him.

'Make sure you leave me all the cleaning up,' said Roger, waving from the gate. 'And if you decide not to wait for me, just leave the door on the latch.' With that he jumped in Gertrude's car and they drove away.

'That's it,' said the Major, stamping his way back into the living room. 'I am done with that young man. He is no longer my son.'

'Oh, dear,' said Grace. 'I expect he is very unhappy and not thinking straight. Don't be too hard on him.'

'That boy hasn't thought straight since puberty. I should never have allowed him to resign from the Boy Scouts.'

'Would you like to eat dinner, or should we call the whole thing off?' Grace asked. 'I can just put everything in the fridge.'

'If it's all the same to you,' said the Major, 'I don't think I can stand that awful Christmas tree a minute longer. What say you we wrap everything in foil and organise a relocation to Rose Lodge where we can have a real fire, a small but living Christmas tree, and a nice dinner for the two of us?'

'That would be lovely,' said Grace. 'Only perhaps we should leave something here for Roger when he returns?'

'I'll leave him a note suggesting he find the turkey's other wing,' said the Major darkly. 'It'll be like dinner and party games all in one.'

Chapter Twenty

Soon after the New Year, the Major admitted to himself that he was in danger of succumbing to the inevitability of Grace. Their relationship had developed a gravitational pull, slow but insistent, as a planet pulls home a failing satellite. In his unhappiness, he had allowed this slow drift to happen. After their Christmas dinner, at which he offered a profusion both of champagne and apologies, he had allowed her to bring him a cold game pie in aspic on Boxing Day. He also accepted her invitation to 'just a quiet, early supper' on New Year's Eve and invited her to tea on two occasions in return.

She had brought him a draft of an introduction to the small book she was compiling on her research into local families and, with a tremble in her voice, asked if he might be willing to take a look at it for her. He had agreed and had been pleasantly surprised to find she wrote quite well, in a journalistic way. Her sentences were plain but managed to avoid both academic dryness and the excess of purplish adjectives he might have feared from an amateur lady historian. With his help, he thought, it might find publication in some small way. He was pleased that they would have this work between them during the dark months of winter.

Tonight, however, would be the second time this week he had been asked to dinner at her house and had accepted. This, he realised, merited closer examination of his own intentions.

'I saw Amina and little George at the mobile library this morning, picking out some appalling books,' said Grace as they finished up their plates of steamed haddock, buttered potatoes, and a homemade winter salad. 'I can't imagine who thinks it's suitable to teach reading through a book of pop-up potty monsters.'

'Indeed,' said the Major, busy picking plump golden raisins out of his salad. They were one of the few things he couldn't abide; with Grace he felt comfortable enough to remove them. She would not comment, but he had an idea that she would make sure to leave them out next time.

'I told the librarian she should exercise more control,' continued Grace. 'She said I was welcome to take over if I didn't like it, and I should be grateful it wasn't all just DVDs.'

'Well, that was very rude of her.'

'Oh, I deserved it completely,' said Grace. 'It's so much easier to tell other people how to do their job than fix one's own shortcomings, isn't it?'

'When one has as few shortcomings as you, Grace, one has leisure to look around and make suggestions,' he said.

'You are very kind, Major and I think you, too, are perfectly fine as you are.' She rose to take their empty plates to the kitchen. 'And after all, everyone needs a few flaws to make them real.'

'Touché,' he said.

After dinner, he sat in an armchair while she clattered dishes and made tea in her small kitchen. She would not let him help, and it was difficult to make conversation through the small pine-shuttered hatch in the wall, so he dozed, hypnotised by the fierce blue cones of the gas fire's flames.

'Anyway, Amina says Jasmina's not coming to the wedding,' said Grace through the hatch. He raised his eyes abruptly, knowing

311

that he had heard but not registered a much longer sentence of which this was merely the footnote.

'I'm sorry,' he said. 'I couldn't hear.'

'I said I had hoped to see Jasmina again when she came for the wedding,' said Grace. 'When she wrote to me, I wrote back right away and asked her to please come and see me.' Her face disappeared from the hatch again and the Major could hear the squeaks and clicks of the dishwasher being set into operation.

'She wrote to you?' he asked the room at large. Grace did not answer, being engaged with manoeuvering a silver tea tray too large for her narrow, sharp-cornered hallway. He went to the door and received the tray from her, angled to squeeze in at the door jambs.

'I really should get a nice little melamine tray,' she said. 'This one is so impractical, but it's about the last thing of my mother's that I've kept.'

'She wrote to you?' The Major tried to keep his voice casual even as his throat constricted with the sudden hurt this information caused him. He concentrated on the task of fitting the tray within the raised brass rail of the coffee table.

'She wrote to me right after she left and apologised for running off without saying goodbye. I wrote back, and I sent a Christmas card—nothing religious on it, of course—but I haven't heard from her since.' Grace stood smoothing her skirt down toward her knees. 'Have you heard from her?' she asked and he thought she stood a little too still as she waited for a reply.

'I never heard from her,' he said. The gas fire seemed to hiss at him unpleasantly.

'It's all a bit strange,' she said and, after a long moment of quiet: 'You still miss her.'

'I'm sorry?' he asked, fumbling for a suitable reply.

'You miss her,' repeated Grace and now her eyes were firmly fixed on him. His own gaze wavered. 'You are not happy.'

'It is a moot point,' he said. 'She made her choice very clear.' He hoped this was enough to change the subject, but Grace only walked over to the window and pulled aside the lace curtain to peer out into the featureless night. 'One feels quite powerless,' he admitted.

The room pressed in on him. The oval mantel clock ticked on oblivious to the shift in tension in the room. The flowered wallpaper, which had seemed cosy, now breathed dust onto the dull carpet. The teapot cooled and he could almost feel the cream drifting to scum on the surface of the milk jug. He felt a sudden horror at the thought of his life boxed into a series of such rooms.

'I have a feeling she is not happy where she is,' said Grace. 'You should look in on her on your way to Scotland. Aren't you going up for some shooting?'

'It's not my place to interfere,' he said.

'It's a pity you can't just storm in and fetch her back,' said Grace. 'She could be your very own damsel in distress.'

'Life is not a Hollywood film,' he snapped. He wondered why on earth she was pushing at him like this. Couldn't she tell he was ready to declare his affection for her?

'I've always admired you for being a sensible man,' she said. 'Sometimes you don't like to speak up, but usually I can tell that you know the right thing to do.' He sensed that what was coming might not be a compliment. However, she seemed to catch herself; she merely sighed and added, 'Perhaps none of us knows the right thing to do.'

'You're a sensible woman, too,' said the Major. 'I didn't come here tonight to talk about Mrs Ali. She made her choice and it is high time I moved on and made some choices of my own. Do come and sit down, dear Grace.' He patted the armchair next to his and she came over and sat down.

'I would like you to be happy, Ernest,' she said. 'We all deserve that.' He took her hand and patted the back of it.

'You are very good to me, Grace,' he said. 'You are intelligent, attractive, and supportive. You are also very kind and you are not a gossip. Any man who is not a fool would be happy to call you his own.' She laughed, but her eyes seemed to be brimming.

'Oh Ernest, I think you just listed the perfect qualities in a neighbour and the worst possible qualifications for passion.' He was shocked for an instant by the word 'passion', which seemed to crash through several conversational boundaries at once. He felt himself blushing.

'You and I are perhaps too—mature—for the more impetuous qualities,' he said, stumbling to find a word other than 'old'.

'You must speak for yourself,' she said gently. 'I refuse to play the dried rose and accept that life must be tepid and sensible.'

'At our age, surely there are better things to sustain us, to sustain a marriage, than the brief flame of passion?' She hesitated and they both felt the weight of the word hang between them. A tear made its way down her cheek and he saw that she had continued to avoid face powder and that she looked quite beautiful even in the rather overly bright room.

'You are mistaken, Ernest,' she said at last. 'There is only the passionate spark. Without it, two people living together may be lonelier than if they lived quite alone.' Her voice had a gentle finality, as if he were already putting on his coat and leaving her. Some contrary spirit, perhaps his own pride, he thought, made him stubborn in the face of what he knew to be true.

'I came here tonight to offer you my companionship,' he said. 'I had hoped it would lead to more.' He could not honestly repeat the word 'marriage' as he had planned a much more gradual increase in intimacy and had not indeed prepared any irrevocable declarations.

'I will not have you, Ernest,' she said. 'I care for you very much, but I do not want to make any compromises with the rest of my years.' She wiped her eyes with the back of her hand, like a child, and smiled. 'You should go after her.'

'She will not have me either,' he said, and his gloom betrayed the truth of everything Grace had said. He looked at her, horrified, but she did not seem angry.

'You won't know that if you don't ask her, will you?' said Grace. 'I'll go and get you her address.'

Grace hugged her arms about her as she watched him try to pull on his coat in the hallway without putting an elbow through one of the many small prints hanging on the wall. He set a sheep on a crag rattling in its black frame and she stepped to steady it. Close to her like this, he was overwhelmed with shame at the shabbiness of his own behaviour and he put a hand on her arm. For an instant, all they had said hung in the balance; he had only to squeeze her arm and she would lose her resolve and take him after all. Such an awful fragility of love, he thought, that plans are made and broken and remade in these gaps between rational behaviour. She pulled away from him and said, 'Be careful on the step, it's very icy.' He had a witty comment to add, inviting her to take a slap at him or something, but he thought better of it.

'You are a remarkable woman, Grace,' he said. Then he hunched his shoulders against the cold and his own failings and stepped into the night.

Telling Roger that the journey to Scotland would include a detour to visit Mrs Ali was not the sort of thing one could successfully manage on the telephone. So, on the Sunday before, the Major tapped lightly on the door knocker at Roger's cottage. The frost was still deep and the sun only a vague promise in the mid-morning sky; he blew on his hands and stamped his feet against the cold as he looked with dismay at the window boxes with their withered holly and dead white roses left over from Christmas. The windows looked smeary, too, and mud on the doorstep suggested that no one was taking care of the place now that Sandy was gone.

He tapped again, the sound reverberating like a pistol shot in the hedges, and saw a twitch of curtain in the cottage opposite. Footsteps, banging, and a muttered curse preceded Roger, who opened the door wrapped in a duvet over flannel pyjamas and sporting flip-flops over his socks.

'Aren't you up?' asked the Major, feeling cross. 'It's eleven o'clock.'

'Sorry, bit of a hangover,' said Roger, leaving the door wide open and trailing back into the living room, where he collapsed onto the couch and groaned.

'Is this becoming a daily condition for you?' asked the Major, looking about him at the room. Takeaway containers sat congealing on the coffee table. The Christmas tree still bristled with black intensity, but its feet were covered in dust. The couch and chaise had slid away from their razor-sharp alignment and now sat askew on the rug, as dazed as Roger. 'This place is a disgrace, Roger.'

'Don't shout. Please don't shout,' said Roger, covering his ears. 'I think my ears are bleeding.'

'I am not shouting,' said the Major. 'I don't suppose you've had breakfast, have you? Why don't you get dressed while I clear up and make some toast?'

'Oh, leave the clearing up,' said Roger. 'I have a cleaning lady who comes tomorrow.'

'Does she really,' replied the Major. 'My, how she must look forward to Mondays.'

When Roger had finished emptying the hot water tank and, from the smell of him, using some expensive men's shower gel, no doubt packaged in a gleaming aluminium container of sporty design, he wandered, squinty-eyed, into the kitchen. He had put on tight jeans and a close-fitting sweater. His feet were bare and his hair combed back in wide stiff lines. The Major paused as he spread some thin toast with the last scrapings of a margarine substitute. 'How come you have all these foreign designer clothes and yet you have no food and your milk is sour?'

'I get all my ordinary food and stuff delivered in London,' said Roger. 'A girl comes and puts it all away in the right place. I mean, I don't mind popping in the gourmet store for a browse around the aged Gouda, but who wants to waste their time buying cereal and washing-up liquid?'

'How do you think other people manage?' said the Major.

'They spend their whole lives toddling down the shops with a little string bag, I expect,' said Roger. 'Sandy took care of it and I haven't had time to get a system in place, that's all.' He took a piece of toast and the Major poured him tea with no milk and cut up a small, slightly withered orange. 'I don't suppose you could pick me up a few things, say on a Friday?' he added.

'No, I couldn't,' said the Major. 'My string bag is quite at capacity as it is.'

'I didn't mean it like that,' said Roger. 'Do I have any aspirin in the cupboard?'

The Major, who had inventoried the cupboards and swept all the dirty dishes into the dishwasher before Roger had rinsed off his soap, produced a large bottle of aspirin and rinsed a glass for water.

'Thanks, Dad,' said Roger. 'Why are you up so early, anyway?'

The Major explained, in as vague a way as possible, that he needed to leave earlier on Thursday in order to visit a friend on the way to Scotland and that he would need Roger to be up with the dawn.

'Not a problem,' said Roger.

'Considering the difficulty I just had in rousting you from your slumbers at eleven o'clock,' said the Major, 'I'll need some more reassurance.'

'It's not a problem because I'm not going to drive up with you,' said Roger. 'Gertrude's been asked to go up early and she wants me to go with her.'

'You're going with Gertrude?' repeated the Major.

'You'll be happy to know I ordered a whole picnic for the trip,' said Roger. 'I'm going to whip out my hamper of cold mini pasties and duck confit on soft rolls with sour cherry chutney and seal the deal with a split of chilled champagne.' He rubbed his hands with anticipatory glee. 'Nothing like a nice long road trip to advance romantic activities.'

'But you asked to ride up with me,' said the Major. 'I was counting on two drivers so we wouldn't have to stop.'

'You never did like to stop anywhere,' said Roger. 'I remember that trip to Cornwall when I was eight. You wouldn't stop for the bathroom until Stonehenge. I really enjoyed the searing pain of that bladder infection.'

'You always remember things out of proportion,' said the Major. 'It cleared right up with the antibiotics, didn't it? And besides, we bought you a rabbit.'

'Thanks, but I'll take Gertrude and a duck leg and avoid kidney stones,' said Roger.

'Don't you think it's unconscionably soon to be pursuing another woman?' asked the Major. 'Sandy only just left.'

'She made her choice,' said Roger. The Major recognised, with a rueful smile, that his son's words sounded familiar. 'I'm not going to let the grass grow,' he added. 'Mark to market and move on, as we say about a bad deal.'

'Sometimes it's a mistake to let them go, my boy,' said the Major. 'Sometimes you have to go after them.'

'Not this time, Dad,' said Roger. He looked at his father with some hesitation and then lowered his head, and the Major understood that his son did not believe he welcomed awkward confidences.

'I would like to know what happened,' he said, turning away to wash dishes. It had always been easier to get Roger to talk when they were driving in the car or engaged in some other activity that did not require eye contact. 'I grew to quite like her.'

'I screwed it all up and I didn't even know it,' said Roger. 'I thought we'd agreed on everything. How was I supposed to know what she wanted if she didn't know herself until it was too late?'

'What did she want?'

'I think she wanted to get married, but she didn't say.' Roger munched on his toast.

'And now it's too late?'

When Roger spoke again, his usual bravado was replaced with a note of seriousness. 'We had a little mishap. No big deal.

We agreed on how to handle it.' He turned back to the Major. 'I went with her to the clinic and everything. I did everything you're supposed to do.'

'A clinic?' The Major could not bring himself to ask more plainly.

'A woman's clinic,' said Roger. 'Don't make a face like that. It's absolutely acceptable these days—woman's right to choose and all that. It's what she wanted.' He paused and then amended his language. 'Well, we talked about it and she agreed. I mean, I told her it was the responsible thing to do at this stage in our careers.'

'When was this?' asked the Major.

'We found out right before the dance,' said Roger. 'Took care of it before we came down for Christmas, and she never told me she didn't want to go through with it—as if I'm supposed to have magic powers of detection, like some psychic Sherlock Holmes.'

'I think you're confusing two concepts,' said the Major, distracted by the metaphors.

'I wasn't confused,' said Roger. 'I made a plan and I stuck to it and everything seemed fine.'

'Or so you thought,' said the Major.

'She never said a word,' said Roger. 'Maybe she was a bit quiet sometimes, but I couldn't be expected to know what she was thinking.'

'You are not the first man to miss a woman's more subtle communication,' said the Major. 'They think they are waving when we see only the calm sea, and pretty soon everybody drowns.'

'Exactly, I think,' said Roger, and then he added, 'I asked her to marry me, you know? On Christmas Eve, before the party at Dagenham's. I felt bad about the whole thing and I was prepared to move our plans along.' He tried to sound nonchalant, but a crack in his voice betrayed him and the Major was suddenly flooded with feeling and had to dry his hands on a towel. 'I mean, I told her maybe we could even try again next year, if I got promoted through this Ferguson deal.' He sighed and his eyes assumed a dreamy look that might have been emotion. 'Maybe a boy first, not that you can really control these things. A boy called Toby and then a girl—I like Laura, or maybe Bodwin—and I told her we could use the little bedroom here as a nursery and then maybe build on a playroom, like in a conservatory.' He looked with confusion at the Major. 'She slapped me.'

'Oh, Roger,' said the Major. 'Tell me you didn't.'

'I ask her to marry me and she acts like I've asked her to eat human flesh or something. I'm laying out my hopes and plans and she's screaming at me that I'm so shallow a minnow would drown in my depths. I mean, what does that even mean?'

The Major wished he had known, coming upon Sandy in the darkened house that night. He wished he had said something at the dance, when Mrs Ali thought Sandy seemed troubled. They might have really done something then. He wondered whether it was his fault Roger had the perceptiveness of concrete.

'I think perhaps your timing was not sensitive, Roger,' said the Major quietly. He felt, in the area of his heart, a slow constriction of sorrow for his son and wondered where or when he had failed, or forgotten, to teach this boy compassion.

'Anyway, who needs that kind of drama,' said Roger. 'I've had plenty of time to consider and now I'm thinking seriously about making a go of things with Gertrude.' He looked more cheerful. 'There's still a lot of mileage in leveraging an old country name like hers, and she's always adored me. Under the right conditions, I might be prepared to make her very happy.'

'You can't negotiate love like a commercial transaction,' said the Major, appalled.

'That's true,' said Roger. He seemed perfectly happy again and rummaged in the bag for an apple. 'Love is like a big fat bonus that you hope kicks in after you negotiate the rest of the term sheet.'

'There is no poetry in your soul, Roger,' said the Major.

'How about "Roses are red, / violets are blue, / Sandy is gone, / Gertrude will do"?' suggested Roger.

'It really won't do, Roger,' said the Major. 'If you don't feel any real spark of passion for Gertrude, don't shackle yourselves together.

You'll only be dooming both of you to a life of loneliness.' He smiled wryly to hear himself repeating Grace's words as his own. Here he was dispensing them as advice when he had only just taken them in as revelation. So, he thought, do all men steal and display the shiny jackdaw treasure of other people's ideas.

As the Major was preparing to leave, Roger suddenly asked him, 'Where are you diving off to, anyway? Who's this friend you're off to visit?'

'Just someone who relocated up north. Grace wanted me to check in on her.'

'It's that woman again,' said Roger, narrowing his eyes. 'The one with the fanatic nephew.'

'Her name is Jasmina Ali,' replied the Major. 'Please show enough respect to remember her name.'

'What are you doing, Dad?' said Roger. 'Wasn't the golf club fiasco enough to warn you off? She's a bad idea.'

'Chimpanzees writing poetry is a bad idea,' said the Major. 'Receiving romantic advice from you is also a bad, if not horrendous, idea. Spending an hour dropping in on an old friend is a good idea and also none of your business.'

'Old friend, my arse,' said Roger. 'I saw how you looked at her at the dance. Everyone could see you were ready to make a fool of yourself.'

'And "everyone" disapproved, of course,' said the Major. 'No doubt because she is a woman of colour.'

'Not at all,' said Roger. 'As the club secretary mentioned to me in private, it's not remotely a question of colour but merely that the club doesn't currently have any members who are in trade.'

'The club and its members can go to hell,' said the Major, spluttering in anger. 'I'll be glad to watch them throw me out.'

'My God, you're in love with her.'

The Major's immediate reaction was to continue to deny it. While he tried to find some intermediate response, something that would express his intention without exposing him to ridicule, Roger said, 'What on earth do you hope to accomplish?' The Major felt a rage unlike anything he had felt toward his son before and he was provoked into honesty.

'Unlike you, who must do a cost-benefit analysis of every human interaction,' he said, 'I have no idea what I hope to accomplish. I only know that I must try to see her. That's what love is about, Roger. It's when a woman drives all lucid thought from your head; when you are unable to contrive romantic stratagems, and the usual manipulations fail you; when all your carefully laid plans have no meaning and all you can do is stand mute in her presence. You hope she takes pity on you and drops a few words of kindness into the vacuum of your mind.'

'Pigs'll fly before we see you at a loss for words,' said Roger, rolling his eyes.

'Your mother rendered me silent the first time we met. Took the witty repartee right out of my mouth and left me gaping like a fool.'

The Major remembered her thin blue dress against an intense green summer lawn and the evening sun catching at the edges of her hair. She held her sandals in one hand and a small cup of punch in the other and she was screwing up her lips against the sweet stickiness of the foul drink. He was so busy staring that he lost his way in the middle of a complicated anecdote and had to blush at the scathing guffaws of his friends, who had been depending on him for the punch line. She had pushed into the circle and asked him directly, 'Is there something to drink other than this melted-lolly stuff?' It had sounded like poetry in his ear and he had steered her away to the host's pantry and unearthed a bottle of Scotch and let her do all the talking while he tried not to gaze at her dress skimming the soft pyramids of her breasts like a scarf forever falling from a marble-sculpted wood nymph.

'What would Mother think about you chasing all over England after some shopgirl?' asked Roger.

'If you say "shopgirl" one more time, I shall punch you,' said the Major.

'But what if you marry her and she outlives you?' Roger asked. 'What happens if she won't give up the house and—well, after all the fuss you made about the Churchills, I don't see how you can just hand everything over to a complete stranger.'

'Ah, so it isn't a question of loyalty as much as of patrimony,' said the Major.

'It's not the money,' said Roger indignantly. 'It's the principle of the thing.'

'These things are never neat, Roger,' said the Major. 'And speaking of your mother, you were there when she begged me not to remain alone if I found someone to care for.'

'She was dying,' said Roger. 'She begged you to marry again and you swore you wouldn't. Personally, I was mad that we wasted so much valuable time on deathbed promises both of you knew were untenable.'

'Your mother was the most generous of women,' the Major said. 'She meant what she said.' They were silent for a moment and the Major wondered whether Roger was also smelling again the carbolic and the roses on the bedside table and seeing the greenish light of the hospital room and Nancy's face, grown as thin and beautiful as a painted medieval saint, with only her eyes still burning with life. He had struggled in those last hours, as had she, to find words that were not the merest of platitudes. Words had failed him then. In the awful face of death, which seemed so near and yet so impossible, he had choked on speech as if his mouth were full of dry hay. Poems and quotations, which he had remembered using to soothe others on those useless condolence notes and in the occasional eulogy, seemed specious and an exercise of his own vanity. He could only squeeze his wife's brittle hand while the useless pleadings of Dylan Thomas, 'Do not go gentle into that good night . . . ,' beat in his head like a drum.

'Are you all right, Dad? I didn't mean to be harsh,' said Roger, bringing him blinking to his senses. He focused his eyes and braced one hand on the back of Roger's couch.

'Your mother is gone, Roger,' the Major said. 'Your uncle Bertie is gone. I don't think I should waste any more time.'

'Maybe you're right, Dad,' said Roger. He seemed to think for a moment, which the Major found unusual, and then he came around the couch and held out his hand. 'Look, I wish you luck with your lady friend,' he said. 'Now, how about you wish me luck at Ferguson's shoot? You know how much this Enclave deal means to me.'

'I appreciate the gesture,' said the Major, shaking hands. 'It means a lot to me. I do wish you luck, son. I'll do whatever I can to support you up there.'

'I was hoping you'd say that,' said Roger. 'Since I'm going up early, there may be some wildfowling, Gertrude says. So how about letting me take up the Churchills?'

꙳ ꙳ ꙳

As the Major drove away from Roger's cottage, leaving his gun box with his delighted son, he had a sinking feeling that he had been manipulated once again. In his mind images played in a tiresome loop. Roger crouched in a duck boat in the foggy dawn. Roger rising to fire at a soaring flock of mallards. Roger toppling backward over the metal bench into the scuppers. Roger dropping a Churchill, with the smallest of splashes, into the fathomless waters of the loch.

Chapter Twenty-one

Would Don Quixote or Sir Galahad have been able to maintain his chivalrous ardour for the romantic quest, wondered the Major, if he had been forced to crawl bumper-to-bumper through an endless landscape of traffic cones, belching lorries, and sterile motorway service areas? He looked to their shining examples as he endured the ugly concrete girdle of London's M25, reminding himself that at least it kept the heaving flabby suburbs from spilling out and suffocating what was left of the countryside. He tried not to lose courage as the south fell away and the motorways became one speeding blur of giant lorries, all racing north as if they had a thousand miles to cover and donated organs in the back instead of cargoes of cold tea, frozen chickens, and appliances. In the fluorescent lighting and faint bleach smell of an anonymous service area somewhere in the Midlands, where he was just another grey-haired old man with a plastic tray, his doubts threatened to overwhelm him.

He hadn't let anyone know he was coming. What if Mrs Ali wasn't even home? The siren call of Scotland with the promised castle banquet and shooting in the heather almost turned his head, but as he put his thumb too vigorously through the cover of a little plastic tub and sprayed his jacket with milk, it came to him that it was precisely Mrs Ali who made the world a little less anonymous. She made him a little less anonymous. He gulped his tea—not difficult, as it was little better than tepid—and hurried out to get back on the road.

〜 ❧ 〜

He felt self-conscious cruising the streets looking for the right road and house number from the letter Grace had given him. Mrs Ali's neat handwriting was crumpled under his fingers on the steering wheel as he checked the thin page again and again against the streets outside. The people on the pavements were now mostly dark-skinned women with children and babies in pushchairs. Some wore the headscarf arrangement of observant Muslims. Some sported the short puffy jackets and gold earrings fashionable among the universal young. He thought he saw a few heads turn to watch him as he passed a knot of young men huddled around the raised bonnet of a car. He overshot the house but was too embarrassed to drive around the block again. Instead, he slipped into an open parking space.

The long street was anchored at one end by a couple of large Victorian mansions, now crumbling and forlorn. At the other end a brick wall indicated the perimeter of a redbrick housing estate filled with six-storey blocks of flats and narrow terraced houses. Metal window frames and blank front doors in one of three colours suggested the limits, artistic and budgetary, of the local housing authority's imagination. Between these representatives of the high and low points of the industrial age was the long row of semi-detached houses built for a prewar middle class of rising aspirations: three bedrooms, two parlours, and indoor plumbing, all serviced by a 'daily' maid.

Some of the semis had been heavily improved since their heyday and were all but unrecognisable beneath their vinyl double-glazed windows, boxy side extensions, and glassed-in front doors. The few that retained their original wooden window frames also had peeling paint and a variety of haphazard window coverings that suggested bedsits. Worst of all, to the Major's eyes, many of the houses, affluent or not, had cut down flowering front yards and paved them over to park multiple cars up against the windows.

The Ali family's house was one of the more prosperous. It retained half a garden with a gravel area on which stood a small two-seater sports car. The elegant effect of the car and the new white-painted windows was overshadowed by the neighbouring house, which bore leaping dolphins on its gateposts and purple shutters around dark wood window frames. The Major was just allowing himself a small sniff of disapproval at such obviously foreign excess when a white woman with streaky hair and a pink fur jacket over green jeans tripped out of the front door in her black patent boots and drove away in a small green car with an 'Ibiza Lover' bumper sticker.

Mentally apologising to the rest of the neighbourhood, the Major marched up to the heavy oak door of the Ali house and stood on the doorstep, staring at the ordinary brass circle of the door knocker. He remembered standing with Mrs Ali outside the golf club, both of them tense with anticipation. He was sure, now, that life could never live up to its anticipatory moments and he became quite certain that today would be a disaster. He looked behind him, thinking perhaps he should make a run for his car. A young man passed slowly on a bicycle, chewing gum and staring at him. The Major nodded and, feeling too embarrassed to shuffle away, turned back to knock at the door.

A young pregnant woman answered. She wore fashionably tousled hair tucked loosely into a scarf and a soft black maternity dress over black-and-white-patterned leggings. Her brown face was attractive but blunt and bore more than a passing resemblance to Abdul Wahid's.

'Yes?' she said.

'Good afternoon, I'm Major Ernest Pettigrew. I'm here to see Mrs Ali,' said the Major in his most authoritative tone.

'Are you from the council?' said the woman.

'Good heavens, no,' said the Major. 'Why, do I look like a man from the council?' The woman gave him a look that said he did. 'I'm a friend of Mrs Ali's,' he added.

'My mother's stepped out to the shop,' said the woman. 'Do you want to wait?' She did not open the door farther or step aside as she said this, and the Major realised she was looking at him with great suspicion.

'Oh, I don't want your mother,' said the Major, understanding his mistake. 'I'm here to see Mrs Jasmina Ali, from Edgecombe St Mary.'

'Oh, her,' said the woman. She paused and then said: 'You better come in and I'll phone my dad.'

ι ʔ ſ

'Is she here?' asked the Major as he was shown into the kind of spare, formal front room that is kept exclusively for guests. Two sofas faced each other across the small gas fireplace, each dressed in crimson flocked silk in a pattern of roses and covered in see-through vinyl. Two patterned wall hangings and a large abstract painting that suggested a blue and grey landscape decked the cream-coloured walls. There were no books and the various small side tables were decorated with lumps of rock and crystal and bowls of dried seed pods and aromatic twigs. Good-quality fabric blinds under a matching blue fabric pelmet hung at the bay window; opposite the window, frosted French doors surrounded by floor-length blue drapes led to another room. The room's finest decorative feature was an oriental rug, a glorious riot of pattern hand-woven from a thousand different blue silks. It was a room, thought the Major, which his sister-in-law Marjorie might admire, and while she would never be seen to use vinyl covers on her furniture she would secretly yearn for such spill-proof elegance.

'I'll get you some tea,' said the woman. 'Please wait here.' She left, shutting the door behind her. The Major selected one of two small, straight chairs that stood at one end of the sofas. They were spindly to an alarming degree but he did not trust himself to sit on a sofa without making alarming trouser-on-vinyl noises. The silence in the room settled around him. The street noises were muffled through the double glazing and no clock ticked on the mantel. There was not even a television, though he seemed to hear the jingling of a game show. He listened hard and thought there must be a TV playing deeper in the house, beyond the frosted doors.

He stood up when the door to the hall opened. It was the young woman, coming back with a brass tea tray that held a teapot and two glasses set in silver cup holders. Two small giggling children slipped in behind her and gazed at the Major as if at a zoo exhibit.

'My father will be home right away,' said the young woman, indicating that the Major should sit. 'He looks forward to meeting you Mr—what is your name?'

'Major Pettigrew. Is Mrs Ali not home?' he asked.

'My father will be here momentarily,' she said again, and poured him a cup of tea. Then, instead of pouring one for herself, she merely shooed the small children out of the room and left, shutting the door again behind her.

A few more silent minutes passed. The Major felt the weight of the room on his head and the pressure of time running through his fingers. He refused to glance at his watch but he could see the other guests arriving in Scotland. No doubt a cold lunch buffet was still set out on a sideboard and guests were seeing to the hanging up of clothes or enjoying a brisk walk around the lake. He had never seen Ferguson's castle home, but it must of course have both lake and cold buffet. These things could be depended upon. In this room, the Major could depend on nothing. It was all unfamiliar and therefore very taxing. All at once, there was a key in the front door and movement in the hallway. Urgent voices seemed to meet as the front door was opened and fierce whispers accompanied the usual hallway noise of coats and shoes being deposited.

The door opened again to admit a broad-shouldered man with black cropped hair and a neat moustache. He wore a shirt and tie and his breast pocket still bore the plastic name tag that identified him, unexpectedly, as Dave. He was not tall, but his air of authority and slight double chin suggested a man in command of some slice of the world.

'Major Pettigrew? I'm Dave Ali and it's an honour to have you in my humble home,' he said in a tone that, the Major had observed over the years, was used by those who believe their home superior to most. 'I have heard all about you from my son, who considers himself greatly in your debt.'

'Oh, not at all,' said the Major, finding himself waved back to his chair and offered more tea. The Major had never liked diminutives and found the name Dave an unlikely moniker for this Mr Ali. 'Your son is a very intense young man.'

'He is impetuous. He is stubborn. He makes his mother and me crazy,' said Dave, shaking his head in mock despair. 'I tell her I was the same at his age and not to worry, but she tells me I had her to whip me into shape, while Abdul Wahid—well, *insha'Allah*, he, too, will find his way once he is married.'

'We were all looking forward to seeing Jasmina—Mrs Ali—when she came for the wedding,' said the Major.

'Yes, I'm sure,' said Dave in a noncommittal voice.

'She has many friends in the village,' said the Major, pressing him.

'I'm afraid she will not be coming,' said Dave Ali. 'My wife and I are going in the Triumph and can barely fit our luggage. And then someone must take care of my mother, who is very frail, and Sheena is due any day now.'

'I appreciate that there are difficulties,' the Major began. 'But surely, something as important as a wedding . . . ?'

'My wife, who is the soul of kindness, Major, said "Oh, Jasmina should go and I will stay with Mummi and Sheena," but I ask you, Major, should a mother, who works seven days a week, miss her only son's wedding?' He ran out of breath and mopped his face with a large handkerchief and considered his wife's many sacrifices.

'I suppose not,' agreed the Major.

'Besides, it will be only the quietest of ceremonies.' Dave slurped at his tea. 'I was willing to bankrupt myself to do it right, but my wife says they will prefer not to make a fuss in the circumstances. So it will be almost nothing—just a token exchange of gifts and not an ounce more than what is proper.' He paused and then looked at the Major with an eyebrow raised in significance. 'Besides, we feel it is important for our Jasmina to make a clean break with the past if she is to be happy in her future.'

'A clean break?' asked the Major. Dave Ali sighed and shook his head in what appeared to be pity.

'She insisted on taking on a large burden when my brother died,' he said slowly. 'A burden no woman should be asked to carry. And now we want only for her to lay down such responsibilities and be happy here in the heart of family where we can take care of her.'

'That is very generous of you,' said the Major.

'But old habits linger,' said Dave. 'Myself, I look forward to the day when I can turn over our whole business to Abdul Wahid and retire, but no doubt I, too, will get under everyone's feet and have a hard time handing over the decisions to others.'

'She is a very capable woman,' said the Major.

'In time we hope she will learn to be content here at home. She is already indispensable to my mother and she is reading the Qur'an to her every day. I have refused to put her in one of our shops. I have told her now is her time to sit back and let others take care of her. So much better to be happily at home, I tell her. No taxes or bills to pay, no books to balance, no one expecting you to know all the answers.'

'She is used to a certain independence,' the Major said.

Dave shrugged. 'She is coming around. She has stopped suggesting to my poor wife new ways to run our inventory systems. Instead, she is obsessed with getting her own library card.'

'A library card?' asked the Major.

'Personally, who has time to read?' he said. 'But if she wants one, I tell her she is welcome to it. We are very busy right now, what with the wedding and opening a SuperCentre next month, but my wife has promised to help her establish proof of her residency and then she will be able to sit home and read all day.'

They were interrupted by a commotion in the hallway. The Major couldn't make out any of the words, but he heard a familiar voice cry out, 'This is ridiculous. I will go in if I please,' and then the door opened and there she was, Mrs Ali, still wearing a coat and scarf and carrying a small bag of groceries. Her cheeks were flushed, either from the argument or from having been outside, and she looked at him as if she were hungry to see all of him at once. Behind her, the young pregnant woman whispered something that made Mrs Ali flinch.

'It's fine, Sheena, let her come,' said Dave, getting up and waving as if to dismiss her. 'It will do no harm to greet an old friend of your uncle Ahmed's.'

'It is you,' she said. 'I saw a hat in the hallway and I knew at once it was yours.'

'We did not know you were back from your errands,' said Dave. 'The Major is passing by on his way to Scotland.'

'I had to come and see you,' said the Major. He wanted desperately to take her hand but he restrained the impulse.

'I was just telling the Major how much you enjoy your reading,' said Dave. 'My brother used to tell me, Major, how Jasmina was always buried in reading. "So what if I have to do a little more so she can read. She is an intellectual," he would say.' His voice twisted with an unmistakable sarcasm at the word 'intellectual' and the Major was gripped with an intense dislike of the man. 'I'm only sorry he worked himself so hard,' added Dave mopping with his handkerchief again. 'Taken so early from us.'

'That is despicable even for you,' said Mrs Ali in a low voice. There was a pause as they looked at each other with equally locked jaws. 'Sheena told me you had a business meeting,' she added.

'Sheena is very cautious,' said Mr Ali, addressing the Major. 'She worries about protecting everyone. Sometimes she even makes people wait in the street for me.'

'Grace wanted me to come and see you,' said the Major to Mrs Ali. 'I think she was expecting you to write.'

'But I did write, several times,' she said. 'I see I was right to worry when I received no reply.' She gave her brother-in-law a look of mild disdain. 'Is this not strange, Dawid?'

'Shocking, shocking—the post office is very bad these days,' agreed her brother-in-law, pursing his lips as if he did not like being addressed by his real name in front of an outsider. 'And I speak as someone who has three sub post offices. We can only put the mail in the bag, but after that we're not responsible.'

'I would like to talk to the Major for a few minutes alone,' said Mrs Ali. 'Should we speak here, or should I take the Major on a walk to show him the neighbourhood?'

'Here will be fine, just fine,' said Dawid Ali in a hurried tone. The Major saw, with a mixture of amusement and hurt, that he was appalled at the thought of them promenading in front of the neighbours. 'I'm sure the Major has to leave very soon, anyway—the afternoon traffic is so bad these days.' He went to the frosted doors and slid them open. 'So we will leave you to chat about old times for a few minutes.' In the back room, a television played low and an old lady sat in a wing chair, a walking frame positioned in front of her. She looked half dead, slumped in the chair, but the Major saw her black eyes swivel toward them. 'If you don't mind, I will not ask Mummi to turn out of her chair. She will not disturb you.'

'I don't need a chaperone,' said Mrs Ali in a fierce whisper.

'Of course not,' said Dawid. 'But we must allow Mummi to think she is useful. Don't worry,' he added to the Major, 'she's as deaf as a post.'

'I must thank you for your hospitality,' said the Major.

'I doubt we'll see you again, clean break and all that,' said Dawid Ali, holding out his hand. 'It was a pleasure to meet such an acquaintance of my brother and an honour that you should come so far out of your way.'

꜀ ꜆ ꜅

After Dawid Ali had whispered a few words to his mother and left the back room, the Major and Mrs Ali moved as far away as possible from the open doors and sat on a hard bench in the bay window. She still held her shopping bag and now she placed it under the bench and shrugged off her coat. It fell carelessly behind her.

'I feel as if I'm just dreaming that you're here,' she said.

'I don't think they'd like it if I pinched you,' he replied. They sat in silence for a moment. It seemed to the Major that it was necessary to break out of the usual kinds of small talk and make some declaration, some demand, but for the life of him he could not find the words to begin.

'That stupid dance,' he said at last. 'I never got the chance to apologise.'

'I do not blame you for the rudeness of others,' she said.

'But you left,' he said. 'Without saying goodbye.' She looked out of the window and he took the opportunity to study again the curve of her cheek and the thick lashes of her brown eyes.

'I had allowed myself to daydream,' she said. 'A fleeting sense of wonder.' She smiled at him. 'I woke up to find myself a practical woman once more and I realised something else.' Her smile faded and she looked serious, like a swimmer who commits to dive in, or a soldier to whom the order to open fire has just been given. 'I threw in my lot with the Ali family a great many years ago and it was time to pay that debt.'

'When you sent back the Kipling, I thought you despised me.' He was aware that he sounded like a wounded child.

'Sent it back?' she asked. 'But I lost it in the move.'

'Abdul Wahid handed it to me,' he said, feeling confused.

'I thought it was in my small bag with all my other valuables, but after I got here I couldn't find it.' She widened her eyes and her lips trembled. 'She must have stolen it from me.'

'Who?'

'My mother-in-law, Dawid's mother,' she said, nodding toward the back room. The Major tried to share her outrage, but he was too happy to discover that she had not meant to return his book.

'Your letters go missing, you are kept from your nephew's wedding, you are asked to leave your home,' he said. 'You cannot stay here, my dear lady. I cannot allow it.'

'What would you have me do?' she said. 'I must give up the shop, for George's sake.'

'If you'll allow me, I will take you away from here right now, today,' he said. 'Under any conditions you like.' He turned and took both her hands in his. 'If this room were not so ugly and oppressive, I would ask you something more,' he said. 'But my need to get you out of here is more important than any considerations of my own heart and I will not burden your escape with any strings. Simply tell me what I have to do to get you out of this room and take you somewhere where you can breathe. And do not insult me by pretending that you are not suffocating in this house.' His own breath came heavy now and his heart seemed to knock about in his chest like a trapped bird. She turned on him eyes wet with tears.

'Are we to run away to that little cottage we once talked about? Where no one knows us and we send only cryptic postcards to the world? I should like to go there now and be done with everyone for a while,' she said. He gripped her hands tightly and did not turn when he heard a wail from the other room, which was the old lady gabbling in Urdu and calling 'Dawid! Come quick!'

'Let's go now,' he said. 'I shall take you there, and if you want we'll stay forever.'

'What about the wedding?' she asked. 'I must see them safely married.'

'Or we'll drive to the wedding!' he shouted happily, abandoning all sense of decorum in his excitement. 'Only come away now and I promise, whatever happens, I will not abandon you.'

'I will go with you,' she said quietly. She got up and put on her coat. She picked up the bag of groceries. 'We must leave now, before they try to stop me.'

'Shouldn't you pack a bag?' he asked, flustered for a moment by the transformation of a momentary passion into cool reality. 'I could wait for you in the car.'

'If we stop for reality, I will never leave here,' she said. 'It is too sensible to stay. Aren't you expected in Scotland? Am I not to help with dinner and then read the Qur'an aloud? Is it not raining in England?' It was in fact now raining, and the fat drops splattered on the window like tears.

'It is raining,' he said. He looked out the window. 'And I am expected in Scotland.' He had forgotten all about the shoot and now, glancing at his watch, he saw that assuming they kept the usual absurdly early hours, he would likely not make it in time for dinner. He turned to see her teetering on her feet. At any moment she would sink onto the bench and the madness of running away would be gone. Her face was already losing its animation. He recognised the tiny moment before his failure would be understood and accepted. He hung in the space of the room, on the cusp of the silence between them and the wailing from the back room. Feet pounded in the hall. Then the Major leaned forward, reached out a hand, and fastened it around her wrist, hard. 'Let's go now,' he said.

Chapter Twenty-two

I need to find a telephone,' he said. They were out of the city, heading west, and already, through the slightly open window, the gloom of the afternoon seemed colder and cleaner. 'I'll have to find a pub or something.'

'I have a phone.' She rummaged in her shopping bag to produce a small mobile phone. 'I think they got me one to keep track of me, but I make sure never to turn it on.' As she fiddled with it, the phone gave a series of jangled beeps.

'Horrible things,' he said.

'Ten phone messages,' she said. 'I suppose they're looking for me.'

At an exit that said 'Tourist Information,' he pulled into a small car park with toilets and an old railway car turned into an information booth. It was closed for the winter and the car park was empty. While Mrs Ali went to use the facilities, he poked at the tiny number buttons and managed, on his second attempt, to reach the right number.

'Helena?' he said. 'Ernest Pettigrew. Sorry to call so out of the blue.'

By the time Mrs Ali came back, her hairline damp from where she had splashed her face with water, he had detailed directions to Colonel Preston's fishing lodge and knew that the key was under the hedgehog by the shed and that the paraffin lamps were kept in the washtub for safety. Helena had been graciously uncurious about his sudden need to use it, though she had refused the excuse of his offer to fetch the Colonel's fly rod.

'You know perfectly well if he ever got hold of it, he would have to face the fact that he's never going to use it,' she said. 'I'd like him to keep his dream a little longer.' As he said goodbye, she added, 'I won't tell anyone why you called,' and he was left looking at the phone and wondering whether the Colonel's whispered stories about Helena might be correct after all.

'We're all set,' he said. 'It's another hour or two's driving, I'm afraid. It's just—'

'Please don't tell me where it is,' she said. 'That way I can disappear even from myself for a while.'

'No heating, of course. Probably a bag of coal in the shed. Not much fishing in the winter.'

'And I brought food,' she said, looking at the shopping bag as if it had suddenly appeared. 'I didn't know what I was doing, but apparently I'm making us a chicken balti.'

He put the bag in the boot, the better to keep the milk and chicken cold. He saw a glimpse of tomatoes and onions and he smelled fresh coriander. There seemed to be some spices and dried leaves in small plastic bags and he felt the squashy contours of a bakery bag containing something that smelled of almonds.

'Perhaps we should stop and get you some—some things,' said the Major, stumbling over images of ladies' underwear in his mind and wondering where to find the shops.

'Let's not spoil the madness of escape with a trip to Marks and Sparks,' she said. 'Let's just drive right off the map.'

The lodge was more a tumbledown sheep shed, its thick stone walls topped with a crooked slate roof and its original openings crudely filled with an assortment of odd windows and doors, salvaged from other properties. The front door was heavy oak and carved with acorns and a medallion of leaves, but the neighbouring window was a ramshackle blue casement, fitted with several extra pieces of wood on one side and missing glass in one of the panes.

The light had all but gone from behind the mountains looming in the west, and a gibbous moon was making its humpbacked way into the sky. Below the lodge, a rough lawn led down to a narrow cove on a lake that seemed to open out like a sea in the darkness. The Major peered at the soft darker rounds of the trees and bushes crowding the property for a sharper silhouette that might signify a shed. He was about to announce a grid-by-grid search for the promised stone hedgehog when it occurred to him that the broken window might allow entry.

It was cold now and Mrs Ali stood shivering in her thin wool coat, the tail of her scarf flapping in a sharp wind off the lake. She had her eyes closed and breathed deeply.

'Cold enough for a frost tonight,' he said. He moved toward her, worrying that she was horrified at the state of the place. 'Perhaps we ought to go back to the village we passed and see if there's a bed and breakfast?' She opened her eyes and gave him an anxious smile.

'Oh, no, it's just so beautiful here,' she said. 'And to tell the truth, even at my advanced age and in the middle of such a ridiculous adventure, I don't think I can quite face checking into a hotel with you.'

'If you put it like that.' His cheeks flushed warm in the darkness. 'Though I don't know if you'll feel that way if we find squirrels in there,' he said, worried about the broken casement. He tightened his grip on the pencil-thin torch he had extracted from its place in the glove compartment and wondered whether the batteries were fresh or whether they were chalky with dribbled acid. 'I suppose we'd better mount an expedition to the interior.'

He could indeed twist the lock from inside the window; he pushed open the door and stepped into the deeper cold of the lodge. The torch gave only a thin bluish beam and he felt his way forward with hands outstretched to ward away the unexpected bang on the knee or knock of head on low beam. The light danced over glimpses of table and chairs, a broken-backed wicker sofa, an iron sink with cotton-curtained cabinets. A large fireplace loomed sooty and dark in one corner, smelling of damp coal. It had been disfigured on one shoulder by the addition of a galvanised container cemented directly into a hole in the chimney so that the heat of the fire could warm water. A couple of pipes with stopcocks led to the unseen bathroom facilities and the welcome possibility of at least a quick sponge bath. An arched opening showed the briefest glimpse of a bedroom. Through another strange arrangement—one patio slider and one French door jumbled together—the lake shone silver and a broad triangle of moonlight fell across the floor and showed large baskets stuffed with fishing gear, dropped as casually as if the owner were going out on the lake again directly. The Major found matches in the obvious place, a tin on the mantelpiece, and, in the low-ceilinged laundry room past the sink area, the promised zinc washtub filled with three paraffin lamps.

'I hope you're not expecting this place to look any better in the light,' he said as he struck a match and reached for the glass shade of the nearest lamp.

She laughed and said only, 'I haven't smelled a paraffin lamp since I was a small child. My father would tell us how it was discovered by an alchemist in ninth-century Baghdad who was trying to distill gold.'

'I thought it was a Scotsman who invented it,' said the Major, burning his thumb and dropping the match as he fumbled with the second lamp. 'But then the most amazing things were being made in the east while we were still getting the hang of wattle-and-daub and trying to find our runaway sheep.' He struck a new match. 'Unfortunately, none of it counted in the end unless you got your patents in ahead of the Americans.'

With the lamps offering their wavering yellow light and a coal fire leaping in the brick hearth, the room began to lose some of its damp crypt smell.

'It's quite charming in here if one squints.' He was opening a bottle of claret that had been meant as a gift to his Scottish host.

'As long as one wipes everything before touching it,' she said, sliding onions into a pan of butter. The rickety stove was powered by a rusty bottled-gas tank just outside the kitchen window. 'The dust seems to be years thick.'

'My former CO, Colonel Preston, has been frail for a couple of years now,' said the Major, looking at the assembled fly rods on the wall. 'I doubt he'll ever visit here again.' He walked to the hearth and tested the water heater with the back of his hand. Then he stood with his back to the blaze and sipped wine from a tea mug and looked at how her hands chopped tomato with a smooth twist and fall of the knife and how she cocked her head in concentration.

'Pity, really; he talks about this place as you or I might talk of—well, of wherever was the most important place in the world to us.' He felt a sadness for the Colonel but it could not hold his attention, because her hair was escaping from its pins and now she stopped to push some strand off her forehead with the flat of her arm. The chicken and spices hissed into the pan and as she covered it with a baking sheet, he could not remember any other place to which he had any attachment at all. The world seemed to have shrunk to fit quite perfectly inside the room.

'And do you have such a place?' she asked, lowering the flame under the pan and straightening up with a smile. 'I know I do not seem to belong anywhere.'

'I always supposed it to be Edgecombe St Mary,' he said. 'My wife is buried in the churchyard, you know, and I have a second plot there.'

'That's one way to feel rooted to a place,' she said. Then she made a horrified O with her lips while he laughed. 'No, that came out all wrong,' she said.

'Not at all,' he said. 'That is exactly what I meant. I always thought it important to decide where one would be buried, and then one could sort of work life out backward from there.'

♭ ♮ ♪

They ate, mopping up the sauce with sweet almond rolls and drinking the wine. She accepted a cup for the purpose of warding off the dampness and drank it cut with water, like a Frenchwoman. 'So, if you want to be buried in Sussex, you probably wouldn't move to—say—Japan?' she said.

'I refuse to answer, on the grounds that I may now prefer to just stay here with you and thereby deprive both Edgecombe and Tokyo of my presence,' he said.

'But we will not stay here, Major.' Her voice was sad. 'Just like the Colonel, we will have to leave and never see it again.'

'True.' He looked around at the fire's dancing shadows on the thick stone walls and the pools of light on the low ceiling from the lamps and the single candle guttering in a broken saucer. They had laid the bedroom's duvet over the back of the sofa to air, and its red flannel added to the warmth in the room. 'You must give me time to think,' he said.

'My husband's body was sent back to Pakistan for burial, something I do not wish for myself, and so I cannot rest next to him. Nor can I be buried in a pretty Sussex churchyard,' she said.

'On some days, days that his wife thinks are bad but which perhaps are good, my friend the Colonel is quite convinced that he is back here,' said the Major.

'So he dreams himself the life he cannot have?'

'Exactly. But we, who can do anything, we refuse to live our dreams on the basis that they are not practical. So tell me, who is to be pitied more?'

'There are real-life complications,' she said, laughing. 'Can you imagine if the whole world decided tomorrow to move to a fishing lodge in the English countryside?'

'It's Wales, actually,' said the Major. 'And they do get a bit funny if there are too many visitors.'

He gave her the nicer of his two pairs of pyjamas, navy cotton piped in white, as well as his camel robe and a pair of wool socks for her feet. He was glad he had packed the extra set after all. Nancy had often chided him for what she called his meticulous overpacking and his insistence on carrying a hard-sided leather bag for all trips. He couldn't abide today's travellers with their huge squashy duffle bags crammed with athletic shoes, balled-up tracksuits, and stretchy multipurpose trousers and dresses made out of special travel fabrics, with hidden pockets, which they wore indiscriminately to theatres and nice restaurants.

From a separate compartment, packed in an oilcloth bag that had belonged to his father, the Major produced a leather wash kit and, with some embarrassment at the intimacy, laid out soap, shampoo, toothpaste, and a small Egyptian cotton towel he always carried for emergencies.

'I'll just run out to the car,' he said. 'I have an extra toothbrush in my breakdown kit.'

'Along with a small barrel of brandy and a spare Shakespeare?' she asked.

'You're laughing at me,' he said. 'But if I didn't have a blanket in the car I'd be pretty cold tonight on that couch.' He thought she blushed, but it might have been the candle flickering on her skin.

When he returned she was dressed in his pyjamas and robe and was combing out her hair with his small, inadequate comb. The wool socks flopped around her slender ankles. The Major felt his breath falter and a new tension vibrate through his limbs.

'It's a very uncomfortable couch,' she said. Her eyes were dark in the lamplight and as she raised her arms to flip her hair back, he was aware of the curves of her body against the smooth cotton of the borrowed pyjamas and the soft robe. 'I'm not sure you'll be warm enough.' The Major felt it was vital to nod, and not to let his jaw fall open while he did so.

'Toothbrush,' he said with difficulty. He held it out by the very tip of the handle because he knew it was important, if he was to keep his composure, that her fingertips not touch his. 'Lucky thing the blanket is cashmere. I'll be perfectly comfortable.'

'You must at least take back your robe.' She stood and slid the robe off her shoulders and the Major found this so sensual that he dug his fingertips into his palms to keep the heat from rising in his face and body.

'Very kind of you.' Panic threatened to overwhelm him just from being close to her. He backed away toward the bedroom and the tiny bathroom beyond. 'I'd better say good night now, just in case you're asleep.'

'It's so beautiful I'd like to lie awake and watch the moon on the water all night,' she said, advancing on the bedroom.

'Much better to get some rest,' he said. He stumbled away from her, found the bathroom door with some effort, and clawed his way in. He wondered just how long he might have to hide out in the bathroom pretending to wash before she would be safely asleep. For a moment, he wished he had brought something to read.

❧ ❧ ❧

The soap and water revived him and also made him feel foolish. Once again, he had allowed his fears, and in this case, perhaps his fancies, to overwhelm his more rational self. Mrs Ali was no different from any other woman, he reminded himself, and in a low whisper he lectured the face in the dim mirror. 'She's deserving of protection and respect. At your age you should be perfectly able to share a small cottage with a member of the opposite sex without getting all carried away like a pimply teenager.' He frowned at his face and ran a hand through his hair, which stuck up like a stiff brush and needed cutting. He decided to make an appointment with the barber when they got back. After a final deep breath, he resolved to march through to the sitting room, uttering a cheery good night as he went, and to allow no more nonsense from himself.

As he walked out into the small bedroom, carrying the lamp, she was sitting up in bed with her knees hugged to her chest and her chin dropped onto them. Her hair spilled around her shoulders and she seemed very young, or perhaps just very vulnerable. When she looked up at him, he could see her eyes shining at him.

'I was thinking about being practical,' she said. 'Thinking of how everything is uncertain once we get back to the world.'

'Do we have to think of that?' he asked.

'So I was wondering whether it might be best if you just made love to me now, here, while we're enjoying this particular dream,' she said. She looked at him with a steady gaze and he found he felt no need to look away. He was grateful to feel a flush of excitement rush through his body like a full tide over flat sand and he saw his ache for her echoed in the high colour of her cheeks. There was no panic or fluster in his mind now. He would not diminish her declaration by asking her if she was sure. He merely hung the lamp on a hook in the beamed ceiling and went down on his knees at the bedside to take both her hands in his and kiss them, backs and palms. As he lifted his face to hers and as her hair swung around them like a dark waterfall, he found words suddenly irrelevant and so he said nothing at all.

∽ ঽ ∫

In the early morning, he stood with a foot raised on a smooth granite boulder by the empty lake and watched the sun dazzle on the frosted reeds and melt the lace of ice on the muddy edge. It was bitterly cold, but he felt the sear of air in his nose as something exquisite and he lifted his face to the sky to feel the warmth of the sun. The mountains across the lake wore capes of snow on their massive rocky shoulders and Mount Snowdon pierced the blue sky with its sharp white ridges. A lone bird, falcon or eagle, with fringed edges to its proud wings, glided high on the faintest of thermals, surveying its kingdom. He raised his own arms to the air, stretching with his fingertips, and wondered whether the bird's heart was as full as his own as he braced his legs against an earth made new and young. He wondered whether this might be how the first man had felt; only he had always pictured the Garden of Eden as a warm, midsummer experience, ripe with peaches and the drone of wasps in the orchard. Today he felt more like man the pioneer, alone in the harsh beauty of a strange new land. He felt upright, vigorous. He welcomed the stiffness of muscle and the faint tiredness that follows exertion. A pleasant glow, deep in his gut, was all that remained of a night that seemed to have burned away the years from his back.

He looked up the slight rise to the lodge, which slept under eaves crusted with ice. A lazy curl of smoke rose from the chimney. He had left her asleep, sprawled on her stomach, her hair in knots and her arms flung careless around her pillow. Too full of energy to remain in bed, he had, as silently as possible, dressed, fixed the fire, and set a kettle of water over a low flame so it would boil slowly while he took a walk. He would have liked to sort out last night in his mind, to categorise his feelings in some sober order, but it seemed all he could do this morning was grin and chuckle and wave at the empty world in foolish happiness.

As he gazed, the French door was pushed open and she came out of the house, squinting at the brightness. She had dressed and wore his blanket wrapped around her shoulders. She was carrying two mugs of tea, which steamed in the air. Smiling under her tangle of hair, she picked her way carefully down the stony path, while he held his breath as if the slightest move might cause her to shy away.

'You should have woken me,' she said. 'I hope you weren't fleeing the scene?'

'I needed to do a little capering about,' he said. 'Some beating of the chest and a spot of cheering—manly stuff.'

'Oh, do show me,' she said, laughing while he executed a few half-remembered dance steps, jumped on and off a tussock of grass and kicked at a large stone with a wild hooting. The stone bounced down the shore and plopped into the lake while the Major winced and shook out his injured foot. 'Ouch,' he said. 'That's about as much primeval man as I can manage.'

'Do I get a turn?' she asked. She handed him a mug for each hand and then spun herself in wild pirouettes to the shore where she stomped her feet in the freezing waters and let out a long, musical yowling sound that seemed to come from the earth itself. A flight of hidden ducks launched themselves into the air and she laughed and waved as they flew low across the water. Then she came running back and kissed him while he spread his arms wide and tried to keep his balance.

'Careful, careful,' he said, feeling a splash of scalding tea on his wrist. 'Passion is all very well, but it wouldn't do to spill the tea.' As they found two large rocks to sit on and slowly savoured their tea and munched on the last two, slightly stale almond cakes, they continued to laugh and to break out, every now and then, into smaller whoops and yells. He offered her a sustained yodel and she sang back to him a phrase or two of a haunting song from her childhood and while the lake lapped at their feet and the mountains absorbed their calls and the sky flung its blue parachute over their heads, he thought how wonderful it was that life was, after all, more simple than he had ever imagined.

Chapter Twenty-three

For the first time ever, the drive back to Edgecombe did not seem like the drive home. Instead it seemed that the closer they got, the more his hopes sank and his stomach tightened, squeezing bile he could taste. He had promised to get Jasmina home for the wedding and they had risen early, before the dawn, rather than go back the night before. Now he kept the car pointed south, roaring past the midlands and ignoring the seductive siren call of Stratford-upon-Avon though it turned both their heads as they sped past the beckoning exit. He coasted grim-faced through the snarls of London's twin airports and for the first time he could remember, he was not cheered when the first signs for the south coast began to appear.

'We are making good time,' she said, smiling. 'I do hope Najwa has remembered to get me the clothes.' She had called on her mobile phone and arranged to have Mrs Rasool let the family know she was coming to the wedding and to have a complete set of suitable clothes waiting for her. He had heard a smothered laugh while she talked and she told him Mrs Rasool was making extra rasmalai for the wedding dinner, which would secretly be in his honour. 'She is very upset with my sister-in-law, who keeps changing the dinner menu and wants the expenses broken down toothpick by toothpick,' she added. 'So she is very happy to know that we will add a pinch of subversion to the feast.'

'Are you sure I should come with you?' he asked. 'I'd hate to be their excuse to back out.'

'Najwa has arranged it so we can wait until we see the Imam arrive before we go in,' she said. 'Then they will not be able to make a fuss. It will drive them crazy, which will be of great satisfaction to me, but they will get their final papers signed and the shop will belong to Abdul Wahid, so what can they do?' Then she was quiet, staring out of the window.

'And you're sure about signing away the shop?' he said.

'I think my husband would be proud to see his legacy passed on. He gave the shop to me, freely, and I will, in the same spirit, give it to Abdul Wahid so that he and Amina and George can live lives of their own as I have been allowed to do.'

'Unselfish acts are rare these days. I admire you.'

'You are not a selfish man, Ernest. You gave up your trip to Scotland to rescue me.'

'If acts of selflessness brought such rewards,' he said, 'we would be a nation of saints.'

They took a small back lane into the village. Rose Lodge looked welcoming in a brief interlude of pale sunshine and they hurried inside to avoid being seen by the neighbours.

There was a still-warm teapot on the kitchen table, together with the remains of a ham sandwich and the day's newspaper, which wore a distinctly crumpled look. In the sink huddled more dirty plates and a greasy carton fringed with dried fried rice.

'Someone's been here,' said the Major in some alarm and he looked around for the poker, intending to check the whole house for intruders.

'Hullo, hullo,' said a voice from the passageway and Roger appeared with a plate of toast and a tea mug. 'Oh, it's you,' he said. 'You could have let me know you were coming. I'd have cleared up.'

'I should have let you know?' asked the Major. 'This is my house. Why on earth aren't you in Scotland?'

'I felt like coming home,' said Roger. 'But I suppose I shan't be welcome here any more.' He glared at Jasmina and the Major weighed the likelihood of his being able to lift Roger by the lapels of his jacket and propel him face first into the street. He thought he could do it but that the struggle might draw unwelcome attention from the neighbours.

'Your welcome here will depend entirely on your own ability to keep a civil tongue in your head,' said the Major. 'I don't have time for your petulance today. Mrs Ali and I have a wedding to attend.'

'I don't suppose it matters to you that my life is in ruins,' said Roger. He tried to adopt a stiff-jawed pose, but the effect was spoiled by the toast sliding off the plate and landing butter side down on his trousers, whence it slid its greasy way down to the floor. 'Oh, bloody hell,' he said, putting down his plate and mug to wipe at his leg with the back of his hand.

'Why don't you sit down?' said the Major, examining the contents of the teapot to see whether it was still fresh. 'Then we'll have some tea and you can tell Jasmina and me all about it.'

'It's Jasmina now, is it?' said Roger as the Major poured tea and handed round the cups. 'I can't believe my own father has a lady friend—at his age.' He shook his head as if this were the final nail in the coffin of his shattered life.

'I refuse to be referred to by a term so oily with double entendre,' said Jasmina as she hung her coat on one of the pegs by the back door and came to sit at the table. She was very composed as she smiled at Roger, though the Major noted a slight compression of the jaw and chin. 'I prefer "lover",' she said.

The Major choked on his tea and Roger actually laughed. 'Well, that'll make the village speechless,' he said.

'Which would be truly wonderful,' she said, and sipped her tea.

'Forget about us,' said the Major. 'What happened in Scotland, and where are my guns?'

'That's my father,' said Roger. 'Goes straight to what's important.'

'Did you sell them? Tell me quick.' The Major tensed, waiting for the pain of the news as one would wait to have a sticking plaster ripped from the skin.

'I did not sell them,' Roger said. 'I told Ferguson where he could shove his all-cash offer and I brought them home directly.' He paused and added, 'Or not so very directly. I came on the train and had a hell of a time with connections.'

'You came on the train? What about Gertrude?'

'Oh, she drove me to the station,' said Roger. 'It was quite an affecting goodbye, considering she had just refused to marry me.'

'You asked her to marry you?'

'I did,' said Roger. 'Unfortunately, I was the second bidder and my terms were not up to par.' He pushed his tea away and slumped his chin into his chest in defeat. 'You see, she's going to marry Ferguson.'

The Major listened in some disbelief as Roger told them how Gertrude had quite won the day in Scotland. It sounded as if she had taken over the place, charming Ferguson's estate manager into agreeing to most of the useful modernisations that Ferguson had proposed and even getting the head ghillie to agree to a restocking plan for the grouse moor. She had found a new cook at short notice through the ghillie's wife, and together they had produced a bountiful menu of feasts and lunches such as Loch Brae Castle had not seen for years.

'On our second day shooting, Gertrude made Ferguson show up in some of the rummiest old tweeds you've ever seen and one old ghillie started crying and had to be given a flask of Scotch and a good slap on the back,' said Roger. 'Gertrude got them from the attics and apparently they were worn by the thirty-seventh baronet, who shot at Balmoral with the King. He told Ferguson he was the spitting image of the old master and you should have seen Ferguson's face.'

'If that's the end of the line of shooting clothes,' said the Major, 'we will all owe Gertrude a debt of gratitude.'

'I suppose it was just her competence,' said Roger miserably, 'but she seemed to get prettier as the week went on. It was positively weird.'

'And Mr Ferguson?' asked Jasmina. 'Did he think she was pretty?'

'He was dumbfounded, I think,' said Roger. 'She's not even tall or anything, but she strode around in her boots and her mackintosh like she'd been living there forever and she got more done in a week than he'd been able to get them to do in a year. It was quite funny to see him jump when some old retainer, who had refused to speak to him ever, suddenly came up and thanked him for "the red-haired lady". After a few days, he took to following her around so she could introduce him all over again to his own people.'

'She found the right setting,' said the Major. 'A place where she belongs.' He could see her quite clearly walking thigh-deep in heather, her paleness perfect for the misty grey light of the north, her hair curling in the persistent mist and the slight stockiness of her figure perfectly proportioned for the low rugged landscape.

'I really blew it,' said Roger. 'I should have gotten in right away, but she was so besotted with me I thought I could take all the time I wanted.'

'And she fell in love with someone else,' said the Major. 'I did warn you love was not to be negotiated.'

'Oh, I don't think they're in love. That's what stings,' said Roger. 'It's a mutual understanding. She gets to stay in the country and run the estates, which is what she really wants, and he gets the acceptance he was looking for and I'm sure he'll feel free to do as he likes in town as long as he's discreet about it.' He sighed. 'It's quite brilliant, actually.'

'But if you loved her,' said Jasmina, 'that would have been the better choice.'

'People like us can't win against people like them,' Roger said bitterly. 'They have all the money, they have the right name. Telling her I loved her, even if it'd been true, wouldn't have helped.'

'What about the guns?' asked the Major.

'I told Ferguson he couldn't have them,' Roger said. 'He got the girl. He cancelled the Edgecombe deal like he was cancelling an order for curtains. He took everything. I'd be damned if I was going to give him the last little piece of me. If Jemima wants to sell her dad's gun, she can do it herself.'

'He's not building in Edgecombe?' asked Jasmina. 'Wouldn't marrying Gertrude just make the building easier?'

'Now he's marrying Gertrude, he fancies a long line of his heirs being lords of the manor here.' Roger sniffed. 'Suddenly it's sacred ground and to be protected at all costs.'

'But he already has a title,' said Jasmina.

'A Scottish title isn't really the same thing at all,' the Major said.

'Especially when you buy it over the Internet,' added Roger.

'I can't believe it,' said the Major. 'This is wonderful news. I must say, I wasn't looking forward to having to choose sides as that awful project became public.'

'It was hardly a difficult choice,' said Jasmina. 'I know you have such a love for this village.'

'Of course, one would have had to do the right thing,' said the Major, but he felt a relief that he would not be called upon to do so.

'Glad you're happy,' said Roger. 'But what about me? I was going to get a big fat bonus out of being in charge of this deal, but right now I doubt I'll keep my job.'

'But you came home to Edgecombe St Mary,' said Jasmina. 'Why did you come?'

'I suppose I did,' said Roger, looking around the kitchen as if surprised. 'I felt so low I just wanted to go home and I guess—I guess I always think of this as home.' He looked bewildered, like a lost child discovered under a bush at the bottom of the garden. The Major looked at Jasmina and she gripped his hand and nodded.

'My dear Roger,' said the Major. 'This will always be your home.' There was a moment of silence in which Roger's face seemed to work through a range of emotions. Then he smiled.

'You have no idea how much it means to me to hear you say that, Dad,' he said. He stood up and came around the table to envelop the Major in a fierce hug.

'It goes without saying,' said the Major, his voice gruff to hide his happiness as he patted his son's back. Roger released him and appeared to wipe away a tear from the corner of his eye. He turned away to leave the room and then looked back to add, 'So do you think maybe we could get Mortimer Teale to put something in writing?'

ᶜ ᵔ ᴶ

It took the Major a fraction of a second to understand the scene as something other than a mere impediment to his own car's forward passage. An ambulance with its lights flashing stood open and empty at the front door of the village shop. Parked next to it, across the road to block traffic, a police car also flashed its lights, its doors flung open and a young redheaded policeman speaking with urgency into his radio.

'Something has happened,' said Jasmina and she jumped out of the car as soon as it stopped and ran to the policeman. By the time the Major caught up she was pleading with him to let her in.

'We're not sure what's going on, ma'am, and my sergeant said to not let anyone in.'

'Is George in there? What happened to them?' said Mrs Ali.

'For God's sake, she's the owner of the place,' said the Major. 'Who's hurt?'

'A lady and her son,' said the policeman.

'I'm the boy's auntie,' said Jasmina. 'The girl is to marry my nephew today.'

'We're looking for an auntie,' said the policeman. He caught Jasmina by the arm. 'Where were you half an hour ago?'

'She was with me at Rose Lodge all afternoon, and she's been with me for the past two days,' said the Major. 'What's this about?' Just then an older policeman, a sergeant with eyebrows as unkempt as a hedge but a kindly expression, came out holding George, who had a large bandage on his left arm and was crying. He was accompanied by Amina's aunt Noreen, who was dressed in a shalwar kameez of white and gold embroidered about the neck with many jewelled brooches and ruined with a large bloodstain and several smudged bloody handprints about George's size. George saw Jasmina and let out a wail.

'Auntie Jasmina!'

'This is her family's doing,' said Noreen, pointing at Jasmina. 'They are criminals and murderers.'

'Is this lady the one who hurt you and your mother?' asked the policeman who was holding Jasmina. George shook his head and held out his arms to Jasmina. The policeman released her and she stepped forward to take him but Noreen put out a hand to stop her.

'He has to go to the hospital, ladies,' said the sergeant.

'What happened here?' asked Jasmina. 'I demand to know.'

'As if you didn't know,' said Noreen. 'You betrayed us with your plans and your lies.'

'Far as we can make out from the boy, ma'am,' said the younger policeman, 'an old lady stabbed his mum with some kind of knitting needle. The auntie's done a runner with a man believed to be the boy's father. Don't know where they went.'

A stretcher appeared, pushed by two ambulance men. Amina lay covered in a sheet, an IV in her arm and an oxygen mask on her face. She made a faint sound when she saw them and tried to raise her hand.

'Mummy!' called George, and Noreen and the kindly sergeant struggled to hold him back.

'Let them help your mummy now,' begged Noreen.

The Major stepped over to the stretcher and took Amina's hand.

'How is she?' he asked a burly ambulance man who appeared to be in charge.

'Must have missed the heart or she'd be a goner, but she's probably bleeding internally. Hard to tell with such a small entry wound.'

'Where's George?' whispered Amina. 'Is he all right?'

'He's right here,' said the Major. 'With your aunt Noreen and Jasmina.'

'Please find Abdul Wahid,' whispered Amina. 'He thinks it's his fault.'

'They gotta get her to the hospital now, sir.' The sergeant's eyebrows were drawn together in sympathy.

'I'll go with you,' said Jasmina. 'He's my great-nephew.'

'You will not,' said Noreen. 'You will stay away from us and you will suffer for your crimes.'

'I'm not to blame and neither is Abdul Wahid. You cannot think it, Noreen.'

'Do you know where your nephew might go, ma'am?' the sergeant asked, writing on a notepad. 'Seems he took off with the old lady.'

'I have no idea,' said Jasmina. She smoothed George's tear-stained face with her hand as the men loaded the stretcher into the ambulance and asked, 'George, where did your daddy go?'

'He said to Mecca,' said George. 'I want my mummy.'

'Mecca—is that a restaurant or a store or something?' said the young policeman.

'No, he means the city I think,' said Jasmina. The Major felt her look at him.

'He said walking to Mecca,' repeated George, hiccupping through his tears.

'Well, if he's walking they won't get far,' sneered the policeman.

'Is Daddy with old auntie?' asked Jasmina. George broke into fresh wails.

'She hurt my mummy with her knitting and she scratched my arm.' He showed the bandage and his body trembled.

'He might be protecting his daddy. Kids'll say anything when they're scared.' The younger policeman was beginning to grate on the Major.

'My nephew was not involved with this,' said Jasmina.

'Put her and her family in jail,' said Noreen as the sergeant handed George up to her in the ambulance. 'They are criminals.'

'We can't rule anything out right now.' The sergeant shut the doors of the ambulance, and the siren began to wail. 'I need to find your nephew.'

'I have no idea where he is,' said Jasmina and the Major marvelled at her blank face and her clear gaze. 'Obviously he's not heading to Mecca.'

'You never know, he might slip the country.' He turned to his companion. 'Better warn the airports and get out a description. Does he own a car, ma'am?'

'No, he does not own a car.' The Major noticed that Jasmina did not mention her own blue Honda, which was not parked in its usual spot. He saw her sway as if she might faint and grabbed her around the waist.

'This has been a big shock, officers,' he said in his most authoritative tone. 'I think I need to take her home to sit down.'

'Are you in the village, sir?' asked the sergeant and the Major gave them his address and helped Jasmina back to the car. 'Stay indoors once you get there,' added the younger policeman. 'We may need to talk to you again.'

～ ？ ◞

Outside Rose Lodge, the Major left the car running while he hurried inside to the scullery. He retrieved his gun box and slipped one of the guns into a canvas carrying slip. Taking a box of shells from the locked cabinet, he shook out a few and stuffed them in his trouser pocket. Then, for good measure, he unhooked a pair of binoculars and a water flask too. He put them in his leather game bag and added a small first aid kit in a tin and an unopened bar of mint cake to complete his preparations. Patting the bag, he hoped he was adequately armed and provisioned to face an insane woman. As he left, he met Roger in the passageway.

'Where are you going? I thought you were dancing it up at a wedding.'

'Got to try and find the groom first,' said the Major. 'Abdul Wahid may be trying to walk off a cliff.' As he hurried down the path, Roger's voice came faintly behind him.

'Pretty extreme way to call things off. Why doesn't he just send her a text message?'

Chapter Twenty-four

The Major knew he was driving faster than was safe in the growing darkness of the lanes, but he felt no fear. There was only concentration and the trees, hedges, and walls tumbling by. The engine's roar was fury enough. No need for either of them to speak. He could sense Jasmina shivering beside him but did not take his eyes from the road. He kept his mind only on the task at hand and as they surged from the carelessly flung outskirts of the town onto the bare grass road to the cliffs, he felt a soldier's pride at an assignment well executed.

'What if we're too late?' whispered Jasmina. The anguish in her voice threatened to tear his composure to shreds.

'We must refuse to imagine it and concentrate only on the next step and then the next,' he said, swinging the car into the empty car park. 'We do what we can do, and the rest is God's problem.'

The cliff on which they had strolled so happily with little George lay in gloom under grey clouds that streamed and feathered at the edges in the growing wind and hung down swollen underbellies black with rain. Out in the channel, curtains of rain already brushed the choppy sea. It was neither dark enough for the lighthouse lamp to make any impression nor still light enough to inspire hope. A gust splattered cold rain on the windshield as they got out.

'We need coats,' the Major said, and hurried to the back of the car.

'Ernest, there's no time,' she said, but she hovered at the edge of the road waiting for him. He strapped his game bag across his chest, slung his gun slip over one shoulder, and picked up his shooting coat and hat. When he handed Jasmina the coat, he hoped the gun was unobtrusive over his shoulder. She seemed not to notice as she put the coat on. 'It's so empty now.' She scanned the endless grass for signs of Abdul Wahid. 'How will we find them?'

'We'll head up to that vantage point,' he said, putting on his hat and looking at the small knoll with its low stone wall and pay telescope. 'Always see more from high ground.'

'Oi! Where d'you think you're going?' A short man emerged from one of the small buildings adjacent to the darkened public house. 'Too windy to be safe out there tonight.' He wore stout boots and jeans with a short work coat and a large reflective vest that made his ample torso resemble a pumpkin. Some sort of harness jingled its loosened buckles around the folds of his waist and he carried a clipboard and wore a two-way radio on a lanyard.

'I'm sure you're right,' said the Major, 'but we're searching for a young man who may be despondent.'

'There's no time.' Jasmina was pulling on his arm. 'We have to go.'

'Jumper, is he?' said the man, consulting his clipboard. Jasmina moaned slightly at the word. 'I'm with the Volunteer Suicide Emergency Corps so you come to the right place.' He made a note on the clipboard with his pen. 'What's his name?'

'His name's Abdul Wahid. He's twenty-three and we think his elderly great-aunt is with him.'

'Not many people jump with their auntie,' said the man. 'How d'you spell Abdool?'

'Oh, for pity's sake just help us look for him,' said Jasmina.

'We'll start searching,' said the Major. 'Can you round up some more volunteers?'

'I'll put out the call,' said the man. 'But you can't go out there. It's not safe for the general public.' He stepped in front of them and made a sort of herding motion with his arms as if they were sheep to be corralled.

'I'm not the general public, I'm British army, rank of major,' said the Major. 'Retired, of course, but in the absence of any proof of your authority, I'll have to demand you step aside.'

'I see someone down there, Ernest.' Jasmina dodged sideways and began to cross the road. The Major created a diversion by saluting the clipboard man and receiving an uncertain hand waggle in response, then followed her.

A man became visible, running toward them up the incline from an area of thick scrub. It was not Abdul Wahid. This man also wore a reflective vest and the Major prepared to avoid him but he was waving his mobile phone in a way the Major understood as an urgent signal for help.

'Oh, no, not him again,' said the clipboard man, who was puffing along behind them. 'You know you're not allowed up here, Brian.'

'No bloody phone reception again,' said Brian. Although he was a compact, fit-looking man, he put both hands on his knees and bent over to catch his breath after the uphill climb. 'Got a jumper south of Big Scrubber,' he went on, pointing with a thumb back over his shoulder. 'Can't get near to talk him in. Some old lady with a weapon and a foul mouth threatened to stick me in the gonads.'

'It's Abdul Wahid,' said Jasmina. 'He's here.'

'You're under caution not to do any more rescues, Brian,' said the clipboard man.

'So you're not going to come and help me grab her?' asked Brian.

'We're not to approach people with visible weapons or obvious psychiatric disorders,' said the man, with the pride of someone who has memorised a handbook. 'We have to call for police backup.'

'It's not like they send a bloody SWAT team, Jim,' said Brian. 'You could save ten people in the time it takes you to call two constables in a Mini Cooper.'

'Is it a knitting needle?' asked the Major.

'Is it that clump of trees?' asked Jasmina simultaneously.

'Yeah, Big Scrubber—or maybe it's an ice pick,' said Brian.

'Don't tell them,' fumed Jim. 'They're the general public.'

'Are you going to radio for help or do I have to go to the phone booth and ask the Samaritans to relay the message?' asked Brian.

'Reception's better at HQ,' said Jim. 'But I can't go unless you all come with me. No civilians allowed.' He sidled over and stood downhill of Jasmina as if preparing to grab her. 'The days of vigilantes like Brian are over.'

'Please, I have to go to my nephew,' cried Jasmina.

'Brian, you seem to me to be a man of action,' said the Major, unsleeving his gun as casually as possible and breaking it gently over the crook of his elbow. 'Why don't you take Jim to get reinforcements and the lady and I will go down and quietly persuade the elder lady to behave.'

'Shit,' said Jim, staring mesmerised at the shotgun. Jasmina gasped and then used the opportunity to turn and run down the slope.

'Shit,' said the Major. 'I have to go after her.'

'So go,' said Brian. 'I'll make sure clipboard Jim makes the right calls.'

'It's not loaded, by the way,' called the Major as he began to hurry after Jasmina. He omitted to mention the cartridges in his pocket. 'Only, the old lady already stabbed one person with that needle.'

'I didn't see any shotgun,' said Brian, waving him away.

As the Major broke into a run, ignoring the danger of turning an ankle on the many rabbit holes, he heard Brian say, 'And Jim'll back me up, because otherwise I'll tell them how he lets me rescue people on his shifts and takes all the credit.'

'That was one time,' said Jim. 'The girl was so out of it I didn't even know she'd already been rescued. I spent two hours talking to her.'

'Yeah, I heard she almost decided to kill herself all over again,' came the faint reply, and then the Major reached the outer rim of the bank of gorse and scrub trees and their voices disappeared.

         ᘓ ᕗ ᒣ

Behind the scrub, he saw Jasmina's small Honda half buried in gorse; a great furrow of mud behind it indicated that it had slid and swerved before coming to a stop. Perhaps Abdul Wahid had planned to simply drive to Mecca.

Abdul Wahid was kneeling close, but not dangerously close, to the edge of the cliff some two hundred feet away. He seemed to be praying, bending his head to the ground as if unaware of any drama in his surroundings. Closer to the Major, two islands of gorse created a narrowing of the grass and here the old lady stood guard, her face as hard as ever but now animated by the sharp in and out of her breath as she pointed her knitting needle toward Jasmina. She held it professionally—pointing down from her fist and ready to thrust like a dagger—and the Major felt sure she was very capable of using it.

'Auntie, what are you doing?' called Jasmina, speaking into the wind and spreading her hands in a gesture of placation. 'Why must we be out here in the rain?'

'I'm doing what none of you knows how to do,' said the old lady. 'No one remembers what it is to have honour anymore.'

'But Abdul Wahid?' she said. Then she raised her voice and called out to him, 'Abdul Wahid, please!'

'Don't you know better than to disturb a man at prayer?' asked the old woman. 'He prays to take the burden on himself and restore the family honour.'

'This is insane. This is not how things are resolved, Auntie.'

'This is how it has always been done, child,' said the old woman in a dreamy voice. 'My mother was drowned in a cistern by my father when I was six years old.' She crouched on her heels and traced a circle in the grass with the tip of her needle. 'I saw. I saw him push her down with one hand and with the other he stroked her hair because he loved her very much. She had laughed with the man who came selling carpets and copper pots and handed him tea from her own hands in her mother-in-law's best cups.' She stood up again. 'I was always proud of my father and his sacrifice,' she said.

'We are civilised people, not some rural peasant family stuck in the past,' said Jasmina, her voice choked with horror.

'Civilised?' hissed the old woman. 'You are soft. Soft and corrupted. My niece and her husband are weakened by decadence. They complain, they make their little schemes, but they offer only indulgence for their son. And I, who should be eating figs in a garden of my own, must come and set things right.'

'Did they know you would do this?' asked Jasmina. The old lady laughed, an animal cackle.

'No one wants to know, but then I come—when there are too many puppies in the litter, when a daughter has something growing in the belly. And after I visit they never speak, but they send me a small goat or a piece of carpet.' She ran her fingers slowly up the shaft of the needle and began to creep forward across the grass, waving the tip of the needle as if to hypnotise. 'They will cry and rant and pretend to be ashamed but you will see, they will give me my own small house now in the hills and I will grow figs and sit all day in the sun.'

The Major stepped from behind the bushes and planted his feet firmly apart, resting his right hand on the stock of the shotgun still broken across his arm. 'This has gone quite far enough, madam,' he said. 'I'll ask you to throw down your needle and wait quietly with us for the police.' She fell back a few steps but regained her composure and a leer crept slowly up the left side of her face.

'Ah, the English Major,' she said. She waved her needle like an admonishing finger. 'So it is true, Jasmina, that you ran away from your family in order to fornicate and debauch yourself.'

'How dare you,' said the Major, stepping forward and snapping the shotgun together.

'Actually, you're quite right, Auntie.' Jasmina's eyes flashed with anger. She stepped forward and held her chin high, her hair whipping about her face in the wind. 'And shall I tell you how delicious it was, you with your shrivelled body and your dried-up heart, who have never known happiness? Would you like to hear how it is to be naked with a man you love and really live and breathe the sensuality of life itself? Should I tell you this story, Auntie?'

The old woman howled as if racked with pain and leaped toward Jasmina, who planted her feet and held out her arms and showed no intention of dodging. Quick with fear, the Major swung up his gun with a shout and, running forward, butted the edge of the stock against the old woman's head. It was only a glancing blow, but her own momentum made it enough. She dropped the needle and crumpled to the ground. Jasmina sat down abruptly in the grass and began to laugh, an ugly robotic laugh that suggested shock. The Major bent down to pick up the fallen knitting needle and slid it into his game bag.

'What were you thinking?' he said. 'You could have been killed.'

'Is she dead?' asked Jasmina.

'Of course not,' said the Major, but he was anxious as he felt the old lady's leathery neck until he found a pulse. 'I do try to avoid killing ladies, no matter how psychotic they may be.'

❧ ❦ ❧

'You're a useful sort in a fight,' said the now familiar voice of Brian. He advanced from behind a bush and bent down to peer at the old woman. 'Good work.'

'Where's the other chap?' asked the Major.

'He's radioed the other volunteers but he's still waiting for backup,' said Brian. 'Shall we go and have a bit of a chat with your nephew and see what he wants?'

'Do you know what you're doing?' asked the Major.

'No, can't say I do,' said Brian cheerfully. 'I must've talked about fifty people down off this bloody cliff in the last ten years, and for the life of me I couldn't tell you how. Bit of a gift, I suppose. Main thing is to act casual and not make any sudden moves.'

Together they walked cautiously down the slope toward Abdul Wahid. He had finished his prayers and was standing with unnatural stillness, gazing out to sea. He did not hunch his shoulders or fold his arms against the cold, although he wore no coat. Only the embroidered hem of his long heavy tunic snapped in the wind.

'He put on his wedding clothes,' said Mrs Ali. 'Oh, my poor, poor boy.' She stretched out her hand and the Major reached to catch her arm, fearing she might run the last hundred yards or so.

'Easy, now,' said Brian. 'Let me get his attention.' He stepped forward and gave a low whistling sound as if, thought the Major, he was calling a gundog to heel. Abdul Wahid turned slightly and saw them.

'Hullo there,' said Brian. He held a hand up in a slow wave. 'I was just wondering if I could talk to you a minute.'

'I suppose you want to help me?' asked Abdul Wahid.

'As a matter of fact, I do,' said Brian. 'What do you need?'

'I need you to get my aunt away from here,' said Abdul Wahid. 'I don't want her to see.'

'Abdul Wahid, what are you doing?' shouted Jasmina. 'I'm not leaving you here.'

'I want her taken away,' said Abdul Wahid, quietly refusing to look at her. 'She should not have to endure this.'

'So you don't want to talk to her?' asked Brian. 'That's fine. If I have the Major here take her away, will you agree to talk to me—just for a bit?' Abdul Wahid seemed to consider this option carefully.

'Please, Abdul Wahid, come home,' said Jasmina. She was crying and the Major reached out a restraining arm, fearing she would try to rush at her nephew. 'I won't leave you.'

'I would prefer to talk to the Major,' said Abdul Wahid. 'I will not talk to you.'

'So I'll get your aunt away to somewhere dry and warm and you'll sit tight and chat with this gentleman?'

'Yes,' said Abdul Wahid.

'He's got a gun, you know,' said Brian. 'You sure you can trust him?'

'What are you doing?' whispered the Major in fierce anxiety. 'Are you trying to provoke him?' Abdul Wahid, however, actually produced one of his short barking laughs.

'Are you afraid he has come to shoot me?' he asked. 'It would not exactly spoil my plans now, would it?'

'Okay, then,' said Brian. 'I think we can make that deal.' He turned to the Major and whispered. 'His laughing is a good sign. I think we should play along.'

'I won't leave,' said Jasmina. She turned her tear-stained face to the Major and he felt the full enormity of what would come next. 'I could never forgive myself.'

'If you don't leave, you may never forgive yourself,' said Brian. 'Best thing to do is give them what they want, within reason. No promises, though.'

'If I leave him in your hands and you can't keep him safe . . .' she began. She turned her face away, unable to continue.

'You may very well never forgive me,' finished the Major. The words tasted bitter in his mouth. 'I do understand.' She looked at him and he added, 'Whoever stays, whoever goes, I fear his death would come between us just the same, my dear.' He took her hand in his and squeezed it. 'Let me play the man's part now and fight for Abdul Wahid and for us, my love.'

'Here you are,' said Brian, taking something from a large backpack. 'Sometimes they like a cup of tea. I always keep a thermos handy.'

He waited while Brian and Jasmina climbed the slope, stopping to collect the dazed but conscious old woman on their way. They did not look back. Out of the corner of his eye he watched Abdul Wahid, who remained motionless. Finally, he turned and walked slowly downhill, flanking left to come parallel to the young man while maintaining a respectful distance.

'Thank you,' said Abdul Wahid. 'This was no place for a woman like my aunt.'

'This is no place for any of us,' said the Major, peering into the abyss of churning whitecaps and jagged rocks that seemed to suck at his feet from hundreds of feet below. 'All this drama is very bad for the digestion.' He stretched his back. 'Come to think of it, I didn't have much lunch.'

'I am sorry,' said Abdul Wahid.

'Would you like a cup of tea?' asked the Major. 'That man Brian gave me a thermos of tea and I have some Kendal Mint Cake.'

'Are you mocking me?' said Abdul Wahid. 'Do you think I'm a child, to be persuaded with food?'

'Not at all,' said the Major, abandoning the casual approach at once. 'I'm just terrified, as you might expect—and a little cold.'

'Is it cold?' asked Abdul Wahid.

'It's very cold,' said the Major. 'Wouldn't you like to go somewhere warm and talk things through over a nice hot dinner?'

'Did you see Amina?' asked Abdul Wahid. The Major nodded. 'Will she live?' he added.

'She asked for you in the ambulance,' said the Major. 'I could take you to her. I have my car.' Abdul Wahid shook his head and rubbed the back of his hand over his eyes.

'It was never meant to be,' he said. 'Every day more complication, more compromise. I see that now.'

'That's just not true,' said the Major. 'You're talking like a fool.' He felt the note of desperation in his own voice.

'So much shame,' he said. 'It hangs around me like chains. I ache to scrape it all off in the sea and be clean for—' He stopped abruptly and the Major sensed he felt unworthy to even mention the name of his creator.

'I know something of shame,' said the Major. He had intended to point out that suicide was not allowed in Islam, but a restatement of rules he already knew did not seem constructive in the immediacy of wind, rain, and a sheer drop of five hundred feet. 'How can we not all feel it? We are all small-minded people, creeping about the earth grubbing for our own advantage and making the very mistakes for which we want to humiliate our neighbours.' As he risked a peek over the sharp chalk edge, his stomach churned at the jagged teeth of rocks waiting below them and he almost lost his train of thought. 'I think we wake up every day with high intentions and by dusk we have routinely fallen short. Sometimes I think God created the darkness just so he didn't have to look at us all the time.'

'You speak of general burdens, Major. What of the individual shame that burns the soul?'

'Well, if you want specifics,' began the Major, 'look at this gun of which I'm so proud.' They both considered the rain beading on its polished stock and dull steel barrel. 'My father, on his deathbed, gave one of these guns to me and one to my younger brother and I was consumed with disappointment that he did not give me both and I chewed on my own grievance as he lay dying before me and I chewed on it while I wrote his eulogy and damn me if I wasn't still chewing on it when my own brother died this autumn.'

'It was your right as the eldest son.'

'I was more proud of these guns than I was of your aunt Jasmina. For the sake of these guns, I let down the woman I love in front of a whole community of people, most of whom I can barely tolerate. I let her leave, and I will never get rid of that sense of shame.'

'I let her leave so that I could acquire all her worldly possessions,' said Abdul Wahid quietly. 'With death, this debt will also be wiped out.'

'This is not the solution,' said the Major. 'The solution is to make things right, or at least to work every day to do so.'

'I have tried, Major,' he said. 'But in the end I cannot reconcile my faith and my life. At least this way, the debt of honour is paid and Amina and George can go on with their lives.'

'How is suicide to be reconciled?' asked the Major.

'I will not commit suicide,' said Abdul Wahid. 'It is *haram*. I will merely pray at the edge and wait for the wind to carry me where it will. Perhaps to Mecca.' He opened his arms and the heavy shirt billowed and snapped in the wind like a luffing sail. The Major felt the tenuous connection of conversation was slipping away from him. He looked around and thought he saw some heads bobbing behind bushes. He waved energetically, but this proved to be a mistake. Abdul Wahid also saw the volunteers and he lost all trace of animation from his face.

'You have kept me too long, Major,' he said. 'I must go to my prayers.'

As he stepped forward, the Major fumbled in his pocket for cartridges and stuck two in the barrels, snapping the shotgun closed with one hand. Even against the rising moan of the wind it made a satisfactory crack. Abdul Wahid stopped and looked at him as the Major took two long steps downhill and began to sidle up between Abdul Wahid and the cliff edge. He was miserably aware of the crumbling and uneven nature of the ground, and his inability to look behind him made his legs tighten until his right calf muscle cramped. Abdul Wahid smiled gently at him and said, 'So, Major, you do intend to shoot me after all?' He opened his arms wide until the wind buffeted his shirt and he stumbled forward a step.

'No, I do not intend to shoot you,' said the Major. He stepped uphill and turned the gun around in his hands presenting the stock end to Abdul Wahid. 'Here, take this.' Abdul Wahid caught the gun as it was pushed into his stomach. He held it, puzzled, and the Major stepped back, uncomfortably aware of the barrels pointing at his chest. 'Now I'm afraid you are going to have to shoot me.'

'I am not a man of violence,' said Abdul Wahid, lowering the gun slightly.

'I'm afraid you have no choice,' said the Major. He stepped forward again and held the barrel end of the gun against his own chest. 'You see, I cannot let you go off this cliff and I intend to spend all night, if necessary, standing between you and the edge. Thus you will not be blown over by accident at any point. Of course, you can always jump, but that was not your plan, was it?'

'This is silly. I could never hurt you, Major.' Abdul Wahid stepped back half a pace.

'If you die here today, your aunt Jasmina will be lost to me, and I do not want to live without her.' The Major struggled to keep his voice even. 'Also, I will not face your son, George, and tell him I stood by and let his father kill himself.' He stepped forward again, pushing Abdul Wahid back. Abdul Wahid moved his hands to grip the gun more comfortably. The Major prayed his fingers were not near the twin triggers.

'You must see that your sense of shame will not die with you, Abdul Wahid. It will live on in your son and in Amina and in your aunt Jasmina. Your pain will haunt their lives. Your wish for death today is a selfish act. I am also a selfish man—from these years of living alone, I expect. I do not want to live to see this happen.'

'I will not shoot you.' Abdul Wahid was almost crying now, his face twisted with anguish and confusion.

'Either shoot me or choose to live yourself,' said the Major. 'I can't face your aunt any other way. How strange to think that we come as a pair now.'

Abdul Wahid gave a bellow of anguish and threw the gun away from him onto the ground. The butt end hit first and the gun gave a roaring boom and discharged what the Major registered as a single barrel.

He felt a white-hot sear of steel shot through his right leg. The force of the close range spun him around and he fell heavily, slipping in the grass. As he rolled, he felt the ground disappear under him. His legs slipped over the edge of the chalk into empty air. There was no time to feel any pain as he scrabbled above his head with his hands and felt his left elbow bump a metal stanchion that had once held a wire fence. He grabbed the stanchion. It held briefly against the tug of his body as he rolled over and then it began to move, the metal squeaking like a dull knife. In an instant, a body landed on his left lower arm and fingers dug at his back to find any grip. His legs jackknifed and his left knee struck the cliff with a pain that flashed like a light in his head. The Major heard the clatter of stones preceding him over the edge. It was so fast there was no time for thought. There was only a brief feeling of surprise and the smell of cold white chalk and wet grass.

Chapter twenty-five

The Major was keen to push away the nagging idea of pain, which started to seep into his head along with the light. It was comfortable in the warm darkness of sleep and he struggled to stay down. A murmur of voices, a clattering of metal carts, and the brief percussion of curtain rings swept aside made him think he might be surfacing into an airport lounge. He felt his eyelids flutter and he tried to squeeze them shut. It was his attempt to roll over that shocked him awake with a tearing pain in his left knee and an ache on his right side that made him gasp. He scrabbled with his hand and felt thin sheet over slippery mattress and knocked it against a metal post.

'He's waking up.' A hand held his shoulder down and the same voice added, 'Don't try to move, Mr Pettigrew.'

'Iss's Major . . .' he whispered. 'Major Pettigrew.' His voice was a hoarse whisper in a mouth that seemed to be made of brown paper. He tried to lick his lips, but his tongue felt like a dead toad.

'Here's something to drink,' said the voice as a straw snagged on his lip and he sucked at lukewarm water. 'You're in the hospital, Mr Pettigrew, but you're going to be fine.'

He slipped away again into sleep, hoping that when he awoke again it would be into his own room at Rose Lodge. He was quite annoyed to discover later the same cacophony of institutional sounds and the pressure of fluorescent lights against his eyelids. This time he opened his eyes.

'How are you feeling, Dad?' said Roger, who, the Major could see, had spread the *Financial Times* over the bed and was using the Major's legs to prop up the pages.

'Don't let me keep you from the stock tables,' whispered the Major. 'How long have I been here?'

'About a day,' said Roger. 'Do you remember what happened?'

'I was shot in the leg, not the head. Is it still there?'

'The leg? Of course it is,' said Roger. 'Can't you feel it?'

'Yes, of course I can,' said the Major. 'But I didn't want any nasty surprises.' He found it quite exhausting to speak but he asked for some more water. Roger helped him sip from a plastic cup, though most of it dribbled uncomfortably across his cheek and into his ear.

'They dug a whole lot of shot out of your leg,' said Roger. 'Lucky for you it missed any arteries, and the doctor said it only clipped the edge of the right testicle, not that he expected it mattered much to a man your age.'

'Thanks very much,' said the Major.

'You also tore up the ligaments in your left knee pretty badly, but that surgery is considered elective so they said either it'll heal on its own or you can join a waiting list and get it in about a year.' Roger leaned over and, to the Major's surprise squeezed his hand and kissed him on the forehead. 'You're going to be fine, Dad.'

'If you kiss me like that again, I'll have to assume you're lying and that I'm actually in the hospice,' he said.

'You gave me a fright, what can I say.' He folded up the newspaper as if embarrassed by his moment of affection. 'You've always been an unmovable rock in my life and suddenly you're an old man wearing tubes. Quite nasty.'

'Nastier still for me,' said the Major. He struggled a moment to ask the questions to which he was not sure he could bear the answers. He was tempted to feign sleep again and put off the bad news. It must be bad, he thought, since there was no sign of other visitors. He tried to sit up and Roger reached over to a button on the wall and the bed raised him into a slanted position.

'I want to know,' he began, but he seemed to choke on his own voice. 'I must know. Did Abdul Wahid jump?'

'Considering he shot my father, I wouldn't have cared if he had,' said Roger. 'But apparently he threw himself down as you went over and grabbed you just in time. It was touch-and-go, they said, what with the wind and the slippery rain, but some guy named Brian threw himself on Abdul and then some other guy came with a rope and stuff and they dragged you back and got you on a stretcher.'

'So he's alive?' asked the Major.

'He is, but I'm afraid there's some very bad news I have to tell you,' said Roger. 'I was going to wait until later, but—'

'Amina's dead?' asked the Major. 'His fiancée?'

'Oh, the girl who got knitted?' said Roger. 'No, she's going to be fine. They're all with her one flight up in women's surgical.'

'All who?' said the Major.

'Mrs Ali, Abdul Wahid, and that George who keeps dunning me out of pound coins for the vending machine,' said Roger. 'Then there's the auntie—Noreen, I think—and Abdul's parents. It's like half of Pakistan is up there.'

'Jasmina is there?' the Major asked.

'When she can bear to be away from you,' said Roger. 'When I got here last night, they were still trying to pull her off your body, and I can't seem to get rid of her.'

'I intend to ask her to marry me,' said the Major, his voice curt. 'No matter what you think.'

'Don't start getting all excited. That testicle is still in traction,' Roger said.

'What's in traction?' asked a voice and the Major felt himself blush as Jasmina came around the curtain wearing a big smile and a shalwar kameez in a yellow as soft as butter. Her hair was damp and she smelled of carbolic soap and lemons.

'You finally went home and took a shower, then?' asked Roger.

'The matron said I was frightening all the visitors with my bloodstained clothes. She let me use the doctors' shower.' She came to the side of the Major's bed and he felt as weak as the day she had held him up, faint from hearing about Bertie's death.

'He didn't jump' was all he managed to say as he clutched her warm hand.

'No, he didn't,' she said. She gripped his hand and kissed him on the cheek and then on the lips. 'And now he owes you his life and we can never repay you.'

'If he wants to repay me, tell him to hurry up and get married,' said the Major. 'What that boy needs is a woman to order him around.'

'Amina is still quite weak, but we hope they will be married right here in the hospital,' Jasmina said. 'My brother and sister-in-law have vowed to stay on as long as it takes to see them settled.'

'It all sounds wonderful,' said the Major. He turned to Roger, who was fiddling with his mobile phone. 'But you told me there was bad news?'

'He is right, Ernest,' said Jasmina. 'You must prepare yourself.' She looked at Roger, and he nodded as if the two of them had spent some time discussing how to tell a sick man something awful. The Major held his breath and waited for the blow.

'It's the Churchill, Dad,' said Roger at last. 'I'm afraid in the commotion of saving you, it got kicked aside or something and it slid over the edge and Abdul Wahid says he saw it smashing on the rocks on the way down.' He paused and lowered his head. 'They haven't found it.'

The Major closed his eyes and saw it happen. He smelled again the cold chalk, felt the futile scrabble of his legs trying to gain some purchase and the agonising slow slipping of his body as if the sea were a magnet pulling at him and, at the edge of his vision, he could see the gun slipping faster, smooth against the wet grass as it inscribed one slow circle on the edge and then went ahead of them over the cliff.

'Are you all right, Ernest?' said Jasmina. He blinked away the scene, not sure whether it was a real memory or just a vision. The smell of chalk faded from his nostrils and he waited for the pangs of sorrow to overwhelm him. He was surprised to find that he could summon no more than the kind of faint disappointment one might feel upon finding a favourite sweater accidentally boiled along with the white laundry and shrunk to a felt mess sized for a small terrier.

'Am I medicated with something?' he asked from behind his closed lids and Roger said he would check the chart. 'I can't seem to feel anything.'

'Oh, my God, he's paralysed,' said Roger.

'No, I mean about the gun,' said the Major. 'I don't feel as upset as I should.'

'You've longed for that pair since I can remember,' Roger said. 'You used to tell me over and over how Grandfather split them up but the day would come when they would be reunited.'

'I longed for the day when I could look important to a lot of people who I felt were more important than I,' said the Major. 'I was arrogant. It must be genetic.'

'That's a nice thing to say to someone who's kept vigil at your pillow all night long,' said Roger. 'Hey, look, I got a text from Sandy.'

'Didn't you just propose to another woman?' asked Jasmina.

'Yeah, but I had a lot of time to think last night and I figured a long text from the bedside of my dying father might do the trick.'

'Sorry to disappoint you,' said the Major. 'You could have impressed her with your eulogy.'

'I'm sorry you lost the gun your father gave you, Ernest,' said Jasmina. 'But you lost it saving a life, and you are a hero to me and to others.'

'Actually, I lost Bertie's gun,' said the Major. He yawned and felt himself growing sleepy. 'Happened to be the closest one to grab. That's not my gun at the bottom of the English Channel.'

'Are you serious?' said Roger.

'And I'm glad,' said the Major. 'Now I won't have to be reminded that sometimes it might have been more important to me than my brother.'

'Oh, shit!' said Roger looking up from his keyboard. 'Now we have to pay Marjorie fifty thousand pounds and have nothing to show for it.'

'I expect the insurance company will take care of that,' said the Major. He struggled to stay awake so he might keep looking at Jasmina's face smiling at him.

'What insurance?' asked Roger, incredulous. 'You had them insured all this time?'

'Insurance was never the issue,' said the Major, closing his eyes. 'When my father died, my mother kept paying the premiums, and when she died so did I.' He opened his eyes briefly to say something important to Jasmina. 'I take great pride in never leaving a bill unpaid—it makes the filing messy.'

'You are tired, Ernest,' she said. 'You should rest after all this excitement.' She laid her hand along his cheek and he felt as a small child feels when the night's fever is cooled by the touch of a mother's hand.

'Must ask you to marry me,' he said as he drifted away. 'Not in this dreadful room, of course.'

∾ ❦ ∾

When he woke again, the lights were dim in the wards and the nurse's desk could be seen as a glow at the end of the corridor. A lamp burned low on the bedside table and he could feel the hospital's central heating breathing as quietly as the patients in the calm of the night shift. A figure sat in a chair at the end of his bed; he called softly, 'Jasmina?' The figure came closer until he could see it was Amina, in a hospital gown and robe.

'Hi,' she said. 'How you feeling?'

'Fine,' he whispered. 'Should you be out of bed?'

'No, I snuck out.' She sat carefully on the edge of the bed. 'I had to come and see you before I left. To thank you for saving Abdul Wahid and for everything else you've tried to do.'

'Where are you going?' he asked. 'You're getting married tomorrow.'

'I've decided I'm not going to get married after all,' she said. 'My aunt Noreen is picking me up first thing and then George and I'll be off to her flat before anyone can make a fuss.'

'But why on earth would you do that?' he asked. 'There are no impediments left to your marriage. Even Abdul Wahid's parents are on your side now.'

'I know,' she said. 'They keep apologising and coming in and out with gifts and promises. I think they've already agreed to put George through medical school.'

'They didn't know about the old lady, I'm sure,' said the Major. 'Such things are unimaginable.'

'It happens more than you think,' she said. 'But I've accepted they didn't intend it. They're deporting the old bag today.'

'Isn't she going to jail?' asked the Major.

'They couldn't find a weapon and I told them it was an accident.' Amina gave him a look that suggested she knew exactly where the knitting needle was. 'I didn't want more shame for Abdul Wahid, and I like his family feeling obligated to me.'

'Are you sure?' he asked, and she nodded. 'So why leave now?' She sighed and picked pills of fabric from the thin hospital blanket.

'Almost dying makes you see things differently, doesn't it?' She looked at him and he saw tears in her eyes. 'It feels like I've loved Abdul Wahid forever, and I thought I'd give up anything to be with him.' She pulled harder at the blanket and a small hole appeared as the threads parted. The Major was tempted to still her ravaging hand but did not want to interrupt. 'But can you really see me spending my life in a shop?' she asked. 'Stocking shelves, chatting to all the old lady customers, going over account books?'

'Abdul Wahid loves you,' he said. 'He came back from the very edge of existence for you.'

'I know. No pressure on me, then?' She tried to smile but failed. 'But it's not enough to be in love. It's about how you spend your days, what you do together, who you choose as friends, and most of all it's what work you do. I'm a dancer. I need to dance. If I give it up to spend my life wrapping pork pies and weighing apples, I will come to resent him. And even though he says I can dance as well, he expects me to be his partner in the shop. He would come to resent me, too. Better to break both our hearts now than watch them wither away over time.'

'What about George?'

'I wanted a proper family for George, with Mummy and Daddy and a puppy and maybe a little brother or sister. But that's just a framed picture on some mantelpiece. It's not real, is it?'

'A boy needs a father,' said the Major.

'If I didn't know that better than anyone, I'd have been off to London tomorrow,' she said. She hugged her arms tentatively around her chest and she spoke in a way that made him believe she had given the matter a great deal of consideration. 'Most of the people who've flung that at me over the last few years haven't the faintest bloody idea what they mean by it. They have no idea what it's like to grow up without one, and half of them can't stand their own fathers.' There was silence; the Major thought of his father's remoteness.

'I think that even if you dislike them, knowing one's parents helps a child understand where he or she came from,' said the Major. 'We measure ourselves against our parents, and each generation we try to do a little better.' As he said this he wondered again whether he had failed Roger.

'George will have both parents; they just won't be under one roof. He'll have me and his auntie Noreen in town and he'll have his father over in Edgecombe along with Jasmina. I hope you'll look in on him, too. He should learn to play chess.'

'Jasmina has fought so hard for the two of you,' said the Major quietly. 'She will be devastated.'

'Sometimes you can't fix everything,' said Amina. 'Life isn't always like books.'

'No, it's not.' He considered the ugly Styrofoam of the ceiling tiles but could find no inspiration there to change her mind.

'I appreciate how much Jasmina has tried to do for us,' she said. 'I want George to have all the family he can get.'

'I hesitate to speak for anyone but myself,' he said. 'I have not yet had the chance to officially ask Jasmina to marry me.'

'You old dog,' she said. 'I knew you two were off doing it somewhere.'

'Setting aside your crude manners for the moment, young lady,' he said in as severe a voice as he could manage, 'I would like to assure you that you and George will always be welcome in our home.'

'You are a very good man, for an old git.' She stood up and leaned down to give him a kiss on the forehead. The Major wondered again at how much love and grief could feel the same as he watched her walk away down the darkened corridor, her legs reflecting their long dancing shadows in the watery polish of the linoleum.

Epilogue

The view from the book-lined room that now went by the name 'The Squire's Morning Room' took in the comings and goings on the terrace and lawn of the manor house. The Major had a full view of Mrs Rasool, resplendent in saffron coat and billowing lime-green silk trousers, who seemed to be arguing loudly and happily into a tiny black headset. The microphone part rested on her cheek like a fat fly. She waved a clipboard and two tuxedoed helpers rushed to assist more guests to the semicircle of white folding chairs arranged in front of a low dais surmounted by a plain canvas campaign tent which flapped in the light breeze of the May afternoon. The Major, half hidden behind the pale linen drape, was glad to have a moment of silent reflection before the wedding. It was meant as a small and deliberately casual gathering of friends, and everything, including the sunny weather, appeared to be cooperating. Yet he still felt the festivities as an impending squall and braced for the ceremonies to break upon his head.

He heard the door open; turning, he watched Jasmina slip into the room and gently close the door. She was dressed in a coat and trousers of old silk that glowed with the ruby-dark softness of fine port. A spider's web of a scarf in a pale Wedgwood blue was spun about her head like a vision. She trod softly across the carpet in low slippers and came to stand at his shoulder.

'You're not supposed to be here,' he said.

'I thought it wrong to leave even one small tradition unbroken,' she said, smiling. She took his arm and they both watched for a while in silence as the guests gathered.

Roger was talking with the musicians—a harpist and two sitar players. Roger ran his hand over the strings of a sitar and the Major assumed he was checking the musician's tuning and opining on the music selections. The groom's side of the chairs was filling up, the men largely invisible between the large bobbing hats. The Major spotted Grace talking to Marjorie, whose hat shook violently with her muttering. The Major could only assume her acceptance of the coming nuptials did not preclude a continued gossiping about their unsuitability.

The Vicar hung about looking lost. Daisy had refused to attend. Alec and Alma were here not speaking to each other in the front row. The Major was very grateful to Alec for standing up for their friendship and quite demanding that his wife accompany him, but now they would all have to put up with her rigid face and her sighs of mortification. As they watched, Alice from next door billowed out from the wide French doors, wearing some kind of batik tent and a pair of hemp sandals. She was accompanied by Lord Dagenham, just back from his annual spring visit to Venice, who had sent word that he would like to receive an invitation but who now seemed rather bewildered to find such strange people waiting on his back lawn.

'Do you suppose Dagenham likes what the Rasools have done with the place?' asked the Major.

'After that incident with the schoolchildren and the ducks, he should think himself lucky things have arranged themselves so profitably,' replied Jasmina. The local authorities had come to hear of the duck shooting fiasco and had promptly closed the school. It was only recently, as part of a long-range plan instituted by Gertrude, the wife of the Laird of Loch Brae, that the Rasools had quietly leased all but the east wing as a country house hotel, allowing ample funds for Lord Dagenham to go back to dividing his time between Edgecombe and other society haunts. It seemed only appropriate that this eclectic affair should be their first catered wedding.

The bride's guests—a very small party made up of an assistant imam named Rodney, Amina and her auntie Noreen, Mrs Rasool's parents, and the man who supplied the shop with frozen produce and had begged to come—now began to cluster on the terrace as if held behind an invisible rope. Abdul Wahid was to lead them to their chairs in a small traditional procession at the appropriate time. He stood to one side with his usual frown, as if he disapproved of all the chattering frivolity around him. He did not look over at Amina. They had developed a strict policy of mutual avoidance, so rigid as to show clearly that they still felt a strong attraction. No doubt, thought the Major, Abdul Wahid also disapproved of the number of dimpled knees and ample matronly bosoms on display in the groom's section. Abdul Wahid tousled the hair of his son, who leaned comfortably against him, knotted tie all askew. George seemed wholly impervious to all the activity and was reading a large book.

The Major sighed and Jasmina laughed at him and took his arm.

'They are a motley and ragged bunch,' she said, 'but they are what is left when all the shallow pretense is burned away.'

'Will it do?' said the Major, laying his hand over her cool fingers. 'Will it be enough to sustain the future?'

'It is more than enough for me,' she said. 'My heart is quite full.' The Major heard a catch in her voice. He turned to face her and pushed back a stray tendril of hair from her cheek, but he said nothing. There would be time to speak of Ahmed and Nancy in the ceremonies to come. At this moment, there was only the pause of quiet reflection pooling between them like sunlight on carpet.

Outside, the harpist improvised a wild glissando. Without looking, the Major could sense the guests sitting taller and gathering their attention. He might have preferred to stay in this room forever and gaze at this face which wore love like a smile about the eyes, but it was not possible. He straightened his own shoulders and offered her his arm with a formal bow of the head.

'Mrs Ali,' he said, delighting in using her name one last time, 'shall we go forth and get married?'

Acknowledgments

A long time ago, a stay-at-home mother in Brooklyn, who missed her busy advertising job, stumbled into a writing class at New York's 92nd Street Y looking for a creative outlet. It's been a long journey since and, as in any good story, I would not have made it without the help of many strangers and friends. So thank you all.

Thank you to my Brooklyn writing community, including writer Katherine Mosby, who first taught me to appreciate the beauty of the sentence; Christina Burz, Miriam Clark, and Beth McFadden, who make up the decade-old writing group with whom I trade blunt criticism and cheap wine; and early readers Leslie Alexander, Susan Leitner, and Sarah Tobin.

Thank you to the accomplished writers who have taught me through the Southampton Writers Conference and the Stony Brook Southampton MFA program. Special acknowledgment to Professor Robert Reeves, teacher, friend, and shameless promoter. He never stops believing in his students. He never wears socks. Thanks also to Roger Rosenblatt and Ursula Hegi; Melissa Bank, Clark Blaise, Matt Klam, Bharati Mukherjee, Julie Sheehan, and Meg Wolitzer; and writing friends Cindy Krezel and Janis Jones.

Thanks to the Bronx Writers Studio, which gave me a First Chapter Award in 2005. Julie Barer read that first chapter and waited three years for the rest of the novel. Thank you, Julie—I now know what it must feel like to win the lottery. Thanks to Susan Kamil, who makes me laugh so much I'd do anything she asks. Fortunately she is also a brilliant editor, so it all works out. Paragraph, workspace for writers, provided me a desk and a community. William Boggess, Noah Eaker, and Jennifer Smith made life easy with their editorial assistance.

In cyberspace, thanks to Tim at timothyhallinan.com for butt-kicking writing advice.

My parents, Alan and Margaret Phillips, always believed I could write and have always supported me. Love to them, to my sister, Lorraine Baker, and also to David and Lois Simonson, who took in an alien daughter-in-law.

Our wonderful sons, Ian and Jamie (who hold the rights to Major Pettigrew action figures), teased me mercilessly until the manuscript was done. My husband and best friend, John Simonson, has always understood this story inside and out and I can never thank him enough—for everything.